TIME'S UP

BOOK 3 OF THE TIME ZERO TRILOGY

CAROLYN COHAGAN

GIRLS WITH PENS

ISBN: 978-0-9995624-6-8

For information, address:
Girls With Pens, LLC
PO Box 301894
Austin, TX 78703
www.girlswithpens.org

This is a work of fiction. Names, characters, places and incidents either are products of the author's imagination or are used fictitiously. Any resemblance to actual events or locales or persons, living or dead, is entirely coincidental.

To the unsung librarians who pass on the love of reading to one student at a time. Keep doing what you do. We need you now more than ever.

Doubt is an uncomfortable condition, but certainty is a ridiculous one.

VOLTAIRE

ONE

"Peace," Tabby says.

"Peace," Juda responds.

"WRONG!" I say. "Do it again."

Scowling, Tabby puts her hands on her hips. "That was perfect," she says. "I didn't look him in the eyes. I didn't stand too close. My voice was soft. What's the problem?"

"You spoke first!" I say, amazed that after four days of practice, she still can't remember that in Manhattan a man always initiates conversation.

As she rolls her eyes, I look at Juda, who looks exhausted. He's spent every day this week helping to train Tabby and every night with his mother Rose in the hospital. His eyes are barely open.

"Maybe turn it into a game," says Grace, who sits on the stoop of the Dixon house. We have to conduct our lessons on the front lawn so our Bees can monitor us. "Like, you're trying to see how long you can go without saying *anything*?"

If looks could kill, Tabby's glare would violently strangle Grace.

Grace blanches, looking away. She's not used to Tabby's harsh manner, plus she's had to be a student herself this week. Having grown up in the basement of Macy's, she isn't used to following the daily protocol set down by the Teachers, the island's religious authorities. Ram, the leader of the Unbound, was suspicious of this, and Grace made up a clever story about growing up in an orphanage and never being allowed outside. She instinctively seemed to know that Ram shouldn't know about the Laurel Society, and I agree. We can't risk him knowing any more of our secrets.

My brother Dekker should also be here helping with Tabby, but as usual, he hasn't shown up. I haven't complained about his lack of help because his presence would aggravate me more. The idea of him teaching girls how to behave makes me ill and angry at the same time; he's welcome to spend his days however he wants.

"What's the point?" Mary lies on the grass next to me, staring at the sky. "Tabby is going to marry Uncle Ruho whether she knows this crap or not. We have to go with her whether we know it or not. So let her make a fool out of herself. Who cares?"

Mary and Grace haven't had problems remembering the rules we've taught them, but they also aren't marrying a divine leader who will scrutinize their manners and etiquette the second we arrive.

"I agree!" says Tabby, heading for the door of the Dixon house.

"No," says Juda. "She's not ready, and we only have five days left."

"I don't even understand why I have to learn all these feeble rules," Tabby says, sweeping aside her bangs. "My fiancé didn't, like, demand it, so why is everyone being so major bossy?"

We've gone through this many times. "Because he sent you the Book!" I say. Uncle Ruho sent Ram our book of scripture as a gift for his bride. "He'll expect you to know the rules that go along with each holy revelation."

"I thought girls *couldn't read*," she says, jutting out her chin.

"He will expect your father or brother to have read the scripture out loud to you."

She snorts. "That'll be the day."

"You'll be punished for making mistakes," Juda says.

He avoids being specific, but images flash through my head: women flogged in the market, brides beaten by new husbands, a woman hanged for not being "pure" on her wedding night.

Tabby paces the lawn like a trapped rat. This is not the glamorous life of a queen that she had in mind. She's as sick of Juda and me as we are of her.

What if she can't learn what she needs to in time? What if she walks up to Uncle Ruho, looks him in the eye, and starts complaining about her journey? What if she takes off her veil?

But maybe, instead of the dark scenes I imagine, he would *send her home*. Maybe, disgusted with his bride, he would send us all straight back to Kingsboro.

This scenario sounds like a reprieve, but I know it would be our undoing. If we return to the Unbound as failures, Ram will destroy our people. We have to remain there long enough to fulfill his inconceivable command: kill Uncle Ruho.

Uncle Ruho claims to be a descendent of God, and Ram thinks this assertion is blasphemous. Ram believes eliminating Ruho will finally trigger the Ascension, when the Unbound's Savior will return and all the Unbound will float into heaven to claim a glorious reward. Ram believes in his theory so strongly that he said that if we don't kill Uncle Ruho he will "blow our island to smithereens."

3

Shaking Ram from my mind, I tell Tabby, "Try it again."

Juda goes over the rule one more time. He's being patient, more patient than she deserves. As difficult as Tabby is, I'm happy to spend this time with Juda. His hair has grown longer than when he was a private guard. It sticks up where he's been running his hands through it in frustration. Though bloodshot, his green eyes are as beautiful as ever.

He catches me staring at him and gives me a shy smile. My instinct is to look away, embarrassed, but instead I maintain eye contact. We have no idea what life will be like when we return to Manhattan, or if we'll be able to see each other at all. This time feels very precious.

The Bee is watching us so most of our communication is with our eyes. I'm amazed how much we're able to say to each other: I'm happy to see you. I'm upset today. I'm afraid of what's coming. I wish I could touch you. Tabby is terrible. How do we get out of this?

After Ram told us we had to go back home, we spent days trying to find a way out of it. Juda told him we were wanted by the authorities, that we would be arrested as soon as we set foot on the island, but Ram told us he had the technology to take care of it. Dekker explained that surely our pictures had been on the Twitcher feed for days—that Uncle Ruho knew what we looked like. Ram was unfazed. I even told him about Mrs. Asher, how she would still be searching for us after the death of her son.

Nothing worked. Ram continued to give us his insipid smile and tell us that it was "God's will" that we carry out his plan and that He would keep us safe. Ram's certainty will be our demise.

Tabby approaches Juda again, and this time she waits for him to speak first. After they've exchanged greetings, he says, "Go get me some water from the kitchen."

Startled, she says, "Go get it yourself!"

Juda throws up his arms in exasperation.

"You have to go and get it, Tabs," Mary says, fanning herself with her hand.

"He didn't even say 'please.'" Tabby looks at me for support.

"It doesn't matter," I say. "If he's your husband, you have to do what he says."

"If he's my husband, he'll have to learn some manners!" Tabby storms into the house.

For the hundredth time, I wonder why on earth Ram chose this girl.

TWO

Living with the Dixons has become very strange. Friends and relatives turn up at the house at all hours of the day to visit Tabby and pray with her. She sits and receives them as if she were the Prophet herself. I know she loves every moment of it. Her parents, Bithia and Gilad, fawn all over her, telling her that she is blessed by God, and they give her whatever she asks for. They even make her little brother Corny be respectful to her.

However, another one of their children is also being sent to Manhattan. Their eldest son, Silas, might as well still be living in the Forgiveness Home. His parents barely speak to him. Bithia cooks for him, and then he takes his food up to his room to eat alone. His parents seem relieved to not have to sit with him through a meal. I've started to take my meals upstairs to join him, and no one has stopped me.

He and Mary were really angry with me when Ram said they had to go to Manhattan, and I don't blame them. Ram told them I'd not only betrayed their location after we ran away from the Forgiveness Home, but that I'd asked for them to be sent away with us. Ram manipulated the entire situation, but he was being honest about one thing: I told him where they were hiding. I thought I was helping them.

I'm slowly gaining back their trust, but it's difficult knowing I have a new secret that I'm keeping. They think we're going to Manhattan only to look after Tabby. I wish I could tell them the truth about our horrible assignment, but I need permission from Grace, Juda, and Dekker, and I don't have it.

I use my dinner times with Silas to teach him what I think he'll need to know to survive the island. Ram hasn't provided him with any special training of his own. Luckily, explaining how males conduct themselves takes about one-tenth as long as teaching a female.

I know Bithia and Gilad are counting down the minutes until I'm gone. I think they would've kicked me out if Ram hadn't told them to host me until we leave. Maybe they would've kicked Silas out, too.

Mary is living at home, which I know she hates. She says her brother Jeremiah, the Sentry, is at least being kind. Dekker is with the Delfords, Grace is with her host family, and Juda is back with the family that sent him to the Forgiveness Home for putting a snake in the toilet. I imagine that's pretty awkward.

This morning, I've been told to be ready and waiting in the Dixon's living room at five a.m. I'm so tired by the daily training that I barely register getting dressed or walking downstairs.

At precisely five o'clock, I hear a rap on the door. I open it to find Mrs. Prue, the bird-like girl who does the Refinement Training. Even at this hour, her hair is in perfect ringlets, her purple dress is pressed, and the lavender carnation on her chest looks freshly plucked.

"Good morning!" she says, much too cheerily. When I don't respond she says, "Come with me, please."

Having little choice, I follow. As soon as my foot leaves the stoop, my Bee flicks into place above me. After a walk through the still-sleeping neighborhood, we arrive at the Leisure Center.

Mrs. Prue guides me through the atrium and down the escalator. When we reach the food court, she takes a hard left to an area I've never been to before: a long pink hallway that smells like a cherry candle. Glass doors line the corridor, and although most of the rooms are still dark at this hour, in the shadows of each, I spot big chairs and sinks like the barber shops in Manhattan.

We stop at the only lighted room. A tall beanpole of a woman motions us inside. She has the smile of someone who knows whether or not it will rain tomorrow.

"This is Gertie," says Mrs. Prue. "She'll be taking care of you today."

"Welcome to the salon!" Gertie says. "We're going to give you a whole new look today, young lady. And I think we'll have a lot of fun!"

I give her a blank stare.

"Have you ever fantasized about a new haircut? A new color? Well, I'm here to make those dreams come true!"

I touch my head. "I like my hair."

The women look at one another.

"Of course you do," says Mrs. Prue. "We should all love what the Lord gave us. But you're part of something bigger now —God's special plan. To fulfill that plan you need to stay safe, sweetie. From what I've been told, you need to look different. Is that wrong?"

I'm confused. "I thought Ram said there was technology to take care of that."

"There is," says Mrs. Prue, speaking slowly, as if to find the perfect words. "But we think it's best if you have the technology *and* you change up your look a bit. Doesn't that make sense?"

Gertie nods with enthusiasm.

"What if I say no?" I ask.

Gertie's face falls as if someone has not only died, but died with terrible hair.

"I'm afraid that's not an option," says Mrs. Prue, her smile big as ever. "You'll do whatever Gertie recommends. It is Ram's desire and God's will. So have a major blast!" She leaves the salon with a wave.

"Let's start by talking about color!" Gertie says, recovered.

I sit in her chair for over THREE HOURS.

When the nightmare is over, my blonde hair is "Tawny Pony"—a dark auburn brown. The length has been shortened by three inches. Gertie wanted to take off more, but I explained that at home I would need to be able to put it back into a bun or ponytail.

Gertie is giddy. "What do you think?"

The overall effect of the "transformation," as Gertie calls it, is very unsettling. I don't recognize myself at all.

I want to cry.

Perhaps it will keep me safer from Ruho and the Twitchers, but what if it keeps Nana from recognizing me?

This is my secret. I haven't even told Juda. None of us wants to go back—we're terrified—but a part of me that I can't share with anyone is actually happy. I can see Nana again. I can check on my father.

Maybe this transformation will make it easier to move around the city to find them, in which case, I should be grateful.

"It's . . . good," I say.

She beams. "I think you look *fab*ulous. Your skin is glowing with the new red tones in your hair! You look at least seventeen. Maybe eighteen?"

I try to smile. She puts a lot of time and energy into her

work, and she's very passionate about it. I manage a "Thank you."

"Mina?!"

I turn my head to see Grace, mouth agape, entering the salon with Mrs. Prue close behind.

"I barely recognized you!" she says.

"I guess that's the idea," I say.

"Whoa. That is just, like, major bonkers."

I touch my hair self-consciously. "They made me do it."

"It looks benny!" she says. "For real."

"Glad you like it," Gertie says, "because it's your turn."

Grace blanches. "But no one . . . I was never . . . No one is looking for me!"

"Ram said to do everyone, so we're doing *everyone*," Mrs. Prue says.

She motions to the chair, so I get up. I give Grace a look of sympathy as she sits down with terror.

"How about a wig?" Grace says. "Wouldn't that be simpler?"

"This is quite a head of hair you've got!" Gertie says, fingering Grace's curls.

"Everyone?" I say. "Does that mean boys, too?"

"Yeps," Gertie says.

My eyes catch Grace's in the mirror. We start to laugh. Maybe this whole transformation thing will be worth it.

"You need to come with me, Mina," Mrs. Prue says.

I'm sad to leave Grace. "Can't I stay and watch?" I ask.

"No, you need to learn how to use Tacts. Let's go."

I reluctantly say good-bye to Grace. As usual, she's putting on a happy face. It helps that her host-mom has been going to the library and getting her as many books as possible. Grace knows we won't have access to books once we return, and so she's trying to gobble up as many as she can. She's given some to me, but I don't read as quickly as she does. I did manage to read her favorite, *Nancy Drew and the Secret of the Old Clock*, and I'm trying to finish her new obsession, *Jane Eyre*, although I have a hard time with some of the older language.

Mrs. Prue guides me back up to the atrium, which is still fairly empty since it's only eight thirty. Sitting at a table near a glass wall is Jeremiah, Mary's brother, the Sentry. As we head for the door I avoid eye contact, but then, to my dismay, Mrs. Prue walks directly toward him.

He does a double take as we reach him. Once he's certain that the girl with the chestnut hair is me, he stands.

"Good morning, Mr. Benjamin," Mrs. Prue says.

"Good morning," he says. "Good morning, Miss Clark."

Miss Clark? How fancy!

"I'll be back for Mina in an hour," Mrs. Prue says, walking away.

She's leaving me with him? *Nyek.*

THREE

Once Mrs. Prue is gone, Jeremiah and I glower at each other. I hate him because he allowed Mary to be abandoned in the Forgiveness Home; he hates me because I helped break her out and we got caught.

Wordlessly, we sit down, and Jeremiah opens a small metal box on the table, revealing several tinier containers. He removes one of the teeny boxes and places it in front of me. "These are your Tacts. I'm here to train you how to use them."

"Why you?" I ask. He seems to want to be here as much as I do.

"Because the more you understand how to use them, the safer you'll be, and the safer you are, the safer Mary is."

"If your family hadn't sent her to the Forgiveness Home, she wouldn't be in danger in the first place."

He grits his teeth. "If you hadn't involved her with your reckless, half-baked plan, she would be fine."

"Have you seen the sores on her stomach? Do you call that 'fine'?" I can't believe the way I'm speaking to this man, but he and his family make me so furious, I can't seem to stop myself.

He crosses his arms, leaning back.

"How can you let this happen?" I ask. "Stop Ram from sending her! She hasn't done anything. She doesn't deserve to go!"

"You think I don't know that!" His voice echoes throughout the empty atrium.

He leans forward and says more calmly, "Ram has decided she's destined to go, so that's that."

I shake my head. "She could be killed."

"No. She won't die, because you and the others will protect her. Because you know it's your fault she's with you."

I wish I could promise him that Mary will be safe, that she'll return here exactly the same girl that she is now, but how can I? "I'll do my best. I promise."

Anger still twists his face.

As frustrating as we find each other, at least our scorn comes from the same place: a love for Mary.

He looks around the room, then uncrosses his arms. "Put in the Tacts."

I open the little box and discover two brown contact lenses. I put them in, but it isn't easy. I hate the feeling of having something in my eyes, and I keep wanting to rub them.

"The left one doesn't do anything except cover your natural eye color," he says. "The right one has all the technology. You won't be able to watch video or cruise the net. You'll only be able to send Nods. Ram wants you focused."

I might be disappointed if I had any idea what he was talking about.

"The lenses are made of antimicrobial nanobots. You can sleep in them and they never need replacing. Do *not* lose them." Over the next hour he shows me how to operate the remarkable right Tact. To start or stop the tiny computer inside, you have to blink six times rapidly. Once it's on, you see a screen similar to the one inside a Twitcher helmet. Then you just have to think of the command you want: up, down, right, left, or enter. According to Jeremiah, the chip in the Tact connects to the synapses of your brain and can understand very simple commands. *Bonkers.*

"This allows you to not only connect with another Tact in Manhattan," he says, "but also to report back to Ram about your progress."

Mrs. Prue arrives to pick me up.

"Thank you," I tell Jeremiah. "You're a good teacher."

He nods, not wanting to accept my compliment.

"Stay safe," he says, but I hear what he means: *Keep Mary safe.*

"I will."

The final stop of the morning is at a red house near Third Street. When Mrs. Prue knocks there is no answer, so she opens the door and calls, "Yoo-hoo!"

When no one responds, she walks right inside, signaling for me to follow. She marches us confidently up the stairs to the second floor. I feel very rude.

Upstairs, we enter what, in the Dixon's house, is the largest bedroom, but here, instead of a bed, there are clothes strewn everywhere. Bolts of fabric lean against the walls—all of them the same eight colors that the Unbound wear.

In the corner, a man sits preoccupied with a strange machine resting on the table in front of him. His red hair is bushy and full above his forehead but clipped short in the back. He wears enormous baby blue glasses that make his eyes look huge. His close-lipped smile has a creepy silver glimmer.

"Hello, John Paul," Mrs. Prue says.

He looks up in alarm, but upon seeing Mrs. Prue his expression changes to delight. Saying nothing, he walks over and gives her a warm embrace.

Now that he's closer, I can see that he holds sewing pins in his mouth.

He removes them. "And who's this?"

"This is Mina," Mrs. Prue says.

"Of course." He gives me a large hug. "Welcome to my sewing studio."

"Thank you." His warmth seems genuine, but I know better now than to trust anyone completely.

John Paul goes to his closet and returns with a huge swath of teal fabric draped over a hanger. "Try it on!" Seeing my blank look, he adds, "It's your new cloak."

"The color is wrong," I say, panicking.

John Paul purses his lips.

"Ruho sent specific instructions for the cloaks," Mrs. Prue says. "The cut must be precise, but John Paul can choose whichever color he wants."

"He can?" My hands start to sweat at the thought of showing up on the island wearing teal. Surely I'll be beaten for wearing it.

"Maybe this Uncle Ruho guy *wants* you to look different?" John Paul says.

I consider this. If we're the only four girls in Manhattan wearing bright teal cloaks, then we'll be very easy to keep track of. *Nyek.* "I'd really rather have one in the traditional color."

"I won't take that suggestion personally," John Paul says, sliding the cloak off the hanger. "I think you might like mine better once you see its major benny feature." He flips the cloak over to show me the inside of the fabric. I see nothing special, but as he holds it up closer, I detect a very faint gold shimmer.

"What's that?" I ask.

"A firewall. It will protect you from being recognized. If a guard tries to scan you, it will send out false information about who you are."

But . . . How . . . ? I'm so confused. "How do you know about the scanning?"

Mrs. Prue answers. "When you first arrived, two of you were wearing guard uniforms. One of you still had a helmet, which had some pretty interesting tech in it—dated, but effective."

John Paul grins with enthusiasm. "Feel better?"

I smile as much as I can, which isn't much.

"Let's try it on and make sure the fit is okay." He holds out the cloak.

It's been nearly a month since I wore one. I throw it over my shirt and pants and it swallows me, the hem falling well below my ankle. The sleeves are too long and the neck is gaping.

"It has to reach to here," I say, pointing high on my neck.

"I *know*," John Paul grumbles. He looks at Mrs. Prue. "Someone didn't measure this girl very accurately,"

She ignores him, shaking her head. "You don't have much time to fix it."

Sighing dramatically, he whips it off my head in one motion.

"How are you coming with the wedding gown?" Mrs. Prue asks.

John Paul beams. "I've been waiting for you to ask." He hurries back to the closet. A moment later he wheels out a mannequin wearing the single most beautiful piece of clothing I've ever seen.

The dress is gold and silver and it doesn't even look like fabric. It appears to be thousands of thick gold and silver threads crossing over one another, like I could stick a finger in-between the layers of shimmering strands. The dress is long sleeved and reaches to the floor, so it will cover Tabby's skin, but anyone can see that it will be extremely form-fitting. She'll have to put a cloak over it until she's alone with her new husband, so the public will never see it, but I don't tell John Paul. I'm sure he would be crestfallen.

"Ohhhhhh, John Paul," Mrs. Prue squeals. "It's . . . It's . . . just . . . ."

"Bioluminescent," I whisper.

"Luminescent! Yes!" she says. When she has finished circling and admiring it, she says, "I now understand why you didn't have much time for Mina's cloak."

Chastened, he says, "The new one will be perfect, I promise! Come here, Mina, and let's measure you properly."

I stand while he takes my measurements. Staring at the stunning wedding gown, I have my first moment of thinking that maybe Tabby's situation is not as bad as I thought.

FOUR

In the evening, I go to the hospital to see Juda's mother, Rose. Dr. Rachel has been treating her for the symptoms of mercury poisoning, but she doesn't have an actual cure. All we can do is wait and pray.

When I enter Rose's room, two strangers stand by her bedside. Are these new nurses? When the boy and the girl turn to greet me, I cover my mouth in astonishment.

Grace's hair has been completely straightened and reaches well below her shoulders. Her glasses are gone and she wears bright green contacts. Passing her on the street, I would never have recognized her. "You look great!" I tell her.

Juda, on the other hand, looks completely bizarre. Gertie has dyed his hair blond, but not white-blond like Silas'—it's more of a bright yellow—and he's wearing square glasses. "Don't say anything," he says with a tight jaw. "I know it's bad."

I try not to laugh. "It's not bad! It's just . . . different."

"You are the *worst* liar," he says, and Grace giggles. He smiles. "You look terrific, though. I like the red."

"I told you it was good," Grace tells him, and then to me,

"And Gertie says this is only the first stage for Juda. She's doing more tomorrow."

"I'm never letting that woman touch me again," Juda says.

"How's Rose today?" I ask, approaching the bed.

"Tired." Juda turns and touches Rose's hand. She's in a deep sleep, breathing hard.

"Her color looks better today," I say. Her cheeks seem pinker than yesterday. I've been trying to see her as much as possible. Dr. Rachel doesn't let me stay here overnight like Juda, but I can visit before dinner.

"Yeah. We had a nice talk earlier," Juda says. "But she's still not eating much."

"Did you tell her?"

"No. I . . . Not yet."

He's been trying to summon up the courage to tell her he's returning to Manhattan, but he's afraid the stress will be too much for her. He might be right.

I take his hand. "I can tell her if you—"

"No. I'll do it. I just need time."

Grace and I exchange glances. Time is something we don't have. We leave Monday.

Four days.

"Dr. Rachel will keep her safe," I say, knowing that it's little comfort.

He nods, and I can see he's trying not to cry.

"I was so mad at her for not telling me about my father. Before we got separated, I was as nasty as I knew how to be. I wanted to make her feel rotten, and I did."

"She said you had a right to be angry. And you're being nice to her now."

"But sometimes I'm still angry." Tears well in his eyes.

"I think that's okay." I hug him, but he doesn't react. "Let's

20

get some water," I tell Grace, wanting to give him space. She quickly agrees and we walk into the hallway.

"She's not doing well," Grace says.

"But she looks better."

"She still won't eat much and her fever is back. What's Juda going to do?"

Juda would never stay behind. Ram has threatened to kill everyone on the island, and Juda won't let all the Convenes die because of him. I feel so helpless. Surely there's *something* we can do.

"Come with me," I say.

"We're not going back in to see Rose?" she asks.

"No. We're going to see Ram."

I don't tell Juda we're leaving because he wouldn't approve of my mission.

It's late and Ram will have already left his office. We need to find his home. Bithia once said he lived next to the Worship Hub, so that's where we walk.

The evenings have become slightly cooler and darker. Fall is coming. The drop in temperature is a relief, but longer nights have always made me nervous—more things can hide in the dark.

"Do you think they're safe?" Grace says in a low voice.

"Who?"

"Rayna. Ayan. Your Nana."

I glance at our Bees, wondering if this is a safe conversation to have. "God willing, yes."

"Do you think we'll be able to see them?" she says.

Does she think about this as much as I do? "It'll be difficult." I speak with my mouth aimed at the ground, hoping the words are inaudible.

"I want to try," she says.

"Yes." I don't say more about it. Ram must know that there

are people we'll want to find when we return. He's counting on his threats to keep us in line, but I don't want him to know any specifics. I decide to tell her one of the other things that's keeping me up at night. "What if Ram wants us to get to the island through the subway? I can't go back down there."

She shakes her head. "Me neither."

"I mean I *really* can't." I've been having nightmares about the subway tunnel—the cold and the dark and even worse, about Damon's body lying at the bottom of the water.

"I think Ram has a different plan."

"Why?" I ask.

"Because Tabby is a bride and he's not going to have a bride arrive soaking wet and smelling like backwater."

I pray she's right.

When we arrive at the Worship Hub, I suggest we walk around it. I'm assuming I'll know which house is Ram's; Bithia has gushed over it at many meals.

As we reach the southern end of the Hub, I see a white house that's at least twice as big as any other. Surrounding the lawn, crawling up trellises, and lining the walkway is every kind of flower you can imagine, and every single one of them is as white as the house.

"That *has* to be it," I say, and Grace agrees.

As we approach the front door, she says, "Are you sure about this?"

I'm nervous, too, but I have to at least try to talk sense into him.

I ring the doorbell. I half expect Marjory to answer the door. I can't picture Ram without her acting as buffer.

A large Sentry opens the door. "Yeah?" he says in a deep, gruff voice. His thick chest and flat head give him the appearance of a tree that just learned to talk.

"We . . . uh . . . We need to see Ram," I say, wishing I

sounded more confident.

"Come to the office tomorrow," he says, closing the door.

"Wait!" I say, throwing myself between the door and the jamb. "Tell him that Mina and Grace are here, and it's urgent."

His shifts his weight, annoyed.

"Please," I say.

"Wait outside," he says, nudging me back onto the stoop.

He shuts the door in our faces, but I smile at Grace. "We found the right house!"

Ten minutes later my confidence is much lower. We're sitting on the white doormat, wondering what to do next, when the Sentry opens the door again. "You can come in."

We jump up. Why does Ram always make people wait? It must make him feel more powerful.

The Sentry leads us sluggishly through the house, which is full of velvet furniture and brightly patterned rugs, just like Ram's dressing room. The smell of something sweet, like burnt sugar, hovers in the air. As we walk deeper into the house, the sound of people shouting radiates from down the hall. I grow frightened. I have no desire to walk into the middle of Ram having a dispute with someone.

The Sentry guides us into a vast living room filled with couches and armchairs, each one holding so many throw pillows that there doesn't appear to be any room left to sit.

Ram is curled up in an armchair big enough for two. He's nested among several pillows, wrapped in a fluffy blanket, with Jezzie's head on his lap. When we enter, her head lifts and she emits a small growl.

Ram, on the other hand, doesn't notice us at all. He's enthralled with a screen on his wall, where colorful images flicker. The shouting noises from earlier emanate from the people on the screen.

It's a movie!

Grace and I say nothing as we watch along with Ram. In an exotic garden, children appear to be eating flowers and grass. A man in purple sings. He eats a leaf off a tree.

The image freezes.

"One of my all-time favorites," Ram says. "It's about how the devil, disguised as the owner of a candy factory, tricks children into failure using the seven deadly sins.

We smile as if we understand.

"Now what is so important that you had to interrupt movie night?" he asks, finally turning to look at us. "Oh my! Who are these glamorous strangers who have arrived in my home?"

Grace touches her straightened hair self-consciously, while I roll my eyes.

"Mrs. Prue did a wonderful job!" he says, taking us in head to toe.

Am I supposed to thank him for changing everything that made me *me*? I won't do it, and I continue to frown.

"Thousands of girls would kill to have makeovers like those so I suggest you learn some gratitude," he says. "Isn't that right, Jezzie?" he asks the dog. "Wouldn't you love a makeover?" He makes kissy noises in Jezzie's face.

"I thought atheists made movies," I say, remembering what Frannie and Susanna told me.

Ram gives me a knowing smile. "Are you afraid that I'm susceptible to atheist ideology, Miss Clark?"

When I don't answer, he says, "I must always be prepared to face the atheist threat, and therefore it's vital that I understand their seditious ways. I confess that in the case of this particular film, they manage to demonstrate *some* morality."

I'm tempted to ask to watch more of the movie and have to remind myself why I'm here. I try to stand taller. "Juda has to stay in Kingsboro."

"That's not possible," Ram says, scratching Jezzie's ears.

"Why not?" I say. "Your dream only predicted five people going to the island, and we still have five without him. He needs to stay with his mother. If you make him go, he won't—"

"Won't what?" Ram says, interrupting. "I believe he'll do whatever I ask, unless he wants his people eliminated."

How can this little man, snuggled in his blanket with his dog, be so cruel?

My heart scuttles at the idea of being separated from Juda again, but I plow forward. "The rest of us can do what you want. We don't need him."

"You may not need Juda there, but God does. He needs someone highly motivated working for Him, and who could be more highly motivated than Juda? The sooner he gets the job done, the sooner he can return to see his mother."

When Ram first told us he was sending us back to the island, he said we were free to do whatever we wanted after our mission was completed, but I'm extremely skeptical. "You're really going to let us come back?"

"Is that what you want?"

Is this a trick question? "I don't want to stay in Manhattan, but we can't exactly just walk out."

"You can tell Juda and the others that I guarantee that once you've eliminated your divine leader, you'll have a means of escape."

"What is it?" I ask, not believing him. "We can't use the subway again. They'll know about it."

"And it's wet and miserable. No, no. My way is much better."

"Tell us now or we won't—"

"That's all. You have no position from which to negotiate, and I have given you something because God likes generosity. Now I would like to get back to my film. Good night."

The large Sentry enters the room. "Come with me, please."

Before we can say one more word to Ram, the Sentry ushers us out of the room and down the hall. He shoves us out the front door, slamming it forcefully behind us.

"That was a major waste of time," I say.

"We *did* get to see part of a movie," Grace says.

Leave it to Grace to find a silver lining.

FIVE

When I get home, I take my dinner to Silas' room, as usual. He sits at his desk, his plate of food pushed to one side, reading the Book with a dismayed expression. His wrist has almost completely healed, and the bite on his ankle from Jezzie has mellowed into a big yellow bruise.

Sitting on the floor with my back against the wall, I balance my plate on my lap and dig in. Bithia has made steak, potatoes, and broccoli with a cheese sauce.

"You should eat that," I say, mouth full, gesturing to his plate. "Food like this is hard to come by at home."

He looks at me, startled, as if he's never seen me before. "I'm not hungry."

"Try. You don't want to be there dreaming of this food."

"I don't want to be there at all."

I have no reply. I feel terrible that I've been with Ram fighting for Juda to stay behind and not for Silas and Mary. They've done nothing to deserve their horrible fate except be friends with *me*. "It's not fair. You and Mary have nothing to do with anything."

"Ram is making a point. He wants all the little children of Kingsboro to know that if you don't conform, some horrible fate awaits you." He closes the Book, leans in, and whispers, "What will the Propheteers do . . . to someone like me?"

Someone like him? It takes me a moment to realize that he means a boy who likes other boys. "How would they know? I didn't know until you told me."

"Yeah, but, somehow I always manage to mess up."

"You can't this time."

"But what if I do?"

The truth is, I have no idea. I've never known anyone like Silas. "You should ask Juda. He had a friend at home who liked boys."

"Really? Can I meet his friend?"

"He died."

His eyes bulge with fear.

"Of the plague," I add quickly. "He got sick."

"Will we get sick?" he asks.

"I don't think so. We just have to avoid the water on the Lower East Side."

"I still can't believe this is happening," he says, hugging himself. "I keep waiting to wake up and find out it's all a nightmare."

If only I could tell him it was.

"I have news." I put down my plate. "Ram says that he'll help us return here after, um, Tabby is settled."

"WHAT?" He rushes over to me on the floor. "What are you talking about? Why didn't you tell me sooner?"

"I just sat down!" I say. "And, um, I didn't know if you'd be happy about coming back here." Lately, he seems to despise everyone in Kingsboro, especially his parents.

"But coming back here doesn't mean we have to stay. We could go to the West!"

It's hard to share Silas' excitement knowing the real prerequisite for our return: killing Uncle Ruho.

Silas' face has changed completely. He no longer looks downtrodden; he seems light and hopeful.

"Maybe everything will be all right," he says.

"When we arrive, Juda will help you. Trust him."

"What about Dekker?"

"Don't trust him," I say. "Don't tell him any secrets. He'll use anything he knows to help himself."

Silas' eyebrows rise up in surprise.

Placing my empty plate on the floor, I say, "I'm not kidding. He's not a very nice person."

"That couldn't have been easy to grow up with."

"Probably about the same as growing up with Tabby," I observe.

He laughs. "Yeah. They're a pair, huh?" His face grows somber. "What if Uncle Ruho doesn't like her?"

I've worried about this, too. "The good news is he'll probably care more about her looks than anything else, and she's a pretty girl. If he expects her to be compliant and dainty—"

"We're totally screwed."

"Yeps."

He goes back to his desk to get his food. He cuts into the steak. "How are you?" he asks me.

I laugh and shrug. The question is too small for the answer.

He nods. "Yeah. I get it. I don't suppose there's anything you're looking forward to?"

"I'd like to know how my family's doing."

"How do you get news there? People don't have Tacts, right?"

"You listen to the radio, but Uncle Ruho controls that. Mostly it's word of mouth."

"So how will you learn about your family if we're staying with Uncle Ruho?"

"That's a good question."

"I'll help however I can."

"Thank you. That means a major lot."

"I think you meant, that's major benny of you." He smiles.

I've been working on my Unbound vocabulary and accent. I can't have Ruho and his people thinking I sound like a Propheteer.

Silas' smile fades. "What happens if they figure out you're a runaway?"

"It's one thing if they figure out I'm a runaway; it's another if they figure out I'm Mina Clark."

"And if they do?"

Silas doesn't know that I witnessed the deaths of Damon and Max Asher. He has no concept of what it is to run away from a marriage or escape the island.

Without looking him in the eye, I say, "It would be very, very unbenny."

As I pass Tabby's bedroom, I see her packing. Making a bold decision, I walk inside. There's something serious I need to talk to her about. "How's it going?"

She shrugs, not looking up. She places a nightgown inside a bag.

"How many bags are you taking?" I ask, awkwardly standing in the doorway.

"Dunno. Four, maybe? Five?"

"Oh. I'm taking one."

"That's dumb," she says. "You're going to want things from here, like, majorly."

"Maybe," I say. "It won't really matter." Nothing from Kingsboro is going to change the fact that I'm back in Manhattan.

The straws Tabby once kept on the nightstand are gone. Thrown away or packed? "Have you said goodbye to Adam?" I ask.

She goes to the closet, pulling shirts off hangers. "Nope."

"Are you going to?"

"What do you care?"

"I guess I just . . . There were people I didn't get to say goodbye to before I left home, and I regret it." I still wish I could tell Sekena everything that happened.

"I'm not you."

"Have you talked to him at all?"

She shoves the shirts violently into the bag. "Nope."

"I'm sorry."

"I didn't say I was sorry about it."

"I guess you can always send him a Nod," I say, "once we're there."

"I don't have a Tact."

"I thought we all had—"

"Ram thinks it would make members of the Unbound homesick if we could talk to friends or family, so we don't get them. Only woolies qualify, it seems." She brushes her bangs out of her face. "Don't you have your own packing to do?"

I've been dismissed. "I just . . . I need to ask you a question." Venturing further into the room, I whisper, "You and Adam . . . "

"What?" She now looks me straight in the eye, her expression daring me to ask about her feelings one more time.

"At home, when a woman gets married, purity is very important, and—"

"Like it's not here?" she says with sarcasm and bitterness.

I plow forward. "If you and Adam—"

"I'm fine, okay." She turns around and drags her hands from head to toe. "I'm pure, virtuous, unsullied, uninfected, untainted, virginal perfection. Are you happy?"

"I am actually. Thanks." I walk out. I felt like one of my aunties asking the question, but Tabby's life could be on the line. I wanted to make sure that *someone* had asked the specific question. Ram has made it quite clear that he does not have any of our best interests at heart. And now I know that Uncle Ruho will get what his contract with Ram demands.

SIX

I try to slow down the next few days, but no matter what I do, I feel like I'm riding a bike with no brakes. The next thing I know, it's Sunday. We leave tomorrow morning.

Tabby and Silas go to the Worship Hub with their family, and when I ask to stay home to pack, no one objects. Now that I'm leaving, my spiritual well-being doesn't seem to be anyone's concern.

I fill the one medium-sized bag that Mrs. Prue gave me. I want to smuggle in so many things: books, food, and, most urgently, a small but very sharp kitchen knife that Bithia uses to slice vegetables. But I assume our bags will be searched as soon as we arrive.

I wish I already had the cloak John Paul made for me— maybe the firewall he put in the lining would conceal the knife —but I won't get the cloak until tomorrow morning, right before we leave.

I decide to put the knife back in the kitchen, but, when I open the drawer, I find my hand won't release it. How can I go back to face Ruho, the Teachers, and the Twitchers empty-handed? It feels like suicide. I take the knife back upstairs and shove it deep among my belongings in the bag. Between the moment when John Paul hands me my cloak and the time I arrive on the island, I'll sneak it into the lining of the cloak. If I can't, I'll ditch it.

The rest of the bag is full of Tabby's old clothing, some green and some yellow, and my own white clothes. The colors won't matter once we're in Manhattan. Even though the clothes are used, they're softer and nicer than anything I ever owned before. I search the closet for a thick sweater, too. I pray we won't still be there come winter, but I would regret not having something warm made out of the Unbound's incredible spider silk.

I try on a blue one that must have belonged to Gilad at some point. When I look in the mirror, I still don't recognize myself. I now wear the brown Tacts full time and am almost fully adjusted to the feel of them on my eyes. My hair is back in its usual ponytail, but the auburn color catches me by surprise every time I catch my reflection. I feel so off-balance, but then when was the last time I felt stable? It would take a lot more than my blonde hair to make me feel like my life was mine again. I let my hair down, knowing I won't be able to wear it this way for much longer.

Tonight we have to meet with Ram one last time. I find myself hoping that he'll give us a reprieve, that he'll have had some vision or dream and that the whole mission is off. But deep down, I know my longing is futile. Ram has no intention of changing course.

I pack the sweater, telling myself that things are different now. I'm not the same person I was when I left home. I was a dumb kid who believed everything her parents told her about the world, and since then I've escaped the Ashers and the Forgiveness Home.

Now I have supportive friends. I miss Sekena, but she always made me feel a bit out of place in the world. Grace, Mary, and Silas make me feel like I'm exactly who I'm supposed to be.

And I have Juda. He's safe and with me every day. Once we're back on the island, he may not always be by my side, but I'll know where he is. More importantly, I'll know his heart. He is mine and I am his, and as soon as we're out of this horrible situation, we'll get Rose and get as far away from Manhattan and Kingsboro as we possibly can.

So I can do this, right? I can go to the island and pretend to be the girl I once was. I can avoid the eyes of men, not speak unless spoken to, and make myself less significant than everyone else around me, because this time, I'll know it's just an act.

———

When I arrive at Ram's waiting room, I see Dekker for the first time in a week. I'm speechless. He's grown as much facial hair as he can, and the beard and his hair are a bright fiery orange—a color I didn't know could appear in nature. He certainly looks nothing like his former self.

Juda is already there, gaping at him.

Dekker raises his eyebrows at me when I walk in. "You look weird," he says.

"Do I look as weird as him?" I ask Juda. He shakes his head.

"I look handsome as hell," Dekker says, smoothing his beard. He looks like a giant kumquat.

Juda's transformation is better than when I saw him at the hospital. His hair is less yellow and more dirty-blond. Gertie must have fixed it. She left it long, which I like. I can get used to his glasses, but I'll never adjust to the new eye color.

"How are you?" I ask Dekker.

"Terrific," he says, with a wide grin. He seems sincere, and, looking him over, I confess there's a new lightness to him.

"Are you happy to be going back?" I ask, aghast.

"Are you nuts? Of course not," he says.

"Then why are you 'terrific'?"

"Wouldn't you like to know?" he says, with a smug tilt of the head.

I look to Juda, who appears as mystified as I am. Maybe Dekker's planning to visit Mother when we return, and the idea is making him chirpy. He always managed to get along with her while I never could.

"Although," he says, "I'd be a lot better if you hadn't gotten us into this mess."

"How is this my fault?" I ask, instantly sick of my brother.

"If you'd just stayed in the Forgiveness Home like you were supposed to—"

"—Ram would still be sending us back," Juda says. "He was going to order us home no matter what, Dekker. Don't you get it?"

Dekker steps forward like he's itching for a fight.

Marjory looks up from her desk, and I hope the boys remember the large gun in the case above her.

Luckily, Grace walks in, distracting everyone. "Peace, Propheteers."

"Evening, Grace," I say.

"Grace?" Dekker says, mouth slightly agape. "You've changed."

"Wasn't that the point?" she says.

I watch my brother watch Grace cross the room. With her straightened hair and lack of glasses, she looks older. You can really see her face—her cheekbones and eyes.

Glaring at Dekker, I say, "She looks different, but she's the same old Grace." I hope he knows I mean *The girl who thinks you're a lunkhead.*

"You can go in now," Marjory says, and the door to Ram's office swings open.

"After you," Dekker tells Grace, and I want to barf.

When we enter, Ram's at his wheel-desk, walking at a brisk rate. "You can remain standing. This won't take long." Closing a screen on his right, he continues to walk and talk. "You'll be leaving tomorrow at eight a.m., after you've said good-bye to your host-families. I'll be seeing you off, and the Unbound can join me or watch live on their Tacts if they so desire. You've done good preparation this week and I'm proud of you." He raises his hands toward the sky. "You're now God's soldiers, and He's looking after you."

I squirm, wanting to say that I never signed up to be a soldier.

"I'm sure you've all been wondering how you're expected to complete your holy mission," he says, jumping off the wheel. "You don't have to worry, because we've thought everything through for you."

Don't worry, he says. Then why doesn't he do it?

"I'll check in with you through your Tacts. I expect thorough updates." He takes a large envelope off his bookshelf. "This contains new identities for each of you. Memorize the information and, it goes without saying, do not take these papers with you." He directs this last sentence at Dekker, as if he's the only one who might make such a stupid mistake.

He hands the envelope to Juda and then returns to the bookshelf. He opens a carved wooden box, removing a tiny cloth pouch. After loosening the strings, he shakes the pouch upside down into his palm. A tiny silver ball no bigger than an aspirin rolls out.

"This little guy may not look like much, but it's the latest in

37

nanotechnology." He holds up the pellet with delight. "If I swallow it, it will land in my stomach and become hundreds of tinier pellets. They'll enter my bloodstream and release tiny doses of Thrombin, which will cause my blood to clot. Eventually I'll succumb to Disseminated Intravascular Coagulation, with millions of blood clots forming throughout my body. To everyone, including my doctors, my death will look like a random, tragic event." He smiles at the cleverness of it all. "So all *you* have to do is pop one of these tiny beauties into Ruho's food."

I shudder as he puts the silver ball back into its pouch. How many times has he used these before?

"John Paul has sewn one of these into each of your cloaks and uniforms so that a search won't discover them. Only one of them is necessary to do the job, but we don't know which one of you will have the first opportunity." He grins at us. "But I know all of you are smart enough and brave enough to pull off this invaluable mission."

Grace looks at me with fear.

"And then you'll bring us back, right?" I say, referring to our last conversation.

Dekker, taken aback, says, "Is she kidding?"

Ram sits down in a beanbag chair. "She's not. I've assured Mina that if you carry out your mission, I'll provide travel out of the city."

Dekker looks elated.

I watch Juda for his reaction. I haven't had a chance to talk to him about Ram's promise. He looks surprised but not as relieved as I'd hoped. He probably doesn't believe him.

"Quit saying 'mission' and just call it what it is," Juda says with contempt. "*Murder.*"

I try to keep the conversation on track. "How can we trust you to get us out?" I ask. "We mean nothing to you."

"I'm hurt that you think that, Mina." Ram puts his hand to his heart. "God gave me a vision of the Manhattan Five and His messages are not to be trifled with. He chose you, and to me you are as precious as anyone in my flock." He actually sounds sincere. "If I abandoned you, I would be no better than a shepherd who led his sheep straight into the mouth of a wolf."

"Instead you're the shepherd who blackmails his sheep," Juda says with contempt.

Ram smiles with patience. "I wish we could have gotten to this place under more amicable terms, but God has a timetable." He gestures to the door. "As do I. I'll see you tomorrow at the big send-off. Get a good night's sleep."

I walk out, glaring at him with all the hatred I can find in my heart.

SEVEN

We file back into the waiting area. We want to look inside the envelope Ram gave us, but we also need to talk far from Marjory's listening ears. Remembering where Silas took me when he wanted to talk in private, I ask the others to follow me.

As we walk down the metal stairs, Dekker begins to whistle.

"Seriously, what's gotten into you?" I ask him.

He grins. "While the rest of you have been stressing out about going home, I've actually been doing something about it."

"This should be interesting," I say.

"I got engaged last night."

Everyone but Dekker stops walking, and he almost bumps Grace down the stairs.

"You *what*?" I say.

"I asked Delilah Delford to marry me and she said yes."

"Why would you do that?" Juda asks, taking the question right from my mouth.

"Because Mr. Delford is not going to let his future son-in-law rot on the island, is he? He'll pester Ram until that future son-in-law is safely back in Kingsboro."

"It's actually pretty smart," Grace says.

"Thank you," Dekker says.

"But you realize once you come back," I say, "you'll actually have to marry Delilah?"

He shrugs. "Whatever."

"Do you even like her?" I ask.

"What does that matter? Her father will give us a house and give me a job. It's a perfect match."

"How did you decide between the two sisters?" Juda asks.

"I could never remember the other one's name," he says.

"You deserve to rot on the island," I say.

"Mother and Father would be proud," he says, defensive. "This is much better than any marriage I would have made at home."

He's probably right.

"And now Ram has promised he'll get us home? I'm a made man." Dekker beams.

"Congratulations," Juda says, patting him on the back.

"Congratulations," Grace says.

I think of the otter daughters and how Tabby could subdue them with a look. They seem like sweet but very meek girls. Dekker will be able to rule the household however he pleases. "Uh, congratulations," I say. "I hope it works out the way you want."

When we reach the ground, I lead everyone through the Leisure Center and down into the noisy food hall. No one stares at us like before, so perhaps our makeovers are working.

We find a table in a busy corner where no one will be able to hear us.

Opening the envelope that Ram gave us, Juda hands out

the papers inside. I scan mine quickly, looking for the item that I know each of us is most curious about: our new names.

Elizabeth Smithson. What? It's major feeble. Can't I just make up my own name? What about Nana's name, Ura? I suppose the name would be in the Twitcher database, so that would be dumb.

"Rufus McDaniel? Are you kidding me?" Dekker says.

I barely suppress a laugh. Is Ram making fun of Dekker?

"I'm not going by this," he says petulantly.

"You have less than twenty-four hours to come up with something else," Juda says.

Dekker scowls at Juda as if he came up with the name.

Grace sucks in her breath as she reads her paper.

"What's wrong?" I say.

"I'm Daphne Butler," Grace says.

"Not bad," I say.

"Daphne was the maiden chased by Apollo. Her father turned her into a laurel tree."

"I think that's good luck," I say.

She shakes her head. "Daphne had horrible luck. She became a *tree*."

"It's just a story," Juda says. "It doesn't mean anything."

Grace sits back, clearly unnerved.

Pulling her against my shoulder, I ask Juda, "What about you?"

"James Thompson," he says.

"Weird," I say, unable to imagine calling him anything but Juda.

"Major weird. What's yours?" he asks.

"Uh . . . Elizabeth."

"That's nice," Grace says. "You can go by Eliza, Lizzie, Beth, Bit—"

"It suits the red hair," Juda says.

"Sure," I say, unconvinced.

We spend ten minutes going in a circle, memorizing one another's names. I decide to go by "Beth." Dekker is angry about "Rufus" and cringes every time someone says it. I tell him to stop it or he's going to get us caught.

Once we feel like we have the new names firmly planted in our heads, we spend time reading the rest of the information: place of birth, parents' names, childhood hobbies, etc.

"Beth" was born in north Kingsboro. Her parents are Justin and Rachel. Her siblings are Mattie and Susan.

Grace puts down her document, face grim. "What do you think of the pellets?"

"Major benny," Dekker says.

I want to punch him. "Nothing about this is benny."

"I mean, they make things a lot easier. We don't have to like, shoot the guy or anything."

"We still have to kill someone!" Grace squeaks and then looks around to see if anyone heard.

"Are we going to tell Mary and Silas?" I ask.

No one thinks it's a good idea to tell Tabby about our "mission," but we've gone back and forth on Mary and Silas. On the one hand, they haven't been asked to be involved with this horrendous deed, so they shouldn't have to suffer knowing about it. On the other hand, they could be so shocked when it happens that they accidentally do something foolish and get us caught. I think we should tell them, but I know them and trust them more than anyone else.

"I think they deserve to know," I say.

"I think they deserve NOT to know," Grace says. I know she hasn't been sleeping very well since Ram told us his plan.

Dekker shrugs. "I really don't care."

"They may be able to help us," I say, unsure how any of us will possibly carry this whole thing off.

"The more people know about the plan, the more likely it is that we get caught," Juda says, looking at me.

He knows how I feel about Mary and Silas, but he feels strongly about keeping our group small. I don't like keeping secrets from anyone in our group, even Tabby, if I'm honest.

"Let's say that we don't tell them for now, but we revisit the question if our needs change," Grace suggests.

Juda nods. "That seems smart."

"Whatever," Dekker says.

"Mina?" Juda asks.

I'm disappointed, but I think this is as good as I'm going to get today, so I nod.

Then Juda says, "This might be the last time we're alone together for a long time."

He's right. Once we arrive on the island, we'll be divided into males and females pretty quickly.

"I've got plenty of time to see you losers. I'm going to go spend time with my future family, thank you very much." Dekker stands and leaves without another word.

As he walks away, Grace watches him. "What do you think about *that?*"

"I'm mostly amazed at Delilah Delford. All the boys in Kingsboro and she chose him?"

"You give him a hard time," Grace says.

I'm astonished. Grace is the smartest person I know. "He once tried to eat a candle."

She giggles.

Juda is ready to get back to business. "We'll use the Tacts to communicate once we're there and try to see each other in person whenever possible."

I've been hanging on to the fact that we have the Tacts. Otherwise, it would be like Juda and I were moving into separate cities.

45

"Right," Grace says, looking at the two of us. "It's going to be major feeble if we can't visit one other."

We sit in awkward silence. There's so much to say about tomorrow, we can't say anything.

Juda and I walk Grace home. Our Bees zigzag above us, so we're not "alone," but at least we're together.

"What happened to you two last night?" Juda asks.

Grace and I look at each other guiltily. We left the hospital without saying goodbye to him or Rose. I don't want to tell him about our failed negotiation with Ram.

"Dr. Rachel said your ma needed rest," Grace says, quick as usual.

"She slept hard last night," he says. "I was relieved."

Changing the subject, Grace says, "How much do you think we're allowed to bring with us tomorrow?"

I wish I knew the answer. "What do you want to bring?"

"Gosh. Shampoo, and soap, and my nice hairbrush. And these pajamas that are so soft, they make you feel like you're sleeping with baby bunnies. And my socks and new shoes—"

"Bring it all," Juda says. "Can't hurt to try."

Grace nods. Underneath her bubbly exterior, I think she's more nervous than Tabby. She's never lived on the island around men before.

When we reach her house, I give her a huge hug. "You'll be fine. I won't let anything happen to you, I promise."

She smiles, but she knows my words are empty. Once we're back on the island, I'll be as powerless as she is.

EIGHT

Once she's gone inside the house, Juda and I walk toward the Dixon's.

One question has been haunting me since Ram's office. "How will we do it?" I blurt.

He takes a deep breath. I don't have to explain what I mean.

"You want to talk about that right now?"

"Yes," I say. "I'm sorry."

"I'll do it if I can," Juda says. "I'm the most . . . uh . . . qualified."

I assume he means because of his training as a guard.

"But you have to take care of Rose! If you get caught—"

"If anyone gets caught, the Teachers will hang us all."

He's right.

"The pellets are tiny," he says. "Someone will have to get really close to Ruho to get it into his food. I don't know if I'll have that kind of access . . . "

"Why would any of us?"

He looks at me sideways. "Tabby is marrying him."

47

"Tabby can't kill him. Ram told us it can't be a member of the Unbound."

"I know. One of you is going to have become Tabby's best friend or attendant or something. Someone has to have the same access to Ruho that she does."

Someone. My stomach drops. It can't be Mary, who's part of the Unbound. And how could it be sweet Grace, who came above ground less than a month ago?

We both know that it has to be me. I stop walking. "I don't know if I can do it."

"I'll do everything I can to think of another way. I promise." He takes my hand.

I can't think about Uncle Ruho or the pellet without feeling dizzy. I concentrate instead on Juda's hand and how nice it is to not have to hide or pull away from him. We walk hand in hand, taking our time.

A breeze whips through the trees. The air crackles with the anticipation of rain, and I savor the sensation of my hair blowing loose around my face.

"This is our last moment alone," I say.

"For a while," he adds.

"Do you think God is keeping us apart?" I ask.

He laughs, but I was only half-kidding.

"I think our challenges only make us stronger," he says.

This sounds like something Rose would say. Besides, Juda doesn't look stronger. He looks tired and thin.

"Are you okay?" I ask.

"Of course."

With his Tacts, I can't look into his eyes the way I used to. They seem flatter, like they don't belong to an actual human, and it's harder to tell what he's thinking.

"Your ma will be fine," I say.

"Of course she will," he says robotically.

"Would you tell me if you *weren't* okay?"

"Yeah." After a moment, he adds, "I think so."

I don't love this answer.

We arrive at the Dixon's house, stopping on the front stoop. Wanting to delay his departure, I say, "I never really told you, uh, how worried I was when you were in the Forgiveness Home. I tried to find you every day."

He smiles, and, for a second, I think I see the old twinkle in his eyes. "I almost fell out of my chair when you walked into my session."

"It wasn't my best thought-out plan," I admit.

"Before then, I'd never experienced happiness and horror at the same moment. I still don't think I'm digesting food properly."

I think he's kidding, but he looks so thin, I wonder if he's not.

Standing on tiptoe, I kiss him.

He kisses me back immediately, as if he's been waiting all night for the chance. He draws me in until I'm encircled by his long arms. I welcome his warm mouth and his body around me. His hair and eyes make him look like a stranger—but this part of him I know. He tastes like honey and smells like fresh cut firewood.

We kiss and kiss, as I wait for the porch light to flicker on, for the Dixons to open the door and scream at us. But they don't. We're able to envelop each other until we're out of breath.

I've always thought that if I were able to kiss Juda for five minutes straight, it would satisfy the longing I have for him, but now I know that isn't true. The longing grows stronger every second, and now I can't imagine any amount of time ever being enough. I think of that bunker, of everything that's happened to us since the time we spent there. What would I do differently if

I could go back? As his kisses grow deeper, I decide that I would never leave.

Once we're in Manhattan, can't we find another protected room? Somewhere on the island, there has to be another safe space where Ram, Uncle Ruho, and the rest of the world will leave us alone.

He leans in, getting as close to my ear as possible. He whispers so that I can barely hear him: "When you see a Nod that says 'Peace and light,' that means 'I love you.'"

Heat rushes to my face. Without turning to him, I whisper just as quietly, "I love you, too."

I feel him smile.

Did I just say that? My heart thuds in panic and without meaning to, I pull away from him.

A bit flustered, he says, "You should get some sleep."

"You, too," I say, knowing that instead of going home, he'll go to the hospital.

His smile fades. "I'm telling Ma tonight . . . that I'm leaving."

I nod, not sure what to say.

He rubs the back of his neck. "I just . . . What if I make her worse?"

"She's incredibly tough. I wish I were half as strong as she is."

He half smiles. "You are."

"She'll understand that you have to leave, that we have no choice."

"I'm thinking of telling her that I'm going there to help the Convenes. I don't want to tell her about living with Uncle Ruho."

His original plan was to return to Manhattan to help the people he grew up with fight their war, so his story would be believable. "She'll be waiting for you when you get back."

"You really think Ram will help us leave the island?" he says.

"Yes, I do." Ram can't just abandon Tabby after Ruho is gone. The Unbound would be beside themselves.

Seeing that Juda's face is still miserable, I add, "I can come with you to tell Rose, if you'd like."

"I'd like it a lot, but I need to do this on my own."

"Okay." I kiss his cheek.

"I'll see you in the morning," he says.

Morning. My dinner threatens to rise back up my throat. "Yeah. See you in the morning."

He kisses me one last time and then leaves for the hospital.

When I finally walk upstairs to my bedroom, I'm fully awake. I change and lie down, but my body snaps with energy. The blood in my veins is like oil heating in a skillet, popping and crackling as it runs from my head to my toes. All I can think of are Juda's words: *someone has to have the same access to Ruho that Tabby does.*

I get up. I double-check my bag, locate the small knife. I take it out. I put it back in. I return to bed. I close my eyes and try to stop my thoughts. I think about Nana—how happy she'll be to see me. How angry she'll be that I had to come back. I focus all of my thoughts on the moment of our reunion.

Next thing I know, I'm in the subway tunnel—treading in the cold murky water, surrounded by squealing rats. The darkness is overwhelming, and as we reach the terminal in Manhattan, a gray hand reaches out of the murky water . . .

"UP AND AT 'EM!" Bithia screeches, as she throws on the lights in my room.

I bolt upright, unaware that I was sleeping.

Nyek. It's Monday.

It's time to go home.

NINE

"We leave in one hour. Don't shilly-shally!" Bithia has no smile for me today.

I shower, going through the three stages of hot water, cold water, and protective sunstop. I put on white pants and a long-sleeved white top. Downstairs, Tabby wears an ensemble similar to mine but in bright fuchsia. She will not get lost in a crowd anytime soon. I guess John Paul made the outfit for her. Her hair is up, fastened with a sparkly gold comb. Her skin is radiant and her lips glossy. She is a ravishing bride-to-be.

Silas is in a navy blue jumpsuit that echoes the uniforms of the Sentries. He would look more imposing if his eyelashes weren't so darn long.

Bithia feeds us a breakfast fit for an army, and I eat as much as I can. Neither Tabby nor Silas eats much. Even Corny feels the tension and attempts to get to the bottom of it.

"Why is everyone unhappy, Daddy?" he asks.

"We aren't unhappy, buddy," Gilad says. "We're proud that our family is part of God's plan."

"We're so blessed," Bithia says, holding back tears.

"And you and Mommy and Daddy are going to have a really benny life after we're gone, okay?" Tabby says in the sweetest voice I've ever heard her use.

Corny looks suspicious.

"Really!" she says. "You're going to be the most luminary people in town. You'll sit in a special place during worship service, and you'll even get to live in a big new house, closer to Ram!"

Corny's eyes grow huge. "Is that true, Mommy?"

Bithia stares at Tabby open-mouthed, as if this is news to her. Tabby smiles at her and then at her father, who looks dumbfounded. He hides his tears by using his napkin to pretend to blow his nose.

Good for Tabby. This is the first non-selfish thing I've ever seen her do.

Corny whines, "Is it TRUE?"

Bithia pats his hand. "Yes, Cornball. It's true. Finish your eggs."

Corny finishes his breakfast with enthusiasm.

When the meal is over, Gilad asks us to gather in the living room in a circle. We join hands while he leads us in prayer. "God, please look over these young pilgrims. Guide them and hold them in Your almighty hands. Give them strength. We will miss each other, but we ask You to allow us all to be reunited next to You in Heaven. So be it."

"So be it," we echo.

We gather our things, which include four huge bags for Tabby, and walk outside, where a black van awaits us. I expect many tears and emotional words, but instead, Tabby stoically kisses each parent on the cheek, ruffles Corny's hair, and steps into the front seat.

Silas' good-bye is more uncomfortable. Neither parent knows what to say. Everyone stares at one another for a while.

Unable to stand it, I take Silas' hand and say to them, "Thank you for giving me shelter in my time of need. God likes generosity." I pull Silas toward the van.

"Wait," he says. He takes a step toward his parents. "I'm sorry I couldn't be different for you."

"Silas, you don't have to—" I begin.

He holds his hand up, silencing me, and continues. "But I'm more sorry that you couldn't be different for me." He turns away and gets in the van.

I step in after him and shut the door. Before we can turn to see Bithia or Gilad's expressions, we're speeding away.

Unlike every other van we've been placed in, this one has rows of seats, and we aren't locked in the back. We're able to see out all the windows. An expressionless Sentry mans the wheel.

We pick up Juda next, who's wearing the same navy uniform as Silas. He looks groggy and distracted as he slides in next to me.

"Where are your things?" I ask.

"Nyek," he says. "Wait a minute!" he yells at the driver. He runs back inside to grab his bag.

Silas and I look at each other, worried. Juda obviously hasn't slept at all. He's in no shape to begin a hard journey.

When he returns with his things, he gives us a weak smile. "Sorry, everyone."

I'm dying to know how his talk went with his mother, but I don't want to stress him out even more. No matter how it went, it couldn't have made him feel good. Once the van is moving, I tell him to try to sleep a little. I offer him the seat by the window. He's barely sat down before he's softly snoring.

Next is Grace. She approaches with two bags, and they're

both stuffed full. Her face is clammy and red and her straightened hair seems to have regained a bit of its frizz.

When she climbs into the van next to me, I see that her eyes are puffy.

"You okay?" I ask.

She looks out the window at the house, where her host-family waves from the front door.

"They're really nice people, and uh . . . " She wipes her nose with her hand. "I may never have a real family again." She presses her sleeve against her damp eyes.

"We're coming back, remember?" I whisper.

"Yeah, if we . . . " Her voice trails off as she remembers Tabby is in the seat in front of us. "If we *do everything right.*"

I hug her as the van pulls away.

Mary is next. Jeremiah carries her bag for her. Her face is neutral, and she doesn't look back at her parents, who stand on the lawn.

Jeremiah slides open the van door, and Mary scrutinizes us all. "Good morning, astronauts. Who's ready to walk on the moon?"

I smile for the first time today.

Taking her bag from Jeremiah, she throws it behind us, on the seat next to Silas.

She turns to her brother. "You're a major dook-wad, but I hope I see you again."

He nods. Is he crying?

"You, too," he says.

She throws her arms around him.

Over her shoulder, Jeremiah glares at the rest us. "Keep her safe."

"We will," Silas says.

After Mary is in the van, I ask her, "Did your brother get in trouble because we hid in his house?"

She sighs. "He's not allowed to take his black exam for at least two more years."

"Ouch," Silas says.

"I'd rather be in his place than mine," she says, waving good-bye to him.

"Yeps," Silas says. "Me too."

Mary spots Tabby in the front seat. "Oooh. You look fab, Tabs." She guffaws. "Fab Tab! I just found your new nickname."

Tabby swings around to glower at her. "You will *not* call me that."

"Got it, Fab Tab." Mary settles in next to Silas.

Dekker is last. Without greeting, he climbs into the very back. Unlike Silas and Juda, he's wearing a green uniform. Perched upon his head is a ridiculous matching beret.

"What are you wearing?" I ask.

"Since I'm the only person who has attended the Lyceum, I'm the senior member of this party. John Paul designed me a uniform to designate my rank."

Mary snorts. "Is your rank 'leprechaun'?"

Dekker looks at her, furious. "Laugh now, but very soon you'll have to obey and listen to everything I say."

"Is that true?" Mary asks me.

With great sadness, I nod.

She turns back to Dekker. "Then before we get there, I'd like to let you know that every time you speak to me from now on, I'll be thinking, 'Shove it up your bumhole.'"

Silas and I laugh so hard that Juda wakes up.

"No one in Manhattan can know you went to the Lyceum," Grace says. "They have to think grew up in Kingsboro, remember?"

Dekker's face contorts in confusion, but he says, "I know that." A second later he says, "What's important is that *you* all

57

know it. Everyone in this van knows that I am the senior ranking functionary."

Mary rolls her eyes, while Tabby gives a sarcastic, "Yeps."

With the seven of us present, Juda, Grace, Dekker, and I use the time to teach the others our new names. Each of us repeats the names over and over until they seem permanently attached to our faces. Still, Juda can never really be *James* to me.

I have the desire to lean forward and talk to the Sentry driving the van, to tell him "If we don't make it back, I want you to know that Ram sent us to murder Uncle Ruho. He made us do it, and he's an evil, horrible man."

But, of course, I don't. I sit there repeating our new names with everyone else as we head toward Ram and the "big send-off." Why can't Ram just call it what it is? Forced deportation.

TEN

The Sentry doesn't stop our van at the entrance to the subway, and I exhale with relief; we'll be returning to Manhattan another way. Driving west for several more miles, we arrive at a neglected park next to the waterfront. We stop next to an ancient playscape, whose derelict swings and rusted slides would depress the most high-spirited child.

A sizable crowd is gathered on the grass, and people gape at us as we jump down one at a time from the van. Ram, waiting to greet us, wears the dapper white suit he wore to Promise Prom. His smile is so large I'm afraid his lips will crack.

Next to Ram stand Marjory, Mrs. Prue, and John Paul. John Paul holds several packages. Our cloaks, finally.

John Paul gives each girl a bundle. Tabby receives two. Her wedding dress must be inside the second. We each say thank you, and he radiates pride.

With the crowd watching, I open mine. As I let the green-ish-blue material unfold, I see the very slight gold shimmer— the firewall. I throw the cloak over my head. A piece of fabric floats to the ground. The veil. I pick it up and shove it into my bag, not yet ready to wear it.

Grace puts her cloak on as well, and I'm grateful. It's very warm outside, and, normally, I would wait as long as possible to put a cloak on. But I have an agenda and the timing is tight. Following suit, Mary and Tabby put theirs on as well. They look strange in the body-hiding garments.

Ram snaps his fingers at two Sentry guards and tells them to carry our bags.

My throat goes dry.

The Sentries take Tabby's things, then Grace's, then Mary's, and just as one reaches me, I blurt, "I need to use the bathroom!"

Everyone turns to look at me.

"It can wait," Ram says.

The Sentry reaches for my bag.

I remember Nana's guidelines and say, "It's lady business."

The Sentry backs away at once.

Ram, at a loss for words, looks to Mrs. Prue.

"I'll take her," she says, smile as perfect as ever. "We'll catch up with you." Approaching me, she says, "This way." She walks away from the water, and I follow with my head down, a bit embarrassed, but some things are more important than pride.

She leads me to a small brick building so old and decrepit it looks like it should be inhabited by trolls. A door has a sign hanging by one nail that reads "Women." Mrs. Prue takes a handkerchief out of her purse and uses it to push open the ancient door. A smell comes out that would knock over a horse.

"I'll wait out here," she says, breathing out her mouth. "Do you have everything you need?"

"Uh . . . yes," I say.

"Then hurry up."

With dismay, I walk into the gloomy restroom. I cross the damp floor and gently push open a stall door, terrified that I'm about to disturb a lair of rats. When the door swings open, I'm ridiculously relieved to see only an ancient toilet.

Once the door is shut behind me, I unzip my bag and shove my hand deep inside. I hid the knife at the very bottom so that it couldn't fall out, but I hadn't counted on not being able to unpack my things to search for it. I feel around with my hand and suddenly feel an acute jab in my wrist.

I can barely keep from crying out.

I'm such an idiot—blindly feeling around for an uncovered knife? Of course I cut myself. At least now I know where it is. I gently move aside my clothing and spot my attacker standing almost straight up between a pair of sandals.

"Hurry up," Mrs. Prue says.

I use a sock to wipe up the blood from my wrist. The cut isn't deep and my cloak covers it. Taking out the knife, I drop it into one of four inside pockets. *God bless you, John Paul.* I pray the firewall really works.

I repack the bag, flush the toilet with my foot, and leave the stall.

"All better?" Mrs. Prue asks with impatience.

"Yes. Thank you."

As we leave the building, she puts an arm around my shoulder, saying, "For the future, dear, nice young women don't talk about 'lady things' in public. It's not modest or sophisticated, and those are both things I think you can be."

I smile, thinking how much smarter Nana is than this woman. "Yes, Mrs. Prue. You're so right."

"Good. Let's catch up with the others."

As we cross the park, I'm amazed at the view, which not only includes Manhattan but the remains of a bridge that once joined Queens to the island. From here, it looks quite majestic, with its pointed towers and latticed frame, despite the bombed-out hole in the middle.

When we arrive at the water's edge, a light drizzle has begun. Mrs. Prue produces a purple umbrella from her purse and opens it above us both. The crowd, now holding their own umbrellas, has migrated and is facing Manhattan. When Mrs. Prue and I finally pass through the throng, we're almost at the water. My friends stand in a line next to Ram, who holds a microphone while Marjory holds a white umbrella above his head.

Next to all of them is something far more terrifying than a subway stop: a drone the size of a taxi with seven seats inside. *Ram expects us to go up in that thing?* My hands begin to shake.

Ram walks to the machine, rubs the side, and says to the audience, "Tabitha and her wedding party will be traveling to Manhattan in style, using our leading technology. You're well-acquainted with our Bees. We call this the Ostrich."

Everyone laughs.

I understand the name. The machine looks like a mashed metal bird holding onto an enormous glass egg.

"It requires no pilot, yet it will fly and land perfectly and then return to us exactly where and when we tell it to. It is our leading conveyance-drone technology."

People clap.

I'm not clapping and neither are my friends. I don't want to get into a flying machine, and I most definitely don't want to get in one without a pilot.

"Thank you for your love and prayers on this righteous occasion," Ram says. "I'm sure Tabitha feels blessed and supported and will be able to represent our people in the way God desires."

To my surprise, and to Ram's it appears, Tabby steps forward and plucks the microphone from his hand. "Thank you, dear people of Kingsboro. I will do my best to represent you, spread love among the Propheteers, and educate the woolie leader in the ways of the Savior."

Mary palms her forehead.

"The rain is ruining Tabitha's hair," Mrs. Prue whines. "Go cover her!" She hands me the umbrella.

Tabby raises her fingers to the sky. "Fear not. You're in good hands, and the Ascension is imminent!"

Ram produces an enormous smile, his little teeth gleaming in the morning sun. "Isn't she lovely?" Grabbing the microphone back from Tabby, he claps, and the crowd joins him.

Tabby rejoins the line, a self-satisfied glow on her face.

I scurry up and cover her in Mrs. Prue's umbrella. Next to me, Mary whispers, "I was hoping maybe you'd made a run for it."

I give her a thin smile.

In the front row I spot old Mr. Groodly, who looks as downcast as ever. He waves meekly. He's the only person watching who understands what we're returning to. The last time I saw him, at Prom, we traded harsh words, but I wave back. All the people he cares about are in Manhattan, and he *still* chooses to stay here.

Ram's voice booms. "And NOW, it is time to say good-bye." He approaches Juda, Grace, Dekker, and me, saying in a low voice, "Remember God is watching you, and so am I. Tick-tock, tick-tock." He then walks up to me, pointing at the Ostrich. "I told you I had a means of getting you in and out. The subway? Why do you woolies have to make everything so complicated?"

Marjory announces it's time for us to board.

We approach the Ostrich with dread. Seven seats cramped inside a glass oval—that's it. I can't see an engine. How does it possibly fly?

The Sentries hand everyone else their bags (I still have

mine). I look at Juda. He's so tired he looks like he might fall over. Does he fully understand what's happening?

"I'll go first," he says. Even in his exhaustion, he's trying to protect me.

I ignore him, hand Tabby the umbrella, and climb inside the egg. He and Grace squeeze in next to me, and then Mary and Silas sit in the seats across from us. Dekker crams his large frame through the entry and heads straight for the single seat at the end. Tabby takes her time outside, waving to the crowd, enjoying the applause.

When she finally boards, she sees Dekker and says, "That's my seat. Move."

"I got here first, sweetie."

Silas laughs.

"What's funny?" Dekker asks.

"I've never seen anyone talk to her that way," Silas says, "and I'm excited to see what happens next."

Tabby takes two quicks steps toward Dekker, pinches his right nipple and gives it a hard twist. He cries out in pain.

"MOVE," she says.

He stands, hitting his head on the ceiling.

Silas laughs again. Dekker sits next to him, saying, "Shut your face."

Tabby sits in the single seat, spreading her cloak out around her. Only now do I notice her sleeves and hem have gold beading, which sets her apart from us. She touches her damp hair, adjusting the comb, then looks out to her adoring crowd. They've seen the incident with Dekker, and they squint in confusion. She gives them a dazzling smile, waving and laughing. They wave back, happy to see that their princess is okay.

A bell chimes once, silencing us all. Seat belts automatically crisscross our torsos.

The bell chimes twice and the Ostrich's door slides shut.

The crowd backs away from the machine. Juda and I look at each other, terrified.

The bell chimes three times, and we lurch off the ground. As Grace yelps, Juda takes her hand. The wind from the rain blows us back and forth as we rise, the glass allowing us to see everything—the ground receding, the people waving, the buildings growing tiny. Overhead, metal blades whirl in near silence.

Before long, we're so high that the crowd of umbrellas becomes a smattering of confetti. Looking down is petrifying, so I face the others. Dekker has turned the same green as his jumpsuit. I close my eyes.

"Do you think we can talk it into taking us to Canada?" Mary says, her voice shaky.

Silas laughs but barely.

Grace gasps. "Look!"

Reluctantly, I open one eye .

"The ocean!" she says.

To my right is an expanse of water bigger than anything I've ever imagined. The rain has turned the waves gray, and the dark rolling water disappears into the horizon—large, beautiful, and ominous.

"Wow," Juda whispers.

"*Peaceful sleep is ever there,*" Grace whispers, "*beneath the dark blue waves.*"

"That's bleak," Mary says.

"Nathaniel Hawthorne," Grace replies.

"Look over there," Silas says, pointing the other direction.

Underneath us, the water divides the land into islands, but farther away, the land becomes solid and goes on and on and on.

"Who lives there?" I ask.

"It looks deserted," Mary says.

Growing up in Manhattan, my world had always seemed so

enormous, but today it seems small. I'm sad to think no one lives out there. Is there nothing beyond the island and Kingsboro?

Soon we're flying over the island itself. After the green lawns and bright houses of Kingsboro, the streets of Manhattan look filthy and ashen. I can almost smell it—the garbage in the streets, the crowds of unbathed people, the hot winds that bring the stench of the goats in the Park. I've missed this world I grew up in. I trust the good smells when there are bad smells, too. I trust noise and crowds and dirt and grime because they're all real. A homeless man with no teeth isn't trying to fool me—he's showing me who he is and maybe asking me to help him out. I'm far more frightened of a man like Ram, who's clean and friendly on the outside but dark and ruthless on the inside.

We swing northward and the Park comes into view. From here it looks enormous! I never understood quite how big it was. Acres of cornfields border acres of wheat. I look for the Boathouse but can't spot it.

"What's that?" Mary asks, pointing west.

Grace looks over. "The canals. They dug them when the sea levels rose."

"We never learned about those in school."

"They're post-Prophet. I doubt your books cover that stuff."

"Weird," Silas says.

We keep flying north, further than I've ever traveled. I find it hard to believe we're still in Manhattan.

As we pass over an area so densely green it could be forest, the Ostrich begins to drop. "We're going down!" Dekker says.

"Relax," Tabby says.

"Any last minute advice?" Silas asks, his nerves apparent.

"Stay out of people's way," Juda says.

"Stay alive?" says Mary.

No one laughs.

We descend lower and lower until I'm certain we're going to land in the top of a tree, but at the last moment, the Ostrich swerves and takes us to a small grass field. The trip has taken no more than twenty minutes. When we were in the subway tunnel, I just wanted the journey to be over. Now I want it to go on forever.

Even through the misty rain, I can spot Twitchers standing on the perimeter of the field. I might throw up. One glance at them and everything the Unbound did for us seems childish and silly—the hair dye, the Tacts, the firewall. *Of course* the Twitchers will figure out who we are. We were moronic to think otherwise.

"Put on your veils," I tell the girls, reaching into my bag. With the Twitchers in sight, no one needs to be told twice.

The Ostrich lands perfectly, like a teacup going into its saucer. The blades slowly stop spinning. The seat belts don't unfasten immediately, making me feel trapped. The temperature also seems to rise dramatically, and my cloak becomes stifling.

Juda takes my hand. "You're shaking," he says.

"So are you," I respond.

He kisses my fingers. It will be the last physical contact we're allowed to have.

I watch as the Twitchers march toward us, large guns in their gloved hands.

"What are they?" Tabby asks, voice shrill.

"Say hello to your new Bees," Dekker says.

ELEVEN

The largest Twitcher steps forward, his voice thundering. "Exit the flying machine!"

It's Captain Memon, the head of the City Guard, the man in charge of all Twitchers. Even if I didn't recognize his voice, I would know the dagger at his side with the emerald sheath.

Tabby rises.

"No," I say. "Boys first."

Dekker smirks at her. Then he, Silas, and Juda stand as tall as they can and exit the Ostrich. Mary, Grace, and I leave next, allowing Tabby to make her grand descent last.

The drizzle feels nice, even through my veil. Mary holds onto me tightly. I imagine seeing a Twitcher for the first time: the black suit, the pointy, reflective mask, the large gun. They're way more sinister than anything in Kingsboro.

I whisper, "You're okay."

She *is* okay. Juda, Dekker, and me? We'll find out as soon as we're scanned.

Before I know what's happening, Tabby exits the Ostrich,

opens her umbrella, and approaches Captain Memon with her head held high.

Oh God. *Don't speak first. PLEASE don't speak first.*

She stops directly in front of him, and, although she's looking straight at him, she waits.

He says, "Peace."

"Peace," she replies.

He looks over her head and speaks to Juda. "Is this Tabitha Dixon?"

"Yes," Tabby says, just as Juda says, "Yes."

"You will teach her to speak when spoken to," Memon tells Juda.

Juda nods once, like a good soldier. Memon doesn't give him a second look, so, hopefully, doesn't recognize Juda from Mr. Asher's house. With his blond hair and glasses, now speckled with rain, Juda looks very little like the boy who worked for Damon Asher.

To all of us, Memon says, "I am Captain Memon, and this is Zebadiah, Uncle Ruho's top religious advisor." A Herald steps out from behind him. The man is old and angular and has maybe three hairs on top of his head.

"Uncle Ruho awaits you," Captain Memon says, and I brace for him to scan us all.

Instead, Zebadiah says, "You will follow me." He pivots and walks away.

Mary begins to walk, but I grab her hand and whisper, "Men first."

After Juda, Dekker, and Silas have followed Zebadiah, we wait for the Twitchers to go, but Captain Memon tells us to walk. I guess his men are bringing up the rear. I don't like the idea of Twitchers where I can't see them.

We climb brick stairs that go on for some time. I'm tired from my short night of sleep, my bag is heavy, and I have to re-adapt to examining my environment while keeping my head down deferentially. I'm grateful that the rain has kept us from a scorching hot day. When we reach the top of the stairs, I hope the elderly Zebadiah will need to rest, but he strides without hesitation up the next concrete path.

I'm momentarily distracted from my shortness of breath by a giant garden full of flowers and plants lush enough to rival anything in Kingsboro. Then the temperature drops several degrees as we're led through a tunnel created by towering trees. I didn't know trees this immense existed on the island. A man sweeping leaves from the walkway looks up as we pass.

"Is that a Herald or a Teacher?" Mary whispers, looking at him.

"A Herald," I say. Juda and I taught her that a Herald is chosen from the top one percent of Students at the Lyceum to become part of Ruho's inner circle. The other ninety-nine percent become Twitchers or Teachers. "Heralds wear gold. Teachers wear red."

When we emerge from the trees, Grace lets out a gasp. On the hill above us is a building that looks out of place and time.

"It's Thornfield Hall," she says with awe.

"It's what?" Mary asks.

"The castle where Mr. Rochester lives in *Jane Eyre*. Just like I pictured it."

"Keep up!" Zebadiah yells.

We follow him up yet another winding path. The surrounding shrubbery is rich green and trimmed to perfection —I can't imagine how much water they must use to keep everything we've seen alive.

As we approach the house, we arrive at a gate—a stone arch with an iron grating. Two Twitchers stand guard. I watch in dread as the one on the right turns on his Senscan.

Zebadiah says loudly, "All guests are required to undergo a

scan before entering the home of his Holiness. Standard procedure."

Feeling lightheaded, I use all my willpower to not look at Juda.

Silas goes first. His scan takes less than sixty seconds, but I'm not worried about him. He's Unbound.

Next is Dekker, and I hold my breath. Dekker swaggers up to the Twitcher, and I want to punch him for his arrogance. The Twitcher scans him, and although he takes slightly longer than he did with Silas, the Senscan turns green, and Dekker walks through the gate.

Juda is next, and I'm so nervous my knees are literally knocking together under my cloak, but he passes and is allowed through the gate as well. Once he's made it, I start to panic for myself. I've seen that the firewall can protect our identities, but can it conceal the knife in my pocket? John Paul never said it would. Maybe I've made a lethal mistake.

Tabby and Mary are scanned with no problem. I tell Grace to go ahead. While she's being examined, I wonder if I can throw the knife into the shrubbery. Or can I once again say that I have to go to the bathroom?

A quick glance back at Captain Memon and his Twitchers tells me no—there's no way out but forward.

It's my turn.

My body is rigid as wood, so I try to relax and be as confident as Dekker. I stride up to the narrow archway. When I approach the Twitchers, I'm close enough to reach out and touch their helmets. I put my hands together to keep them from shaking.

I watch the Senscan move up and down my body. I try to think of any word in the human language besides *knife*. I remember my omming and start to count backwards from one hundred, but before I can reach eighty-five, the light on the

Senscan turns green. Exhaling with unspeakable relief, I walk under the stone arch.

I did it. We all did it. The firewalls worked.

This time. I want to get rid of the knife as soon as possible. *It's not worth it.*

I try to focus on where we're headed next. Zebadiah makes a left and leads us through an outdoor passage that has a stone wall on one side and half a dozen open arches on the other. We enter the house, and the first room is round with dusty brick walls. I've never seen anything like the ceiling. I can't describe it, except it sort of feels as if I'm inside an animal, like I'm seeing its skeleton—brick columns reach all the way to the highest point in the ceiling and everything that holds the room together seems to jut out like ribs. The room also looks like it might collapse on top of us.

While the rest of us ogle, Tabby closes her umbrella, smoothes her cloak, and tries to fix the back of her hair.

"Whoa." Grace tugs on my cloak, gasping. "We're in the Cloisters!"

"Quiet!" says Zebadiah without turning around.

The Cloisters. I remember Father saying that Uncle Ruho's home looked like it had "been there a thousand years," which I thought was an insult, but he said it was beautiful: "a castle meant for a king." I would've thought Uncle Ruho would want to live in the most modern house with the most electricity on the island. This place looks like it still uses candles.

Zebadiah keeps walking, taking us through a long, imposing room. The stone walls and floor provide the same coolness as the tree tunnel. Sculptures stare down at me. A painting on the wall looks like a dog with a mustache. To my left are more open archways, these revealing a lavish garden tucked into the center of the building.

We pass through the most magnificent doorway I've ever

73

seen—marble angels fly above our heads. The doors themselves have been sculpted with flowers and horses breathing fire. What could it all possibly mean? I'm so preoccupied by my surroundings that at first I don't notice the group awaiting us in the next grand room. Ushering us inside, Zebadiah proclaims, "Your Eminence, your special guest has finally arrived!"

Now it's my turn to gasp. The posters around the city have never showed Uncle Ruho to be a desirable man, but they presented someone far more attractive than the man sitting on the throne in front of us.

This man is grossly overweight, and the pastiness of his skin suggests he has never set foot in his fancy garden or anywhere else outside. Dark moles are scattered across his fleshy face; his hair is sparse and gray. He slumps awkwardly to his right, like a giant ham unable to right itself.

Beside me, a whimper escapes from Tabby.

Oh my God. Poor Tabby.

I take her hand, knowing that she will only make things worse if she reacts badly to him. She trembles as if she's caught a chill.

Zebadiah says, "I present your fiancée, your Holiness." He motions for Tabby to step closer. She doesn't move.

Uncle Ruho lifts his wobbly chin in displeasure.

I whisper, "Two steps and bow your head." Before he can get angrier, I move forward, pulling Tabby with me.

Ruho looks her up and down carefully, as if he can see through her cloak. He sucks his teeth, motioning for her to come closer. When he begins to stand, two Heralds rush over to help him. Once he has his balance, they step away.

He seems very unhealthy. If he were ill, it would solve so many problems!

"Peace," he says.

"Peace," Tabby responds.

He shuffles forward and takes her hand, inspecting it. He lifts it to his dry lips and kisses it. Looking to his men, he says, "If the rest of her is as delicate and lovely as this hand, then I am a happy man."

Tabby seems unsure whether she should respond, since he didn't address her. "Thank you, Uncle—sir."

"You are to be my wife. You will call me what my mother called my father: Beloved."

"Thank you . . . Beloved."

"Your hair is like spun gold." The fingers of his left hand rub her palm, and then he runs them up her wrist, enjoying the feel of her skin.

I hold her hand tighter, terrified she might slap him.

He keeps running his hand higher and higher up her sleeve. I can't see Tabby's face, but I imagine her expression would slice through stone.

"Take off your shoes," he says. "I need to see your feet."

"Your fiancée has had an arduous journey. She should rest." A woman I hadn't noticed steps out from a dark corner. She wears the brown veil and cloak of a Matron. She has spoken without permission, but no one rebukes her.

Ruho doesn't acknowledge her. "Show me your feet!" He reaches down for Tabby's shoes.

"Miss Tabitha wants to freshen up before lunch, correct?" the Matron says.

Tabby nods with frenetic energy.

Ruho now frowns at Tabby like a toddler. "Get her out of here."

With the help of his aides, he sits back down.

The Matron approaches us, her hair pulled back in the kind of tight bun favored by my mother. The one or two gray strands embroidered throughout the brown suggests she's also near my mother's age. "The girls will come with me. The boys will go with Zebadiah."

Our separation. It's here.

Juda gives me a last look. It's the tiniest of smiles, meant to soften my fear. I wish he could see my face, so I could give him a reassuring look back.

Zebadiah leads him, Dekker, and Silas out through a side door. I wish I knew the house well enough to know where they were being taken. The Matron snaps her fingers at Grace, Mary, Tabby, and me. We follow her back the way we came, through the long hall.

"Girls have not been allowed into the Cloisters until now, so the arrangements for your accommodations have been made hastily." She speaks in a quick, efficient manner. "You must adapt and keep yourselves out of the way. You're to speak to no one except me. Ever. Do you understand?"

"Yes, Matron," Grace and I say, and then Mary and Tabby echo our words.

"You'll call me Mrs. Hypat."

"Yes, Mrs. Hypat," we say.

Matrons are always "Mrs." because they're married to God.

"Tell me your names," she says. "I already know Miss Tabitha."

"Mary."

"Daphne," Grace says.

"I'm Beth," I say, the name sticking to the roof of my mouth.

We pass through the round room again, but instead of going out the exit, we turn right, entering another huge hall. This one has a wood ceiling and a tapestry as long as the wall. Trying to look at the figures in the tapestry, I trip over my cloak. I catch myself and don't hit the ground, which is lucky, since Mrs. Hypat doesn't slow down.

We're soon following her down a spiral staircase. At the bottom, she stops in front of a pair of modern glass doors. "This used to be the Treasury. His Holiness thought it was appropriate for you to stay here, since his bride is his 'newest treasure.'"

Mary sniggers as we're led through the doors into a vestibule with wood walls covered in carvings. Is anything in this place not carved? People and animals protrude from old-world scenes. I don't have time to scrutinize them since Mrs. Hypat leads us straight into the main room.

The space is very odd, with concrete floors and a plaster ceiling—much newer than the rest of the house. Even stranger, there are display cases pushed against the walls, which appear to be full of silverware and jewelry. A large bed stands awkwardly in the center of the room. There's nothing else in the way of furniture. "His Eminence thought you'd be better off as far away from the men's quarters as possible."

"Where are the other rooms?" I ask, removing my veil. The girls follow my lead and remove theirs.

"This is it, for now," Mrs. Hypat says. She keeps her veil on, but I can sense her taking in our faces. She spends a long time looking at Tabby. Will she report back to Uncle Ruho if she decides Tabby is inadequate?

"Where are the other beds?" Mary asks.

"Where is . . . anything?" Tabby asks with dismay.

"As I said, the accommodations are new, so you'll make do with no griping." Mrs. Hypat points at a door in the corner. "The bathroom is located through there. I will fetch you when it's time for a meal or if Uncle Ruho requests you. Other than that, you will remain here and pray. Do you understand?"

"No, I major don't!" says Tabby in a hostile tone. "I've come here to be married, not to be shut in like an inmate. Tell Uncle

Ruho, my *beloved*, that I will walk around his house and his grounds as I please, or I'll return home immediately."

I'm shocked at Tabby's words, but I don't think nearly as shocked as Mrs. Hypat. A terrible silence fills the room. She takes two slow steps toward Tabby, and I wait for her to bring out her Taser.

But she doesn't. Instead she says, "I will take your request to his Holiness."

"Good!" says Tabby. She sounds confident, but I can see in her eyes that she has no idea what she's doing.

Mrs. Hypat walks to the door. "I would take care how many requests you make of him, however. You don't want to spend all of his benevolence before you're even married."

"Benevo-what?" I ask when she's gone.

"It means, like, goodness," Grace says, sitting on the bed.

"I think he spent that a long time ago," I say, joining her.

"Well done though, Fab Tab," Mary says. "We can't stay locked up in here all day."

Tabby glares at the three of us. "Get off my bed."

"There's nowhere else to sit," Mary says, gesturing at the room.

"Then sit on the floor!" Tabby says. She marches to the bathroom, slamming the door behind her.

After an awkward silence, Grace says, "She deserves to be upset. I wouldn't want to marry an old man."

"Especially one that looks like a sick toad," Mary says.

"Shhhh," I say, not wanting Tabby to hear.

"What? She totally knows what he looks like," Mary says.

"You don't have to rub it in," Grace says, jumping down and approaching the bathroom. She places her ear on the door. "You okay, Tabby?"

When she gets no answer, she knocks.

78

"Die!" Tabby says.

Grace shrugs, returning to sit on the bed. "When do you think the wedding will be?" she whispers.

"Whenever it is," I say, watching the bathroom door, "It will be too soon."

TWELVE

Mrs. Hypat returns with the news that while we are forbidden to walk unaccompanied through the house, we've been given access to the gardens, as long as we keep our veils on and do not interact with the Heralds. It's not much, but it's better than nothing.

After midday prayer, Grace suggests we explore the center garden. I agree; our room is already making me claustrophobic.

When we arrive outside, I'm disappointed to see how small the garden actually is. I could take twenty strides and cross the entire thing. A fountain stands in the middle and the sound of bubbling water fills the air. A fountain! When most of the city is *desperate* for water!

I stroll with Grace, hoping to get a private word, but Mrs. Hypat stays close. "So what is a 'cloister' anyway?" I ask Grace, trying to make casual conversation until we're alone.

"It can mean a couple of things—a convent or a monastery —but here it refers to the covered walkways, like the ones that line the garden." She points to the stone arches around us. "There are a bunch of them here, which is why it's the 'Cloisters'—plural. Some rich guy brought them over from the old world, like, two hundred years ago."

Grace has perfected the Unbound accent.

"Aren't you a smarty pants?" Mrs. Hypat says.

"I, uh, like to read," Grace says.

"Too bad," Mrs. Hypat says, and I think she means it.

"What's that?" I ask, pointing to the huge tower that looms above us. It must be five stories tall.

"We call that *the keep*. His Holiness sleeps there."

"Where are your chambers, Mrs. Hypat?" Grace asks.

Mrs. Hypat clears her throat. "I have a room on the south side of the grounds. However, now that there are females in the house, I imagine I'll be moving in here."

I can't tell if this is good news or bad.

"How long have you worked here?" Grace asks her.

"I don't work," she says sharply. "It's against the law for women to be employed."

"Of course." Grace's voice is contrite.

"I was brought here when I was twelve years old, at the divine request of his Eminence, to help in the laundry room. He has never thought a man could wash a garment properly." She raises her chin. "By fifteen I was running the laundry room, and by eighteen I was in charge of every linen and uniform on the premises, including manufacturing."

This sure sounds like work to me. "Do you still do that?" I ask.

"I am currently acting as the nanny for Uncle Ruho's young bride and her attendants," she says pointedly, "but I hope to return to my duties soon."

Neither Grace nor I have a response to this.

I walk toward the keep, hoping to shake off Mrs. Hypat. As I move one foot in front of the other, my eyesight goes blurry, and I bump into her.

"Sorry," I say. Letters have appeared over my right eye. My Tact is showing me a message—my first Nod!

Think Mrs. Old Bat ever going 2 leave us alone?

I stifle a laugh. It's from Grace, who innocently crosses the garden. How does she walk and type so well?

Deciding to send a response, I blink rapidly six times, then concentrate on the up-down movements that control the keyboard.

Vrry fonny.

I'm not so good at typing. I need to practice so I don't fall down or get caught. I take a seat alone under one of the arches, planning to spend some time training with my Tact, but Mrs. Hypat takes a seat next to me. She's like glue, this woman.

"How was Miss Tabitha chosen?" she asks.

Tabby now sits on the other side of the garden with Grace. "Um, she's a very appealing and special girl," I say, having no clue how to respond. What did Ram tell these people?

Leaning in, she says, "If there'd been a search here, the line would've reached for miles. Thousands of women would have killed for the opportunity to have a life free from the fear of starvation and poverty."

She leans in even closer. Her skin radiates with the smells of lavender and lemon, which is a strange contrast to her prickly personality. What does she look like, I wonder?

"Did lots of girls want to marry him?" she asks.

What do I say? This feels like a trap, but I can't make a proper judgment without seeing her expression. I trace the cut on my wrist, now closed. "Would you . . . want to marry him?"

She snorts, and I'm relieved.

"Appalling. Why would I marry my own father?"

"Oh, uh, I'm so sorry. I didn't know." Mrs. Hypat is Uncle Ruho's *daughter*? But he's never been married. And if she's telling the truth, why is she living here like a servant?

"No one knows outside these walls," she says.

"Then why would you tell me?" I ask, baffled.

"You're never leaving here, just like me."

Standing, she walks over to the other girls, and I'm left to digest her jaw-dropping revelation.

At lunchtime, we're marched through the building and brought to a doorway flanked by Twitchers on one side and Juda, Dekker, and Silas on the other. They stare straight ahead, like soldiers, although Silas accidentally glances at us as we pass by. He looks shellshocked. It's hard not to talk to them, to ask about their treatment and accommodations. I try to catch Juda's eye, but he's well trained at standing guard.

We enter a room with stained glass in the windows. An enormous dining room table sits in the middle. I'm famished and ready to sit down, but Mrs. Hypat tells us that only Tabby will be eating. The rest of us will stand against the wall and make sure she doesn't need anything.

"Like salt?" Mary asks in annoyance.

"Like anything," Mrs. Hypat says sharply.

We wait fifteen minutes for Uncle Ruho to arrive, and my legs are already tired by the time Zebadiah helps him sit down. I shift my weight to my left side, causing Mrs. Hypat to whisper, "Stand up straight."

The first course is soup, and we all watch in horror as Ruho spills most of it down his purple and gold tunic. I can only imagine the disgust on Tabby's face.

She takes only a few sips of her own soup. I taught her how to eat with her veil on, but she had a hard time getting the hang of it. To be fair, I've always hated it myself. There's no talking until the second course. A Herald in an apron proudly presents goat head with a side of potatoes.

Tabby picks up a fork and knife but has no idea how to cut into the goat head. I rush over to help. "May I?"

She allows me to take the utensils. I begin to slice from the tender part of the cheek.

"How old are you, Beloved?" Ruho asks, breaking the silence.

"Sixteen," Tabby answers.

He frowns. "Ram said fifteen."

"I only turned sixteen, like, last week," she says, the lie slipping easily from her mouth.

He smiles. "Lovely."

"How old are you?" she asks.

I stop cutting the meat. The air seems to leave the room.

"What's that, Beloved?" he asks.

From his place against the wall, Zebadiah stares daggers at Tabby.

Please don't say it again, I think.

"How OLD are YOU?" she says, louder.

"Stop it," I whisper.

Then, suddenly, Uncle Ruho laughs uproariously. For a moment, I think he may choke on his goat. "Oh, Beloved. You are a spark. I am sixty-four years old."

"And when will you be sixty-five?"

"Why?"

"So I know when to get you a gift, of course," she says sweetly.

She is really unbelievable. I place several choice cuts of meat on her plate and return to my place at the wall.

"January first."

"A very auspicious day," Zebadiah chimes in.

I could have told her that. January first is a holiday for the whole city.

The moment that Ruho has finished his meal, he wipes his mouth and says, "I think we should discuss the wedding, don't you?"

Tabby clears her throat as if she's been waiting for this question. "Yes. I think we should hold off until the days are cooler so that more people will want to attend."

Zebadiah smiles at Uncle Ruho, who says, "People will want to attend no matter what day we choose, even if I say the location is inside this goat skull."

"Of course. I meant no disrespect," Tabby says, cutting a potato. "I just thought we would want our guests to be comfortable."

"We want our guests to be loyal. That is it."

She nods, taking it in.

"Then maybe you should stage some sort of competition," she says with excitement. "And only the winners get to attend the wedding. Wouldn't it be entertaining to watch people fight for the honor of your company?"

He smiles. When he's happy, he sort of looks like a big, chubby baby. "You are intriguing, and I like the way you think."

"But, sir," Zebadiah says, "we have already announced the date."

"Of course we have," Ruho says. "We will proceed as planned and be married on Thursday."

That's in *three* days. Tabby's body goes slack.

Uncle Ruho slowly stands, telling her, "You may stay for dessert and tea or anything else you may like. I have meetings." With Zebadiah's help, he walks out the door. Heralds quickly clear his plate away.

Mrs. Hypat says, "The rest of you may now sit down."

Grace, Mary, and I sit in the chairs closest to Tabby. Mrs.

Hypat sits in Uncle Ruho's spot at the head of the table. The Herald with the apron returns with two more goat heads but no potatoes. He places one in front of Mrs. Hypat and one in front of the rest of us. When he's gone, Mrs. Hypat says a quick prayer and then gives us the signal that we may remove our veils.

When Mrs. Hypat pulls her own veil away, I have to force myself not to react.

"Go ahead and stare. I know you want to," she says, picking up her utensils.

The left side of her face is stunning: smooth skin with a high, carved cheekbone, full lips, and remarkable mahogany eyes. The right side—I can hardly describe it—looks caved in. The skin appears melted as it adheres to bones that are crushed inward. I can't help but think of a roast in the oven, one side cooked and one side raw. My God. *What could have happened to her?*

"Oh, Mrs. Hypat," Grace says, on the verge of tears.

"I don't need your sympathy, Daphne," she says. "It happened when I was born. Problems in the birth canal. And it has its blessings."

"Like what?" Mary says, ever nosy.

"If you must know, this face is the only reason I'm here. His Holiness has proclaimed that I cannot possibly be divine if God has cursed me with such a deformity. Therefore, his Eminence is not threatened by me, and I'm able to safely live out my life. I cannot say the same for the rest of my siblings."

"Siblings? There are more of you?" I blurt out before I can stop myself. I haven't even had a chance to tell the others that Mrs. Hypat claims to be Uncle Ruho's daughter. They share looks of confusion.

"It's time to eat," she says, reaching for her platter.

"You can tell us. We're your friends," I say.

"Hardly. You are Apostates. I want one thing in this world and that is to leave it for the next. Every moment I spend with you heathens endangers my chances of entering Paradise; however, his Holiness has ordered it, and so I will do what I must."

"You're being kind to strangers. The Book says this is a virtue, does it not?" I ask.

She squints at me. "You think you're clever, Beth, but spending twenty-four hours with the most holy of texts does not make you a theologian."

"But does it say it?" I say, surprised by my own daring.

"It does, but it also says—"

"My understanding, although it is *far* inferior to yours, is that being kind to one's neighbor, whether one knows him or not, is the one of the greatest acts a follower of the Prophet can perform."

She scowls.

"And where does it say that exposure to someone different threatens your entry into Paradise?" I ask.

"Apostates are the worst kind of sinners. They believe that—"

"What *do* we believe?" Mary says, interrupting. She turns to Tabby. "This should be good."

"You believe that our Prophet is a liar," Mrs. Hypat says.

"I believe *our* leader is a liar," Mary shoots back.

Mrs. Hypat looks baffled and then irritated. "I said it was time to eat."

Mary looks at the single goat head. "This is it?"

"You'll find that is ample nourishment. You must be resourceful and waste nothing."

"You can have mine," Tabby says, pushing her goat's head toward us.

"Nonsense," Mrs. Hypat says. "You must be round and nubile on your wedding night."

"I'm fine with the potatoes," she says, shoving a big bite into her mouth.

"I'd be fine with potatoes, too," Mary says, watching jealously.

Grace pulls the tray with our goat head toward herself. She begins to slice it with expertise. "We didn't get this much at, uh, the orphanage. It was a special treat." She turns it around. "The tongue is the best part."

"That is major disgusting," Tabby says.

Grace smiles as she takes her first bite.

"You will all eat," Mrs. Hypat says, "and clean your plates. I won't lose my standing in this household because of spoiled foreigners!" Her flash of anger causes the disfigured side of her face to contort until it looks demonic.

We eat the rest of our meal in silence.

THIRTEEN

We spend a dull afternoon in the back garden. I pretend to study the flowers while I work on my Tact typing skills. Grace asks for paper and pencil so she can sketch the foliage, and Mary takes a nap.

Tabby pulls petals off of a white daisy. Her glorified days as a princess in Kingsboro are over, and the reality must be settling in. I assume she's absorbing the news that her wedding will be in three days. I wonder if she's thinking about Adam. I know she cares about him more than she wants to admit.

Who would she approach if she needed to talk? Mary is Unbound and probably understands her situation the best, but I don't think they've spent any real time with each other. She and I have been living in the same house, and I'm the only one here who knows about Adam, but she made it very clear from the beginning that she can't stand me. I sense she would eat Grace for breakfast. She must feel very lonely.

We pray at sundown.

"Again?" Tabby asks, and I almost laugh.

Back in Kingsboro, we explained that prayer happens three

times a day, but, like most of the other rules, it never sank in. Mrs. Hypat's shocked face at her complaining is almost worth all the trouble Tabby gave us.

After prayer, Mrs. Hypat brings us blankets and pillows. "You'll make do with these for now. I'm working on getting more mattresses."

As soon as she's gone, Grace, Mary, and I pile the blankets on the concrete floor, doing our best to make a soft surface. We lie down in a circle.

All day I've been dying to talk with them alone. "You won't believe what Mrs. Hypat told me out in the garden: she said she was Uncle Ruho's *daughter*."

Grace's jaw drops. "No way."

"That is major crazy," Mary says.

"Is that why she was talking about not being 'divine' and all that?" Grace reaches for a curl on her head that's no longer there.

"Do you think she's telling the truth?" I ask.

"Who would lie about that?" Mary looks nauseated.

"How many siblings do you think she has?" I say, still astounded by the idea.

"Even one is shocking," Grace says.

"You never heard of him having children before today?" Mary asks. We shake our heads. "How would he keep them a secret?"

"I guess you can do a lot of things when you're *divine*," I say with disgust.

"Where do you think the other ones are?" Grace whispers.

I shudder to think about it. *I am able to safely live out my life here. I cannot say the same for the rest of my siblings.*

"If there were women he wanted to be with, why didn't he just marry one of them?" Grace says.

"Maybe none of them *wanted* to be with him," Mary says,

and Grace's eyes narrow into angry slits. I'm sure she's thinking of her own mother.

"Shut up and go to sleep," Tabby says from above us.

"Easy for you to say, Fab Tab," Mary snaps. "You've got a bed."

Tabby bolts up. "Marry the drooling prune, and you can have the bed. How about that?"

Mary doesn't answer.

"That's what I thought. So shut your hole and go to sleep." She lies back down and throws the blanket over her head.

Mary looks at me, sighs, then rests her head on her pillow.

I stop thinking about Mrs. Hypat and start wondering how Tabby would feel if she knew that we'd been ordered to do away with her repugnant fiancé. Would she be horrified or thrilled?

I lie there considering this, growing more and more convinced that she would be incredibly relieved. And why should she be tortured by the belief that she'll have to spend the rest of her life with a gruesome old man? I'm ready to wake her up when I remember I have a way to consult with the others.

I blink my eye rapidly six times, and a screen appears in my Tact. I slowly type out my message to Juda, Dekker, and Grace: *Tabby n bad state. Want 2 tell her about pellet.*

I've barely hit send when an answer appears.

Under NO CIRCUMSTANCES r u 2 tell Tabitha about mission. Would endanger all of u. Repeat. Under NO CIRCUMSTANCES. W/God, Ram

What's happening? I didn't write to Ram!

With a horrible sinking realization, I understand that he must be monitoring all of our messages. *God is watching you, and so am I,* he said before we left.

We have no privacy. I can't talk to Juda without Ram

reading every word. I want to cry. The Cloisters just became even more of a prison.

A new message appears: *Do u understand, Mina? W/God, Ram*

Feeling sick, I respond: *Yes.*

Good. Need update, plz.

An update? I can't imagine what he wants me to report after only one day.

A new feed appears on the screen: *Met Ruho. Wedding n 3 days. Learning his routine. W/God, Juda.*

So Juda has also just learned that Ram is monitoring everything we write. He must be as startled and frustrated as I am.

Ram writes: *God shines his light upon u. Always remember y u r there.*

As if I could forget.

FOURTEEN

We're still sleeping when Mrs. Hypat walks into our room, loudly clapping her hands. "Up, up, up! His Holiness would like to see Miss Tabitha immediately in the assembly hall. You must get her bathed and dressed in the next ten minutes."

Mary groans from the floor. "Ten minutes? She won't even be able to brush her teeth."

"Bathed and dressed," Mrs. Hypat repeats. She claps again. "NINE minutes, Miss Tabitha."

Tabby rolls over in bed, her eyes still closed. "Tell my beloved I don't like to eat when it's still dark outside."

"I'll do no such thing. It's time for the daily briefing. He's invited you to join him, which is a great honor, something only one other woman has ever experienced."

"Who?" Grace asks.

"Not that it's any of your business, but me," Mrs. Hypat says, standing up straighter.

"Why don't you take my place today?" Tabby asks crankily.

"Because I wasn't invited. You were." I sense resentment in Mrs. Hypat's answer. "EIGHT minutes."

Tabby opens her eyes. "Fine." She rolls out of bed and stomps into the bathroom.

Mrs. Hypat turns to the rest of us splayed across the floor. "Don't just lie there. You're going, too."

The next eight minutes are chaos as we throw on cloaks and veils and try to make our hair as neat as possible. As Mary predicted, none of us has time to brush our teeth.

Mrs. Hypat gives us a quick inspection. As she examines us, I'm keenly aware of the knife in my pocket, which creates a slight lump in my cloak. Luckily, we're in enough of a hurry that she doesn't seem to notice. "Let's go, ladies!" she barks.

She escorts us briskly up the stairs, never pausing to see if we're keeping up. We don't go far, crossing one room and then entering another with old tapestries covering every wall.

Uncle Ruho sits on a throne, like yesterday, but today, several other men sit beside him. Zebadiah and Captain Memon are among them.

"What took you so long?" Ruho asks as we enter.

"I had no notice," Mrs. Hypat says. "The girls weren't—"

"I hate excuses," he says. "Never be late again."

"Yes, your Eminence," she says, bowing low. She leaves the room.

Ruho leers at Tabby. "I have to deal with running this ungrateful island, and your presence will soothe me. Sit there." He points to the far wall, where four chairs await. We cross the room and sit, giving Tabby the seat closest to Ruho.

"You were saying . . ." he says, looking at Captain Memon, who glares at us before continuing. He obviously does *not* feel soothed by our presence.

"Sixteen Convene rebels were eliminated yesterday, along with five Deservers. We lost four of our own men," Memon says. "I'm concerned that the daily death count continues to rise."

I instantly become more awake. Daily death count? He must be talking about the war.

"Send tanks into the streets. Do what you need to do!" Ruho says, sending spittle onto Memon.

"As I've already advised, your Eminence, if you kill civilians, I fear you will lose the loyalty of your people."

"My people will always love me!"

"Of course, your Holiness," the men around him murmur.

"But what if the Convenes win, your Eminence?" Memon says.

"That's a possibility?" Ruho says, alarmed.

"They're greater in number."

"How did you let you this happen? You should have kept weapons out of their hands!"

Memon's voice rises. "I tried to sweep the entire city a year ago, and you said no!"

Ruho's voice rises to match him. "No! I precisely remember that I thought it was a tremendous idea!"

Memon's eyes flicker with frustration and anger as Zebadiah cuts in with a calm tone. "Nevertheless, your Holiness, here we are."

Uncle Ruho seems about to yell at him as well, but he thinks twice and smiles. "I assume that the ceasefire for my wedding day won't be a problem?"

Zebadiah gives Captain Memon a worried glance. "We're doing everything we can," he says, "to spread the word."

Memon begins to list the safety precautions for the wedding day.

I lean in to Tabby. "Ask what's going on."

"No way," she whispers back.

"Please," I ask, wishing I had leverage with her. "It's really important."

"Back off."

"Don't you want to know if your new realm is at war? Maybe you're in danger," I say, wondering if I can frighten her into helping me.

She doesn't answer.

"What if I lend you my Tact?"

She turns her head away.

"What if I make Mary stop calling you 'Fab Tab'?"

She clears her throat and says loudly, "Beloved. Is the island at war?"

Wow. I had no idea the nickname bothered her so much.

Captain Memon stops speaking and gives her a terrifying glare. A sixteen-year-old girl has just cut him off.

Looking at Tabby, Uncle Ruho speaks in a slow, ominous voice. "You're young and foreign and don't know our ways, so I'll forgive your mistake this *one* time, but you're NEVER to speak again unless you've been spoken to, understand?"

"Yes, Beloved." Tabby reaches over and pinches my thigh. I squeak.

Sucking his teeth, Ruho looks at the men around him. Then he looks back to Tabby and smiles. "Don't be alarmed. The island is experiencing a . . . small conflict. Recently a terrible man, a Deserver named Clark, poisoned the water supply of the Convenes—a branch of my people. It was a horrendous act of terrorism. The people seek justice, and until this insurgent Clark is found, they're busying themselves rebelling against *me*, if you can believe it. Clark can't hide forever, and as soon as my men execute him all of this violence will come to an end. God has told me so. The whole thing is a tragedy. Many good people on both sides have died."

I stay in my chair, not making a sound, but I want to scream. I want to run to Ruho, shake him, and yell, "You LIAR! You did it! YOU poisoned the water! NOT my father."

A terrorist.

Father is a wanted terrorist who will be executed as soon as he is tracked down.

I sniff as I hold back tears. Next to me, Grace takes my hand. She understood Ruho's words—the lie that he's created.

Ruho's men continue to discuss the city: the water and food distribution, energy shortages, transportation issues, and what to do with the fuel that Ram is supplying as part of the marriage agreement. It all blurs together.

When we get back to the room an hour later, I wait impatiently for Mrs. Hypat to leave us alone.

As soon as she shuts the door, Grace says, "Oh my gosh, Mina. Are you okay?"

I drop onto the hard floor and pull off my veil. "No."

Mary, alarmed when she sees my face, says, "What happened?"

Grace realizes that I'm not going to explain, saying, "The man that Uncle Ruho said poisoned that water, is, uh, Mina's father."

Mary's eyes go wide. "No way. Why did he do it?"

"He didn't!" I say, furious at her for asking.

"Sorry," she says. "Ruho said—"

"Ruho is a lying sack of dung," I say.

"Keep your voice down," Grace says, sitting on the floor next to me.

"*He* did it," I say. "Uncle Ruho and his backstabbing friend, Mr. Asher. They tricked my father into helping them, and now they've blamed Father and called him a . . . " I can't finish the sentence.

"Terrorist," Grace whispers.

"It's my fault," I say. "If I hadn't run away from the Ashers, the Laurel Society never would've learned about the mercury, and none of this would've happened."

"And Convenes would still be dying," Grace says. "You're

not thinking straight."

I can hear the logic of what's she saying, but somehow I still know it's my fault that Father is a wanted man. "Maybe if I hadn't left the island, I could've told people the truth about Mr. Asher and the mercury."

"The Laurel Society knew the truth, and I'm sure they told people—lots of people!" she says. "But Ruho spread a different story, and he probably managed to do it a lot faster."

"What's a Laurel Society?" Tabby asks, sitting down in front of us.

Grace and I look at each other, realizing our mistake. "It has nothing to do with you," I say.

"That guy, Captain Lemon, wanted to bash my brains in for interrupting him today, and I did that for you. So I think you, like, owe me some information," she says.

What's the least I can tell her? "It's a group of women."

"And?" she asks.

"They don't like Uncle Ruho."

"And?"

Grace jumps in. "They named themselves after the Greek myth of Daphne and Apollo, and they represent the fundamental right of women to be equal citizens."

"Major yawny," Tabby says, standing and heading for her bed.

I smile at Grace.

Mary whispers, "So can this Laurel Society help save your father?"

With despair, I say, "They don't help men."

"I'm major sorry," Mary says. "It's awful."

I excuse myself. I need to be alone.

Once inside the bathroom, I send Juda and Dekker a message. I don't care if Ram reads it. *Father missing. Ruho blamed him 4 bad water. City @ war.*

Ram's response comes quickly: *Do NOT get distracted. Stick w/mission. U will c your father n Heaven. W/God, Ram*

After another minute, a message from Juda appears: *Ruho traitor 2 his people. Your father is good man. So sorry. Peace + light.*

I write back: *Peace + light.*

I wait a while to hear from Dekker. Could he have removed his Tact?

Five minutes later, I finally hear from him: *UnTrue. U r imbecile.*

What else should I have expected? When we were in Kingsboro, I told him about Father, Mr. Asher, and the mercury. At first, he acted as if I were a hysterical girl who'd made up a dramatic story to get attention. Annoyingly, after Juda confirmed the facts, he believed me. I assume that the same thing will happen here. As soon as Juda or another man tells him about father, he'll believe it. I don't know why I even bother.

Will he worry about Mother? If Father's on the run, did she go live with my aunties? Or has she gone to join an order of Matrons? It's hard to imagine. Dekker has always been close to her, and he'll freak out if he isn't sure of her whereabouts.

My sweet father, who only wanted to help people, is a wanted man. Is he living in the streets? Does he have friends who will help him? Will I ever see him again?

Ruho is ready to sacrifice him with no conscience. He told the lie to Tabby so easily, like he almost believed it himself.

All the deception that's been presented to me in my life—by family, by elders, by friends—comes rushing back. I thought I could survive coming back here. I thought I was so tough that the poisonous lies that infect every crevice of this city wouldn't effect me. I'm such a fool.

FIFTEEN

The next day, I have no desire to leave our room. I want to be alone to think. To my dismay, Mrs. Hypat tells us she wants to give us a tour of the house after breakfast.

The meal is a silent affair. Uncle Ruho is agitated and doesn't speak to Tabby, who I think is relieved. Grace and Mary seem as depressed as I am. As we've settled into a routine of eating, walking in gardens, and sleeping, we can feel our lives shrinking, as if we are transforming from growing plants back into hard, dried seeds.

I'm desperate for communication with Juda, to talk to him about my father without the listening ears of Ram. As soon as our food has been cleared, I ask Mrs. Hypat, "When do the boys eat?"

"That's no concern of yours, Beth," she says with sharpness. "Boys and girls do not eat together."

"Tabitha is allowed to eat with family, and therefore, she would like to eat with her brother, Silas, at meals," I say. This whole idea is a gamble.

"I doubt—"

"And I would like to eat with my brother, Rufus, and Daphne would like to eat with her brother, James." I know that Grace's and Juda's cover stories have nothing to do with being brother and sister, but I assume they will both go along with my fabrication.

"All those boys are your brothers?" Mrs. Hypat asks.

To my relief, Grace and Tabby join me in saying, "Yes, Mrs. Hypat."

"Our parents wanted them here to protect our honor and family name," I say, knowing this is an answer Mrs. Hypat can respect.

"I will consult with his Holiness, but I wouldn't get your hopes up."

"Thank you, Mrs. Hypat," I say, already feeling a little better.

Mrs. Hypat's tour begins in the Unicorn Room, where the briefing was yesterday. "The tapestries in this room are very valuable," she says in her knowing tone. "They're over six hundred years old. Together, the panels tell the story of the hunt and capture of a unicorn."

Most of the pictures are straightforward, showing a hunting party of men with dogs searching through a forest for a magnificent white unicorn.

"What is this panel?" I ask, pointing to the one near the entrance.

"That is the unicorn purifying the water," Mrs. Hypat says. "A unicorn horn was thought to have mystical powers."

I can't help but think of father, who like this unicorn, purified water for his people and then was punished. The panels showing the capture of the unicorn are brutal; the otherworldly animal meets its end pierced by spears and attacked by dogs.

"Here he is reborn." Mrs. Hypat points to a tapestry which presents the unicorn alive and well within a circular fence.

"How do you know this panel comes after the others?" Mary asks.

"Because he has the wounds from the spears. See?" Grace says, pointing to the bloody scars on the unicorn's body.

"So he's reborn, but he's still a prisoner?" I ask.

"It's a sad story," Grace says.

"It's major gruesome," Tabby says.

"It's a wonderful story of resurrection. A masterpiece!" Mrs. Hypat admonishes us. "Let's move on."

I take a last look at the heartbreaking unicorn as she leads us back to the dining room. "This was once the 'Early Gothic Hall,' and it has many wonderful examples of stained glass. Aren't the windows remarkable?"

Various people and scenes have been cut out of colored glass and placed in the windows. The light coming through bathes the floor in shades of pink, yellow, and blue. I often find myself studying the rays of color while we wait for Uncle Ruho to finish his meals.

"For many years the property of glass that allowed it to transmit light while remaining intact was equated with the idea of a virgin birth, like the one experienced by our Prophet."

"There's no animal in nature that cares about virginity." I hear myself quoting Silas. "So why do we make such a *big deal* out of it?" Everyone turns toward me. "It's true."

Mrs. Hypat is not happy with my interruption. "As a reminder, I'll be checking your bedsheets the morning after the wedding, Miss Tabitha."

"Ew. Why?" Tabby asks.

"For blood, of course. The Heralds will want to see it."

Tabby has no response.

I pat her shoulder. "It's normal here. Relax."

She turns to me, unnerved. "You people are freaks."

Mrs. Hypat continues with the tour, leading us through several more rooms. They begin to blend together, as she describes painting after painting and sculpture after sculpture. I'm relieved when we finally return to the Treasury.

"How much education did you girls have at home?" Mrs. Hypat asks, removing her veil. Once again, I experience a quick intake of breath. I don't know that I'll ever get used to her damaged face.

Once all veils are removed, Mary says, "We learn to read at four, and then we continue with school until we're seventeen. Some people keep studying until they're twenty-one. Some people even longer."

"Even the women?" she says, incredulous.

"Yes," Mary says, rolling her eyes. "Even the women."

"Marvelous," Mrs. Hypat says to my bewilderment. "You must miss it."

"Yes," Mary says.

Tears spring into my eyes, as I think of the education in Kingsboro that I was promised and that I will never have.

Mrs. Hypat notices. "Now, now, dear. We'll find ways to keep your brains busy. Like our tour today."

"It won't be enough," Grace says, depressed.

"God has chosen you to be here, so it is sufficient in His eyes."

Tabby sits on the bed. Instead of the bored expression I expect, her face looks pallid and tense.

Replacing her veil, Mrs. Hypat heads for the door. "I will see you at lunch. Peace."

The second she's gone, Tabby goes into the bathroom and slams the door.

"What now?" Mary says.

Grace shrugs. "Maybe she's upset because Mrs. Hypat reminded her she can't go to school anymore?"

Mary raises an eyebrow. "Are you serious?"

"Just leave her alone for now," I say, tired of reacting to every tantrum Tabby throws. "Can we please discuss Mrs. Old Bat?"

"What?" Mary says.

"She approved of the education you had. That's pretty radical for a relative of Uncle Ruho's."

"Maybe she was just testing us, to report back to Zebadiah on how immoral we are," Grace says.

"She's a grumpy old witch either way," Mary says.

We continue to discuss Mrs. Hypat, until, after fifteen minutes, Grace says, "Do you think Tabby's okay?"

I hadn't noticed she was still in the bathroom.

"Should we be worried?" Mary asks.

"She did look a little sick," Grace says.

Getting up, I knock gently on the door. "Tabby?"

No answer.

"Are you okay?" I put my ear against the door. "If you don't say anything, we're going to get worried."

After more silence, I try the door. It's locked.

I say to Grace and Mary, "Can you give us some privacy?"

Grace looks hurt, while Mary looks intrigued.

"Let's go to the garden, *Daphne*," Mary says. "We'll discuss daisies or some crap."

As soon as they're gone, I say, "Tabby, is this about Adam?" There's no response, but I continue. "I would be upset, too. You said you didn't love him, but I didn't really believe you. I saw the way you looked at him at Promise Prom, and the way he looked at you. I know you really care about each other, and you must really miss him, and it must be hard to know you're going to marry someone else, someone you don't really know. Maybe you would feel better if you talked about it, you know?"

I wait and nothing happens. Out of ideas, I decide to join the others in the garden. I'm almost out of the room when the lock on the bathroom door *clicks*. I guess it's an invitation?

When I open the door, I'm startled to see Tabby crouched in the corner. Her eyes are red and puffy.

"What's wrong?"

She stares at the ceiling. "Go away."

"You unlocked the door."

She gives me a deep Tabby sigh. She traces the tiles on the floor with her finger. "What Mrs. Hypat said before, about the sheets . . . "

My shoulders tense.

"I just . . . " she says. I can tell she doesn't want to continue. "What if . . . I don't . . . bleed?"

Panic sweeps through me. "I asked you while we were still in Kingsboro. I told you how important it was! And *now* you're telling me you're not a virgin?"

Her face is a strange shade of puce. "I—I . . . I'm not sure."

I'm bewildered. Do the Unbound have a different definition than we do? Silas said that virginity was something men made up to protect property, so maybe it's possible for different societies to have their own definitions?

I clear my throat, unsure how to proceed. "In Manhattan, being a virgin means you've never had, uh, sex."

"Duh," she says, in her usual Tabby tone.

"So how can you, um, not be sure?"

"Mrs. Prue, she taught us about manners and being lady-like. She never really explained . . . more."

Unbelievable. Our rules are much stricter than those of the Unbound, but the moment I got my menses, my aunties sat me down and told me *everything* I needed to know about my wedding night. The information they gave me left little doubt about the status of one's virginity. How can a society care so much about purity and then not supply adequate information?

Tabby squirms under my astonished gaze. I've never seen her so vulnerable, even when she told me about Adam. Plopping down on the tile, I take a deep breath and dive in. "Let's start with how babies are made . . ."

For ten minutes, Tabby says nothing. She listens as if I am the most fascinating person in the world. She nods a lot and cringes several times. By the time I'm done, she seems calmer and back to herself.

"Well?" I ask, knowing her next statement could make the difference between life and death.

"I'm fine."

Before I even know what's happening, I'm hugging her. I didn't realize how much tension I was holding in my body.

"Praise the Prophet," I say.

In a wrenched voice, she says, "*I don't believe in the Prophet.*"

"Praise *whomever*," I say, laughing.

She pulls away, wiping her eyes. "I'm sorry about, like, your dad."

"Thank you." I'm surprised she even remembers.

A second later, her face hardens, and she says, "Don't tell the others about our conversation, or I will make your life major miserable."

Same old Tabby. "Of course you will." Standing, I offer her a hand. "You okay?"

"I think I need another minute."

I leave her. She may have found some reassurance in what I told her, but she now has to contemplate what her wedding night with Ruho will physically entail. I shudder at the thought.

She only has two days left.

We need to help her. We have the means. We *should* help her.

By the time I reach the garden, I've made up my mind, and I send a Nod: *Want 2 administer pellet b4 wedding.*

The answer is immediate: *Splendid. W/God, Ram.*

SIXTEEN

By the time I'm in bed that night, Grace, Juda, and Dekker all know that we need to get a pellet into Uncle Ruho's food by Thursday.

The question is *how?*

We send frantic Nods back and forth.

I explain that I can get close to Tabby during mealtime, but she's on the other side of the table from Ruho. Juda thinks the best idea is to try to get it into Ruho's food while it's still in the kitchen, but I'm concerned that the pellet could accidentally go into Tabby's meal.

We tell her not 2 eat her food, says Grace.

4 what reason? I ask.

U r clever + u'll think of something, chimes in Ram.

I hate his relentless presence in our conversations.

I can xplore kitchen after lunch 2moro, says Juda.

That only leaves us dinner tomorrow. One chance. *What if they won't let u n?* I ask.

Tell them u want 2 ask chef about wedding food, Grace says.

BEnny iDea, Grace, Dekker says. I didn't know he was here, he contributes so little.

Perhaps u can do it @ wedding? Ram suggests.

Whole city will be @ wedding, Grace writes, just as I type, *Would b caught immediately!*

I'm not interested in Ram's ideas. He doesn't care if we get caught; he just needs Uncle Ruho dead.

Will leave it 2 u. Just get it done! I can almost hear Ram squawking the words.

Get back 2 us about kitchen, Juda. I sign off.

I sleep badly and am up before the sun.

I go into the bathroom, locking the door. I examine the corner of my cloak, until I feel the tiny pellet sewn inside. Holding the fabric up, I pick at the threads. Suddenly, the pellet pops out. It lands in the sink and circles toward the drain. My hand shoots out and, just as the pellet is about to be lost to the pipes forever, my fingers grasp the small silver ball.

I exhale with relief, but then, remembering what the pellet can do, I almost drop it again. What if it can enter my blood-stream some other way than my mouth? Is it safe to have it against my flesh? I drop it quickly into an inside pocket. How can something so small be so deadly?

I think of the knife in my other pocket, whose presence has been making me more and more nervous. I may have made it through a Twitcher scan, but I don't know how many more days my silhouette will survive Mrs. Hypat's inscrutable gaze. Any day now she's going to notice the pointed outline in my cloak.

I quietly walk back into the bedroom. I return the knife to

my bag, praying that I don't run into a situation where I need it on hand.

I then wake Grace and pull her into the bathroom. Once inside, I tell her that I've put the pellet into my pocket for easy access.

Her eyes widen. "I'll do the same." She picks the threads of her cloak, and, with more skill than me, eases the pellet from the fabric. She places it with care into her pocket.

"Today is it," she says. "I can't believe it. Do you think—"

A knock on the door causes us both to jump.

"What's going on in there?" Mary asks.

I open the door. "Nothing. We, uh, just wanted to talk and didn't want to wake you guys."

"It didn't work."

"Sorry."

I feel strange lying to Mary, who's been by my side through so much. Will I tell her the truth when it's all over? The idea of telling her what we're being forced to do fills me with shame.

I can't look her in the face as we leave the bathroom.

At breakfast, I stare at Ruho the whole time. I hate his fat face, but does he deserve to die? He's denounced my father as an insurrectionist. He's started a war that has led to the deaths of who knows how many Deservers and Convenes. He helped poison the water of innocent people, including children.

Even if he does deserve to die, am I able to be the one who does it? I remind myself that Juda will be the one who actually puts the pellet in the food. The tension in my stomach doesn't go away.

———

After breakfast, I ask Mrs. Hypat if we may explore the grounds. We're allowed to enter any garden, and I remember passing through several large ones outside the house on our first day. Mrs. Hypat says we may, and, of course, she escorts us.

The air is crisp and fresh. Heralds trim hedges and rake leaves. The south garden is magnificent but feels as artificial as the painted lawns of the Unbound. Tabby and Mary are seeing the pleasant side of the island, the trimmed and organized side. Juda, Dekker, and I know how fake it is. It must be so easy for Ruho to live here and pretend that the whole island is like this. No wonder he and Ram have become friends. They both live in fantasy lands.

I have little understanding of where we are. From flying over the island, I know that we're far north of the park. But how far? I can't spot the skyline of Manhattan. It's creepy. The trees in every direction are too dense to see through, like the rows of corn in the Park, and I can't see far enough to figure out where I am, which is major frustrating.

Once Ruho is dead, we have no idea what will happen. Even if Memon and Zebadiah don't suspect us, they'll no longer have a use for us, which is dangerous. How long will it take for Ram to send the Ostrich? If he doesn't send it right away, we have to be prepared to run. Will we know where to go?

"Beth! Come here!" Grace waves me over. She, Mary, Tabby, and Mrs. Hypat are staring up at a group of trees.

As I walk closer, my ears are assaulted by an urgent screeching. It reminds me of the old rusted swing set in Palmer Park that Dekker and I liked as kids, but this is more like hundreds of swings creaking at once.

"Starlings," Mrs. Hypat says as I reach her. "They're migrating."

I scan the trees until I spot the black birds hidden in the shadows of the leaves.

"It's not even fall yet," Grace points out.

"It gets earlier and earlier each year," Mrs. Hypat says. "We're lucky to see them at all."

The shrieking stops abruptly; an eerie silence fills the air. The birds from one tree dart into the sky. Taking their cue from the first group, the starlings from the other trees take flight. There must be thousands of them. They swarm above us, dipping and diving.

"What are they doing?" I ask, mesmerized.

"Gathering everyone—they don't want to leave anyone behind," Grace says, impressed.

They start their deafening metallic cry again. They circle two more times and then land in the next group of trees, only thirty feet away.

"That was a whole lot of hoopla for not very much progress," Mary says.

Mrs. Hypat turns to her. "And yet, they will make it all the way across the country, a few feet at a time, losing as few of their flock as possible."

"They're heading south, right?" Grace asks.

"Of course. To a warm winter." Mrs. Hypat walks toward the birds. "I'm going to get closer to watch the next swarm." Mary and Tabby join her, while Grace and I hang back.

"At least we know which direction is home," Grace whispers.

By home, I know she means Macy's.

"We have no idea how far we are," I say. "Plus, there's a war on, so crossing the city will be a lot more dangerous than it used to be."

"If we could tell Rayna we're here, I'm sure she'd help us."

I wish there were a way. Then I could tell Nana, too. "We have to be ready to go. Anytime."

"You mean after we've used the pellet?"

"Yes, and everything depends on being able to escape the

house." How closely are the Twitchers watching us? They wouldn't be expecting us, "members of the Unbound," to go fleeing into the night. What would we have to gain? We walk in silence for a while.

Out of nowhere, Grace says, "I miss Kingsboro. Is that wrong?"

"I don't . . . I can't really say."

"Don't you miss it at all?"

"I miss talking freely to everyone."

"Especially Juda?" she asks teasingly.

I smile with shyness. "Yes."

"I miss my family, but I also miss . . . " Her voice becomes tight. "I thought the people there were special, and because of what my host-family said, I thought *I* was special. I really liked what they had to say about the world and God. It made so much sense to me. When they were worshipping, there was so much love in the room! And then Ram . . . He turned out to be . . . He's an awful man. And then it all went away. What am I supposed to believe now? *Who* am I supposed to believe in?"

I understand her disappointment. Mine has become a permanent ache in my belly. "I was so excited about school and that library you told me about."

"There were so many more books I wanted to read, so many classes I wanted to take! But was it wrong to want those things if a bad man was providing them?" Her tone becomes sheepish. "I have a confession. Even though Ram is evil, and I hate him more than anyone I can imagine—I still want to go back. Am I a terrible person?"

Who am I to answer this? "I don't think so." My mother was pretty terrible, but I still miss my home. "I think the important thing is that you recognize that Ram is capable of bad things, and you don't let yourself be fooled by him again."

"I could *never* trust him again."

"And maybe question him when he tells you about God."
I've been thinking about this a lot lately. "Both Ram and Uncle
Ruho say they have a direct line to God. They're *certain* of it,
and they tell people what to do based on it. But they can't both
be right—because they hear such different things."

"Unless God is playing a big joke on everybody."

"It's not a very good joke."

"No." Her voice becomes shaky. "I'm scared we're not
going to make it back to Macy's or Kingsboro. What if we have
to live in the Cloisters forever?"

"We *won't* get stuck here." I refuse to live the rest of my life
watching Uncle Ruho eat soup.

Tabby, Mary, and Mrs. Hypat walk back toward us, three
dark columns against the green grass. I search the sky, and the
last of the starlings have flown out of view. Our getaway won't
be nearly so easy.

SEVENTEEN

That afternoon, we get a long Nod from Juda: *Went 2 kitchen. Meals put on long table b4 Heralds pick up + take upstairs. Dekker 2 make diversion—I will put pellet n food. Will put n both meals, 2 b safe. B SURE Tabby does not eat 2night.*

Affirmative, Grace replies.

Yeps, replies Dekker.

"How will we stop Tabby from eating?" Grace asks me.

"I think we have to spill her food somehow. I can't think of any other option. Unless we tell her."

"If we spill her food, and then Ruho dies, won't people be suspicious that we knew something?"

"The pellet is above and beyond any tech that they have here," I say. "If it works the way Ram says it will, then it will take twenty-four hours to take effect. His people will never suspect the food." I have an anxiety-producing thought. "After dinner, we *have* to remove the other one from Tabby's food, so no one finds it."

"Twenty-four hours isn't leaving a lot of extra time before the wedding night."

I've thought about that a lot. The wedding is tomorrow, so the pellet needs to take effect before tomorrow night. "We're cutting it very close."

As I dress for dinner, my hands are shaking. Mary is talking nonstop about a fight she once saw at the Forgiveness Home over a baked potato, and I want to ask her to *please stop talking.* The sound of her voice is making me major tense. *Any* sound is making me tense: footsteps on the floor above us, the bathroom door opening and shutting, Tabby's incessant sighing. My blood is rushing through my body so quickly, I swear it aches. Dinner is at six o'clock. I am sitting and ready at five fifteen.

Finally, at five forty-five, Mrs. Hypat comes to collect us. Grace gives me one last nervous look before she puts on her veil. I put mine on and walk out last. As I climb up the stairs, I put my hand on the wall to steady myself. I am ill with nerves. All of a sudden, a Nod from Juda appears in my eye: *PLAN IS OFF!*

Nyek.

What happened? Did he get caught? My throat threatens to close. *Oh God.* What if they caught him trying to put something in the food? We're walking through the hallway, with Mrs. Hypat just ahead, so I can't speak with Grace, who also will have read the message.

That's it then. That was our last chance, and now it's gone. Tabby will have to marry Uncle Ruho tomorrow, and then she'll have to spend the night with him. I want to apologize for failing her, but she doesn't even know what we were trying to do.

When we arrive at the dining room, the boys aren't standing guard outside. I'm right. *Juda was caught.* I walk on trembling legs into the dining room, and there the boys are—sitting at the table with Uncle Ruho.

Juda looks at me. Even with the veil, he knows my red hair. He gives me a quick nod, so everything must be okay.

"I will eat with your brothers tonight," Uncle Ruho tells us, "and determine if you will be allowed to dine with them in the future."

"Thank you, Beloved," Tabby says, sounding dazed.

Mary, Grace, and I line up against the wall with Mrs. Hypat, as usual.

"*Everyone* shall eat with me today," Ruho says.

Zebadiah gestures to the seats across from the boys, but when Mrs. Hypat reaches for a chair, Uncle Ruho says, "Not you."

She snaps her hand back, returning to the wall.

Sitting across from Juda, I end up closest to Uncle Ruho, whose face is even worse close up, with bits of dry skin that need to be scrubbed off. He smells like Auntie Purga the month she decided that garlic would cure her constipation. He doesn't look at me or acknowledge my presence.

Three Heralds arrive with trays of food. Uncle Ruho and Tabby each receive pork chops, steamed spinach, and sweet potatoes. The rest of us get ham hocks.

As I look longingly at Ruho's delicious meal, I realize that it's within reach. If he could be distracted for a few seconds, I could surely drop the pellet right into his spinach. Or Juda could.

Blinking six times, I type: *Can do it.*

Juda's face is completely relaxed as he listens to Zebadiah say a prayer over the meal. When Zebadiah is finished, Juda says, "Peace," and lifts his fork. At the same time, he gives me an almost imperceptible nod.

I hope no one notices my hand shaking as I take hold of my own fork.

With a mouth full of pork, Uncle Ruho says, "Which one of you is the brother of my Beloved?"

When no one answers, Tabby says, "Silas."

"No one spoke to you!" Uncle Ruho shouts at her.

Her body gives a little jump.

"I am," Silas says, alarmed.

Ruho stabs a piece of meat as he sizes Silas up. "I should've guessed. You have similar hands."

Silas looks at his hands with curiosity.

"How many Kingsboro men were courting your sister?"

Tabby's figure goes rigid.

"She was very popular," Silas says. "She could've, uh, married anyone she wanted."

Tabby's body relaxes. Was she worried he was going to say, "You were her only chance at marriage"? He's smarter than that.

"And did you leave your wife behind?" Ruho asks him.

"Uh . . . Yes," Silas says. He grows very serious. "It was very sad. I miss her . . . every day."

Tabby begins to laugh and then stops abruptly. I think Mary kicked her under the table. *What's wrong with her?* Silas having a wife in Kingsboro is a story that will keep him safe here.

"How about the rest of you?" Ruho asks the boys, waving his knife.

Dekker and Juda look everywhere but at Uncle Ruho.

"You," Ruho asks Dekker. "Did you leave a wife behind?"

After a moment of contemplation, Dekker says, "I'm still searching for the most pious woman, your Holiness."

Silas' face betrays confusion, since he knows Dekker is engaged to Delilah Delford. But I know how Dekker's mind works. If he'd said he had a fiancée in Kingsboro, Ruho would know that he wanted to return there and would never be loyal to him.

"Very good," Ruho answers, impressed. "And you?" He looks at Juda, who shifts uncomfortably in his seat.

"No, your Holiness. I have not married."

"Why not?"

"I haven't, uh, had the opportunity." He gives me the quickest glance.

"Well, there are plenty of opportunities here. We'll make you a good match in no time!"

Juda returns to his meal. I know that he won't pay attention to what Ruho is saying, but I can't help but feel a surge of jealousy. What if Ruho decides to pick a bride for him?

Focus, I tell myself.

"I'm curious about your people." Ruho wipes his mouth. Has he finished eating? "Is it true you burn anyone you consider an infidel?"

Mary begins, "Are you fu—"

Dekker cuts her off. "No, your Holiness. That's only a rumor."

I get a Nod from Juda: *Distract him.*

I cough, but Ruho keeps talking to Dekker. I cough again but louder this time. He still doesn't turn. So I produce a loud hacking cough that suggests I'm choking to death on the ham hock.

Now everyone looks at me, including Uncle Ruho.

"Are you okay?" Silas asks.

I keep coughing, trying to give Juda as much time as possible. I'm bent over, so I can't see him clearly.

"Get the girl some water," Uncle Ruho says with irritation.

A Herald shoves a glass in my face, and I have no choice but to take it. As I gulp down the water, I look at Juda, but I can't tell from his expression if he was successful or not.

I'm considering what my next distraction could be when Captain Memon enters the room. He whispers to Zebadiah, who in turn whispers to Uncle Ruho.

Ruho, clearly annoyed, says, "Show her in."

Zebadiah stiffens. "Accepting this woman's presence again and again in your home is highly improper."

"Show her in!" Ruho repeats.

Zebadiah and Captain Memon give each other a look.

"Yes, your Eminence." Zebadiah nods at Captain Memon, who marches out of the room and returns with a petite woman flanked by three private guards. Her cloak and veil are black and made of the finest silk.

Uncle Ruho makes her stand a long while before he says, "Peace."

"Peace. I haven't heard from you in some time, your Eminence."

I stiffen. I know that voice.

It belongs to Mrs. Asher.

EIGHTEEN

I'm ready to stand and flee when I remember that my veil covers my face and that my hair is now red.

Uncle Ruho tries to sit up a bit. "My dear Mrs. Asher, you know that I would've been in touch if there were anything to report."

Mrs. Asher's hair, the same silky brown that I remember, is pulled back in a taut ponytail. Her voice is full of righteous anger. "You promised me you would find the devils who killed my son and husband, and you've found nothing!"

"We've tried every possible—"

"You've not tried hard enough! Perhaps it's time for me to stop supplying oil to your Grace's regime."

Ruho leans forward. "Perhaps it's time for me to seize the assets of an unmarried woman!"

She laughs sharply. "You couldn't find my assets with a map."

Tabby snickers.

Mrs. Asher walks closer to the table. "I would think that locating the daughter of a terrorist would be a top priority, your

Eminence, something that would pacify your people while you locate her murderous father."

Dekker's eye twitches. *Perhaps now he'll believe me about Father and everything Ruho has blamed on him.*

"His Eminence is quite capable of deciding for himself what is a top priority," Zebadiah says.

Juda sits only a foot away from Mrs. Asher, and he has no veil to cover his face. *I want to send him a Nod, but I dare not distract him in any way. I tell myself to breathe. Mrs. Asher hasn't noticed him yet. His back is to her, his hair is now blond, and he's wearing glasses. His head is down, frozen. He knows her voice better than I do. He spent half of his life in her household.*

Is she still using the same guards? Scrutinizing them, I think the one on her right looks vaguely familiar. If he's worked for the Asher's for a long time, he'll be able to identify Juda, too. I become queasy.

"I'm here today," Mrs. Asher says, "because I heard your bride has arrived." Her eyes land on Tabby, whose ornately adorned cloak and place at the head of the table have given her away. "I want to talk to her."

"Out of the question!" Ruho says.

"She's come from the other side of the wall, where we know my husband's murderers are hiding. It's insulting that she's here. You should never have let her come before the Apostates gave up his killers!"

She approaches Tabby, leaning in and getting right in her face. *To my right, Grace puts a light finger on my thigh, a reminder that I must remain calm.*

Mrs. Asher, inches from Tabby's face, says, "Peace."

"Peace," Tabby responds. She slumps back in her chair, suggesting she could care less about who this woman is.

In a light tone, Mrs. Asher says, "You must be absolutely

charming. If you were chosen from all the girls in your region, I can only imagine what a beauty you must be!"

Tabby gives her an insincere, "Major thanks."

"I look forward to your wedding day, as does everyone in the city. It's the event of the year—no, the decade! If you need anything, *anything* at all, you let me know. I'm Gabrielle Asher, and I have access to everything you could possibly want or need while you're here." She sticks out her bottom lip in a pout. "How you must be missing things from home! But I assure you that we have wealth and luxury here, too. All you have to do is tell his Holiness that you want to see me, and I'll whisk you away. You can stay in my guest room. Half of the penthouse will be yours, and we'll have a wonderful time—eating fabulous food and buying gorgeous clothes. Doesn't that sound fun?"

Tabby sits up, and I start to perspire. I've been the victim of Mrs. Asher's charm, and she's hard to resist.

"I just have one question for you," Mrs. Asher purrs.

"Yes?" Tabby says, a new longing in her voice.

"Have you seen them?" Mrs. Asher says, straining to remain cheerful. "Teenagers—a boy and a girl. We think they emerged somewhere in your area, around a month ago. Do you know anything about them?"

Grace stiffens beside me. She's now as frightened as I am.

Tabby breathes heavily, and I can imagine her weighing her options.

I evaluate her allegiance to us—does she have any? Maybe after our moment together, when I explained the details of reproduction, she feels some sort of bond? I pray that after our few days here, she understands that giving us up would be a fatal betrayal.

"I . . . " Tabby begins to speak and my mouth goes dry. "I don't know them, but . . . they sound major feeble."

Praise God.

Mrs. Asher, still close to Tabby's face, says, "You sound unsure."

To my surprise, Mrs. Hypat steps forward. "She's young and impressionable, Mrs. Asher, please—"

"She's an empty-headed girl!" Ruho says, clearly ready to be done with Mrs. Asher. *Does* he care about catching the "devils" who killed her family? Probably not, when I think about it. Mr. Asher knew that Uncle Ruho helped him poison the water and now he can't tell anyone about it. Ruho is probably relieved he's dead.

As Mrs. Asher backs away from Tabby, Captain Memon approaches. "Time to leave," he says, his voice as deep and threatening as the rumble of a tank.

Walking back to the center of the room, Mrs. Asher says, "I thank you for your audience today. I look forward to your wedding, and I wait for news about my husband and son that will sustain the relationship that the Asher family and his Holiness have always enjoyed."

Before Uncle Ruho can even say, "Peace," Mrs. Asher has left the room.

By the time I've begun to breathe normally and regained my senses, I look down to see that Uncle Ruho's dinner plate has been cleared. I look to Juda who sends a one word message: *negative.*

We had one chance and we missed it. The wedding is going to happen.

After dinner, Mrs. Hypat takes longer than usual to leave our bedroom. I suspect she wants gossip about the runaways that Mrs. Asher is looking for, but we stay silent as long as she hovers. As soon as she's gone, I expect we'll converge on one another and start chattering, but instead, a deep quiet takes over the room.

Finally, Tabby breaks the silence. "So you dirtbags killed people?"

"No. It wasn't like that." I go to sit by her. The second I reach the bed, she stands and walks away.

"Give me one major reason I shouldn't turn you into that woman."

Where do I begin? "We didn't kill Mr. Asher. His son did. And—"

She puts up a hand. "I don't want to hear it, actually. I should've known you were a bunch of criminals and creeps."

I look to Grace, hoping she might have an idea on how to persuade Tabby, but she looks blank.

"So now what?" I ask.

"I don't know," Tabby says. "I need to think about it."

"Oh, please," Mary tells her. "Don't be a major wheedle." She looks at me and Grace. "We didn't think the Manhattan Five left the island because life was good. I've been here less than a week, and I already have a list of people I'd like to knock off."

I almost smile. "I was supposed to marry Damon, Mrs. Asher's son." I explain to Mary what happened when I stayed in the Asher's apartment, and how Damon and his father hunted me down. Mary's mouth hangs open as she listens to every word. Tabby pretends not to be interested, but I can see her listening from the corner. I'm ashamed as I describe how we led Damon into the deep part of the water, knowing he couldn't swim.

"Wow," Mary says when I'm finished. "That's major—I don't know—just major."

Grace nods. "It was."

Mary continues. "What's the story with Mrs. Asher? She

seems . . . slippery."

Mary is so smart. When I told Jeremiah I loved her, I wasn't lying.

"She starts off really nice, pretending to be your friend, but it's because she wants something. She'll betray you in a heart-beat. She promised Tabby a penthouse, but she's just as likely to send her to the Tunnel."

"What is that anyway?" Mary asks. "It sounds like some-where you go mining."

"It's like, uh, an underwater prison. Inescapable," Grace says.

"My grandmother was sent there for five years," I say. My heart pounds. All that water above you, living in some tiny little cell, it's my version of Hell.

"So what do we do about this lady?" Mary asks.

"Avoid her at all costs."

Tabby looks disappointed, and I feel sorry for her. It must have been a relief to believe, even for a moment, that there was a luxurious escape from the Cloisters.

"Can you stop talking already?" she says, changing into a nightgown. "Tomorrow is a really big day for me, and I'd like to get some sleep."

"Sure, Tabs," Grace says. She goes around the room, turning off the lights. "Anything else you need?"

"My own room."

There's a strained silence as we all realize that this is our last night with Tabby in the Treasury. Starting tomorrow, she'll be sharing Uncle Ruho's room as his wife.

I can't remember the last time I felt that I had failed someone so badly.

I blink six times and send Ram the update: *No success.*

He responds at once: *2morrow is another day!*

His exclamation point makes me want to vomit.

NINETEEN

The next morning, Tabby refuses to get out of bed. Mrs. Hypat let her sleep through breakfast, which was surprising, but now it's almost ten o'clock. The rest of us are dressed in our best clothing with our hair washed and styled.

Mrs. Hypat returns, expecting Tabby to be ready. "Is she even awake?"

Knowing she is, I say, "Tabby, you have to get up. We have to leave soon, and you still need to bathe."

"You really think he cares about body odor?" she says without raising her head.

"Don't you want to put on your pretty dress?" Grace asks.

"You wear it."

"We should unpack it." I open one of Tabby's bags, finding assorted clothes and shoes. At the bottom, I spot a handful of straws, mementos of her time with Adam. She would kill me for seeing them.

Her third bag contains the bundle with her wedding dress. When I pull it out, the gold and silver threads catch the light, causing the dress to sparkle like a diamond.

"My goodness," says Mrs. Hypat.

"Wow," says Mary, who also hasn't seen it before. "Razzamatazz."

Tabby lifts her head to glance at the dress and then lets it drop right back down on the pillow.

Mrs. Hypat gathers Mary, Grace, and me together, whispering, "You have got to do something, or Ruho's people will."

We look at the sad, unmoving lump in the bed.

"Tabby," I approach her, my voice rising, "If you don't get out of bed right now, Captain Memon will come down here and drag you out of bed. He'll throw you into that shower and he won't give a damn about your modesty! I beg you, in the name of the Savior, please do this on your own, before things get ugly."

I'm astonished when she sits up. When I see her dark-pitted eyes, I understand that she didn't sleep all night.

"Let's start with a shower," I say, hoping the water will help.

For the next hour, she acts like a child who can do nothing for herself. After the shower, we brush her hair, get her into the dress, and put on her shoes.

Mary explores Tabby's bag for makeup options. "Eureka! She brought concealer!" Mary runs over with a tube of something. She squirts a bit of tan goop onto her finger and is about to put it under Tabby's eye when Grace says, "No one's going to see her face. She'll be wearing a veil."

Mary freezes. "Oh. Right."

"Uncle Ruho will see her tonight," Mrs. Hypat says matter-of-factly.

"He doesn't care about my face," Tabby says, speaking in a monotone.

My mother wanted my face to look nice for my Offering. I thought it was in case other women saw me without my veil in the kitchen. A girl on offer always wants the gossip about her looks to be positive. But my mother actually wanted my face to look good because she planned to set my cloak on fire during my Offering. She wanted to make sure my suitors got a good look at the product that was hitting the market.

I push away Mary's hand. "Leave her alone. She doesn't need it."

Mary returns the makeup to Tabby's bag. "I don't get why John Paul worked so hard on that dress if it's going to be hidden by a cloak."

"Wait till you see what he designed!" Grace says, going back to the bundle. She pulls out a cloak and veil made of the same gold and silver thread as the dress.

We tell Tabby to stand, and Grace drapes the cloak around her. It's not like a regular cloak, in that it doesn't go over her head or cover her whole body. It drapes around Tabby's shoulders more like a cape, with the right side hooking onto the left shoulder. The result is very modest, allowing glimpses of the dress when Tabby walks.

"Major chic!" Mary proclaims.

"Hair up or down?" Grace asks. "Tabby?"

When she doesn't answer, Mary says, "What's quickest?"

"Down," I say.

"People will love the color," Mrs. Hypat says, "and Uncle Ruho loves the length."

"Mmmhmm," Grace says, beginning to brush it again.

All at once, Tabby begins to cry.

"Oh gosh. Did I pull too hard?" Grace stares at the brush like it's a weapon.

"I wanted to wear my hair up," Tabby says.

"We can still do that. We might have time." Mary looks at Mrs. Hypat to confirm.

"And I wanted a dress without sleeves."

"Uh, I don't think we have time to fix that," Grace says.

"Not now." Tabby sniffs. "I mean for my real wedding . . . to someone else."

"To Adam?" I say with gentleness.

"To ANYONE!" she says, crying harder.

Mrs. Hypat looks at us with a mixture of helplessness and urgency. "We don't have time for this!"

"Give her a minute!" I snap. "She's marrying someone fifty years older than her—"

"Whom she doesn't love—" Grace adds.

"Who looks like a toad!" Mary says.

"She has a right to have a good cry!" I say. I'm filled with rage that we weren't able to give Ruho the pellet yesterday. Even if we give it to him today, it won't take effect until tomorrow. It could save Tabby from a lifetime of marriage, but it can't save her from her wedding night.

Mrs. Hypat is baffled. "I'm sorry. I thought Miss Tabitha had chosen this path and that it brought her great spiritual pleasure."

"Uncle Ruho is your father, and look how he treats you," Mary says. "Why do you think he'll treat his wife any better?"

Mrs. Hypat steps back, stung. "He treats me . . . I am lucky to serve in his household."

"He treats you like a lapdog and you know it," Mary says.

I flinch. Being cruel to Mrs. Hypat won't solve anything.

"I'll wait in the hallway. She has ten minutes." Mrs. Hypat puts on her veil and leaves the room.

Grace gives Mary a scolding look.

"What? I was being honest."

"You're not helping the situation." Grace turns to Tabby. "Are you okay?"

Tabby has stopped crying but is back to her inert state. I wish I had something positive to say. I take her hand. "This won't be forever. He's old. I PROMISE. This ISN'T forever." I look deep into her eyes, trying to convey the truth of what I'm saying.

Grace spreads Tabby's waterfall of white-blonde hair over her shoulders and then snaps on the gold and silver veil. After we've put on our own veils, Mary and I each take one of Tabby's arms.

As we walk her out the door, Mary says, "You're going to be luminary, Tabs."

Mrs. Hypat exhales with relief when she sees us. "Praise the Prophet. She looks like an angel descended from heaven!"

We're almost to the stairwell when Tabby says, "I forgot something." In a sudden show of strength, she pulls away from Mary and me and rushes back into the Treasury.

We wait, and then we wait a little longer. "I'll check on her," I say, concerned.

Entering the Treasury, I don't see her. My heart pounds. What lengths would Tabby go to to avoid this marriage? I slowly open the bathroom door.

I'm dumbfounded by the scene inside.

Tabby stands at the sink holding my knife. She's surrounded by bits of blonde hair. It fills the sink and covers the floor where she stands. She's chopped it crudely with the blade and the result makes her look like a boy who's escaped from the madhouse.

I say the only thing I can think of: "Did you go through my things?" I look back in the room at my open bag.

Saying nothing, she brushes past me, a big smirk on her face.

TWENTY

Jaws drop when I usher Tabby back into the hallway, but we have no time to stop and discuss what's occurred. We rush up the stairs and through the Late Gothic Hall.

When we reach the main entrance, Mrs. Hypat says, "Miss Tabitha, take that cape and cover your hair. We don't need his Eminence reacting before the wedding. We're on a schedule."

I'm sure this is contrary to what Tabby had in mind, because she doesn't move. Mary unhooks the cape from Tabby's shoulder and lifts it up over her head. She then drapes it as best as she can. Tabby lets her. Her rebellion for the day seems to be finished.

"That'll do for now," Mrs. Hypat says, still frowning.

Once we leave the house, we're led south by a small army of Twitchers through the park. Our footsteps cause every squirrel in our path to flee, and I'm reminded of the people on the sidewalks who ducked out of the way when Grace and I were disguised as Twitchers.

The temperature is pleasant, but I can tell it's going to turn into a hot day. No one has told us where we're going, and Grace and I have been guessing where the ceremony might be: she thinks Lincoln Center, and I said maybe Carnegie Hall, the city's largest prayer center.

The path under our feet turns to gravel as we approach a line of gleaming white cars, running and waiting. Mrs. Hypat points to one near the back. "You girls will be in that Hummer. Miss Tabitha and I will ride closer to his Holiness."

Climbing up the big step into our car, I almost rip my cloak. Once inside, I offer a hand to Grace and Mary. The interior is so expansive, we each have a row to ourselves. Two armed Twitchers sit up front, and they don't even turn around when we enter. The seats are white leather, and I'm nervous that my hands might leave a mark.

Mrs. Hypat approaches the open door, and I'm stunned when she says, "Your brothers will join you."

A minute later, Juda, Dekker, and Silas climb in after us. They're wearing the gold tunics of Heralds and look very odd.

Juda slides in next to me in the back row, taking my hand. "Hello," he whispers.

"Hello," I whisper, giddy at his touch.

"Do you know where we're going?"

"Not a clue."

As a Twitcher approaches the Hummer door, I jerk my hand away from Juda's. The Twitcher slams the door shut, gives the car a bang on the ceiling, and we begin to move, engine roaring. Juda takes my hand again.

"I'm major excited," Grace says over the motor. She sits in front next to Dekker. "This is my first big wedding."

"They're, uh, long," Dekker says. Seemingly out of conversation about weddings, he adds, "This is a gas car."

"How do you know?" she asks.

"It sounds different than a battery," he says. He's always loved cars. "Can you imagine how much gasoline each one of these relics uses?" He uses a nicer tone with Grace than he uses with me.

"What else do you know about antique cars?" Grace asks, and he's off and running.

Silas asks Mary, "Do they make you dress up for the wedding even though you're all covered up?"

"Yes. We'll take off our cloaks when it's just women."

I'm happy they're all talking and that the engine provides enough noise that Juda and I can talk privately. Leaning into him, I say, "When Mrs. Asher came in yesterday, I nearly peed myself."

"I can't believe she didn't spot me," he says. "I worked for her for nine years!"

I can't believe it either. He was close enough for her to touch.

I lower my voice. "What did you tell Silas about the things she said?"

"The truth. Did you tell Tabby and Mary?"

"Most of it. Tabby was . . . difficult."

"Will she turn us in?"

"I don't think she has anything to gain. For now. How did Silas respond?" I'm worried about what he must think of me.

"He was a bit freaked out, but I think he understands why we did what we did."

Looking at the back of Silas' white-blond head in the seat in front of me, I think of the long conversation he and I should have. I know that he can sympathize with not wanting to marry the person your parents want to you marry, but that doesn't mean he understands why we would leave Damon to drown.

Putting his mouth right against my ear so Silas and Mary can't hear, Juda says, "I was on my way to the kitchen with the pellet when Zebadiah showed up and said we had to join Ruho for dinner."

"I'm the one who said you were our brothers," I say with regret. "I didn't know he'd suddenly want us to eat together."

"Don't feel bad. It was a clever idea."

As quietly as possible, I say, "I hoped you'd put the pellet in while I was coughing."

"Zebadiah was watching me like a hawk, like he was afraid I didn't know how to use a knife and fork or something."

As buildings go by, I wait for something to look familiar. Old brick apartment buildings crumble next to collapsed subway tracks.

"Is this how the whole city looks?" Mary asks, dismayed.

"Naw," Dekker says. "No one lives this far north anymore. Too far from good water."

At least, so we thought. All this time, Uncle Ruho has been hoarding gasoline and water. If only I could tell the world. He would probably find a way to twist the truth, just like with my father. Men like Ruho are shatterproof.

"I feel awful for Tabby," I say.

"Me, too," Juda says. "How is she?"

"Pretty bad."

His face is grim.

"We have to try again as soon as possible," I say.

"I should be able to get access to the kitchen as soon as Ruho has another meal."

"Good." I bite the inside of my mouth, worrying. "And after? What will we do?"

"Go back to Kingsboro," he says, as if it's obvious.

"If Ram doesn't send the Ostrich for us right away, we have to have a plan."

"They won't know it was us, remember? The pellet is unde-tectable." Even as Juda says this, I hear the nerves in his voice. We're trusting Ram's words completely. If the pellet isn't as advanced as Ram claims, we'll all hang.

"I don't want to stick around," I say.

He sighs. "Me neither, but if we bolt immediately, they'll *know* it was us."

I've also started to worry that if the Twitchers spot the Ostrich, they might shoot it down.

I hesitate over my next words. "I'd like to see Nana."

He looks out the window. "I figured." When he turns back to me, he has a small smile. "I have family I'd like to see, too."

Of course he does. During all my time thinking of Nana, I've never considered that Juda still has family here as well.

"But I have to get back to Ma as soon as possible, even if it means not seeing my uncles or helping the Convenes."

"Of course." I slide closer to him, checking to see if the Twitchers are paying attention. "How did she take the news? When you said you were coming here?"

"Not well." His forehead creases. "She was really worried about me, about all of us. And now no one is visiting her . . . " His head hangs.

"Have you heard from Dr. Rachel?" She promised to check in with him, using the Tact.

"This morning," he says. "She said Ma was the same, no better, no worse."

"At least she's not alone. Dr. Rachel is with her."

"It's not the same."

Wanting to change the subject to something lighter, I ask about Juda's life in the Cloisters. I learn that he, Dekker, and Silas share a room with several Heralds. The arrangement sounds awkward, but at least they all have beds. During the day, they're expected to stand guard during every meal, read the Book, and pray three times a day.

I tell him a bit about our routine and that three of us sleep on the floor. I also tell him that Mrs. Hypat is Uncle Ruho's daughter. He's as floored as I was.

"He never even looks at her!" he says.

"It's baffling."

"How can she stand it?"

Thinking of all the women and girls I've known, I say, "Her life could be worse."

We reach midtown, and the sidewalks are full of Twitchers but no one else. They carry guns much larger than the ones I'm used to.

Silas watches them, his face tight with alarm. "Is this normal?"

"They're probably enforcing the ceasefire for the wedding," Juda says.

Silas gapes out the window. "There are . . . a lot of them."

"Try to remember that they're on our side," Juda says.

He's technically right. Since we're members of the wedding party, the Twitchers are *our* guards. How major bizarre.

Leaning forward, I whisper to Silas, "How are you?"

He raises an eyebrow, as if this is the dumbest question he's ever heard. I remember when he asked me the same thing back in Kingsboro, and I felt the question was much too small for the answer.

I try again. "I mean, has anything . . . bad happened?"

Giving me a weak smile, he says, "So far, so good."

I smile back. I'd love to give him a hug, but the driver would probably see and we'd be in big trouble.

The car comes to a stop and the engine ends its roaring. I'm desperate to talk to Silas and Juda more. When will we get to speak again? Maybe not until Ruho is dead.

The driver opens his door and climbs out of the car. Taking advantage of his absence, I give Juda a quick kiss through my veil. He looks around nervously but then smiles at me. "Peace and light."

"Peace and light," I respond.

Our door opens, and we clamber out of the Hummer. I look all around, trying to get my bearings.

I can't believe it. We're in back of Madison Square Garden. Juda gives me a look of shock. Public executions happen here in front of crowds of thousands. *This* is where Uncle Ruho wants to be married? At least Tabby doesn't know what normally occurs here.

As the driver leads us across the street, my pulse accelerates as I realize that we're only blocks away from Macy's. I could be there in five minutes. An electric current seems to zip through my body as I think of getting to the Laurel Society and seeing Nana.

Slowing down my walk, I wait for Grace. When she reaches me, she says, "Mina, we're—"

"I know," I say, before she can finish. Even though she spent her whole life underground, Grace, thanks to her books, knows this city better than I do.

"What should we do?" she asks.

"Nothing. For now." Will there be a moment during this long day when we could sneak away?

"Your city is a mess," Mary says, approaching on my left. "And it stinks."

"Yeah," I say, inhaling deeply. "Isn't it great?"

As Twitchers open a heavily guarded door, a Herald shepherds us inside Madison Square Garden. He walks us through twisted passageways until we reach a door with a handwritten sign that says "Bride."

The Herald separates us from the boys and orders us to enter the room, and as soon we do, he shuts the door and locks it behind us. I have no idea where the boys will be taken. I don't imagine the groom wants their company.

Tabby and Mrs. Hypat are already here. Tabby paces the floor, while Mrs. Hypat sits in a chair. This dressing room is nothing like the one Ram uses. This one has folding metal chairs and bars on the windows. I shudder, knowing that many prisoners must have been kept here.

We remove our veils and sit down.

"How many people do you think will be watching?" Tabby says, a new energy in her voice.

"The stadium holds twenty thousand, I believe," Mrs. Hypat says.

She touches her newly shorn hair. "Nobody told me."

"It is the wedding of our divine leader," Mrs. Hypat says. "If you had any sense, you would've known, child."

"What should I do?" Tabby asks me.

"Keep the cape over your head. It looks good," I say, hoping it won't slip during the ceremony.

"You don't need to do anything but sit there and be quiet," Mrs. Hypat says. "Lots of people will be approaching his Holiness and speaking, but your role is to be stoic and look beautiful."

"How do I look beautiful if I'm covered?" Tabby asks.

"Your spirit is beautiful." Mrs. Hypat spreads her hands. "You exude piety and grace."

Tabby rolls her eyes.

"It sounds easy, but it's hard work," Mrs. Hypat says. "The ceremony will last for six hours."

Grace nudges me, and I know what she's thinking: Surely we can find a way within all that time to sneak out.

"Six hours!" Tabby looks at all of us, aghast. "What if I need to pee?"

"I suggest you do it now." Mrs. Hypat points to the bathroom. "I suggest all of you go. You'll all be on stage with her."

My heart sinks as I look at Grace, whose face has fallen. There will be no sneaking away while twenty thousand people have their eyes on us.

When we're ready, Mrs. Hypat gathers us at the door. "This is it, ladies. I would like to say that although I've not always understood or approved of your Unbound ways, I have enjoyed observing the rituals and intricacies of female friendship, something I have never enjoyed. As Miss Tabitha begins her life as his Holiness' wife, I hope you will continue to support her in the manner that you did today."

We're so surprised by the warm remark, that we're left speechless.

She pulls down her veil and opens the door.

TWENTY-ONE

As we enter the arena, I'm flabbergasted by the size of the place and the number of people already here. The seats snake up so high that the ones on top look as tiny as coat buttons. The noise is overwhelming. People are chatting as they find seats, and I imagine that most of the guests are as gossipy as my aunties. Men sit in the front and women are relegated to the back, in the button seats.

Uncle Ruho already sits on stage, perched on an enormous throne. I imagine this is so the audience didn't have to see him limp in. He wears purple and gold brocade and, bizarrely, his gray hair is now brown. He must have dyed it this morning. I'm sure it was meant to make him look younger, but instead he looks even more pasty, and the brown shade seems to accent his moles.

Mrs. Hypat tells us that Tabby will be introduced and that we will escort her to the gold pillow at Ruho's feet. Then we will sit on our own pillows at the edge of the stage. At least we don't have to stand for six hours. Mrs. Hypat and the boys, our "brothers," get to sit in the audience.

We wait on the sidelines for what feels like an eternity as the crowd finishes seating themselves. I think it has added another hour to the ceremony. Ruho already looks exhausted and irritable. I wonder if *he* peed.

"Where are the decorations? The flowers?" Mary asks, frowning out at the stage.

"Usually at the dinner afterward."

"It's all so . . . beige. And it kind of smells like old man sweat."

Finally, Zebadiah takes the stage. Today he wears gold from head to toe and resembles a polished candlestick. His entrance quiets the crowd. He leads a prayer and then welcomes everyone: "This is the most joyous of occasions—the wedding of our Divine Leader. His Holiness waited until God sent the most perfect girl, and he had to be patient, but God always has a plan, and He delivered to his Eminence the most appealing, the most pious, and the most fortunate girl that has ever walked the planet Earth. This noble creature will ensure the peace between our people and our neighbors. I give you Miss Tabitha Lorraine Dixon!"

I note that he didn't mention the huge amount of fuel that comes with a marriage to Tabby.

We walk onstage to applause so loud I think it will blow us back into the wings. I look to Tabby for her reaction but can't see her face through her veil. She must be completely overwhelmed. She's shaking as we lower her onto the gold pillow.

"Remember . . . you're *luminary*," Mary whispers in her ear before we walk away to seat ourselves.

Zebadiah speaks again. "His Holiness will now receive his gifts."

Men begin to file down from the seats and get in line. Each of them holds a box or envelope in his hand.

"What's happening?" Mary asks.

"It's traditional for the couple to accept gifts at the opening of the ceremony," I say. "This is also when male friends and relatives share advice for the marriage. Then Heralds bless the union and the couple says vows. Then all that's left is prayer and the women's song."

"Women's song?"

"Women aren't allowed to give gifts or advice, so at the end of the ceremony, they sing a song to the couple."

"Feeble," Mary says.

"It's a beautiful song," I say.

"It's FEEBLE," Mary says. "When I get married, I want *all* the advice to come from women. Let men sing some dumb song."

Weddings have always been this way, but what she says makes sense. If the women in Tabby's life had lined up to give her advice before she left home, she would've arrived with a *lot* more knowledge than she did.

The next few hours are spent watching Uncle Ruho receive his gifts and hear praise from his people. A man will approach him, head down in supplication, and after Ruho has said "Peace," the man will lavish him with affection. If Ruho doesn't think the praise is high enough, he begins to praise himself until the supplicant understands that he needs to say more. Some grovel to the point of tears and wailing.

"Is this guy for real?" Mary whispers.

"He's no worse than Ram," I say, remembering how much Ram loved applause.

"If Ram and Uncle Ruho were in the same room, how would God be able to shine enough light on them both?" Mary says with disgust.

I can't help but search the faces of the guests for people I know. Is Grandpa Silna in line? Or Mr. Husk, Sekena's father? Looking up at the thousands of women patiently waiting in the

149

upper tiers, I wonder if Sekena could be here. She doesn't like to leave the apartment, but I could imagine her being excited about the divine wedding. I would give anything just to hear her voice.

After the last man has finally paid homage, Zebadiah comes forward again and faces Uncle Ruho and Tabby. He begins reading from the Book, but I can't hear the words.

"Why isn't he facing the audience?" Mary asks.

"The ceremony is for the couple, not the guests. How does it work in Kingsboro?"

"Ram has on a mic, so we can all hear every word that he says."

"Ram marries everyone?"

"Since I was a kid, yeah."

I consider this as Zebadiah closes the Book.

Grace leans in. "Maybe we can still sneak away."

"There are thousands of people watching the stage," I say, feeling this should be obvious.

"After. What if we, sort of, just get 'lost in the crowd' for a while?"

I imagine this. Would they send Twitchers to look for us? How important are we as "attendants to Miss Tabitha?" Tabby would probably raise a stink, not wanting to go back to the Cloisters alone. What if we got caught sneaking into or out of Macy's, giving away the location of the Laurel Society?

"We can't," I say, my heart breaking. "It's too risky."

"We may never be this close again," Grace says.

"I know."

Zebadiah helps Ruho rise from his throne and kneel on the ground next to Tabby. Zebadiah leans into them, murmuring, and then he waits. The crowd goes silent.

This is it. Tabby and Ruho are saying their vows.

None of us can hear a thing, but as soon as Zebadiah turns around, people begin applauding.

"It's over," I say.

"They're married?" Mary asks.

"Yeps," Grace says.

Mary sighs. "This was the most depressing wedding I've ever been to."

"He hasn't even seen her hair, yet," Grace says.

I hope he's not too angry. Tabby was being rebellious when she cut it off, but she wasn't considering how punishing Uncle Ruho could be.

"Let's pray she doesn't say anything about *his* hair," I say.

Tabby and Zebadiah help Ruho back into his throne. Traditionally, the married couple would exit the stage hand in hand, but I think that Ruho still doesn't want people to see him walking.

Zebadiah says to the crowd, "Thank you for witnessing this divine union. God smiles on you all. Peace."

With that, the people start to file out, and I realize we're going to have to sit here until they're all gone.

"I don't know how much longer I can sit up straight," Mary says.

I know what she means. My lower back aches, and my rear end has lost all feeling.

We wait over an hour for the arena to empty. Twice, I fall asleep sitting up.

When not one person is left in sight, Ruho finally stands. Zebadiah and another Herald rush over to help. I can't hear anything specific, but Uncle Ruho seems to be complaining quite a bit as he walks off stage.

Tabby stands, frozen. Is she supposed to go with him or come with us? She looks at us for help. As much as I hate to do it, I point toward Ruho. She's now his wife and needs to be by his side at all times.

She follows Zebadiah and her new husband. They disappear into a dark hallway.

The rest of us are escorted outside to another big white car, but this time, the boys will be traveling separately. Before I know what's happening, we're headed back to the Cloisters.

How can I have been so close to Nana and done nothing? We still seem near enough that if I screamed she might be able to hear me. The urge is so overwhelming, I almost roll down my window and start to holler. But I don't. I swallow the howl, and disappointment sits like a rock in my belly.

TWENTY-TWO

When we return to the Cloisters, the house is surrounded by hundreds of flickering lights. As we walk up the long path, I discover that candles have been placed in small paper bags full of sand along every pathway. The effect is magical.

Inside the house itself, Heralds scurry about with flowers, food, and extra chairs. Every room has been transformed into a banquet hall full of candles and fine tableware. Golden bowls of white hydrangeas rest on every spare surface in the house. The smell of roast meat drifts through the halls.

"Wow," Grace says. "It's stunning."

"I wonder who's invited," I say.

"From the looks of things, only major fancy people," Mary says.

"What are *we* supposed to do?" Grace says.

"Are we still able to talk to Tabby?" Mary says.

"I think so," I say. One can usually talk to a bride after a wedding, but I've never been to a divine one before. "Let's find her."

We wander the rooms, where Heralds continue to arrange platters and centerpieces.

We discover Tabby already seated, alone, at a colossal table in the Late Gothic Hall. She sits at one end with her head down, her cloak still raised above her head.

"Tabby!" Grace cries.

Mrs. Hypat, who waits in the shadows as usual, rushes up. "You can no longer call her that!"

Several Heralds also turn to give Grace an admonishing look.

Grace's voice becomes timid. "I mean, uh, your Eminence?"

"That's better, Daphne." Mrs. Hypat pats her shoulder. "You can also call her 'your Holiness.'"

Mary stifles a laugh. "That's gonna take some getting used to."

Mrs. Hypat returns to her dark corner.

"You okay?" I ask Tabby.

"What do you think?" Tabby says without looking at us.

"What can we do?" Grace asks.

"Burn down this building," Tabby says without hesitation.

Grace laughs uncomfortably, but I know Tabby isn't kidding.

"I would if I could," I say. If I can put a pellet in Ruho's food tonight, I will.

"Maybe you should—" But we never get to hear Mary's suggestion, because Uncle Ruho appears in the doorway, Zebadiah close on his heels.

"Beloved! What a joy to see you." Limping slowly into the room, he plops himself into the cushioned chair at the head of the table.

Grace takes several steps backward and stands against the

wall, which seems like a good idea. Mary and I do the same. Ruho doesn't seem to notice us.

"What a tremendous crowd! Have you ever seen anything like it, Zebadiah?" Ruho says. I've never seen him in such a good mood.

"No, your Eminence. Largest I've ever seen."

"There must have been, what, eighty, ninety thousand people there?"

Zebadiah smiles at him. "Uh, yes. Probably more."

Mrs. Hypat told us the stadium could hold twenty thousand.

"Tremendous crowd. Tremendous." He looks at a Herald pouring water into all the goblets on the table. "Did you hear about the crowd?"

Without looking at him, the Herald says, "It was tremendous, your Holiness."

Uncle Ruho beams. "Exactly!" He looks at Tabby. "Come here, Beloved."

She doesn't move.

"Come here!"

She stands with great reluctance.

"Closer!" he says.

She takes a few steps toward him.

He pats his lap. "Here!"

She takes another slow step, seeming to weigh her options.

"Don't make me tell you again," he says in a more ominous tone.

She walks to his chair, hesitates, and then perches on his cushion right next to him, which is wise. I'm not sure his lap could handle the weight of her.

He puts an arm around her. "Isn't that better?" With his other arm, he strokes her leg.

I wait for her body to stiffen, but it doesn't. She's more like a rag doll. As he pulls her in to nuzzle her, everything about her is limp and indifferent. How can he not notice? Or maybe he does, but he doesn't care.

What if I embraced Juda, and his body went slack? The thought is major embarrassing. Even if I had the physical strength to keep him in my grasp, why would I keep subjecting him to my affection? The moment he signaled disinterest, I'd be humiliated.

A man who doesn't notice his partner's physical discomfort is not a good man.

Ruho strokes Tabby's head, causing her cloak to fall back. Her chopped hair is exposed.

"What . . . What in the Prophet's name is that?" Ruho says, touching her head. "*Who* did this to you?"

Her voice is full of fear as she whispers, "I did."

Ruho looks around the room, fuming, until his eyes land on Mrs. Hypat. "*You* allowed this? You let my new wife turn herself into a *boy?*"

Mrs. Hypat steps forward, and I'm terrified on her behalf. What can she possibly say?

"I am sorry, your Holiness. I was negligent."

She's taking responsibility for something she had no control over. I was the one who reached Tabby first, and it was already too late. Tabby did this and no one else.

To the shock of us all, Ruho violently rips off Tabby's veil.

As the Heralds in the room turn their faces away, Mrs. Hypat surges forward. "No, your Holiness. You mustn't—"

"I am finding your company tiresome, Hypat. We no longer need you tonight."

"But—"

"I said GO!" Ruho yells.

Mrs. Hypat flinches, then walks out of the room with her usual crisp cadence.

Uncle Ruho stares at Tabby's exposed face, which is covered in nervous blotches. He grabs her chin, turning her head left and right, as if she were a horse he just bought.

"I should have you beaten for cutting off your hair. It was at least half of your beauty."

She stares silently at the ceiling, his hand around her jaw.

"I could do that, but I'm a generous man, and it's our wedding day. So I will let you make it up to me." I hold my breath, waiting to hear what he means. "You will sit here all evening and show my guests what an adoring wife you are. Without your beautiful hair, you will just have to show them your beautiful face."

Exhaling, Tabby tries to smile. "Of course, my beloved."

The Heralds give one another appalled glances. This is highly unorthodox. I can't imagine what the guests will think, but Ruho is the Divine Leader, so no one dares to tell him he's being improper. Zebadiah looks like he might have a coronary.

Guests begin to arrive fifteen minutes later. I would guess that by eight o'clock, two hundred men have filled the rooms of the Cloisters. Many of them come to our hall to pay their respects to Uncle Ruho. They have already praised him at the wedding ceremony, but it seems that one can never flatter him enough.

Twenty men sit at the dining table in our room. They're served pheasant and steak and many luxuries such as chocolate, oranges, and strawberries and cream. No one has told us if or when we will eat.

Tabby remains seated in Ruho's chair. She picks at his dinner, and he lets her, destroying any hope I had of sneaking the pellet into this meal. The men at the table are free to stare at her, and they do. I think I'm more uncomfortable than she is; she grew up with men looking at her face.

She's in full Tabby performance mode. Every now and then she rubs Ruho on the back or whispers something in his ear. She even gives him a kiss on the cheek. Ruho is thrilled. Tabby always does better when she has an audience.

Some men at the table look just as uncomfortable with her bare face as the Heralds, while others are mesmerized by her. One oily man at the table brazenly asks Ruho if he is worried that God may not absolve this transgression. Uncle Ruho laughs, saying, "The great thing about being divine is that you can always absolve yourself."

The whole event is dreamlike in its bizarreness.

When the meal is finally over, the men take forever to leave. They linger, talking and talking about nothing, each one loving the sound of his voice more than the last. I worry that they'll stay until morning. Thankfully, the Heralds begin to extinguish the candles in the candelabras, a definitive sign that it's time to say goodnight. They're probably worried about Uncle Ruho, who, after his long wedding and lively dinner, is falling asleep at the table.

When the last guest has left, Tabby stops performing as quickly as an instrument that someone has stopped playing.

Ruho hardly seems to notice. "Where's Zebadiah?" he asks.

Zebadiah is at his side within seconds. "Yes, your Eminence?"

"We're ready to go to my chambers."

"Yes, your Holiness."

Zebadiah picks up Tabby's veil from the floor, handing it to her with disgust, as if she were the one who'd thrown it there. She reattaches it.

Zebadiah then helps Ruho to rise and leads him, still

jabbering about the size of the wedding crowd, out of the dining room. "There were a hundred thousand people there!"

Tabby walks slowly behind them.

We don't have a chance to say anything to her on the way to her wedding night. But really, what is there to say? I whisper a prayer for her under my breath.

TWENTY-THREE

When we finally return to our room, I'm exhausted beyond belief. We were allowed to eat leftovers from the feast, and the combination of standing for so many hours and the rich food has made me long even for my spot on the concrete floor.

Upon seeing the bed, all of us seem to realize at the same moment that Tabby is no longer here to claim it. The three of us jump on the mattress with glee.

Giggling, Grace says, "Who gets to sleeps here?"

"We can rotate," I suggest, hoping I get the first turn.

"We can all sleep here, I bet," Mary says. "You and Grace sleep the regular direction and I'll sleep toe to head." We try it out, and sure enough, we all fit.

"I can't believe Tabby had all this space to herself," Grace says.

"It's okay," I say. "She deserved it."

As we lie there in silence, I'm sure we're all thinking of the same thing: Tabby alone in the tower with Uncle Ruho.

I shiver.

Grace climbs out of bed and goes into the bathroom. A

second later, she comes right back out. "Whoa. It's major freaky in there."

When Mary and I join her, I see Tabby's blonde hair covering the sink and floor.

"I still can't believe she did it," Grace says. "Her hair was razzamatazz."

"Yeah. It was formidable," Mary concedes.

Perplexed, Grace asks, "What did she use?"

"Uh, a knife," I say. I wonder if I should admit it was mine, but I'm distracted by the fact that it no longer appears to be in the bathroom. "Do you see it?"

We search the floor, behind the toilet, and anywhere else it might have fallen, but it's not here.

"Maybe Mrs. Hypat found it?" Grace suggests.

"Then why aren't we in trouble?" I say, beginning to panic.

"Are you sure Tabby left it here?" Mary says.

"I thought she did . . . " I swear she dropped it into the sink. "But maybe she took it with her."

"Why would she take it?" Grace asks.

Mary and I look at each other, and from her dark look I know she's having the same thought that I am. "*Oh, God.*"

I dart out of the bathroom, grabbing my veil. I snap it on as I run out of the Treasury.

"Mina, wait!" Mary calls.

I sprint up the stairs and have reached the Unicorn Room before I realize that I don't know how to reach the tower. I close my eyes, pulling it into memory as I see it from the central garden.

I realize I'm on the wrong side of the building. Heralds are still clearing tables as I race the other direction. They look up at me, confused, but don't stop me.

I reach the northeast corner of the building but find no entrance to the tower. I want to scream. Then I remember the stairs that lead down to the kitchen. I take them two at a time. When I arrive at the bottom, I discover two hallways.

I start with the one to my right. I almost run headfirst into two Twitchers.

The taller one says, "What are you doing here?"

"I, uh, needed some broth for my companion. She's ill."

"The kitchen's the other way," he says with contempt.

"Oh! Thank you," I say, bowing so low I almost fall forward.

They pass by, muttering about having to deal with women in the building. I'm lucky they aren't Heralds, who know I shouldn't be here without Mrs. Hypat. I turn around, walking with them and then turning toward the kitchen. *Thank the Prophet,* they don't come with me but head up the stairs instead.

Waiting until I hear them reach the main floor, I return to the first hall. I'm extremely relieved when, thirty feet in, I discover a staircase. Looking up, I see what must be five flights. This is it.

I run up the stairs, passing closed door after closed door. Mrs. Hypat said that Uncle Ruho slept at the top of the tower. How does he get all the way up here? He can't possibly walk.

When I reach the fifth floor, I'm winded and sweat trickles down my forehead. Anxiety has seized every emotion in my body. At the top of the staircase is a door with no guard. Perhaps Ruho wanted privacy for his wedding night? The two Twitchers I met were probably his usual surveillance.

Now that I'm here, I realize that I have no plan beyond finding the room.

What kind of emergency would cause someone to knock on this door? *Think, Mina.* I could say the building is under attack, but what will Ruho do when he realizes it isn't?

I could say Tabby forgot something in the room. A gift for his Holiness? But then what gift will I give him?

"A kick in the rear," I can hear Mary answering.

Tabby herself is the gift. We have nothing else.

The clock is ticking while I stand here like an idiot. I can't wait too long. I have to tell Tabby about the pellet. I have to tell her there's hope!

Before I lose my nerve, I bang on the door. Not sure what story to tell, I decide I'll know which is best when Ruho opens the door—if I get the chance to speak. He may fling me back down the stairs.

No one answers.

Do I dare knock again? I think of everything we have to lose and bang on the door a second time.

After a slight pause, I hear, "Who is it?" It's Tabby.

"Beth, your Holiness."

I'm about to explain that the kitchen is on fire when the door flings open.

Tabby, wild-eyed, stands in front of me wearing a long white nightgown. From the waist up, she's drenched in blood.

I'm too late.

TWENTY-FOUR

"I messed up major bad," she says.

"Get back inside," I say.

She stumbles backward, and I follow, my heart racing with panic and dread. I secure the door, take a breath, and look around. I'm in a large, opulent room filled with gold furniture and multicolored velvets. Lit candelabras surround a round bed, which is unmade. In the middle of the bed lies Uncle Ruho. He is halfway through a state of undress. His eyes are open and full of disbelief. His skin is yellow and waxy and his mouth forms a terrible grimace. Protruding from the right side of his neck is my knife.

I try not to gag. *Oh, Tabby. Why couldn't you have waited?*

Her eyes dart around the room, as if she expects bats or Twitchers to come flying out of the rafters.

"It's okay," I say. "We just have to stay calm."

"It's not OKAY!" she says. "He's dead!"

"You're the one who brought the knife!" I shriek.

Her voice gets small. "I . . . j-just wanted to keep him away from me. I never planned—" She stares down at herself. "He was kissing me, and t-touching me, and I told him to stop, but he wouldn't. He wouldn't stop. All I knew was I *had* to make him stop. And then there was all this blood. Everywhere." She moans.

I grab her shoulders. "I understand why you did this. So will Mary and Grace, but Zebadiah and Captain Memon will NOT. We have to get out of here before they discover what's happened, okay?" She nods, wiping her eyes with her sleeve. She only manages to smear more blood onto her face. "First, you have to get cleaned up." I scan the room, then point to the far wall. "Use that sink over there, and I'll find something clean for you to wear."

I enter Ruho's enormous closet, my whole body trembling. Picturing his body lying feet away, I feel faint. The look on his face is so horrible—somewhere between a laugh and a scream. I have to stop thinking about it if we're going to get out of this.

After taking a minute to gather myself, I find a tunic that's big and plain and could be a simple dress on Tabby. When I bring it out, she's wiping the last of the blood off her face. Her hair is wet and looks clean, or clean enough. It's an odd blessing that she cut it off and didn't have much to wash. She throws the tunic over her naked body. As she uses a clean towel to rub her hair dry, I catch a glint of light on her hand.

"Show me your hand," I say.

Squinting her eyes shut, she holds it out toward me. "Is it blood?"

"Where did you get that ring?" I ask.

She opens her eyes to study the large ruby on her forefinger. "He gave it to me, in the car, after the wedding."

"Take it off."

Without a word, she slides it off and hands it to me. I search the room. "It's not jewelry. It's a *collar,* and it will track you wherever you go."

Her voice rises an entire octave. "SMASH IT! Flush it down the toilet!"

"We don't want it to suddenly turn off. It's better if everyone thinks you're in this room for as long as possible."

I don't need to bother hiding it; as soon as Ruho's body is discovered, Tabby's disappearance will be apparent. I place it by the sink.

"You need a cloak," I tell her. She can't go outside in just a tunic. I search the room until I find her abandoned cloak in the corner on the floor.

"I'm never going to blend in wearing a wedding cloak," she says, rubbing her hands in desperation.

"It's nighttime, and you don't have anything else!" We don't have time for her to be contrary. I wrap the cloak around her and hook it at the shoulder. The fabric sparkles like shattered glass. "Try turning it inside out."

She removes the cloak, flips it around, and repositions it. The fabric is still the gold and silver of the wedding dress, but it's not nearly as shiny. "It will have to do," I say. Between her chopped platinum hair and her shimmering cloak, if we make it into the city, she'll stand out like a peacock in a pigeon coop.

I'm thankful I wore my cloak and veil here, but everything else in my room will have to be left behind.

"When we get to the bottom of the stairs, we have to walk through that short passageway, go up the stairs, and then make it to the south entrance." Already escape seems impossible. Twitchers or Heralds could be in any part of the house, and there's no excuse in the world for Tabby to be anywhere but with her new husband.

"No, we don't." She points to a nook near the door. "That's an elevator. My belov—Uncle Ruho couldn't walk all the way up here. It leads to the ground floor, really close to the north exit."

Praise the Prophet.

"I need to tell the others what's happening," I say.

I type into my Tact, *Emergency! Ruho dead. Must leave NOW. Meet @ north exit.*

On the one hand, Tabby has solved our problem, and Uncle Ruho is dead. On the other hand, she's done it in a terrible and violent way that cannot be hidden, and we don't have time to come up with a decent escape plan.

Responses start to flood my Tact.

What's happened?

R U okay?

Hallelujah + God bless. May he rest n peace. This one is from Ram.

I type my answer: *Meet us NOW.*

"Let's go," I tell Tabby. Securing my cloak and veil, I try not to look at the corpse on the bed.

Tabby snaps on her own veil and pulls her cloak over her hair. She walks to the elevator with determination, never looking at the body on the bed. She presses the down button, and the engine of the elevator whirs as the car slowly heads up to our floor. I try to use omming while we wait, but it's no use. My mind is flooded with all the problems we'll face trying to leave the grounds. We hear a clank as the elevator finally arrives, and we lurch forward as the doors open.

We both gasp. Standing inside, like the shadow of death, is Mrs. Hypat.

TWENTY-FIVE

"Beth, you weren't in your bed," Mrs. Hypat says.

"No, I, uh—"

"Mary said you were concerned about Her Eminence, but I couldn't imagine you would do anything as inappropriate as come here. You will leave with me at once." She reaches for my arm and, instinctively, I jump back.

This is a mistake. I've given her a clear view into the room.

She sucks in her breath.

Before we can stop her, she exits the elevator and approaches the corpse.

Tabby tugs on my cloak, pulling me toward the elevator. Can we dive into it and hit the button in time? As I have the thought, I hear the doors clank shut behind us.

Mrs. Hypat circles the bed, examining the bloody body from several angles. With her veil still in place, I can't see her face. She abruptly sits in a purple chair in the corner, placing her hand on her heart.

"Are you okay?" I ask.

She holds her other hand out, signaling I should stay back.

Folding back her veil, she takes several big gulps of air. Like me, she seems ready to be sick at the sight of the corpse. "He does not look peaceful," she says.

I go to the sink, fetching her a glass of water. She accepts it but only takes the slightest sip.

"Did you do this?" she asks me.

I realize that now that Tabby is cleaned up, I am an equal suspect.

"I did," Tabby says in a shaky voice behind me.

Squinting at Tabby, Mrs. Hypat finishes her water, stands, and walks toward the door.

"Where are you going?" I ask in a panic.

"To alert Zebadiah," she says matter-of-factly.

"Wait!" Tabby says. "I thought you were supposed to look after me!"

Mrs. Hypat gives her a fierce scowl, indicating that Tabby has pushed the limit of her caretaking.

Her hand is on the doorknob.

"He poisoned the Convenes!" I blurt.

She pauses.

"His Holiness and Mr. Asher! They used parts from an old mercury plant to build the pipes, and it poisoned the water supply, and then they blamed it on someone else: a man named Zai Clark."

"Rubbish. Why would you know that?"

"Because Zai Clark is my father."

"What are you doing—?" Tabby says.

If nothing else, I'm stalling.

Hypat looks at me, confused. "That makes no sense."

"I'm . . . I'm one of the people that Mrs. Asher is looking for. I grew up here, as a Deserver."

"You killed her husband and son?"

"No. Mrs. Asher wasn't there. She doesn't know what

happened."

"Why on earth would you return to Manhattan?" she asks, thankfully taking her hand away from the doorknob.

Keep talking, Mina. "Ram made us."

"Why?"

This question was inevitable. I settle on a half-truth. "He wanted people with Tabby who knew the island, who could consult with her and teach her about the Book." She studies Tabby, who doesn't know any different.

"I was at the Asher's apartment two months ago," I say. "I heard Mr. Asher talking to Captain Memon about the water treatment plant and the Convenes. Uncle Ruho paid Mr. Asher a lot of money to make sure the mercury was there. Juda's—I mean James' mother is really sick from it."

"That's true," Tabby says.

"I know he's your father but—" I say.

Mrs. Hypat interrupts, "I know his cruelty."

"He was an awful man who killed a lot of people, and he was forcing Tabby . . . You know why she did this," I say.

Mrs. Hypat stares at Tabby for what feels like forever. "You've been very stupid."

This I agree with.

"You cannot hide this crime," Mrs. Hypat says. "The entire city knows you were the only one with him tonight."

I should have told Tabby about the pellets our first day here. How could I have been so dumb? I can't believe I listened to the others.

Mrs. Hypat purses her lips. "If I don't report this immediately, I'll be executed right beside you."

"But you're the heir!" I say. "You're the only descendent of the Prophet!"

She blows out air: *pfft.* "His Holiness wanted a boy—"

"Who cares? He got a girl! And the Prophet was a girl. The

Heralds know that. They've been going along with him all these years, but they know the Prophet was a woman."

Mrs. Hypat's eyes search the room in doubt.

I continue. "Will the people want a leader who is divine or not divine? The Heralds will lose their authority without someone who is descended from God."

"You're descended from God?" Tabby says, impressed.

I nod at her with enthusiasm. "She is."

"I'm no leader," Hypat says.

"Of course you are. You run half this place already."

Her head lifts. "I do." I'm beginning to feel hopeful until she says, "I can't protect Tabby. No matter who I am."

Tabby gives her a pleading look. "No one will check this room until morning. Can't you at least let us have a head start?"

Mrs. Hypat begins to pace. I can imagine all the thoughts going through her head: who knows I'm in this room right now? What if Tabby and Beth are caught and tell on me? What if *I* am blamed for this murder?

Does she really have anything to gain by letting us go? She can turn us in and still be the heir.

My tact fills with a message: *No pellet activated. What happened?*

It's from Ram. The pellets have some sort of activation signal? *Nyek.*

Is Ruho dead r not? he writes.

I ignore him, focusing on the matter at hand: Mrs. Hypat and why she should help us.

"If you let us go," I say, "we'll spread the word throughout the city that Ruho poisoned the water, and that you are the rightful heir."

"I could have anyone do that," she says with sharpness.

"Not tonight," I say. "If you don't let people know that you exist *right now* then Captain Memon could have you executed without a second thought. It will be like you never existed, and he can take charge."

Her eyes widen at this reality.

"But if people on the island know you're alive, you will be safe." I hope this is true.

"The people will be excited, but once they see my face, they'll know I'm not divine, just like Father said."

"Why would they see your face? You will have the veil on in public, just like the Prophet," I tell her.

"That is major feeble," Tabby says. "Don't cover your face. If you're in charge then you can tell women to stop covering their faces, if they want to, right? That's what I would do. I think your face, is, like, kind of major fierce. Everyone thinks I have no backbone because I'm small and blonde. *No one* will want to mess with you. Even the men."

"You're a simple-headed girl who's always gotten everything she's ever wanted because of her looks. You know nothing." Mrs. Hypat turns back to me. "How would you spread the word?"

"We'll go to the large group of women I know in midtown, and they'll be very happy that a woman is now in charge. They'll want everyone to know immediately."

"I would be giving you an enormous amount of trust, Beth."

"Mina. My real name is Mina."

"We need to go," Tabby says with anxiety. I give her a look which I hope tells her to be patient. If we don't get Mrs. Hypat on our side, we won't be able to leave at all.

What else could I possibly say to bring Mrs. Hypat to our side? I'm out of ideas. I'm trying not to let her see the terror that I feel.

Mrs. Hypat clasps her hands in front of her. I can see she's made a decision. I brace myself. "I'll give you your head start. Zebadiah will come to wake his Holiness at nine a.m. sharp, and when he discovers this crime, the whole city will come for you."

Nine a.m. It's eleven now, so that gives us ten hours to escape.

Tabby rushes toward her. "Thank you! I knew you would—"

Mrs. Hypat holds out an arm to block her. "Before you are found, you will tell everyone you meet that his Eminence poisoned the Convenes, that God has punished him with death, and that his daughter, Esther Lydia Hypat, is taking over."

"Of course," I say.

"If you are caught, I will deny this conversation ever happened and offer you no aid or clemency. Do you understand?"

Tabby stops smiling. "Yes."

"Yes," I say, relieved but frightened for what lies ahead.

"You should use the elevator to leave," Mrs. Hypat says.

"Yes," Tabby says. "And then out the north door."

"No. Go down two more levels to the cellar. You'll find a tunnel that leads to the garage. His Eminence couldn't walk across the grounds and he refused to let anyone see him in a wheelchair."

Tabby nods with new understanding. "He made me walk to the house by myself after the wedding."

"The Hummers are still in the driveway. A ring of car keys will be in his Eminenance's pocket."

We all look at the body with dread.

"Tabby," I say. "That's all you."

TWENTY-SIX

After Tabby has found the keys, we say good-bye to Mrs. Hypat.

"Thank you," I say.

"You must hurry." She pushes the button for the elevator.

Tabby's head tilts as she studies Mrs. Hypat. "I wasn't very nice to you."

"I'm used to it."

"Well . . . enjoy being in charge," Tabby says as the elevator arrives. "People have to be courteous to you now." We step inside and get one last glance of Mrs. Hypat as the doors close. She stands tall, her gnarled face lifted with poise.

When the doors shut, I hit the button for the ground floor, not the cellar.

"What are you doing?" Tabby asks.

"We have to meet the others. I sent them a Nod."

"We need to leave!" Tabby says.

"Don't you want Silas to come with us?"

She makes a low groaning sound.

Another Nod from Ram appears in my Tact: *Dead or not dead?*

Dead! I type back.

How? he asks.

What can I say? I retype *DEAD!*

The door opens on the ground floor, and we're greeted by an empty silence. *Nyek.* No one is here yet. We step out into the stone passageway.

"The banquet hall is there, and the exit is that way," Tabby says, pointing to the left and then to the right.

Do the others know where to go? "Wait here," I tell Tabby.

"No way," she says, following me.

We tiptoe down the passageway until we can see the banquet hall, and then we find a statue to hide behind.

We wait.

Ram sends me Nod after Nod, but I continue to ignore them. After we've stood there five minutes, Tabby whines, "Why aren't we leaving?"

The truth is, I'm becoming incredibly anxious as well. Every second we stand here is precious time wasted.

Suddenly, two shadows come racing through the banquet hall and into the passageway. I'm about to have a heart attack before I make out the teal cloaks of Mary and Grace.

I hug Grace. "Thank the Prophet."

"What's going on?" she asks, breathless.

"Did you see the boys?" I say.

"They aren't here?" Mary asks.

"We have to leave them," Tabby says, walking away.

"No!" I say, pulling her back. "We have to give them more time."

Where r u? I type to them.

There's no answer.

"How long do we wait?" Mary asks.

I don't have a response, because I'm not in any way prepared to leave without the boys.

We stand there, staring at one another. Another five minutes goes by.

"Mina . . . " Tabby says.

"I KNOW." I don't want to hear it.

"I'm sure they're fine," Mary says. "They'll be right behind us."

"Let's go!" Tabby says.

Unable to believe the words coming from my mouth, I whisper, "Fine. Let's go."

Go 2 cars I write the boys. How will they get past the guards without Ruho's tunnel?

Tabby sprints toward the elevator like the building is on fire. Mary and Grace charge after her. I move slowly, looking back into the banquet hall several more times. I run after the girls, my heart breaking.

The tunnel to the garage is nicer than I was expecting. It's clean and well-lit, with a smooth glossy floor. A folded wheelchair rests against one of the tiled walls. We can see where we're going, but we'll also be easily spotted by anyone else who enters. If Ruho isn't in the tunnel, does anyone else have reason to be here? I pray not.

We don't speak. All sound seems amplified down here, from our footsteps to our breathing.

We're walking at a brisk pace when from somewhere behind us comes a rattling sound, like a chain sweeping across a pipe. Perhaps the elevator is going back upstairs. Perhaps someone wants to come down. Without a word, we all break into a run.

We don't stop until we reach the end of the tunnel, which ends at another elevator. The four of us rush inside and Grace punches the one button on the panel. As we wait for the doors to close, we look back down the long white tunnel, waiting for someone or something to come after us.

Blessedly, the doors shut before we see anything.

When we reach ground level, the elevator opens to reveal an old subway stop. Ruho must have used an old train tunnel to build his fancy wheelchair passage.

A ramp leads outside. Asking the others to wait, I tiptoe up it very quietly. When I reach the top, the long fleet of Hummers is only yards away. I could kiss Mrs. Hypat. I promise myself I will do right by her.

I sneak back down the ramp and whisper to the others, "The cars are right outside. We have a lot of keys with a bunch of markings, but we don't know what any of the markings mean. We just have to try them on every car until we find one that works. Mary, can you drive?"

"Those things are twenty times bigger than anything I've ever driven!" she says.

"But can you do it?" I say.

"I can try."

"Good." I ask Tabby for the keys. One by one, I slide them off the ring and hand them out—multiple keys to each of us. "Try them on the door of every car. As soon as one works, signal with a whistle."

Creeping up the ramp, we search the night for guards. The moon is waning, which gives us cover but makes it difficult to see anything. I worry about Tabby's glittery cloak.

When it seems the coast is clear, I whisper, "Go!"

We run, scattering among the vehicles.

Tabby tries the car nearest to us, and Grace takes the second, so Mary and I head for the third and fourth. I try my first key, hand shaking. The key goes into the slot but won't turn. *Nyek*. I try a second key. Nothing. The third key is no good. I move onto another car.

I repeat the same process with the same results and move to the next car. Each attempt seems longer than the last. How can we *all* be failing? I'm moving on to my fourth car when I finally hear a sharp whistle. Looking to see where it came from, I spot someone waving around the tenth car. I scurry toward them.

Grace is still waving when I arrive. Mary and Tabby didn't hear her whistle.

"You opened one?" I say, relieved.

"No," she says. "People are coming."

Nyek. Squinting into the darkness, I can just make out three shadowy figures heading toward us from the direction of the house.

I whistle, hoping Tabby and Mary will come running. We now have no choice but to escape on foot. Our head start has been wasted. As the men draw closer, the tiniest amount of moonlight catches the refection of white-blond hair.

Silas!

When I walk forward, Grace tugs on my cloak, urging me back.

"It's the boys," I whisper, running.

At the noise of my feet, the boys freeze. Alarm turns to elation as they see my cloak.

"Mina!" Juda says.

Rushing to him, I throw my arms around him. "Where were you?"

"We couldn't make it to the north exit, so we went out the south one."

"We waited for you. Why didn't you message us?"

"I can't type and run. Sorry."

"Can you keep your voices down please?" Dekker says. "I'd like to get out of here alive."

"Then hurry," I say, hastening them to the line of Hummers.

Mary runs up. "I found one!" she announces, pointing to a car.

"I found the boys!" I say, my heart galloping.

"Perfect timing," Mary tells them. "Your carriage awaits."

"Whoa," Silas says. "You guys are incredible."

"Why, thank you. We are," Mary says, leading us to her Hummer.

"I'll drive," Dekker says with authority.

"I'd rather have Mary," Tabby says, running up.

"You can drive?" Dekker asks Mary.

"Of course," she says.

"Women here aren't allowed," he says, as if we care.

"Shocking," Mary says.

"How about we go with the guy who was a professional driver?" Silas says, looking at Juda.

"That works." Mary hands Juda the keys.

He unlocks all the doors. Everyone piles in, while I circle around and get in the passenger seat. The engine rumbles to life. Will it bring Twitchers running for miles?

The second I shut my door, Juda jolts us forward, and Grace shrieks.

"I thought you knew how to drive this thing!" Dekker says from behind us.

Juda ignores him, examining the control panel of the enormous vehicle.

"Do you know where you're going?" I ask him above the noise.

The car weaves in the gravel and then bumps onto the old paved road. "South."

I look behind us, waiting for the lights of another car to appear. When we've made it twenty blocks with no signs of being followed, I face the front.

This is it. We've escaped the Cloisters.

And soon we'll become the most wanted people in Manhattan.

TWENTY-SEVEN

Our Hummer is the only car driving through the old parts of the city, like a grizzly bear roaming an empty forest. We rumble down an avenue called Fort Washington, which I've never even heard of. At night, the abandoned neighborhoods feel sinister and menacing. What if the car breaks down or runs out of gas? We'd be stuck in this no man's land, and who knows who or what might live out here now?

"How did you get past the guards at the gate?" I ask Juda, removing my veil. The dark glass of the windows will hide me from prying eyes.

"We have Silas to thank for that," he says, laughing.

We all look to Silas sitting in the very back next to Mary. He says sheepishly, "I, uh, had a picture of my gorgeous wife and we gave it as a bribe to the guard."

"Your gorgeous wife?"

"It's a really good picture of Susanna."

Susanna is his best friend in Kingsboro. I laugh. I guess there are advantages to photographs being rare.

"What happened back there, Mina?" Grace asks.

Dekker, next to her, juts out his chin. "Yeah. We deserve an explanation,"

I wait for Tabby to say something, but she doesn't. "Tabby?" I say.

Everyone looks at her. Sitting in a small space behind the driver's seat, she shrinks in her seat. "You tell them."

Does she want me to explain, or does she expect me to make up a lie? "Um. Uncle Ruho is dead, like I said in my message. He was . . . uh . . . Tabby killed him."

"Holy crap!" Mary cries.

"Whoa," Dekker says.

Silas asks, "How did it happen?"

"It doesn't matter," Tabby says.

"She was defending herself," I say.

Juda clenches his jaw, and I know he's thinking of when Damon tried to assault me. I have to wonder: if I'd had a knife that night, would I have done the same thing as Tabby?

"It must've been awful. I'm major sorry, Tabs." Silas puts a hand on her shoulder. "Although, I'm not sorry that you won't be spending your life with that pig."

"He was disgusting," Dekker says.

Grace doesn't say anything; she just gapes at Tabby in awe.

Juda says, "I'm sorry none of us were there to protect you."

"I protected myself," Tabby says. She stares defiantly out the window.

She won't want to hear it from me right now, but I think what she did was very brave. "Mrs. Hypat let us escape," I tell Grace. "It was major surprising. We promised to spread the word about her being the rightful divine heir. She warned us Ruho's body would be discovered by nine a.m."

"Will our parents still get their new house?" Tabby asks Silas. "Do you think they'll get kicked out because I killed my husband?"

"I don't know, Tabs," Silas says gently. He looks at her with concern, like she may still be in shock. "We don't know how Ram will respond."

"You told Ram what happened, right?" Dekker asks me with enthusiasm.

"Uh, yeah," I say.

He leans forward. "What did he say? When is he sending the Ostrich?"

Dekker must've turned off his Tact, or he would have seen the dozens of messages from Ram. "He wants information," I say.

"Write him again!" Dekker whines.

"I don't think he'll like what we have to say."

"We should stay still," Dekker says, sounding frantic. "Ram said as soon as Ruho was dead, he'd get us out, so there's no reason to run away! He'll definitely send the drone."

"Wait, what do you mean 'as soon as Ruho was dead'?" Silas says. "How did you know he would die?"

Nyek.

When no one else answers, Grace says in a small voice, "Ram sent us here . . . to kill Uncle Ruho."

"Who is 'us'?" Silas asks.

Dekker rubs the back of his neck. "The Propheteers, woolies, whatever."

"What the Hell?" Mary says, mouth agape.

Tabby's head snaps up. "*You* were supposed to kill him?" Her voice becomes a growl. "Then why didn't you?"

"We, uh, tried, but—" Dekker's voice trails off.

"YOU." She glowers at me. "You made me feel as if I'd done the most sickening thing possible when you saw the blood. But *you* were going to kill him?"

"Not with a knife—"

"Let me out of this car!" she screams.

"This isn't a good place," Juda says in a calm tone. "Maybe—"

Tabby lunges forward, grabbing his arm. The car swerves to the right. We all scream as it hits the curb of the crumbling sidewalk.

Tabby keeps shrieking. "You let me think I was going to spend my whole life with that broken-down, slobbering TURD!"

The Hummer grinds over old concrete and we're about to hurdle into an apartment building when Juda veers left, propelling us back onto the street with a hard bounce. After a few swerves, Juda is able to bring the car back to a reasonable speed.

But even as the car stabilizes, Tabby becomes more furious. "I stabbed him! And you . . . I didn't . . . I hate you all." She suddenly begins to bawl—big uncontrollable sobs that make her whole body shake.

"She stabbed him?" Dekker says. "That's hard-core."

"We tried to do it before your wedding night, Tabs. We wanted to, I swear," I say.

"You guys are weasels," Mary says, patting Tabby's back. "What else are you lying about?"

"Nothing, I swear," I say.

"Yeah, right," Silas says, glaring at me.

"Ram wanted us to trigger the Ascension," Grace says.

"Why would you keep that from us?" Mary says, voice rising. "After everything we've been through?"

"I wanted to tell you," I say, ashamed.

"She did," Juda says, and I'm grateful. "Ram wouldn't let us. He thought the more people who knew, the more likely we were to get caught."

As I hear the explanation again, it sounds so weak. I can't believe we listened to Ram.

"I think we're missing the bigger picture," Grace says.

"What?" Mary yells.

"According to Unbound scripture," Grace says, "'no faithful adherent' to your Savior may harm the 'false king' because murder is a sin. A nonbeliever must assassinate the leader for the Ascension to occur. Ram told us he would BOMB the island if one of us, a Propheteer, didn't kill Ruho."

A new tension fills the car.

"So we'll LIE!" Dekker says. "We'll tell Ram that I killed him!"

With growing alarm, Silas asks, "How much does Ram already know?"

"He knows we didn't use the pellets he gave us for the uh, assassination," I say, ashamed to say the word out loud. "They must have a signal in them." I have a horrible thought. "Everyone give me your pellet!" As Grace, Dekker, and Juda hand me the pellets, I say, "What if he's using them to track us?" I roll down my window.

"Wait!" Grace cries. "What if an animal eats one?"

"So they kill some rats! Who cares?" Dekker cries. "Toss 'em, Mina!"

We're still in a deserted part of town. I'm not worried about people stumbling upon the tiny pellets, but Grace is right. Any number of small creatures could eat them. "Does anyone have something I can put them in?"

"For the love of the Prophet!" Dekker says. He leans forward, grabs the pellets out of my hand, and throws them out the window.

Grace cries out and then silence fills the car. I roll up the window. Dekker sits back with his arms crossed. Tabby watches Grace wipe away tears. "Are you kidding me? Over rodents?"

Dekker watches Grace, and I almost think I see guilt in his eyes. "We had to get rid of them," he says. "It was Mina's idea."

"We have to focus!" Juda says, keeping his eyes on the dark street. "Ram knows we didn't use the pellets, but that doesn't mean he knows exactly what happened."

"That's what I've been saying!" Dekker says.

"I think we should tell him things went according to plan," Juda says.

Everyone agrees this is the best option we have right now. We settle on a narrative, and I'm selected to send the Nod.

My Tact has gone into sleep mode. I blink it on and see even more messages from Ram demanding to know what's happening. I type our careful answer: *Dekker killed Ruho. Lost pellet. Used blade.* I send the Nod.

A second later we receive the reply: *OUTSTANDING. Stand by 4 instructions.*

"Excellent," Dekker says. "He'll send the Ostrich!"

"No, he won't," I say.

"Why not?"

Everyone groans, but Grace says patiently, "Because he'll wait to see if the Ascension happens, and when it doesn't, he'll know we lied. And then he'll start the bombing."

"How long will he wait?" I ask.

We look at one another, each hoping the next person can tell us.

Silas says, "Unbound scripture says the Ascension will begin within one day of the false king being destroyed, so I think that means Ram expects it to happen within twenty-four hours of . . . when did you tell him Ruho died?"

"Eleven p.m." A time burned into my mind forever.

"Ram promised us," Dekker says, crushed. "He said that we were his sheep, and he was our shepherd who would look after us."

"You're all so feeble," Tabby says. "If the Ascension happens, you're heathens, so you'll be sucked into Hell; if it doesn't happen, Ram will bomb you and your city to the ground, and you'll *still* go straight to Hell. It was lose-lose from the start, you chumps."

Irritated, Dekker sits back in his seat.

"That's not helpful, Tabs," Mary says.

Tabby's right, though. We should have realized that Ram never had any intention or interest in bringing us back to Kingsboro. If I'd thought more about his deepest beliefs, I could have seen that his trust in the Ascension put us in a no-win situation.

"We have to find a safe spot," Juda says.

"Does that exist here?" Silas asks with doubt.

"I think we should head to the Lower East Side," Juda says. "I have family there."

"I think we'd be safest underground with the Laurel Society," Grace says. "Don't you, Mina?"

Before I can respond, Juda says, "Macy's is in the middle of the war zone."

Grace tells Tabby, "There's a group of women there who will protect us."

"They'll protect *us*," I say. "We don't know if they'll protect the boys."

"Why not?" Silas asks.

"It's complicated," I say with reluctance, "but it's sort of a *matriarchy*, like you taught me about, and they usually only welcome women."

"A matriarchy doesn't only welcome women. It's just led by women," Silas says.

"I'm sure they'll let the boys in. This is an emergency," Grace says.

I want so badly to agree with her. I'm dying to drive straight there, to see Nana, and tell Ayan everything that's happened. I know they'd help me. But I remember how Rayna and many of the women reacted when I showed up unannounced with Juda.

They wanted to throw him out immediately, and he was one boy, not three.

"I don't think we can go, Grace. We have to go east for now," I say. "We'll find a way to go soon, just you and me." We have to tell them about Mrs. Hypat, like we promised, and we have to warn them about the bombs. Thank God the women are already underground. Their basement survived one bombing already, so maybe it can survive another.

Grace tries to smile, but I know she's crushed, because I'm crushed, too.

"We'll go to my uncles'," Juda says. "We'll get some sleep and reassess in the morning. Agreed?"

We murmur our consent, but I guarantee no one feels good. If Ram bombs the island, nowhere will be safe.

TWENTY-EIGHT

I don't really understand where we are until Fort Washington Avenue hits Broadway, which I know will take us all the way to Houston Street. As we get farther south, Grace points things out to Mary and Silas. They don't seem as mad at her as they are at the rest of us Propheteers, but it's pretty hard to be mad at Grace.

At 116th Street, she says, "That used to be a university called Columbia and across the street was a college only for women, called Barnard! Can you imagine? When the Teachers took over they burned the library and chiseled women's names off every building.

"What happened to the students?" Mary asks.

"I'd rather not talk about it," she says.

She's quiet until we reach the 60s, where she tells them about Lincoln Center and then points out my apartment building. "And that's where Mina and Dekker used to live."

"Really?" Silas says, gazing up at the high rise.

The building is completely dark, which isn't so unusual at night, but I'd expect at least the lobby lights to be on.

"It looks abandoned," Mary says.

"They're probably just conserving energy," Dekker says, "because of the war."

I can't read his face. Ever since Mrs. Asher arrived during dinner, Dekker has known for certain that Father has been denounced as a terrorist. He's said nothing to me about it. If he had his way, he'd probably make Juda stop at our building so he could check on Mother. The idea has no appeal for me.

"What's this?" Mary asks, intrigued.

We're entering the Theater District.

"Oh, uh, I don't know much about this area," Grace says.

"C'mon. You know about everything," Mary says.

"This is where women sell themselves for money," I say.

"You know that?" Dekker says, floored.

"Don't you?" I say with innocence.

"I wouldn't expect Manhattan to have such a place," Mary says.

"Everywhere in the world has such a place," Silas says.

"Even Kingsboro?" I say, surprised.

"Of course," he says.

"Where?"

"Remember where Promise Prom was? Well, behind the Earth sphere—"

"Why are we talking about this?" Tabby says.

"It seemed relevant," Silas says.

"Something's wrong," Juda says.

"What do you mean?" The hair on my neck prickles.

"This is the only part of the city that stays busy no matter what time it is."

Scanning the quiet streets, I say, "You think the war has shut the area down?"

"Over there!" Grace says, pointing to our right.

A small band of men with rifles has turned onto the street.

The men have long facial hair and wear loose tunics—Convenes. As soon as they see our Hummer, they begin firing.

Remembering that they can't see through the dark glass, I cry out, "They think we're Twitchers!"

We all duck, but the bullets bounce off the side of the car. Even the ones that hit the windows don't penetrate the glass. *God bless Ruho's armored vehicle.*

"Turn around!" Dekker yells at Juda.

But Juda hits the gas, speeding by the shooting men.

We seem to be in the clear until we cross 45th Street, where we hear more gunshots. We can't see where they're coming from. A man screams. Without warning, a Twitcher runs into the street in front of us. He waves his arms above his head. Juda slams on the brakes to avoid running him over.

The Twitcher runs to Juda's window, banging on the glass.

"What do I do?" Juda asks us.

If we drive away, he'll alert everyone that our car should be stopped.

"Put on your veils," I tell the girls, while snapping mine on.

The Twitcher bangs again.

Juda rolls down his window an inch, not exposing his face. "What is it?" he says in a deep, annoyed voice.

"I have an injured man. I need to commandeer this vehicle."

"Negative. I have a full load."

"My wounded trooper has priority. Leave your men here."

"My orders are—"

"I just told you what your orders are. Step out of the car, son."

Juda's foot slams on the gas pedal and we careen forward. The Twitcher is still screaming at us as we swerve over a curb and onto 44th Street. Juda takes a hard right onto 6th Avenue, rocking us all to the other side of the car. We're going the wrong direction down a one-way street, but since we're the only car in sight, Juda keeps going.

"Awesome!" cries Dekker.

Juda's face tells me he's aware the situation is not awesome. Twitchers will now be on the lookout for a runaway white Hummer. He takes a left onto 42nd Street and we hurtle past Bryant Park. The great lawn, once known for its market on Saturdays, is now covered with tanks being guarded by hundreds of Twitchers.

"Get us away from here!" Dekker screams.

Juda screeches down 5th Avenue.

"That used to be the city library," Grace says, pointing to a crumbled corpse of a building.

"No one cares, Grace!" Tabby yells.

Juda drives faster and faster down 5th. We pass a few more clusters of Twitchers but none of them tries to stop us. If they have word that we should be detained, we're going too fast for them to try.

"Did you know Uncle Ruho had tanks?" I ask Juda.

"No," he says, eyes locked on the road.

"They must be a hundred years old," Silas says.

"The fuel . . . " Dekker says. "It's unfathomable. Like this car times twenty."

"Now we know what Ruho was going to do with the fuel Ram gave him," Grace says.

"I'm glad you put an end to that, Tabby," Silas says.

She doesn't respond.

When we reach 8th Street, Juda turns east and doesn't stop for one light or stop sign. We fly through the night like a drone.

As we approach 1st Avenue, Grace screams. Juda slams on the brakes just in time to avoid hitting a horse crossing the street. I grip the dashboard so hard, I leave marks in the leather. An old Convene stares at our car with bug-eyes as he follows behind his mare. I touch Juda's shoulder. "We're on the east side. You can slow down."

"Maybe," he says. "I'll feel better when we're south of Delancey."

No one says anything for a long time, I assume because we're all picturing the horrifying accident we almost had. When we finally reach Houston Street, Juda says, "The Hummer is too conspicuous. We should walk from here."

He cruises the car to an old tenement building on Avenue A. When we spill out the doors, I gulp the outside air, grateful to be alive. Grace runs to the edge of the sidewalk, throws off her veil, and vomits. Of all of us, she's probably been inside a car the least. I can't imagine she'll ever want to be in one again.

Approaching her, I put a hand on her back. "You okay?"

She nods, wiping her mouth. "Sorry."

"Don't be sorry."

"We need to get going," Juda says, looking around.

"Can't we rest a minute?" I ask. Grace still looks green.

"Sorry, Grace. It's too risky to stay still," Juda says.

I understand his urgency. I'm relieved to be out of the conspicuous Hummer, but now I feel like a tortoise with no shell.

Juda smiles at Grace with pity. "Is there anything I can do for you?"

"Never drive me anywhere again," she says.

"I promise," he says, putting the key in his pocket.

Grace takes a few deep breaths. Dekker picks up her veil, handing it to her. She snaps it on, saying, "Let's go."

Juda leads us further south, keeping us in the shadows of the sidewalks. I'm horribly aware of our John Paul-designed cloaks, which seem to glow bright teal even in the dark. The boys' jumpsuits appear too fitted, with overly wide shoulders, and Tabby's cloak glitters like it's made of stars. Any Convene would instantly know we're foreigners. My whole life used to be about blending in, and now I feel as visible as a blinking light.

The entire Lower East Side is Convene territory, reaching from Canal Street up to Houston and from the Bowery to the East River. I've never spent any real time here, except for the occasional errand for Nana when she wanted specific spices or herbs.

Once you cross Houston, you can sense an immediate change. The buildings aren't as tall or modern. Street signs have rusted and never been replaced. Oil lamps line the streets and can be seen in apartment windows. At night, they give the whole neighborhood a warm orange glow.

"What's that smell?" Tabby asks.

"Horses, probably," Juda says. "We're near a stable."

"It's something else . . . " She gives the air a long sniff.

"The lamps." He inhales and smiles. "We use fresh fish oil to keep the neighborhood lit."

Tabby wrinkles her nose in disgust.

Out of the darkness ahead, a man appears. He has a salt-and-pepper beard, a brown tunic, and a sizable rifle resting on his shoulder. The hair on my neck and arms stands on end as he walks straight toward us.

"Don't panic," Juda says. "Let me talk to him alone."

Juda approaches the man. We can't hear what they're saying, and time slows as I wait for the man to arrest Juda or shoot him.

But instead, the man hugs him.

A moment later, Juda waves us over. "This is Dodo, an old friend of my Uncle Mal's. He didn't recognize me with the blond hair."

"Or the glasses! Quite a disguise, Udi!" Dodo laughs. "These are yer friends?"

I haven't heard Juda's nickname "Udi" since Rose fell ill. Hearing it makes me feel safe.

"You should meet everyone," Juda says, "but it's more important that we get off the street."

Juda suddenly has a bit of a Convene accent; I smile.

"Of course, of course!" Dodo says. "Mal will be delighted." We follow him back in the direction he came from. Juda gives me a smile, and I'm filled with relief. Maybe our luck is turning.

TWENTY-NINE

On Broome Street, Dodo and Juda lead us into an apartment building I would've guessed was abandoned. The front door has no lock or doorman, and a baby carriage missing a wheel rests lopsided in the lobby.

"Is a baby in there?" Mary asks, worried. Investigating, she coos. "Kittens!"

Dodo laughs. "Yeah, our rat-catcher had a new litter."

Mary reaches in to pet one of the fuzzy newborns.

"I wouldn't do that unless ya want fleas," Dodo says.

Mary snaps back her hand.

The elevator looks like it hasn't run in fifty years, and its metal door is propped open with a crowbar. Inside, I spot a mattress with a figure curled up in thin blankets. Does someone live in there?

Walking deeper into the lobby, Juda opens a side door and waves us up the stairs. He keeps an eye on the street as I pass him. Dodo leads us up, and on each landing we encounter another mattress, sometimes two. We try to step delicately over sleeping people, but more than a few open their eyes to scowl at us.

Do these people always live here, or is it because of the war?

Finally, when we've climbed six flights and reached the top floor, Dodo opens a door to the hallway. The tang of trash mixes with the sharpness of cured meats and heavy stews. Personal items line the hallway—clothes, chairs, pots and pans. Do they belong to the people in the stairwells?

When Dodo finally stops at a door, he doesn't knock. Instead, he bursts into the unlocked apartment, bellowing, "Look who I brought ya, my friend! Udi is home!"

The man inside, who was certainly dead asleep, looks up from his bed in astonishment. I recognize Rose's dark skin and eyes, but this man's face is longer and his mouth wider. "Udi?" he says, squinting.

Juda crosses the room in three steps and embraces the man. "Mal! I'm so happy to see you."

"We thought ya were *dead*." Mal, Juda's uncle, doesn't hug Juda back, as if he might be a ghost. "You and yer ma just . . . disappeared!"

Mal has the nasal, long-voweled accent of a Convene, stronger than Dodo's.

Juda makes a huffing sound, dismissing his concerns. "We left the island."

Dodo and Mal look astounded. They both start speaking at once: "How? What was it like?" "Do they have fuel?" "How's the water?"

"I'll answer all your questions," Juda says, "But first, I have news. We need Jiol."

Mal stands. He startles me by pushing his bed up into the wall, springs groaning. "Wake him," he tells Dodo.

Dodo leaves at once.

Mal walks into a tiny corner kitchen to put water on to boil. His apartment is unlike any home I've ever seen. It's incredibly small, no bigger than most living rooms. Every nook and cranny is used for something. Chairs hang from hooks on the wall. Dishes are stored in baskets under a small sink. The dining room table folds down from one wall and the bed from another. One brightly patterned rug covers the entire floor and the smell of licorice tea permeates the room. Some might find the home too cramped, but I think it's cozy and inviting.

Reaching into a cubbyhole, Mal retrieves a metal tin. "Corn cookies—not fresh today, but fresh enough." Handing the tin to Grace, he looks down at his pajamas. "'Scuse me." He draws a curtain across a wire that runs diagonally between two walls, creating a perfect nook of privacy.

After taking a cookie, Grace passes the tin around. Grabbing one, I bite into it and the combination of sweet and salty seems to revive my whole body.

I tell Juda, "Thank you for getting us here safely."

When he looks at me, his eyebrows are knitted together with worry. He whispers, "How will I tell them about Ma?"

"Just be honest." As hard as it might be, I'm happy that he'll finally have family support. He needs people around who've known his mother a long time.

Uncle Mal pushes back his curtain and emerges fully dressed in a tunic and pants. He's also brushed his hair and put on socks and slippers.

Without warning, Dodo bursts back into the apartment. The guy doesn't seem to know how to make a small entrance. A man who I assume is Uncle Jiol trails behind him.

Jiol, lacking the height of Juda and Mal, possesses the short squat body of Rose. He wears a solemn expression that doesn't change even as he says, "Udi, what a relief!"

Juda towers over him as they embrace. Separating himself, Juda says, "This is Silas and Dekker."

"Peace. Good to meet ya," Jiol says. "Dodo says you've got news—"

"And this is Tabby, Mary, and Grace," Juda says, going against custom. Usually, if men are gathering to discuss important business, the women are ignored.

Jiol, thrown by the interruption, says, "Peace. Good to meet ya, too."

"Peace," the girls reply.

"And this is Mina," Juda says, taking my hand. "The girl I love."

I'm glad no one can see my face, because I'm sure I'm turning twelve shades of fuchsia.

Jiol looks concerned, but Mal smiles from ear to ear. "Udi! You rascal. That's terrific! When didya get hitched?"

"We, uh, didn't, Uncle."

Jiol looks at our intertwined hands. "Then I assume it'll be any day now?"

"Things have been a little too chaotic to think about wedding bells, sir," Mary says behind me.

"Of course," Mal says, but Uncle Jiol's expression tells me that he thinks there's always time to make the moral choice.

Mal removes compact chairs from the hooks on his walls, unfolding them for each of us. Soon we're all seated, holding warm mugs of tea.

I hesitate to drink.

Mal, sensing my uncertainty, says, "Don't panic. The water's been brought in from the Inwood Spring uptown."

I'm embarrassed. Why would Mal use tainted water? I sip the delicious tea.

All attention turns to Juda. Mal and Jiol, who looked

nothing alike to me a moment ago, now have their eyebrows raised in identical expressions of curiosity.

Without preamble, Juda says, "Uncle Ruho is dead."

"Dead?" Jiol says. "Nonsense. He was married this morning in front of the whole city."

"We know. We were in the wedding party. We anticipate the body will be discovered tomorrow at nine a.m., which is when the Heralds will be checking on him. Once they find him, every Twitcher in Manhattan will be searching for us, so we understand if you don't want us to stay. "

He didn't say it was Tabby, but he's said enough to let them know it was one of us.

"We need a place to spend the night and figure out our next step, but more importantly, we need to warn you and all of the Convenes that the leader of the Apostates, a man named Ram, is most likely going to bomb the island."

The uncles are slack-jawed.

Juda told us we were coming here because it was a safe place to stay. He never mentioned that his uncles might say no. But I can't blame him for his honesty. They should have all the facts before they harbor wanted criminals.

"How soon will the bombin' begin?" Uncle Jiol says.

"We don't know," Juda says, "but we think it will be by the end of tomorrow." Juda gives them a quick explanation of the Ascension and why Ram wanted us to kill Ruho.

"We wondered why the Apostates had sent that old man a bride. It made no sense! I told you, Jiol. No sense!" Mal says, sounding superior.

"What kind of bombs do the Apostates have?" Jiol asks.

Juda looks to the members of the Unbound.

Silas speaks for the first time. "At home, the Purists, uh, people who don't like you folks on the island, always brag about our bombs. They say each one could destroy a building."

"How many do you have?" Mal asks.

Mary's quiet, halting voice suggests she would rather do anything than speak. "Um, my brother works for the military. He once told me our weapons reserve was, um, 'major spectacular.'"

"Why would your leader want to kill innocent people?" Jiol says, bewildered.

"Isn't murder a sin where you come from?" Mal asks Mary.

When Mary says nothing, Silas speaks again. "As Juda explained, Ram expects your leader's death to lead to the Ascension, which my people have been waiting their whole lives for. If it doesn't happen, then Ram needs to give them something else, so they don't replace him. Some of my people think that the Ascension can't happen not only because of Uncle Ruho, but because of all of the heathens—you and your people—who are worshipping the wrong God. They'd be happy to see you bombed." He looks at the floor, ashamed.

"And your God would sanction this butchery?" Mal says angrily.

"Oh please, Mal," Jiol says. "Think of the number of people here who would be perfectly comfortable with the extermination of the Apostates. We cannot throw stones." He turns to us. "You'll stay here, no question. We won't have you roamin' the streets."

I hear exhales of relief from Mary and Dekker.

"But *don't* talk to anybody and *don't* leave the buildin'," Jiol says.

"We need to find 'em some new clothes," Dodo tells the uncles. "They look like they came from Mars!"

Mal agrees, his expression turning grave. "Mrs. Asher's been comin' to the neighborhood and offerin' a large reward for information about you, Udi. Normally our neighbors look after one another, but these are desperate times."

Mrs. Asher. She seeps into everything like tainted water.

"We'll be careful," Juda says.

"That lady has her own army of guards. We'll set up a twenty-four hour watch," Jiol says.

"Thank you," Juda says.

"We should let you sleep," Mal says. He looks at Dodo. "We'll need help. I don't have room for seven."

"I can take the boys," Jiol says.

"I'll talk to Mrs. Jane," Dodo says, and once more, he bounds out of the apartment like a Labrador retriever.

Mal refills our tea mugs. "And yer ma?" he asks nervously. "Where is she?"

"She's still in Queens," Juda says, unable to look him in the eyes. "She has the Plague."

Both uncles mutter quick prayers.

"The medicine in Queens is much more advanced than here," I say. "Rose's doctor is taking very good care of her."

No one seems comforted by my words.

"I'm trying to get back to her as soon as I can," Juda says.

"I'm sure you are," Mal says, patting him on the back.

"We'll get word to Jordan tonight about Ruho and the bombin'," Jiol says. "He'll want to talk to you as soon as you've rested."

I assume that Mal is talking about Jordan Loudz, the leader of the Convenes. "Can I talk to Mr. Loudz tonight?" I ask.

"We'll pass along information," Mal says.

"I'd rather talk to him myself," I say.

"You'll meet him tomorrow," he says. "Now you need sleep."

"I have news that needs to be shared immediately."

Tabby nods at me in agreement.

"And I'll tell him, as I've said," Mal says.

"It'll be fine," Juda tells me. "You can trust Mal."

Disappointed, I say, "Please tell Mr. Loudz that Uncle Ruho has a daughter named Esther Hypat at the Cloisters, and she is Ruho's rightful and only heir. She had nothing to do with his death nor the contamination of the Convene's water supply. Uncle Ruho was responsible for the mercury poisoning—he and Max Asher. I believe, if given a chance, Mrs. Hypat could be an honorable leader."

"I will tell Jordan exactly those words," Mal says with an assuring tone.

"Thank you. Her life could depend on it."

"I can't wait for you to meet Jordan," Juda tells me.

My father liked Jordan, and I know Juda trusts him, so I hope he can be relied upon to tell the truth to everyone on the Lower East Side. I also hope Jordan doesn't believe any of the nonsense that Ruho made up about my father.

Dodo barges back in the door, causing me to jump. I've become more anxious knowing Mrs. Asher is on the prowl. Dodo says, "Mrs. Jane can take the girls."

We say goodnight to Uncle Mal and Uncle Jiol. Juda insists that he would rather talk with them than sleep.

"You gotta sleep, Udi," Mal says. "You need energy for tomorrow."

I'm relieved when Juda agrees.

Dodo drops Silas, Juda, and Dekker off at Jiol's apartment, which is next door, and then leads Grace, Mary, Tabby, and me down one floor. He barges into Mrs. Jane's apartment just as he did Mal's. "I got the girls!" he announces.

"Hush!" Mrs. Jane says, pointing to children asleep in their beds.

Chastised, Dodo backs out the door waving, with a mischievous smile.

As soon as he's left, Mrs. Jane takes off her veil, revealing a round, pleasant face, with dark circles under both eyes. She looks like she needs sleep more than we do.

Her apartment is the same size as Mal's, but beds take up half the space. I count six children. She whispers at them, forcing three of them to share with the other three. She offers us their abandoned spaces. *"Please, sleep!"* she whispers.

"There was more room in the last place," Tabby whispers to Mary

"It's more appropriate for us to stay with a single woman than with a single man," I whisper at them, smiling at Mrs. Jane.

"Whatever," Mary says. "It's a bed." She yanks off her cloak and veil and climbs into the nearest one without taking off her shoes.

The rest of us take off our veils, cloaks, and shoes. Grace gawks at Tabby who's wearing only Uncle Ruho's tunic, but she says nothing. They clamber onto mattresses.

"It smells funny," Tabby says, and I shoot her a look that says that if she speaks again, I will turn her into the Twitchers myself. She turns her back to me.

I regret my nasty look. The girls are still very angry with me, and I need to be nice if I want them to forgive me.

I thank Mrs. Jane again and climb into the last bed. I'm exhausted, but I don't fall asleep right away. *What are we doing here?* We were supposed to be on the Ostrich on our way back to Queens, not sleeping in some strange apartment on the lower east side waiting to be bombed. Nothing has gone according to plan, and once again we're completely at the mercy of a group of men.

THIRTY

With everything on my mind, I only manage to sleep a few hours. As soon as I have any consciousness at all, I begin to panic about the day ahead. How many hours until Zebadiah find's Uncle Ruho's corpse? Did Uncle Mal talk to Jordan Loudz last night? Will Ram really drop his bombs? Are Nana, Father, and Sekena in safe places?

Despite the early hour, I get up.

"What's wrong," Grace asks groggily.

"Nothing," I say. "Go back to bed."

I thank Mrs. Jane for her hospitality and tell her that I'm returning to Uncle Mal's apartment. Her face tells me that she thinks such an early visit is rude. "If no one's awake yet, come back here," she says. "And *don't* talk to anyone in the halls."

"Yes, Mrs. Jane," I say.

I quietly leave the room and walk down the hallway. When I enter the stairwell, one of the families sleeping on a mattress is already awake. A mother bounces a baby on her knee. "Peace," she says.

"Peace," I respond, trying to keep my Deserver accent hidden. I wonder what she thinks of my bright cloak?

When I get upstairs, I nervously knock on Mal's door. To my relief, he answers right away, cup of tea in hand. "Come! Come!" he says, looking both ways down the hallway.

Juda sits in front of an enormous breakfast. His fake glasses rest on the table and he holds a cup of tea, staring into space. When he notices me, he says, "You couldn't sleep either?"

I half smile.

"Dodo arranged a little welcome feast," Mal says.

I'm so touched. Food is surely harder to come by now that there's a war, and this meal looks amazing.

"He's always been a good man," Juda says, wiping crumbs off his jumpsuit.

"He always liked yer ma," Mal says with a smile. "Please, sit down. Have a bite," he tells me.

Taking a chair, I eat an egg, some goat's cheese, chunks of thick oaty bread, and a slice of meat that, as soon as I put in my mouth, I know is squirrel. I confess, when it's warm and served with other food, it isn't half bad. Juda smiles at me, giving me a teasing nudge as I finish it.

"It was all delicious," I say, handing Mal my empty plate. "Tell Dodo thank you." He smiles at me graciously.

"Time to wake Jiol," Mal says, reaching into a low cubbyhole and pulling out a shoe. He walks to the wall that holds his bed and bangs on the brick with the heel of the loafer.

The noise makes me jump, but Juda laughs. "Still too lazy to walk next door, Uncle?"

"What's the point?" Mal says. "He hears me just fine."

"So does the rest of the building," Juda says, raising an eyebrow.

Ignoring him, Mal asks, "Who needs more tea?"

Before the water is boiled, Jiol walks in the door. He looks hassled and irritated, but he looked the same way last night, so I can't say if anything has changed. He sits, saying nothing as Mal fills his plate with food.

As soon as we have our tea and Jiol is eating, Mal says to me, "So, we understand you were engaged to Damon Asher?"

Startled, I look at Juda, who appears just as mystified as me. "How did you know that?" Juda asks.

"Mrs. Asher has told everyone that Udi stole you away during the night and then murdered her husband and son so he could keep you."

"It's not true!" I say. "Juda was—"

Jiol puts a hand up to silence me, which is maddening. "Mal said she said it. He didn't say we believed it." He gives Juda his intense stare. "We know she's spreading lies, but we must know the truth."

Juda sits up straighter.

"We have no judgment. We're only lookin' for the facts. We need to know if you killed Max and Damon Asher."

Juda crosses his arms, frowning. "Why?" I'm puzzled by the defensiveness in his voice.

"If you're innocent," Mal says, "perhaps we can dissuade Mrs. Asher from pursuing you. We could find the person who did it and have them—"

"There is no other person."

Mal looks crushed, while Jiol frowns.

"But I didn't kill anyone," Juda says. "Damon shot his father. He meant to shoot me." From the guilt in Juda's voice, you would think he *had* shot Mr. Asher.

Before Mal or Jiol can respond, Juda continues. "Damon followed us into the subway. He wanted to massacre us all. He was so enraged that he walked into the water without knowing how to swim, and he drowned."

Mal's eyes bulge from his head.

"The truth can't help us," I say. "Mrs. Asher will never believe our version of events."

"Even if she did, she'd still want us shot," Juda says.

Mal and Jiol sip their tea, and I can almost see the wheels turning in their heads.

Jiol stops drinking. "Why would Damon chase you when he was the one who shot his pa?"

"He wanted to kill Mina because she didn't want to marry him." Juda clears his throat. "He wanted to kill me because he and I had just found out that we had the same father."

Mal runs his hand through his hair, the way I've seen Juda do a hundred times.

Placing his elbows on the table, Juda looks deeply into his uncles' eyes. "Now it's time for you to tell me some truth. Did you know that Mr. Asher was my father?"

Mal looks down at his mug of tea, while Jiol stares at the wall behind us. Their silence is their answer.

Juda's face pinches. "How could you have kept that from me all this time?"

"We promised yer ma," Mal whispers.

"All that time I spent in his home, working for him, being treated like a piece of spit by his son, and you knew!"

"We thought it was for the best," Jiol says.

"*Why?*" Juda says.

"If you'd known, would you have continued to work there?"

"NO!"

"Exactly," Jiol says. "Rose wanted you safe, getting a strong education, eating healthy food. You had all those things. You're a good kid, Udi, and if you'd left, you would've given up yer best chance at a decent upbringin'."

Having spent time with the Ashers, I take issue with the phrase "decent upbringing."

"Yer ma was tortured by the decision, believe me," Mal adds. "Jiol and I sat at this table many nights comfortin' her, convincin' her that you wouldn't turn out like Damon."

"So she wanted to bring me home?" Juda says, voice breaking.

"At times," Jiol says. "But mostly she felt she was doin' the right thing."

Reaching out, I touch Juda's arm, not caring about the uncles' disapproval.

He takes big mouthfuls of breath, trying to remain calm. "How did they even meet?"

This has been my big question since the day I read Rose's letter aloud to Mrs. Asher.

Jiol looks at Mal, frowning.

"I think you owe me the truth," Juda says. "I'm eighteen years old."

"Yeah, you're old enough, I suppose," Mal says.

"Our father worked for Mr. Asher," Jiol says. "He was a doorman in one of his buildings."

"No one ever told me that," Juda says, bewildered.

"When me and Jiol were boys," Mal says, "we got the measles. Ma decided it was dangerous for Rose to be in our apartment, so she told Pop to take Rose to work with him. He was against it, but Ma insisted. So Pop took Rose, who was sixteen, to the buildin' where he worked, and she sat behind the desk with him.

"Mr. Asher came into work every mornin', Pop greeted him, and Rose didn't say a word, like a good girl. She says she sat in her veil and drew pictures of the trees outside the window, and when she got bored of those, she drew Pop. And when she got bored of him, she drew Mr. Asher. One day, he noticed her pile of drawings and asked to see 'em. She tried to say no, but Pop didn't wanna be rude. When Mr. Asher saw dozens of sketches of himself, well, that was it. He decided Rose was in love with him. He started to bring her little gifts and to flirt with her. He was handsome and had a lot of money and Rose, well, she was young and impressionable. Mr. Asher wooed her for a long time, and they were in love. Really. You gotta know that, Udi. It was our pop who forbade the marriage. He didn't want Rose to be a second wife. He knew she was strong-willed and wouldn't take the back seat to anyone."

Jiol chuckles. "No, she would not."

I find it hard to imagine Rose in love with Mr. Asher. He must've been very handsome, as handsome as Juda, but I can't conceive of him as gentle or loving. But why else would she have fallen for him?

"Were you ever going to tell me?" Juda says.

"Rose was plannin' on it," Jiol says. "She wanted you to be out of yer pop's house first."

"She didn't feel like she was deceivin' you," Mal adds. "She thought she was protectin' you."

Juda's eyes grow red. "She was sick in a hospital bed, and I was mad at her for lying to me. I knew I should just get over it, but I couldn't."

"You were with her every day," I say. "That's the important thing."

"But in my heart I was angry. God could see that. What if Ma knew it, too?"

"You have plenty of time to tell her that you forgive her, Udi," Mal says with gentleness. "And to ask for her forgiveness."

"No. We're never getting out of here," Juda says. "That's clear now."

I'm shocked to hear him say it, even though I've started to feel the same way.

"If God desires it," Jiol says, "you'll be back by her side."

His statement rings empty to me. I used to take solace in hearing that God had a plan, that He always knew best, but now it sounds like something to say when you can't think of anything else.

THIRTY-ONE

The others trickle in for breakfast. Dekker and Silas arrive an hour after me, and Mary, Grace, and Tabby show up a few minutes later.

Grace gives Juda and me a smile, but Tabby and Mary don't. They're still mad that we didn't tell them about our orders to kill Uncle Ruho, and I don't blame them. I would be mad, too. Silas isn't openly angry—he's just quiet.

Mal serves them food, and, halfway through the meal, Tabby pokes at her plate. "What is this, anyway?"

"Squirrel," Mal says pleasantly.

Dekker drops his fork with a clang onto his plate. "*What?*"

"I'm gonna barf," Tabby says, covering her mouth.

"I'm sorry for my friends' rudeness, Uncle Mal," Juda says through gritted teeth. "They aren't used to foreign food."

"Not at all," Mal says. "Adjustin' to a new culture can be difficult."

I want to expose Dekker and say he's from here, but it would only hurt Mal's feelings, so I don't.

"Thank you for breakfast," Mary says politely.

"Yes, thank you," Silas says, in a tone that seems to apologize for his sister's lack of manners. Neither he nor Mary ate the squirrel, but they gobbled up everything else.

There's a knock on the door. Tension fills the room as we wonder if a friend or an enemy has arrived.

Mal says in a calm voice, "Yes?"

"Peanuts for sale," a man says.

Mal smiles. "That'll be Jordan."

Standing, Jiol opens the door and reveals a twenty-something man with thick, curly black hair and a disarming smile. His clothes are not new, but they're tidy and well-fitting. His intense eyes scan the room, and when they land on Juda, they light up with pleasure. "Praise the Prophet, Juda. What a relief to see you!" He crosses the room as if he's been here a thousand times.

"Great to see you, too, Jordan," Juda says, standing to hug him.

So this is Jordan Loudz, the leader of the Convenes. Father mentioned him often and Mother hated hearing his name. I'm not sure what I thought he would look like, but this man is so handsome and confident, I feel tongue-tied.

Jiol grabs Jordan a chair off a hook. We're too many to sit around the table, so Mal clears the dishes and pushes it up against the wall. We use the whole room to make a circle, and even then, it's tight.

Mal makes brief introductions.

"Mina and Dekker Clark?" Jordan says, smiling. "Yer father is Zai!"

We nod.

"What an excellent man."

"Thank you," Dekker says.

I'm relieved. Jordan seems to still consider Father respectable.

"So you did it?" Jordan says. "You left the island?"

"Yes," Juda says.

Jordan laughs. "I prayed the rumors were true. I can't wait to hear every detail, but first, it seems we have more important things to discuss. Ruho is dead?"

"Yes," Juda says.

"Why haven't we heard anythin' about it?" Jordan's stare is so penetrating, I imagine it would be hard to lie to him.

"We were promised twelve hours until the news would be released, so we could escape." Juda glances at the clock on Mal's wall. "That time ends in two and a half hours."

"Someone helped you escape?" Jordan asks.

"Mrs. Hypat," I say. "Mal told you about her last night. She let us go because she trusted us to spread the word about her father and to help legitimize her leadership."

Jordan, looking disconcerted by my entry into the conversation, says, "Why would you want to support anyone in that family? They've been suppressin' and starvin' us for generations."

"She's a decent woman who deserves a chance to prove herself. I hope you'll help us make that known."

"Which one of you killed Ruho?"

No one speaks.

"Why does it matter?" Juda says.

"Whomever it was will be in great danger—wanted by the Heralds and Twitchers."

"We know that," Tabby says. Her veil is on, but I know she's rolling her eyes.

"We believe the Apostates are going to start bombing the city tonight," Juda says.

"Why?" Jordan asks.

Juda explains how Ram ordered us to murder Ruho and why it had to be someone who believed in the Prophet. He gives a brief explanation of the Ascension and then says, "The wrong person killed Ruho, and, as a result, we haven't fulfilled our side of the bargain. Ram will punish us by dropping his bombs."

"I don't understand," Jordan says. "How could you let the *wrong person* kill him?"

"Some of us were not given *full information*," Mary says, crossing her arms.

"Exactly," Tabby says, crossing her arms as well.

Restarting our fight is not what we need right now. "It was very complicated," I offer. "It was beyond our control."

Jordan stares at his hands for quite a while. His eyes appeared brown when he first arrived, but reflected in the morning light, they almost look gold. "If this *Ascension* occurs, Ram and his followers will float into the sky to sit by God?"

"If they've lived devout lives," Mary says.

"And do we think this Ram," Jordan says, "is open to negotiation?"

"We don't know. He told us to 'standby'." Juda sounds very tired.

"How are you communicating?"

"We have something called Tacts in our eyes that allow us to send messages."

Jordan smiles. "Fascinatin'." Crossing his legs, he says, "The important question is, does Ram truly believe in this Ascension, or is he just trying to gain control over Manhattan?"

We look at the members of the Unbound.

Silas brushes his bangs out of his eyes. "He's a believer. He's been in charge since I was a kid, and his whole world has always centered around the Ascension."

"That's too bad," Jordan says. "He'd be easier to bargain with if he preferred money or power."

"He likes those things, but he thinks he'll have more of both in Heaven," Tabby says.

Jordan rubs his thumb across his lips. "If he believes that a person born in Manhattan needs to kill our divine leader to bring about his Ascension, then maybe *that's* the thing we have to offer him."

"It's too late," Tabby says as if Jordan is a moron.

"You claim we have a *new* divine leader, and isn't one the same as the last?" Jordan says.

As his meaning sinks in, I grow cold. "You want us to offer to kill Mrs. Hypat?"

"If it'll keep him from bombin' the city and killin' every Convene and Deserver, then yes."

Tabby waves her hands. "She saved us. She let us go. We'd be dead if it weren't for her!"

"She's done nothing wrong," I say, letting a growl seep into my voice.

"Even if she were a terrible person," Grace says, "which she isn't, why would her murder help anyone? She'll die, the Ascension *still* won't happen, and Ram will *still* bomb the city. So you've killed an innocent woman and bought us, what, like, twenty-four extra hours?"

Jordan nods at her. "I hear you. You'll have to convince Ram that with Mrs. Hypat you did everythin' *exactly* as he asked, so if his Ascension doesn't happen, it's his fault, or his God's fault, not yers."

Mary produces a strangled laugh. "You're bonkers. We could never convince him of that."

"I might be able to," Jordan says, "if you let me negotiate with him."

No one speaks.

"Give me one of yer Tact things, and I'll talk him into a new arrangement."

221

"No," I say. "I won't murder Mrs. Hypat for some crazy bargain that has almost no chance of working. None of us will."

"No," Grace says.

"Nope," Mary, Silas, and Tabby say.

"No," Juda says, sighing. "We have to think of something else."

"I respect yer choice." Leaning back in his chair, Jordan steeples his fingers. "But you still have to get ahead of this thing. Reports of Uncle Ruho's death will spread quickly, and so will the news about who did it." He looks at Tabby. He has guessed it was her. "Ram is bound to hear the talk. He has a contact inside the Cloisters that arranged Ruho and Tabitha's marriage, so you have to assume that contact will tell him the details of Ruho's death."

Who is it? Zebadiah? Memon?

We thought we had twenty-four hours after Ruho died before Ram would start bombing, but now it seems we might only have until the moment Ram speaks to someone inside the Cloisters.

Jordan continues, "You need to tell the truth to Ram yourselves and then negotiate with him any way you know how, appeal to his righteous side. Those of you that grew up with him are our best resource for what kind of argument will be the most effective, so you need to brainstorm together. Jiol, can they use yer apartment for a while?"

"Of course," Jiol says.

"In the meantime, I need to speak with Dekker and Mina alone," Jordan says.

"Why?" Dekker demands.

"It's about yer father."

THIRTY-TWO

My stomach drops. "Juda can stay."

Jordan gives him a look I can't read, and Juda stands, kisses the top of my head and says, "I'll be right next door."

I watch with dread as everyone, including Mal and Jiol, files out the door. Jordan scoots his chair closer to me and Dekker. His voice is softer than before. "As you may know, I was friends with yer father. He did many great things for the Convenes."

I wait for Dekker to make some snide comment about our mother hating Father's work with Jordan, but he doesn't.

"Do you know where he is?" I ask, trying to keep my voice even.

"As soon as you told yer father about the mercury, he was determined to stop the bad water from reachin' any more Convenes. We told as many people as we could that it was poisoned, but Uncle Ruho started sayin' the water was fine, that the news was a hoax. People started drinkin' it again. Zai decided he had to destroy the plant."

I can't imagine Father making this decision; he spent his life building it.

Jordan takes a deep breath. "We helped him find ammonium nitrate and kerosene. He used his credentials to get back inside the plant. He detonated the explosion and . . . he just couldn't get out in time. I'm very sorry for you both. He was a noble man."

I look at the cracked green paint on Mal's wall and the crumbs of bread on the floor. I know I have a few seconds of normalcy left before Jordan's words sink in, and I have to feel them.

"You're sure?" I say, thinking of when Mother said Nana was dead, and it was a lie. "Maybe he got out and no one saw."

Jordan smiles gently. "I was there. I saw him . . . after. He didn't suffer."

My breathing stays normal. My eyes are dry.

"Who knows how many lives he saved," Jordan says.

"You're telling me that my father died like some common insurgent?" Dekker's cheeks are covered in red splotches.

"I'm tellin' you he died a hero," Jordan says, thrown by Dekker's reaction.

"No. You're saying he turned against Uncle Ruho, blew himself up, and won't go to Paradise."

"He's in Paradise," I say, certain of it.

"Says the person who's never read the Book!"

"I've read it more times than you!" I snap back.

"You stupid—"

"You've had a shock, and this is awful news," Jordan says patiently. "Zai was incredibly proud of you both." He looks at me. "He told me how you showed up at his house in a Twitcher uniform. He couldn't believe how clever you were."

"What about me?" Dekker says, indignant.

"He was so pleased that you were together, helping each other," Jordan says.

"Sure. He was so pleased, he killed himself!" Dekker stands, his chair screeching in protest. "Where is our Mother?"

I didn't even think to ask about her.

"I'm afraid I don't know," Jordan says.

"Because you're just a pinhead Convene!" Dekker heads for the door.

"Dekker!" I say.

"Don't leave the building!" Jordan says, his voice of authority returning.

"I'm not a child. I'll do what I want!" Dekker walks out, slamming the door.

"Don't worry. Mal and Jiol will stop him," Jordan tells me. "But that's the kind of scene you cannot be makin' while you're here. You can't draw attention to yourselves." He continues to ramble on, offering strategies on how to stay out of sight. I hear nothing he says.

Father is dead.

I'll never see him again. Never hear his voice. Never hear another one of his jokes. When I left the island, I thought I might never see him again, and yet I knew he was here, walking around, smiling at his favorite meals, and frowning at my mother's complaints.

And now he is not.

"You okay?" When I don't answer, Jordan says, "My pa died when I was yer age. He worked for a construction company under horrible conditions—no helmets, no safety harnesses, no supervision, nothin'. One mornin' a beam fell and knocked him off the scaffoldin'. He fell two stories and no one bothered to take him to the hospital. After he died, no one suffered any consequences: the man who dropped the beam, the man who ran the site, the man who owned the buildin'. It was like my pa was just a piece of wood that'd split down the middle and been thrown away. He died for nothin'. I was angry for a long time, most of my life in fact."

"I'm sorry," I say.

"Yer pa didn't die for nothin'. He made a conscious choice to break into that plant. He died for a cause he believed in. He was saving lives—probably thousands. You should sleep well knowin' he was a hero."

"You aren't angry anymore about your father?"

"Sometimes, but I channel the anger into our work. When the Convenes achieve equality in this city, men won't have to work under conditions like my pa." He stands. "Wish I could stay. I need to get people to the basements of their buildings, prepare for the bombing."

"You don't think we'll be able to negotiate with Ram?"

"We need to plan for the worst. You can stay here for a bit, but soon you should head to a lower floor."

I don't want to be alone. I don't want to think about Father. It's too painful.

When we open the door, Mal and Jiol aren't standing in the hall. We find them next door, preparing to move to the basement. Jiol's apartment, unlike Mal's, is completely spare, and one wonders how he lives in a space with no furniture or basic necessities outside of a chair and mattress. I don't even see clothes except the ones he's wearing.

No one in the room has seen Dekker.

"You should find yer brother," Jordan tells me. "We can't have him roamin' the buildin' throwing a tantrum."

As much as I don't want to be around Dekker, Jordan is right.

"I'll help you," Juda says, standing.

"I need to speak with you," Jordan tells him. "I have a few more questions about Kingsboro and the Unbound."

"I'm okay," I say. "I'll find him."

"Take care of yourself," Jordan says, his golden eyes shimmering. "Peace."

"Peace," I say.

As I leave the apartment, I realize that I forgot to ask him about the Laurel Society and whether the women there are surviving the war.

THIRTY-THREE

I send Dekker a Nod: *Where r u? Return NOW*.

The quick response is: *Suck pavement*.

I go down the stairs, checking each floor. The furniture and possessions in the hallways don't help my search. From a distance, every stack of blankets looks like it could be a slouching seventeen year old boy.

When I've reached the lobby with no luck, I panic. Did he go outside?

Hearing a stirring from the elevator, I remember the person I saw in the shadows yesterday. Hesitantly, I approach. I squint into the darkness, bowing slightly to show respect.

Someone sits up from the mattress, a person so aged I'm not sure if it's a woman or a man. They have a dried apple of a face and little hair, and when they smile, they produce a gaping black hole of a mouth. Unsettled, I try to smile back.

Do I speak first? If this were a woman, she should be wearing a veil, but we also seem to be in her home, which means she's free to do as she pleases.

When they say nothing, I say, "Peace."

They nod.

"Did you see a boy?" I ask. "A very large boy?" I raise my hand to show them Dekker's height. "I guess he's more of a man now." They tilt their head. "He probably looked angry or upset."

They nod again, giving me a flicker of hope.

"Did he leave the building?" I ask.

They smile, nodding over and over.

My insides fold in on themselves. *Nyek.*

"You were very helpful," I say, wishing I had some food to offer. "Peace."

Walking to the front door, I poke my head out and look up and down the street. The sun is rising, and amber light creeps up the sidewalk as men open up storefronts. One would think it were an ordinary day. *They have no idea what's coming for them.*

With relief, I spot Dekker's green jumpsuit and red hair about two blocks north.

Do I dare leave the building? Mrs. Asher is out there. *What are you thinking, Dekker?* His green jumpsuit makes him stick out like a walking blade of grass. I have to get him back inside.

I scurry out the door and march as fast I dare up the sidewalk. My clothes are conspicuous, too. When will Dodo find us new ones? The blocks seem unreasonably long this morning, and my frustration with my brother grows with each step. When I finally catch up to him, I tap on his back.

He jumps.

"You need to come back to the apartment," I say. "You can't be outside!"

"And you can't tell me what to do." He starts to walk away, but I grab his sleeve.

Knowing that being pushy will get me nowhere, I change my tone. "Are you okay?"

"Leave me alone!" he barks.

"It's okay for you to be upset, Dekker. Dad is gone and—"

"Why should I care? He never even liked me."

My anger at him weakens. "That's ridiculous."

"He thought I was stupid."

I let go of his sleeve. I had no idea he felt this way. "Of course he didn't. He loved you."

"He thought I was an ass. And now I can never prove anything else."

"No, he—"

"Go away."

"But you're wrong—"

"I said GO AWAY." He storms across the street.

Nyek.

What should I do?

There's no talking to him when he's like this. He shouldn't be wandering the streets, but it's even more dangerous for me, a girl on my own. Anyone could interrogate me at any moment. Taking a deep breath, I head back to Mal and Jiol's building. Dekker knows the stakes. He'll come back when he's ready.

I hurry back upstairs to Jiol's apartment. When I walk inside, I find everyone except Juda sitting on the floor, huddled around a piece of paper. Mal and Jiol are in Jiol's minuscule kitchen, packing food into boxes.

Seeing my friends grouped together like this, hard at work on a problem, fills me with a swell of emotion. The news of my father makes me want to go to each of them and tell them how much I love them, even Tabby. Time is so precious, and the danger closes in every minute. My eyes tickle with tears, and I know I'm about to lose it. I can't possibly tell them yet what Jordan told me. I don't have the strength. "Well? Have you come up with anything?" I ask them.

Grace, barely looking up, puts down her pen. "First, we

talked about blackmail, and whether we had any information to use against Ram."

"For example," Mary says, "do we think the Unbound would care that he told you to murder Ruho?"

"I major *don't*," Tabby says. "If people thought it was going to make the Ascension happen, they would ignore a tsunami."

"Anything else we can use?" I ask.

"Nothing," Mary says. "No secret babies. No secret wives."

"Or husbands," Silas adds.

"He's major boring," Mary says.

"And we can't threaten him," Grace says. "We have no decent weapons of our own."

"Since your tanks can't float," Tabby says.

"And he doesn't seem to have any one person that he loves more than any other," Grace says.

"What about Jezzie?" I say.

"The dog?" Mary asks.

"You're going to tell him that if he bombs the city you'll sneak into Kingsboro and hurt his dog?" Grace says with shock.

"I'm exploring all avenues. Don't be mean," I say.

"I don't hate the plan," Silas says. "Jezzie *bit* me."

"Moving on," Grace says. "We've decided the best idea, like Jordan said, is to appeal to his faith, to convince him that killing thousands of innocent people is not what his Savior would want. In fact, the Savior would disapprove and will punish all of the Unbound for such a grave sin."

"How will you convince him of that?"

"With scripture, of course," Mary says.

"You have some with you?"

"No, unfortunately," Mary says. "We've been sitting here trying to remember everything we can from the Book of Glory that might be relevant. I was pretty relieved when you walked in. I need a break."

"We don't have time for breaks," Jiol says from the kitchen.

"Yeah, yeah," Tabby says, waving a cup. "Can I have some more tea?"

Jiol scowls but puts water on to boil.

"Shouldn't we move to the basement?" I say, remembering Jordan's warning.

"Soon," Jiol says. "Our basement is small, and I'm in no hurry to share it with every resident of this buildin'. Don't fret. Me and Mal are packing up supplies to take down."

Staring at the paper, Grace clicks the pen on her teeth. "What about that section in the sixth part about not taking revenge?"

"How do you know that?" Mary says, amazed. "Did you read the entire Book of Glory while you were in Kingsboro?"

Grace shrugs. "I wanted to go to school, and my family said it would help."

"*I've* never read the whole thing," Tabby says.

"Shocking," Silas says.

The door opens and Juda walks in. He gives me a look of pity, which I turn away from. When he sits on the floor next to me, he places his hand over mine. He says what I've already guessed: "Jordan told me. I'm so sorry."

"Oh no, Mina." Grace covers her mouth with her hand. "Not your father."

When I don't answer, Juda says, "He died a hero. He saved thousands of people."

Grace crawls across the circle and embraces me.

"He was a good man," Juda says.

I forget that Juda met my father. When Mr. Asher and Father were negotiating my marriage contract, Juda was the go-between. They didn't speak much, but I'm grateful that Juda got to spend some brief time with him.

Juda tells the others how my father blew up the plant.

"He was so brave," Grace says, awe in her voice. She releases me, wiping her eyes.

Mary, on my right, throws her arms around me, saying nothing. Tabby, to my surprise, joins her. Have they forgiven me?

"I'm so sorry we lied to you," I say softly.

"You were in an impossible situation," Mary says. "Right, Tabs?"

Tabby remains silent.

"*Right,* Tabs?" Mary repeats.

"I'm sorry about your father," Tabby says.

That's okay. I'm grateful if she can forgive me even a little.

Silas gives me a sad smile. "He sounds major impressive."

"He was." I wipe away tears.

"Can we get you anything? Or do you want to be alone?" Mary says.

"I want to keep working on stopping Ram," I say.

Mal brings me a cup of tea. "We're very sorry about your father. Jordan has very good things to say about him."

"Thank you." I take the tea. Clearing my throat, I ask Silas, "What do you have so far?"

He hands me their piece of paper. I inhale, clear my head, and read it. The quotes about murder are surprisingly similar to the ones in our Book. The word choices are different here and there, but the overall message is the same: ending life is a sin.

I hold up the paper. "So who's going to contact Ram to make this appeal?"

No one speaks.

I scan the circle, considering each person. Mary and Silas are out of the running—they've been in the Forgiveness Home for their own sins, so Ram can discount them. Juda is also known as a subversive. Tabby is, well, Tabby. She has no patience or negotiation skills. That leaves Grace.

Of course it should be Grace. She's the smartest of us all. She's patient, thoughtful, and sincere.

"I nominate Grace," I say, explaining my reasons.

Everyone quickly agrees, but Grace says, "You're overestimating me. I think Ram is terrifying."

"He's not terrifying," Mary says. "He's a lying, scheming bully, and he isn't worth all the goodness in your pinky."

Grace's brow furrows. "Can I see the paper again?" After I hand it to her, she reads it over and over. After some time, she says. "If I'm going to do this, I need to be alone. I can't do it with all of you watching."

"Everyone out!" Mary says, standing.

When Mal and Jiol continue to pack food, Mary says, "You too."

Startled, Jiol says, "Are you orderin' me out of my own home, girl?"

"Yes," she says.

His jaw tightens.

"If you wouldn't mind stepping next door, *please*," she says. "Grace is trying to save the entire city."

He drops a loaf of bread into the box, and, followed by Mal, leaves the apartment.

The last to leave, I give Grace a hug. "Are you sure you don't want me to stay?"

She nods.

"We'll be right next door. You're going to be major outstanding."

She lifts her veil and takes in several deep gulps of air. I shut the door just as she blinks six times to activate her Tact.

THIRTY-FOUR

Back in Mal's apartment, we wait on pins and needles. I know I could turn on my Tact, tune into Ram and Grace's conversation, but Ram would see that I'd joined, and I don't want to cause a distraction.

Where is Dekker? I can't believe he hasn't come back yet. A tiny voice wonders if he plans to come back at all, but I push it aside. I can't worry about that right now.

Mal holds up a pile of towels. "While ya have a few minutes, I suggest ya take advantage of the shower. Once we're underground, there'll be none."

Tabby wrinkles her nose. "Ew."

"We've also collected some plainer clothing for ya," Jiol says, pointing to a pile in the corner.

"But these clothes protect us," I say.

"I explained that to Uncle Mal," Juda says. "But we can't have the other tenants asking about our strange clothes when we're in the basement."

I understand the argument, but I also feel very safe within

my firewall. Am I ready to abandon Beth and be Mina Clark again, scannable and traceable in every way? "Can we put the new cloaks over our old ones?" I ask, deciding this is a very clever idea.

Walking to the stack of clothes, I dig until I find the black cloak of a married woman. I shake it out and throw it over my teal cloak.

"It was a nice idea," Mary says.

"What's wrong?" I look down to see that the hem of the black cloak is shorter than the teal one by several inches. The sleeves of the teal cloak also peek out in an obvious way. "I just need a bigger cloak is all," I say. I proceed to try on every cloak in the pile, and each one has the same problem: the bright teal shows somewhere.

"We could hem the teal cloaks," I say.

The idea is greeted with half-smiles.

"There's no time, child," Jiol says, packing up Mal's food.

"I think you have to let it go, Mina," Juda says gently.

I refold the cloaks. He's right. The boys have to change clothes no matter what—they can't cover their jumpsuits with tunics—and I have to find the courage to join them.

"I'm showering," Tabby says, rummaging through the stack of clothes. I imagine she's ready to get out of Uncle Ruho's tunic and that shimmering cloak.

"There's only the one bathroom down the hall, so everyone must be quick," Mal says. "There's no hot water, so I don't imagine you'll want to dawdle much anyway."

"What?" Tabby says, dismayed.

"Just think of it as stage two of your shower at home, without the stage one," I say, although I don't relish the idea of a cold shower myself.

After Tabby leaves, I ask Mal, "Can I help with anything?" I need to do something with my hands.

"We've packed up most of the food," he says. "Why don't you and Juda check the flashlights and make sure the batteries are fully charged?"

Six flashlights are laid out on the table, the batteries inside worth as much as all the food that Mal has packed. I pick up the volt meter sitting on the table, while Juda unscrews and empties all the flashlights. One at a time I touch the probe to the batteries and make sure the reading is close to 1.6. We discover one that is only 1.35, which means it's fifty percent charged. Mal frowns at the news. "I'm gonna have words with that energy merchant on Monday."

"I hope we're still here for you to have those words," Jiol grumbles.

"That's not funny," I say.

"Sorry, dear," Mal says. "Jiol's humor becomes very black in times of crises."

Tabby returns from the shower in the plain black cloak and veil of a local married woman. Her short wet hair sticks straight up. In a hostile tone, she says to Mal, "You said cold, not *major-glacial-ice-cube-freakin'-freezing.*"

Silas laughs, which cuts the tension that fills the room.

Suddenly Grace fills the doorway.

She walks into the apartment with tentative steps. I wish I could see her face behind the veil; I can only go with her unsteady body language, which isn't encouraging.

"Well?" Mary says.

"He wouldn't listen," Grace says. "The more I quoted, the angrier he got, like he thought I was trying to prove I was more devout than him or something. So I tried to explain that everything that had happened with Ruho had been a giant mistake, that Tabby felt her life was in danger, that he was the one who wouldn't let us tell her about our plans. He didn't care. He was . . . just awful . . . " She begins to sob. "He quoted violent, primitive texts about horrible punishments for non-believers."

"Solomon quoted those to me when he wanted to scare me for being 'sexually immoral,'" Silas says. "They're monstrous."

"They're medieval and Ram knows it," Mary says. "He's using them as an excuse because he's major fuming."

"What now?" I ask.

"We need more information about his intentions," Jiol says. "Didn't you say your brother was in the military, Mary? Can you contact him with your eye thingy?"

Jeremiah. I'd almost forgotten. "That's a great idea. I'm sure he'd talk to you!"

She frowns.

"What's wrong?" Juda asks.

"Ram will be reading every word," Mary says. "I don't want to get Jeremiah into more trouble."

Mal says, "When Jiol and I were young, we had a codeword for when either of us had lied to our mother, so the other would know to go along with the lie. Do you have anything like that?"

Jiol smiles. "Ah yes. *Puddles.*"

Mary bites her lip in concentration. "I don't think so."

"Your life is at stake, Mary. He'd want you to contact him," Grace says.

We all nod in agreement.

"I'll try," Mary says. "But I can't promise anything."

"Good girl," Jiol says.

I cringe, knowing that the condescending term might change Mary's mind, but she seems focused on her new task. She borrows Grace's Tact, putting it in her eye like an old pro. She blinks six times. This time, I turn mine on so I can follow along.

Mary writes, *Jeremiah. This is Mary.*

240

A few seconds later a reply appears: *Prove it.*

Mary doesn't hesitate. *Your feet smell like rotting eggs.*

Mary! R u ok?

Fine. What is happening there?

Every 1 sitting n Hub waiting 4 ascension 2 happen, praise the Savior.

Mary writes, *Praise Him. I long 4 my moment 2 rise & sit by my beloved Savior.*

She says to me, "He'll know something is wrong. I would *never* say that."

We wait and then wait some more. Jeremiah doesn't answer.

"What happened?" Mary asks.

"Maybe he decided it wasn't you," I say.

"Do you think Ram saw our Nods and cut us off?" Mary asks, dismayed.

"What should we do?" Grace says.

"Is there anyone else we can contact?" I say. "What about Dr. Rachel?"

Suddenly, Jeremiah is back, writing, *Sorry. Had 2 program secure line. Ram ordered Sentries 2 prepare arsenal 4 assault. U MUST LEAVE MANHATTAN NOW.*

How??? Mary writes.

ANY WAY U CAN.

Mary writes, *Send Ostrich!*

Drones on lock-down, he says.

You must stall. NEED TIME.

After much too long, he writes, *Can delay a few hrs. HURRY.*

And then he's gone.

Mary and I sit in stunned silence. What does "a few" mean?

"If I abandoned you, I would be no better than a shepherd who led his sheep straight into the mouth of a wolf." That's what Ram said before we left. Ram is a wolf, and I always knew it.

"What did your brother say?" Jiol asks anxiously.

In a monotone voice, Mary says, "Prepare for a bombing."

THIRTY-FIVE

Uncle Mal and Uncle Jiol will go door to door telling every person in the building that they must go into the basement as soon as possible. They'll also keep an eye out for Dekker.

They tell us not to move yet, but sitting around the apartment is awful. I want to run around the neighborhood, warning everyone about the bombing and telling them about Mrs. Hypat, but Jiol insists it's too dangerous for us to leave the building. Not only is Mrs. Asher looking for us, but Uncle Ruho's body will be found in less than an hour. We don't know when the Heralds will make the news public; who knows how people will react? Jiol says there could be both riots and parades.

I remember I need to change before we head underground. I decide to take Mal's advice and take a quick shower. At least it's something to do. I head down the hall, holding my new clothes and a towel in my arms.

The bathroom takes "basic" to a new level. The room is all tiled—the ceiling, walls, and floor. The shower head is on the ceiling, and there's a drain on the floor, but there's no stall, so the water will spray over the entire room, including the sink and toilet. Where am I supposed to put my towel and clothes? They'll get soaked no matter where I put them.

I spot a small hook on the back of the door where I can hang my towel. Even here, I imagine it will get damp. Taking off everything, I wrap myself in the towel and place my clothes, dirty and clean, just outside the door. Then I hang the towel on the hook, count to three and turn the shower handle.

Ice cold water shoots down from the ceiling. I try to jump away, but there's nowhere to escape to. I hop back and forth, covered in goose pimples, as I use the shampoo that sits on the sink.

There's a knock on the door. I squeal as I reach for the towel. Then I remember I need to turn off the water first.

"WHAT IS IT?" I screech.

"We have to go. NOW," Juda's voice says.

"Why? Wha—"

"NOW."

What's happening? My mind races as I cover myself as best I can. "Hand me my clothes."

The door opens and two arms come in, holding my new clothes. I grab them and shut the door.

As fast as possible, I slide on the pants and top over my slick skin and throw on the black cloak. I use the towel to scrub at my hair, which is still full of shampoo.

When I step out of the bathroom, Juda is waiting, holding out my shoes and veil.

"What's happening?" I say, as I struggle to pull on the shoes.

"Dekker's back. He saw Mrs. Asher and her men headed this way. We've been ratted out."

Nyek.

"Mal is taking us out the back exit."

244

My feet squish in my shoes as Juda leads me down the hall. I run my fingers through my hair, hoping to pull out some of the froth. We turn a corner and find the others already waiting. Dekker laughs when he sees me, but Grace elbows him in the ribs.

"One of my neighbors has given you away," Mal whispers. "We can no longer put you in the basement, and we must be quiet going down these stairs."

I flinch as he opens a rusted exit door that screeches so loudly people must hear it in Queens. He holds it open and we enter the stairwell. We rush down the steps as fast as we can. When Mal shuts the door behind us, the scrape echoes like a truck dragging a dumpster.

There's nothing to do but move faster. We race down the six flights. Who gave us away? Surely not sweet Mrs. Jane. When we reach the bottom, we're winded and anxious. There are three different exits, and Mal is still a good two flights above us. Why didn't he just tell us which way to go?

When he finally reaches the bottom, he has to stop to catch his breath. He points to the door on our right, so we rush through it. Luckily, it isn't as rusted and loud as the last one.

We're in an alley, and I'm completely turned around with no sense of north or south.

Behind us, Mal says, "We're goin' to Dodo's. Udi knows the way."

"We should split into couples," Juda says, "so we don't attract attention."

"She's lookin' for a couple—you and Mina," Mal says. "We'll divide into two groups. You and Mina will go with Grace and Dekker. Silas, you and I will go with Mary and Tabby."

Juda agrees, and we divide quickly.

"If you're confronted by guards or Twitchers," Mal says,

"the best thing to do is scatter. They aren't sure who they want from our groups, and we want them to stay confused."

"If we get separated, meet up at the spot where we left the Hummer," Juda says. "Everyone remember how to get there?"

We nod.

"Take Norfolk Street to Dodo's," Juda tells Mal, "and we'll take Clinton."

Mal claps Juda's shoulder. "See you there."

I don't say goodbye to anyone because I refuse to believe I won't see them again in minutes.

THIRTY-SIX

Once on Norfolk, we walk at a regular pace, and I find it almost impossible not to run. With his new blond hair, Juda seems to be lit from within, and I wish he could borrow Grace's veil to cover his face. I have to keep reminding myself that Mrs. Asher doesn't know his new hair and glasses.

We've walked two blocks and have almost reached Rivington when I spot her. I can't see her face, but I don't need to. I would recognize Mrs. Asher's perfectly coiffed hair and ornately draped fabric anywhere. She's leaning against a shiny black car, looking up at the building we just left, as if she might see us in a window.

We have to walk right by her.

Has everyone else noticed her? I hope so. I don't want anyone to react to her when we're only a few feet away. We need to walk in a normal fashion, making no abrupt movements or sounds. If she continues to look up, we might be okay.

I'm feeling relieved that at least she's alone, but then I spot a guard in the driver's seat of her car.

Stay calm, I say to myself.

We stroll past her, two married couples running morning errands.

She studies our group.

Why did she stop looking at the building? Nothing about us should be conspicuous. We have a blond man, a red-haired man, a curly-haired blonde, and me . . . the sodden-haired girl.

Nyek. Mrs. Asher is probably gaping at the shampoo in my hair, thinking *Who would leave the house like that?*

We're almost at the end of the block, seconds from turning onto Rivington.

"Halt!" a man yells.

In a low voice, Juda commands, "Don't turn around."

But when I hear "Halt!" again, I swivel my head and see Mrs. Asher's driver marching toward us.

"Stop them!" Mrs. Asher shrieks.

"Scatter!" Juda yells.

I sprint north.

"They're MURDERERS! Stop them!" Mrs. Asher yells. From the sound of her voice, she's running, too.

I speed up.

I've forgotten how hard it is to run fast in a cloak and veil. My feet keep getting tripped up in the hem, and I can't see properly through the veil.

"You'll never catch me!" Juda cries, loud enough to hear down the block. He must be trying to steer Mrs. Asher away from me.

I make a hard right, running across Stanton Street.

I hear footsteps behind me. Mrs. Asher didn't fall for Juda's trick, or maybe she thought it would be easier to catch a girl than a boy.

When I hit Suffolk, I make a sharp right, circling back to Rivington. Turning left, I discover an alley. I duck inside and crouch behind a dumpster.

I breathe fast and hard.

Where are the others? Did anyone get caught? I take big slow gulps of breath, trying to calm down. We agreed that scattering was the best strategy, but I hate not knowing what's happening to everyone else.

Aware I'm being reckless, I peek out from behind my hiding place, hoping to see someone or hear something that will explain what's going on. I wait for the commotion on the street that will mean Mrs. Asher's guards are about to find me, but I hear nothing—no screeching voices, no running feet.

I send a group Nod: *What's happening?*

Come 2 car! comes Dekker's quick response.

Praise the Prophet. They're safe.

I wait a bit longer. I creep to the entrance of the alley and take the briefest of glances up and down the street. Nothing.

I lift my cloak slightly, dash onto the sidewalk, and run toward Avenue A. I don't know if I've ever run so fast. I reach the old tenement building and approach the big white Hummer. Figures huddle behind it.

"Mina!" Juda comes out, lifting me off my feet. "We were starting to worry."

"I was hiding. Sorry."

"Don't be sorry. You were being safe." He puts me down.

The second group—Mal, Mary, Silas, and Tabby—are also here. Why didn't they go to Dodo's? "What happened?" I ask.

"We heard Juda yelling and decided we'd better hide fast," Mary says.

"Where's Grace?" Juda asks me.

"She's not with you?" I ask.

"No, she ran after you," Juda says. "We thought you were together."

"I was alone the whole time." I start to panic. Were the feet

I heard behind me not Mrs. Asher's? What if I was running from Grace?

"She probably got lost," Silas says.

"She knows the city better than any of us," I say, mind reeling. "We have to find her."

"Mrs. Asher is still out there," Juda says.

"I don't care," I say, ready to return to Norfolk. "I'm going to look for her."

To my surprise, Dekker says, "I'll come with you."

"No! Use your Tact," Juda says.

Of course! I blink six times to activate it and send Grace a Nod. *Where r u?*

"That's not going to do you any good," Mary says in a tiny voice.

"Why?" I say, irritated.

"Because I still have her Tact in my eye."

Grace gave it to her to message Jeremiah. Dread fills me from head to toe. "She can't be far. We have to find her." I start down the street.

"Don't be stupid," Mal says, grabbing my arm. "I'll go. No one is lookin' for an old man."

"You shouldn't risk—"

"I'm the smart choice and you know it," Mal says. "I'll retrace our steps."

I begrudgingly agree. If I'm captured, I can't help Grace.

"Do you still have the keys for this car, Udi?" Mal says. "It's the safest spot for you to hide until I return."

Juda pats his pants pockets. Sure he left them in his Unbound jumpsuit, I try to think of another hiding place for us. Juda holds up the key. Sometimes I just love him so much.

We watch Mal walk back down Avenue A. He moves far too slowly for my liking. By the time he reaches Broome street, Grace will have had time to walk back to the Cloisters.

The six of us pile back into the car that we thought we'd abandoned for good. The interior is hot and stuffy, but I confess, I have a new appreciation for its opaque windows and bulletproof construction.

Once settled, we don't speak much. Grace's absence is heavy among us—the glowing wick cut from a candle. Her chirpy enthusiasm can be annoying, but now that it's gone, everyone's energy is heavy and dark. I try to remember all the stressful occasions that Grace and I have experienced together and how it would have felt without her. It's hard to do.

This is all my fault. Why didn't I turn around and see that the person running behind me was Grace? Why didn't she call out to me? I curse myself over and over.

A knock on the window startles me out of my daydream. Mal's face presses against the glass. Juda opens the back door and lets him inside.

Mal's face tells me everything. I feel sick. "I saw her on Essex. She was surrounded by two guards and a Twitcher. Mrs. Asher was yellin' at her, askin' about the people 'who murdered her son.'"

Everyone looks like they've been punched in the stomach.

"They put her in a car and drove north," he says.

Eyes filling, I say, "We have to turn ourselves in. We can't let her suffer on our behalf."

"Turnin' yourselves in won't save her. Then Mrs. Asher would have three of you instead of one!" Mal says.

"Is there any way to rescue her?" Juda asks, his voice grave.

"Normally, I'd go to Jordan, but he's preparin' everyone for the bombin'. I'm sorry, children."

Sorry isn't good enough. Mrs. Asher and her guards don't even know about the bombing. They could take Grace up to the penthouse, or decide to stand right in the middle of the street at the exact moment Ram decides to unleash his weapons. "We owe Grace more than this," I say. "We have to at least *try*."

"We don't have any guns," Juda says.

"We have to focus on getting to a safe place before the bombing, and then we can think about yer friend," Mal says.

"No," I say, hating him. There has to be another way. Grace wouldn't give up on me. She'd remember some crazy plan from some old book she read and know exactly what we should do. Picturing her in the Macy's library, wearing big glasses and pouring tea, makes me want to cry. She had such a nice, peaceful life, with people who cared about her, and I had to go and ruin it.

I straighten up. "I know someone who can help us."

"Who?" Juda says.

The only other human who loves Grace as much as I do: "Rayna."

THIRTY-SEVEN

I give Mal a brief explanation of the Laurel Society. He seems trustworthy enough to keep the information secret, and he's not going to let us leave him unless he knows where we're going.

"The women there, they love Grace," I explain. "They have computers, and they'll be able to tell us where Mrs. Asher has taken her." I hope this is true. If Mrs. Asher takes Grace back to her penthouse, will anyone officially report it?

"The girls will have to go alone," Juda says. "The boys will go to Dodo's."

"No. You have to come with us," I say. "Once we locate her, we'll need your help, and we can't waste any time!" Finding Grace is too important to worry about rules.

"We're not allowed there and you know it," he says. "We've already been through this."

"I don't care if you're allowed or not. This is an emergency, and Rayna will understand as soon as I explain the situation."

"I think we should go with Mina," Dekker says.

I raise my eyebrows. "You do?"

"If it's the only way to save Grace, then yeah."

"Thank you," I say, amazed by his agreement.

"She wouldn't leave us behind," Mary says.

"I'm willing to try—" Juda says, but I can see the skepticism in his eyes.

"This is daft!" Mal says. "If you walk all the way there and are turned away, you're exposing yourselves to danger for no reason at all. It's much better for you to go to Dodo's, where it's safe!"

"How is it safe?" Juda says. "Mrs. Asher knows we're in the neighborhood, the neighbors are no longer trustworthy, and bombs are about to drop! Nowhere is safe!"

"How can this group help you?" Mal says. "They're just *women*."

My last bit of patience evaporates, water boiling into steam. "And you're just a *man* who's never been out of this neighborhood, let alone off this island. You've never been sold into marriage, and you've never run for your life because your family cared more about its dignity than it did about your death!"

No one speaks.

"I'm sorry, Uncle Mal," Juda says. "Mina is just upset—"

"Do not apologize for me!" I say. "I am sick and tired of apologizing to men, when they should be apologizing to me."

"Here, here," Mary says.

Uncle Mal's mouth has fallen open. I'm sure no girl or woman has ever spoken to him this way.

"You've been very good to us, Mal," I say, taking a deep breath, "and I will never forget your kindness, but we have to go our own way now. Grace is our new priority. Right?"

Everyone except for Juda nods. I'm sure he's considering his ma. "I understand if you want to stay," I tell him.

"No," he says, brow furrowed. "I'm coming with you."

Mal lifts his head in defeat, but, thankfully, he's not cross.

"Make sure you're underground as soon as possible." He embraces Juda. "Please be careful. And come back as soon as you've found your friend."

"I promise," Juda says. "Tell Jiol and Dodo I'll see them soon."

Mal gives him a half smile, and anyone can see he doesn't believe him.

As we walk up Broadway, I think over the quick turn of events. I wholeheartedly believe that the Laurel Society is our best bet for locating Grace, but that doesn't mean I'm confident we'll be able to do anything with the information.

What could Mrs. Asher possibly want with her? As far as she knows, Grace knows nothing about her husband or her son. *Grace, please keep your wits about you. LIE. Don't admit you were at the boathouse or in the subway. If she thinks you were a part of her family's death, she'll NEVER let you go.*

Juda told me that when I was a prisoner of the Ashers, he spent a lot of time outside their building, staring up at the penthouse, trying to figure out how to rescue me. He never told me if he came up with a decent plan.

Or maybe Mrs. Asher has taken her to the Lyceum for questioning. Dekker knows the building well, but thousands of Teachers and Students reside there. How could we possibly save her?

Anxiety is making me unsteady. We walk as three couples, yards apart: Juda and Mary, me and Silas, and then Dekker and Tabby. We don't want to lose sight of one another this time. Once again, I want to run down the street, sprint if I can, but all logic says to walk normally.

Silas walks on my left, acting as my husband. "I'm really sorry about your father," he says.

I don't even know what he means for a second—the idea of Father being gone is too new. I'm not ready to be the-girl-missing-a-parent. "Uh, thanks."

"He sounds like a good man."

"Yeah."

"Do you want to talk about it?"

"Not yet."

"Okay." A few moments later he says, "Can I ask you about something else?"

"Maybe."

"Why are you so sure this group of women can help us?"

"They have technology and guns."

A moment later, he says, "Have you ever used a gun?"

"Not really." I carried one when I was dressed as a Twitcher, but I never shot it. "You?"

"No. And I never will."

"Even if your life is in danger?"

"Nope. I don't believe in them."

"I thought everyone in Kingsboro loved guns." I remember the huge gun in the case above Marjory's desk. "Kalyb told me that the Unbound hated the female president because she tried to take away people's guns."

"Or maybe it was just because she was female," he says.

I sigh. "Maybe."

"Are you scared?"

"Yes," I say without pausing. The idea of losing Grace has me petrified. "You?"

He scans the sky. "I'm scared of the bombs." A few steps later, he says, "I'm really scared of being stuck here. I just . . . I can't believe this is how you grew up."

"Which part?" I ask.

"All of it. The cloaks. The violence. The subservience."

Two months ago I wouldn't have really known what he meant, but now I've seen other ways to live. The Unbound promised a life that they couldn't deliver—education and equality for girls—but at least they gave me a vision of a world to aspire to.

"I suppose I thought it might be better for you here," I say, "being a man."

He shakes his head, almost laughing. "I've been terrified the whole time. What if I look at someone the wrong way? What if I say the wrong thing or move my body in an odd manner? I've been major conscious of every breath, movement, and word since the second we arrived. It's exhausting."

"Welcome to the world of women."

"Welcome to the world of being a molley. I've had to be careful most my life, but never with the idea that the penalty was, like, death."

I should've known that suppressing oneself wasn't new to him. "I'm sorry. It's probably scarier than being a woman."

"It's not a contest. There's no prize for being the most terrified."

I like the way Silas puts things.

"I was the most frightened of that Zebadiah," he says.

"More than Captain Memon?" Zebadiah seems so frail.

Although there are few people on the street, his voice lowers. "I saw him eyeing a lot of young Heralds. You learn to notice these things. That man . . . likes the male form."

"What a fraud."

"*Hypocrite* is the word you're looking for." A block later he says, "I wondered about Dekker for a while."

"Really?" I try to hide my shock. I don't want him to think that I would be disappointed if Dekker liked boys. I've just never considered it before. "Why?"

"He keeps everyone at such a distance, like he's afraid of people getting to know him"

"I think he enjoys being a jerk," I say.

"He was sweet when we were living in the Cloisters. He taught me a lot about the Heralds and how I should behave around them."

"But you don't think he's . . . "

"A molley? No. He's obviously crazy about Grace."

"*What?*" Surely I haven't heard him right.

"You haven't noticed? He sits up straighter when she's in the room and kind of gazes at her."

I'm floored. Dekker *did* agree with me quickly when I said we should go to Macy's. I glance behind me, and his walk is stiff and strange. *He's just as worried as I am.*

"Wow," I say, because I can't think of anything else.

"God works in peculiar ways," he says.

I hadn't perceived any of this before now. I wonder if Grace did?

We've reached 34th Street. Juda and Mary turn west and when we turn to follow them, we see they've stopped dead.

Juda takes Mary's elbow and continues to walk west until he reaches an alleyway. He ducks inside and, moments later, we follow. I hope that when Dekker and Tabby turn behind us, no one notices.

When we're all safely in the darkness of the alley, Juda says, "Twitchers were stationed in front of the south entrance."

"How many?" Dekker asks.

"Twenty or so."

I can't breathe. Have they found the Laurel Society? "What were they doing?" I ask.

"I tried not to stare at them for long." He prowls to the front of the alley and looks around the corner. When he returns he says, "They're sort of just—standing around. Their guns are holstered."

I don't know what to do. We can't get by them. Is the Laurel Society still in the basement? They may have been swept out weeks ago. "What about the north door?" I say.

"We'll have to walk the long way around."

"Then we do it." We don't have any other plan. "Let's go up 5th Avenue."

We all agree and Dekker, taking the lead, strides to the entrance of the alleyway. He looks toward Macy's, but instead of stepping out and heading east, he continues to stare.

"What is it?" I whisper.

"Something's happening," he says.

Sliding in behind him, I peek around his shoulder. The Twitchers are alert. Some are typing and others are talking to one another. A few of them take guns out of their holsters. I grab the back of Dekker's tunic and pull him back into the alley.

Mary says, "What's happening?"

"They're mobilizing," Dekker says.

"They look like they're receiving down-net," I say.

Juda's eyes widen. "It must be nine o'clock, the time for Zebadiah to find Uncle Ruho's body."

Dekker inhales sharply. "Aw, man, you're major right."

"What will they do?" Mary asks.

"We don't know. This has never happened before," I say.

"Do you think they'll start looking for Tabby?" Silas asks.

"They'll start looking for all of us," Juda says.

We stay in the shadows of the alley. After five minutes, I carefully check the street again.

"Juda," I say. "They're *gone*."

He joins me. Every single Twitcher has left the block.

"Could it be a trick?" I say.

"If they knew we were here, they'd just come and get us," he says. "They outnumber us four to one." He rubs his neck. "They were probably told to head to the Cloisters or maybe the Lyceum."

We wait a while longer to make sure the coast is truly clear, then we run across 34th Street. For a stressful moment, I can't find the hidden entrance. Thankfully, I remember a demolished clock tower that Grace mentioned. Once I locate it, Juda helps me move aside wood, metal, and garbage to reveal the rusted door. We pry it open with difficulty. The six of us squeeze through and then pull it shut firmly behind us.

We're inside the basement. *I can't believe we're here.*

The moment I have the thought, an alarm begins to ring.

THIRTY-EIGHT

"What's going on? Where *are* we?" Tabby asks, needled by the jangling alarm.

"It'll be fine," I say. "They know me." I take off my veil, wishing myself that the bell would stop. I take comfort in the familiar sight of the shining white hallway and the slight smell of Chanel No 5.

A second later, a dark figure comes racing up the hall at top speed. It's Rayna, and she's pointing a gun straight at our heads. Panicked, Dekker throws up his fists, and Rayna's eyes flash as she locks in on him.

"Rayna, WAIT!" I cry.

It's too late. She tackles Dekker and they go sprawling. I wait to hear the shot from her gun as it hits the floor, but, praise the Prophet, it doesn't go off.

Dekker flails, trying to punch her in the face, but she easily slips her arm under his neck and begins to choke him.

"Rayna!" I yell again, as I watch Dekker's face turn purple.

She looks at me with rage. Taking a moment to absorb my red hair and brown eyes, she finally says, "Mina?"

"Let him go! He's my brother!"

She looks at Dekker with hostility. She releases his neck but doesn't let him go. "What the HELL are you doing here?" she asks me.

Dekker coughs as he tries to free himself.

"Don't worry," I say. "No one saw us."

"We've been surrounded by Twitchers for weeks. Of course they saw you!" Freeing Dekker, Rayna stands up and walks to the door behind us, yanking at a hidden wire. The alarm stops. Grabbing her pistol from the floor, she tells Dekker, "You're lucky I had the safety on."

He continues to cough. Mary and Tabby remove their veils, relieved.

"The Twitchers left," I say.

Rayna frowns. I'm not sure if she's skeptical of my news or just unhappy to see my face.

"When they heard Uncle Ruho was dead," Juda adds.

"Dead?" Her eyes flicker. "How do you know?"

"I killed him," Tabby says, lifting her chin.

Rayna looks her up and down. "Then *you* can come in."

"We have a lot to tell you and Ayan," I say. "We all have to come in."

Rayna, prickly as ever, looks tired. Her spiky blue hair looks faded and overgrown, like a plant that needs watering. She seems thin and less substantial than the last time I saw her. "You know better than to bring men here. They can't come in."

"Why don't we wait outside?" Silas says, nervously eyeing Rayna's gun.

"Uncle Ruho's body has been found," I tell Rayna. "We're wanted criminals, and the boys' faces are known. They can't be out on the street."

"I don't care about them and neither will Ayan. The Laurel Society is—"

"They have Grace," Dekker says.

She stops. "Who does?"

"Mrs. Asher. The Twitchers," I say. "We're here to get her back."

Her mouth purses as she glares at the boys. "What do they have to do with it?"

"We're here to help," Dekker says.

Rayna looks the boys up and down, saving a particularly nasty look for Juda. "How long has she been gone?" she asks.

"An hour, maybe more," I say.

She grinds her teeth. "You can come in to talk to Ayan, but the boys are staying here."

"No. They're coming inside with us. No one knows the Asher's apartment better than Juda, and Dekker knows the ins and outs of the Lyceum." I look at Silas, at a loss. "And Silas is an expert in climbing buildings."

He raises his eyebrow in doubt.

"You're pushing it, Mina," Rayna says.

"You're wasting precious time. We have to find Grace now. If they decide she doesn't know anything, God knows what they'll do to her."

Lip curling, she says, "Don't speak to anyone—"

"And keep their faces down. They know," I say.

After scowling at me a few more seconds, she walks away, down the hall.

"She's, uh, friendly," Mary says.

"I'd like to say she gets better . . . " I say.

We catch up to Rayna, who says tightly, "When you triggered the alarm, I was sure the Twitchers had finally found us."

"If they don't know you're here, why were they outside?" I ask.

"We're dead center of the war zone. They decided it was a

convenient spot to make camp. We've been stuck inside for weeks."

"Is everyone okay?" I ask, noticing that the halls don't seem as well-lit as before. When she doesn't answer, I grow alarmed. "How's Nana?"

"She's, uh, in the infirmary," Rayna says.

"Why?" I feel dizzy.

"She needs food," Rayna says.

"You're out of food?" I think of all the food I've left behind: the banquet at the Cloisters; the breakfast at Mal's. How could I have arrived with nothing?

"No, but we're rationing tightly, and your grandmother has refused to take her fair share. Stubborn old coot."

"That's not nice," Mary says.

"Why? It's accurate." As we reach Ayan's quarters, Rayna tells me, "I'll tell Ayan about Uncle Ruho and Grace. You should go see your grandmother."

As much as my heart pulls me toward the infirmary, I know that the boys will have no chance if I leave them alone with Rayna.

"No. I'll see her after we talk to Ayan," I say.

"She won't let them stay, whether you're here or not," Rayna says, a nasty grin on her face. She knocks on the door.

Inside the office, Ayan is conferring with Gray, the cook. I walk in with Rayna and Ayan is confused, but she smiles when she eventually recognizes me. As the boys enter, her alluring face goes dark.

"What's this?" she asks Rayna.

"Mina claims that the Twitchers have left our perimeter. She says that Uncle Ruho is dead and that this one here is the one that did it." She jerks her thumb at Tabby.

Ayan's mouth drops open a little. She says to Gray, "Check that the Twitchers are truly gone. If they are, alert our contacts to leave food in the usual places." Gray rushes out.

"Why are they here?" Ayan says, looking at the boys.

"Grace has been taken by Mrs. Asher," Rayna says. "They're here to help her, which is the only reason I allowed them inside." She glares at the boys, as if we all didn't already know how unhappy she was with them.

Without a moment's thought, Ayan says, "The girls can stay. The boys cannot. We can begin a computer scan—"

I knew her words were coming, yet they fill me with rage. "It's an emergency!" I say. "Grace is missing. We have nowhere else to go."

"As I said, *you* can stay . . . "

"And the boys can go die on the street?"

"They can do whatever they want, as long as they leave us alone."

"I told you, Mina," Juda says, glaring right back at Rayna. "Their hatred for men is greater than their love for Grace."

"I don't believe that," I say. "Ayan, tell me that's not true."

"It's not about hatred. It's about protection." She looks at the boys and her voice isn't unkind. "We have survived against horrible odds for many years, and it's only because we abide by very strict rules. As soon as we start to break them, we'll perish."

"I think we should ask *everyone*," I say.

"I have final say here," Ayan says, eyes narrowing.

I march out of the room before she can say another word.

"Mina!" she yells after me, anger overcoming her composed voice.

I rush to the basement's main room, where, as I expected, the majority of the Laurel Society is having breakfast. I'm thrown by how thin and haggard the women look. Several of them are so weak that they lie on pillows as others spoon broth into their mouths. Pushing my intense worry about Nana aside, I say loudly, "I need to speak with all of you."

The women look up from their food in wonder. Most of them know me from the first night I dined here, but I look different now, so I say, "I'm Mina Clark, Ura's granddaughter, and I want to tell you that Uncle Ruho is dead. I know because I saw the body. The Twitchers outside your doors left when they heard the news. Food should be available very soon."

The room stirs as my words sink in.

"Dead?"

"What?"

"How?"

Soon cries of "Praise the Prophet!" rise up.

I know I should tell them about the bombs that are coming, but, selfishly, I first need their help rescuing Grace.

"The reason I'm here is because Grace has been taken. I've come to ask for the Laurel Society's help in getting her back."

All the women nod, which is a good start.

"I have friends with me. Those friends include three boys— one of them is my brother, Dekker. I trust these boys with my life. I'm not asking you to let them move in. I'm asking you to let them inside long enough for us to figure out where Grace is. If they stay on the street, they'll be arrested and executed."

Tabby, Mary, and the boys linger in the hallway just out of sight. "Come here," I say, motioning to them. They walk with timidity into the room, producing a chorus of gasps. Several women shrink in on themselves.

"Don't be frightened," I say. "They won't hurt you. They only want to help."

"Get out!" a woman yells.

"They must leave!" says another.

"What have you done?" a girl yells at me.

Soon they're all yelling at me.

Ayan enters. She gives me a look of pity, as if I've tried to convince a roomful of blind people that they can see.

"Everyone be calm. The boys are leaving. You're all safe." She looks at the boys, tilting her head back. "It's time for you to go."

My head drops. Why is everywhere I go exactly the same? *Someone* is always unwelcome or unacceptable. I'm exhausted with trying to fight it.

Walking to my side, Mary puts her arm around my shoulder. She whispers, "Amazing that people who've spent their entire lives being discriminated against are so eager to discriminate against others."

She's right. It's upside down. And I'm sick of it.

"What's wrong with you people?" I say, surprised to hear my voice. "You sit around talking about the problems with Uncle Ruho and the Teachers and how they don't treat women fairly, but you treat men unfairly. You don't know these boys, you don't know anything about them. And yet you decided immediately that they're your enemy. How is that any better than men deciding you're dumb and worthless because you're women?"

The women have stopped yelling, but they still look angry.

"I left this island, and I hoped for a new, better world. So did Juda and Dekker, who were with me." I point to them. "But when we got to Queens, we were different from other people, because we were from Manhattan, and we suffered because of it. Juda was tortured and I was electrocuted with rods. Silas was considered inferior by his own people, and he was starved and forced to wear a backpack of rocks for weeks at a time. Mary has scars on her stomach from the horrific belt she was forced to wear. And then we come here, where the people I love are supposed to be, and you tell me that half of us can't come in because we don't meet your requirements?

When will the requirements stop? When will everyone be equal?"

I want to scream and beat on the walls.

Rayna continues to stand with her arms crossed. She looks at Ayan, who studies me with a creased forehead.

"There's a difference between tolerance for all," Ayan says, "and allowing a fox into a chicken coop."

"Only if you assume all males are foxes!" I say. "And how can anything change if you make that assumption? You'll have to hide down here for the rest of time if you assume that every man is your enemy. You're not rabbits who need to avoid every other creature. You're people. And there are other people out there who want to help you. And others who need your help. PLEASE."

"I can't allow—"

"Why don't you ask them?" I say, gesturing toward the rest of the Laurel Society. "Don't they get a say?"

"Absolutely," Ayan says, smirking. "How many of you ladies want these boys to leave immediately?"

Hands raise into the air, but it's not all of them, and my pulse quickens with hope. I say, "And how many of you feel it's time to live in a wider world of acceptance?"

Hands go up, but I can't tell if it's as many as the ones who said no.

Ayan's brow furrows.

"This is the time, Ayan," I say. "Ruho is dead. We get to decide what the new world will be. Not him."

The women whisper as Ayan stares at our group, hands on her hips. I'm tempted to get on my knees and beg, but I force myself to stand tall and meet her gaze.

"Let them use the computer," a voice says.

"No! Make them leave!" someone else says.

"Let them stay an hour. It won't kill us," Gray says.

"Maybe they're spies, and there are more men on the way!" someone says, causing a new unrest.

Mary looks at me, frustration in her eyes.

"These women are major bonkers," Tabby says.

"You have no idea what they've suffered," I say. "You escaped your marriage. Most of them didn't."

She says nothing else.

"How about we let Rayna decide?" Ayan says.

Rayna's eyebrows shoot up.

"Rayna is head of our security," Ayan says. "Would everyone agree to let her decision stand?"

"Aye," the group says together.

I look at Juda. We both know what this means: we've lost any chance we had.

Rayna frowns as she scratches the back of her head.

"Think of Grace," I say to her. "Think of her room and her stuffed animals and her Nancy Drew books and—"

"Shut your hole," Rayna says. "I've known Grace a lot longer than you. You don't need to remind me who she is."

I draw back.

She fingers the gun in her holster. "I don't know why Mina brought these boys here. I don't know what she thinks they have to do with saving Grace or why she didn't just leave them on the street to fend for themselves."

I start to answer, but Mary gives me a look that tells me to stay quiet.

"But I do know she was smart enough to get off this island and survive long enough to make it back. She survived living with Uncle Ruho and escaped after he was killed. So she's not a complete dingbat."

I'm amazed by this compliment.

"If she believes that Grace has a better chance of staying alive if these boys stay here for an hour or two . . . " She pauses, taking a breath that seems to cause her pain. "Then we should let them stay an hour or two."

I'm speechless. *Rayna*, of all people, has come down on our side. Ayan's mouth has gone slack, but she soon gathers herself, telling the women, "Then it's decided. We will grant the boys two hours. Stay in your rooms if you don't want to encounter them. And that is that."

As Rayna walks back toward the hall, I say, "Thank you. I can't believe you—"

"Come with me to the computer room," she says, not interested in my gratitude.

First, I have one more very important thing to do. I approach Ayan and whisper, "I need to tell you something else. Will you join us?" She looks harried but nods. Once in the hall, I continue, "We have good reason to believe that bombs will be dropped on the city today. By the Apostates. You should be safe down here, but you shouldn't send Rayna or anyone else outside."

"Including your boys?" she says sharply.

"We'll leave just like we promised, but I thought you should know."

Ayan rubs a thumb against her lip. "How trustworthy is the information?"

"Very," I say. "I also need to tell you about Esther Hypat." I brief her on Mrs. Hypat's history and role in our escape. I assure her that Hypat knew nothing about the mercury in the water (a scheme that Ayan has known about since my last visit). I share my belief that Mrs. Hypat could make a decent leader. As I explain all of this, I think of Jordan Loudz's suggestion that we offer to kill Mrs. Hypat, and I have to hold back my rage.

"Fascinating," Ayan says. "Thank you for the information." She walks back into the main room. As we follow Rayna down the hallway, I hear Ayan say, "Ladies, we need to get ready for emergency procedure six."

Juda walks next to me. "You did really well."

"I got us two hours. Whoopee."

"It's a lot better than nothing. The way you spoke to those women was really impressive."

"I was just mad."

He smiles. "It works for you."

When we reach the computer room, he gives me a soft smile and says, "We've got it from here."

"What?" I say, confused. Does he think only the boys can understand a computer?

"Go see your grandmother," he says. "You'll find us after."

My chest grows heavy.

He's right. It's time to see Nana.

THIRTY-NINE

Before I leave, I ask Dekker, "Do you want to see Nana?" She's his grandmother, too, after all.

"Naw. She would barely know who I was. You go."

I'm relieved. I asked not because I want him to join me, but because it felt like the right thing to do.

Mary reaches into her cloak pocket and pulls out one of Mal's corn cookies. "Give this to your Nana."

"You might need it for yourself." We don't know how long it will take for the Laurel Society to access food.

"But I'm not starving." She places it in my hand.

"Thank you, Mary." Carefully, I put the cookie into a pocket, hoping it won't crumble.

I hurry to the infirmary, which I used to pass on the way to meals. It's a medium-sized room that's kept sparkling clean and always has the lights on.

Walking inside, I spot Nana at once, asleep in a bed in the corner. All the beds are full, and most of the women are as old, if not older than, Nana. Regina, the Laurel Society's healer, helps one woman drink water.

As I approach Nana, Regina looks up. Perplexed, she says, "Mina?"

I wave hello, and she gives me the signal to be quiet.

I've looked forward to this moment for so long, but for some reason, I'm nervous. She told me to leave the island and never come back. What if she's angry or disappointed? After everything that's happened today, the last thing I need is Nana's disapproval.

I pull a chair up next to her bed so I can watch her sleep. Like Rayna, her face is too thin. Her eyes look sunken and her skin has a gray sheen. She smells bad. I saw Rose when she'd gone less than a week without eating and she looked like her soul had been sucked out. Nana already looks dead.

I work hard to keep back the tears. I focus on her breathing.

Eventually, Regina comes around to give her water. She wakes Nana ever so gently, then helps her to sit up.

Nana squints at me with one eye open. "Mina?" She sounds bewildered.

I try to smile.

"Did I die?" she says, reaching out to me.

"No, Nana. I'm really here."

"Why?" she says, suddenly petulant. "I told you to leave!" She finishes her sips of water and shoos Regina away.

"I did. And then I came back. To see you."

"What happened to your lovely hair?"

I touch it self-consciously. "I had to dye it so people wouldn't recognize me."

To my relief, her eyes fill with excitement. "How was it out there?"

What do I tell her? I should focus on the positive. "The Apostates, they . . . didn't burn us at the stake. A family took me in, and they lived in a big house. There was a lot of electricity and light. I got to go to a big party and wear a pretty dress."

"Who cares about a dress. Are they going to help us? Did you tell them about the women here?"

That's what she thought? That the Apostates would come here and help the Laurel Society? "No, Nana. They only care about helping themselves."

She takes a deep rattling breath. "I should have known."

"Rayna says you need food?" I ask.

"Rayna is uptight."

"You don't look good, Nana."

"That's rude, Chickpea." She slumps back down into the bed.

"You need to eat something."

"Did you bring me a banana?" Her eyes regain some sparkle.

"No, but I do have this." Pulling the cookie out from my pocket, I wish it looked as appetizing as it did sitting in Mal's pretty tin.

"Thank you, but I'm not hungry."

"Yes, you are! I can tell by looking at you!"

"I never liked cookies. Too sweet."

I raise an eyebrow at her lie.

"You should give it to your mother."

"You're confused, Nana," I say, frustrated. "I think you need more sleep."

"Marga is here," she says, petulant again. "She'll want to see you."

Humoring her, I say to Regina. "Is my mother here?"

"Marga? Yes. She's in your grandmother's room."

My skin turns icy, and my chest grows heavy. The woman who was giddy to sell me into marriage is down the hall. "How did she get here?"

"I'm not sure," Regina apologetically. "I think your grandmother sent Rayna to find her when your father disappeared."

"Both my girls are with me," Nana says, patting my hand. "Life is good." She closes her eyes.

How can she forgive my mother so easily—forget everything that's happened between them?

"She's tired," Regina says. "I think you should go."

"I just got here."

"You can come back this evening, but she needs rest."

Nana opens her eyes, and worry must be written all over my face, because she says, "Don't fret. I won't croak while you're gone."

I force a smile. "You'd better not. I went to a lot of trouble to get here, and I have a lot to talk to you about."

"I refuse to miss one word," she says groggily. "And don't forget to give Marga the cookie."

I kiss her forehead, and Regina shoos me out of the infirmary.

And now, I suppose, I have to go see my mother.

FORTY

On my way to Nana's room, I stop and rethink. I should really tell Dekker that Mother's here. At least *he'll* be happy about the news. If he goes to see her, maybe I don't need to.

No law exists that says I have to. I'm relieved to know that she's safe, that she's not living on the streets, but I'm not prepared to interact with her. As hard as the last month has been, I have to admit I've experienced an amazing sense of liberation not being under her roof waiting for her next admonition or slap.

If I see her now, I can only imagine the criticisms waiting for me. The list of things I've done wrong must be long enough to wrap around the island.

When I open the door to the computer room, everyone turns to look at me. Expressions are grim.

"Any luck?" I ask.

"Not yet," Juda says. "But we've just gotten inside the system."

"As I've explained," Rayna says, "Because Grace wasn't scanned as a child, she won't be in the system. She may not come up at all, so I'm searching for any young women between the ages of sixteen and seventeen who were arrested today."

"Are there a lot?" I ask.

"More than you can believe," Mary says.

I'm suddenly regretful that Grace was scanned as *Daphne* while we were at the Cloisters, and not *Grace*. Without her teal cloak, Daphne no longer exists.

"How is your grandmother?" Silas asks.

"She's, um, tired. She's sleeping." I don't want to talk about how worried I am about her. "Dekker, I need to talk to you."

He looks suspicious.

"We won't be long," I say.

"Come straight back," Rayna says. "As soon as we find something, we need to be ready to act."

As soon as we've stepped out, I say, "Mother is here."

"What?" His eyes light up. "Where?" He looks around, as if she might be standing down the hall.

"She's in Nana's room."

"Take me," he says, as excited as I've seen him in weeks.

I stick my head back into the computer room. If I'm going to see Mother, I need backup, and Dekker doesn't count. "Mary, could I borrow you for a minute?"

Juda knows more about my history with my mother, but I can hardly walk into her room with a boy. Mary seems unlikely to put up with any nonsense. I've seen her physically fight with someone and it was impressive. I want someone who will inspire me to be tough, and I would be embarrassed to be any less fierce than Mary is.

"What's going on?" she asks as she joins us.

I lead them down the hall. "We're going to see my mother."

"Oh! I didn't know she was here."

"Neither did I."

"You don't sound major excited."

"Our relationship is . . . complicated."

When we reach the room, I hesitate, so Dekker knocks.

"Who is it?"

Hearing Mother's voice sends goose pimples across my skin. I feel five years old.

"Your son!" Dekker says with pride.

"Dek-k-k-ker?" she coos.

"You go in first," I say. "Have some time alone."

Without responding, he charges into the room. "Mother!" he cries, shutting the door.

Left behind, Mary and I look at each other with resignation.

"Are you going to tell me *why* your relationship is complicated?" she asks.

"She wanted me to marry Damon, no matter who he was or what he did to me. She tried to have me arrested by Twitchers." I shrug. "And she's just always preferred Dekker."

"How could anyone prefer that dimwit over you?"

I laugh. This is why I brought her.

She looks around, studying the structure of the hallway and ceiling. "Are we actually safe here? It's not exactly a fortress."

"They've hidden here for decades. Think how close those Twitchers were. They still didn't find them."

"I don't quite understand who these women are. If they're so smart and tough, why don't they escape like you did?"

"They're here to help people, not abandon them." I feel a pang of guilt as I say this. "They take in women trapped in unlivable circumstances, and, when they can, deliver food to women who need it. I'm pretty sure they gave food to Rose when Juda was just a baby." The baskets of food were either from the Laurel Society or Mr. Asher. I prefer to think they were from Ayan.

"Has your grandmother always lived here?"

279

"No," I say. "She lived in an apartment off Union Square. After she broke her hip, Ayan brought her here. They're old friends."

"Really? Benny."

"They were in the Tunnel together."

"Now *that's* a story I'd like to hear."

"Me, too, actually." Nana has always been stingy with the details. "Nana was sentenced to several years for teaching my mother to read. I've never heard why Ayan was there or for how long. Everyone is pretty private here."

"Do you think they miss men?"

I can't speak for all of them. Grace was very curious about Juda when he arrived. She had no experience with boys and was pretty thrilled to get to meet one. But other women seem happy to leave their men behind. I bring up something I've never really wanted to talk about. "They don't allow men here, but they also don't allow male babies."

She raises an eyebrow. "Are little boys banging on the door, begging to enter?"

"No, dummy. Some women flee their homes with their children. They can come here with their daughters but not their sons. Don't you think that's feeble?"

She studies the floor, as if she regrets her remark. "That's awful. They just abandon them?"

"The women fear what the boys will become; but also, they know that their husbands will look for their wives and daughters for a while, but they will spend a *lifetime* searching for a son."

"But still. To leave them behind . . . "

"I know."

"Are they . . . happy here?" she asks.

"I think . . . sometimes. It seems like a hard life, but I don't know if it's harder than what they had before."

"If they were willing to leave behind their sons, I can only guess that what they left behind was unendurable."

We look each other in the eyes. I'm glad that she isn't sitting in judgment of these women, which would be easy to do.

The door opens, and we hear Dekker saying goodbye to Mother. "I love you, too. I'll be back soon. I promise."

Stepping outside, he shuts the door. His smile disappears at once. "She looks terrible," he whispers.

"She probably needs to eat," I say.

"Don't upset her," he says.

"Maybe I shouldn't bother her," I say, sure that everything about me will "upset her." "Did you tell her I was here?"

He nods.

"It sounds to me like this is a band-aid you need to rip off immediately," Mary says.

I hate that she's right. Resigned, I knock on the door. "You should go back to the computer room," I tell Dekker.

He walks away, saying, "Show respect."

"Come in," Mother says.

Mary and I walk in the room to find her curled up in Nana's bed covered in what looks like every blanket and quilt in Macy's.

"Hello, Mother," I say.

Her head lifts, but her body doesn't. She looks frail and washed out but not nearly as sick as Nana. "Mina? . . . You look . . . strange."

"I changed my hair."

"Isn't it nice to see her though?" Mary says in a voice sweeter than a ripe peach.

Mother's face still only registers confusion. She looks at Mary, whose foreign accent must only be confounding her more. "Who are *you*?"

"I'm Mary, Mina's friend from Kingsboro."

When Mother doesn't respond, Mary adds, "From across the river."

"An Apostate?" Mother pulls her blankets in tighter.

"She's friendly, Mother. She doesn't want to hurt anyone."

"Even if I did, all I have is a veil and maybe, uh . . . " Mary pats her pockets. "A tissue."

I smile, but Mother does not. She spent my whole childhood telling me about the horrors of the Apostates, so one of them trying to be funny isn't going to change her mind.

"I would like to speak with my daughter alone," she says in the high-handed tone I grew up with.

"Okay." Mary heads for the door.

"Stop," I tell her. "I want Mary here."

Mary hesitates, not knowing what to do.

"Mary, *go*," Mother demands.

"We're no longer in your house, Mother, and I don't have to follow your rules. Either Mary stays or we both go. Your choice."

"Insolence. Ingratitude. I should've known that if I saw you again, this is what I would get."

"Ingratitude? What exactly is it you want me to be thankful for? Teaching me I was worthless? Selling me into a marriage to a lunatic? Or reporting me to the Twitchers?"

Her eyes flare with rage, but I can see she's too weak to come at me. She might even be too weak to lift herself from the bed. This should elicit sympathy from me, but it doesn't.

"I believe you're the one who should be grateful," I say. "Nana took you in and gave you a bed even after you betrayed her. She went to the Tunnel because of you. She should have spat in your face, and instead she welcomed you inside. But I know you're poison. It's only a matter of time before you betray the women here."

"*Me*? The *traitor*? Your father is dead, and it's your fault! If you'd gone through with your marriage everything would be fine. He would still be here; we would still be in our nice home; there wouldn't even be a war! You destroy everything you touch!"

Mary gives me an anxious look.

I've spent many nights thinking about the mistakes I've made and what I might have done differently. If I'd married Damon, I never would have met Ayan and Rayna, never would have learned about the poisoned water, never could have told father what was happening. Perhaps the Convenes would never have figured out that the water had mercury in it. They wouldn't have declared war on Uncle Ruho, and perhaps Mother and Father would still be living safely at home.

I shake the thoughts from my head. When I had these worries before, Grace reminded me that if I had behaved differently, "Convenes would still be dying."

"You're right, Mother," I say. "I told Father about the mercury in the water, and he destroyed the plant. He saved thousands of lives. He knew what he was doing. I'm sure you'd be happier if no one knew about the mercury, but that's a reality neither Father nor I could live with."

"Get out," she moans. "I'd like to go back to sleep now."

I can't leave yet. Mother might have the answer to one question that has plagued me since the day I left our apartment. "How is Sekena?"

Mother closes her eyes, pretending to sleep.

I reach into my pocket. "Nana wanted me to give you this. She wouldn't keep it for herself."

Her eyes flip open and widen when she sees the cookie. She grabs for it, but I pull it just out of reach. "How is Sekena?" I repeat.

"She joined the Matrons," she says through a clenched jaw.

"What? When?" I'm horrified.

"Weeks ago. She was too expensive for the Husks, and they knew they were never going to marry off that girl."

The sorrow in my heart is physically painful as I picture sweet Sekena donning a brown cloak. "Do you know which residence?"

"Give me the cookie first," she says.

"No."

She glares at me. "I think her mother said it was on 37th Street."

"You think?"

"I mean, she did."

I put the cookie on the table by the bed.

Mother's hand darts out from the blankets to snatch it. She sniffs it briefly and then devours it in three bites, like some feral animal.

She doesn't say thank you or good-bye. She rolls over to let us know she's done with us. We walk out, and once the door is shut, I can breathe properly again. "Thanks for staying with me," I tell Mary.

"Sure." She bites her lip. "Who's Sekena?"

"My best friend and neighbor. She, uh, well, it's sort of like she joined the Fallen. She can never get married or have a family."

"Oh. I'm sorry. That's . . . feeble."

We walk back toward the computer room. "I wish I could see her," I say. "I need to warn her about what's coming."

"Too bad she doesn't have a Tact."

"Yeah, I know."

"Those things your mom said about the war—my mother gives me a guilt trip about eating chocolate. She's got nothing on your mom."

I almost smile.

"Mina, when these women kick us out of here, the bombing

may have started. We don't know how long Jeremiah can delay it."

"We have to hurry back to Mal's or Dodo's," I say. "They'll put us somewhere safe."

"You think we can rescue Grace and then make it back to the Lower East Side in time?"

"It's possible," I say, even though I'm not sure it is. "But you can always stay here. They'd be happy to have you."

"I don't want to separate."

"Me either," I say.

When we arrive back at the computer room, I give her a hug. "Thank you."

"For what? I just stood there."

"And it meant everything."

When we walk inside, the energy of the room has completely changed.

Juda, unable to look at me, whispers, "We found her."

FORTY-ONE

"Where is she?" Mary asks.

When none of my friends answer, Rayna says, "In the Tunnel."

I close my eyes, wishing I could close the door and reenter. Maybe it would change the answer.

"How did they get there so fast? Didn't they want to question her? Didn't they—" I can't finish my sentence. Despair has seized me.

"She didn't talk," Rayna says. "She didn't give them any information, and this is her punishment." She smiles. "Brave little twerp."

"That's it, then," Dekker says, looking devastated. "We've lost her."

"Don't say that," I say, dizzy.

"*No one* escapes the Tunnel," he says quietly.

"That isn't actually true," Rayna says, sitting on the desk.

"What do you mean?" I say.

"A woman here escaped the Tunnel only days before her scheduled execution."

We all wait in dumbfounded silence.

"Ayan," Rayna says.

Ayan was in the Tunnel at the same time as Nana. I always assumed they were released together, but Ayan escaped? Hopeful, I say, "So you think she would know how to break out Grace?"

"No," she says, and I glare at her. Why did she bring it up?

"But the person who got her out might," she says, glaring right back.

"Who was that?" Juda asks.

Without looking at him, she says, "Me."

My mouth falls open. "You broke Ayan *out of the Tunnel?*"

"She got me out, too, in a way."

"What do you—" Mary asks.

Before she can finish the question, Rayna has grabbed a piece of paper and a pencil from a drawer. She tells us to gather round.

"Here's the Tunnel compound." She draws a large rectangle next to a small one. "This whole building is called the 'guardhouse.' The front part is the 'control room,' where the majority of the Twitchers stand guard for an attack. Outside is 'No Man's Land'—a block of concrete and barbed wire."

She taps on the larger rectangle. "This is the 'intake room,' modern construction. The prison cells reach back under the water from there. There are actually three tunnels—one for boys and men, one for women, and one for girls. Each tunnel is approximately a mile and a half long." She draws three long, thin rectangles behind the square. "There's no entrance or exit from the other side."

I shudder.

She draws a new big square disconnected from the others. "This used to be a bus station. Several streets branch out from it. This one . . . " She draws a looping street. " . . . is a ramp that leads to the guardhouse. It's been closed off for decades. We could use it to access the roof, most of which is ancient. It wouldn't take much to carve a hole into it."

The rest of us stare, dumbstruck. She can't possibly be serious.

"And then what?" Juda asks. "We'll be surrounded by Twitchers and thrown into cells ourselves."

Dekker nods in frantic agreement.

"Not if we make the hole in the right place." She draws an x on the corner of the building. "The Twitchers are stationed in the control room and at intake. But here . . . " She points to the x. "That's a weapons room. The guards only enter it during an emergency, so it's almost always empty. It's a safe place to enter, and we would gain access to firearms."

"How could you possibly know all this?" Dekker asks.

She holds his gaze for a long time, and then, seeming to decide she has no choice but to answer, says, "I used to work there."

"That's a bunch of crap," he says, standing taller. "Women aren't allowed to work."

"Nonetheless . . . " she says, trailing off. "We can argue about this or we can help Grace. Which is it going to be?"

Dekker's eyes narrow.

"We want to save Grace," I say. "Keep talking."

"Once we all have guns, we leave the weapons room and enter the cells. Grace will be in the north wing, with the other teenage girls."

"Are you saying we're going to shoot our way into the cells?" I ask.

"Do you expect them to give her to us politely?" she says.

"I won't use a gun," Silas says.

I don't feel good about it either. I've never shot anyone. "Can't we use Tasers instead?"

Her voice is tight. "You would have to be close enough to a Twitcher to touch them to use a Taser, and *they* will have guns. You'd be dead before you've even turned the Taser on."

"If it's a surprise attack, Tasers could work," Juda says.

"Six kids with no experience. You aren't exactly a stealthy bunch."

"We could be," I say.

"Who says we're all going?" Tabby says, arms crossed.

Of course.

"Maybe I want to stay here."

"Then stay here," I say. "No one will force you to help. Just like no one forced me or the others to help you when you killed Uncle Ruho."

She pouts. "That was different. We were escaping a horrible situation, not walking into one."

Looking her up and down, Rayna says, "It's better if she stays here,"

"Yeah, I can like, look after your grandmother or something," she says to me.

"Or her mother," Mary says, smirking.

"Sure, Tabby." I don't have time to worry about her right now. "Is everyone else in?"

As nervous faces greet me, my heart grows heavy. It hadn't occurred to me that not everyone would be ready and willing to do whatever was necessary to save Grace. But they aren't as close to her as I am. Why should they risk their lives for her? Rayna is suggesting a plan that seems like suicide.

"I'm going," Juda says, giving me a smile. He's always cared for Grace.

Rayna gives him a nod.

Mary's forehead creases. "I want to help, but I'm not sure how much of a *warrior* I am."

"We don't need warriors—" I say.

"I'm afraid, I mean, like, genuinely afraid I'll be a liability. I don't run fast. I don't know how to punch. I can't even make a decent *hoot* sound to warn you that people are coming."

I laugh, but no one else does. "I can't do any of those things, either," I say, "but it doesn't matter. Right, Rayna?"

"If she says she's useless, then—"

"I didn't say I was *useless*," Mary says, frowning. "I said I wasn't a warrior."

"I'll come," Silas says with a nervous voice, "but as I've said, I'm not using a gun."

"Rayna, if we all had Tasers," I say, "is there any way to make your plan work?"

She glowers at Silas, sighs, and looks at her drawing. "Maybe after dark, when the patrol is smaller—but we can't risk waiting. We have to do this before the bombing starts."

"Wouldn't the bombing distract the Twitchers?" Juda says. "They'd have a lot more to think about than some small bumps coming from the roof."

"It's too dangerous," Rayna says, shaking her head.

"Maybe wait until tomorrow," Tabby says. "For all you know, half the Tunnel will be blown to bits by then."

I give her a look that tells her to shut her mouth.

"You don't think Uncle Ruho's death is causing chaos in the guardhouse right now?" I ask, thinking about the Twitchers who left 34th Street. "They must be trying to sort out who's in charge and whether or not things are supposed to go on like normal."

Rayna wags her finger at me. "That's true." She stares at her map. "Okay, Mary, I may have a way you can help."

Mary perks up.

"The rest of us will leave here at ten-thirty a.m.," Rayna says. "At precisely a quarter to noon, you'll send a message to the Tunnel using this computer." She points to the machine behind her. "Your message will say 'All unessential staff to report to the nearest prayer center immediately.'"

Tabby rolls her eyes. "I could do *that*."

"That's brilliant," Juda says.

"How many men are unessential?" I ask.

"If they're being ordered to mourn their Divine Leader," Rayna says, tapping her hand on the desk, "I would imagine over half of them will leave. Maybe three-quarters."

I inhale deeply. Maybe this plan will work.

"And then what do I do?" Mary asks.

"That should be it," Rayna says. "If we only have to face twenty-five men instead of a hundred, we have a good chance of pulling this off."

"After we find Grace, how do we get out?" I say. "The same way we got in?"

"That depends on how many Tasers we can get our hands on."

"Will there be some in that weapons room?" Juda says.

"We can't count on it," she says. "Most Twitchers have one on their belts and don't ever lock it up."

I don't understand Rayna's plan completely yet, but I say, "I think I know where we can get Tasers." It's a long shot, but at least it's on the way to the Tunnel.

FORTY-TWO

After we've gone over Rayna's plan several times, she tells us we have twenty minutes to prepare to leave. I run to the infirmary to say goodbye to Nana. Seeing me, Regina frowns. "I told you not to return until tonight. You'll exhaust her."

"I won't be here tonight," I say, my guilt unfolding.

Once again, Nana is sleeping. I don't want to wake her. Her breathing is steady, which is a relief.

"I have to leave, Nana," I whisper. "I have to save Grace." Even though she doesn't stir, I feel compelled to keep talking. "I wish I could stay. More than anything. But Grace wouldn't leave me in the Tunnel, so I can't leave her. I don't know if I'll be back this time." We didn't think I'd be back when I went to Queens, but this feels different. "Our plan is, um, major bonkers. At least Rayna is going . . . "

I don't know what else to say to her sleeping body.

"Rayna told us she used to work at the Tunnel and that she broke out Ayan. I wish you were awake and could tell me about it. We didn't get to have our big talk. You haven't told me about being in prison. I didn't get to tell you all about Kingsboro and what life is like off the island. I wanted to tell you about Bees and Tacts and Refinement Training. And I read two novels— Grace's Nancy Drew book and *Jane Eyre*, which I didn't really like at first. But I've been thinking about it more, and I like how Jane creates her own family out of the friends she finds, not from the family she was born with." Realizing this could hurt Nana's feelings, I add, "*You'll* always be my favorite family. If I come back tonight with Grace, I'm going to bring you some food, I promise—a big feast, maybe a roast chicken like my first night here."

She opens her eyes half-way.

Grinning, I say, "You like the sound of chicken, huh?"

"You brought some?" she says.

"No, but you'll have food soon, I promise." I take her hand. "I have to leave."

"Again?" she says.

"I'm so sorry."

"Is it important?"

"Very."

"Okay. Well, bring me back something interesting."

"I'll try." I try not to let her see my sadness.

"God is proud of you," she says.

She's wrong. I don't pray anymore. I don't obey His rules. I'm not even sure which God is real.

"God loves you," I tell her. If God exists, then I know this is true.

"Find me as soon as you get back; tell me everything," she says, eyes closing again.

"I promise." I stand. Before I leave, I tell Regina that a food delivery is coming, and that she has to make sure Nana is among the first to eat. She says that she'll be on the top of the list. We both hope Nana will comply.

Wiping my eyes, I leave the infirmary to meet Rayna and

the others in the utility room. Rayna has put on a Twitcher uniform, while three other uniforms still hang from hooks. Grace and I lost the other two.

"Put this on," Rayna says, handing a uniform to Juda.

Unable to look at her, I say, "I thought you couldn't use them anymore, because of what Grace and I did."

"I don't think Twitchers will be taking the time to scan other Twitchers today," she says. "Too much going on."

Juda puts the jumpsuit on over the clothes Mal gave him.

Rayna hands the other two uniforms to Dekker and Silas.

"What will I do?" I say, dismayed.

"Act as our prisoner."

"Why can't Dekker be the prisoner?" I ask.

"Because I saw you as a Twitcher, and you were two feet too short," she says.

Dekker laughs as he puts on the jumpsuit.

Out of nowhere, Silas says, "Tabby's not a coward."

"No one said she was," Juda says.

"I'm sure you were thinking it, or that maybe she's just a wheedle. She likes Grace, a lot, she just . . . she told me she can't kill anyone ever again. And I get it."

"I get it, too," I say softly, thinking of Ruho's bloodied body.

"I just wanted you to know she's not a jerk, at least, not this time."

"She's better off here," Rayna says. "Every Teacher and Twitcher in the city will be looking for her soon." She gives the boys helmets and helps them connect the down-net wires to the uniforms. Within moments, I am surrounded by Twitchers.

She gives them a quick run-down on how the equipment operates and how she's wired the helmets to communicate with one another without Twitchers being able to intercept the messages. I'm frustrated not to be a part of their conversation circle, but Mary has given Grace's Tact to Silas, which means I can communicate silently with everyone except Rayna. *I'll be fine.*

"We only have four guns. I assume you know how to use one?" Rayna asks Juda and Dekker. They say they do, and she gives each of them a standard Twitcher handgun. She puts the other two in her own holsters.

Remembering an important detail, I warn them, "Don't tell the computer to do a second scan."

"Why?" Silas says in the metallic voice the helmet causes.

"Just don't," I say, recalling the mortifying moment I saw a Herald's naked body.

Mary and Tabby are waiting outside the room when we exit.

"I think I should come with you," Mary blurts.

"Your job is very important," Rayna says. "You have to stay."

"Tabby can do it."

"I taught you, and I don't have time to teach her. We have to leave." Rayna walks toward the main hall and we follow.

"I'm not doing enough," Mary insists.

Rayna doesn't stop. "You're two able bodies among a group of starving women. When the food arrives, help feed them. When the bombs come, comfort them. And if we don't come back, you'll be the only ones able to tell Ayan about the world outside of this island. Your survival is important."

Mary and Tabby's faces are solemn as they absorb this information. I hadn't considered all these details, that staying here is just as crucial as leaving.

When we reach the main room, Ayan is there with most of the women who were at breakfast. When she sees us, she stands, crossing her hands in front of her. "Rayna, this is outrageous. You can't possibly leave us today, of all days."

"It's Grace," Rayna says, walking toward the exit.

"I know, and I'm sorry. But this mission is pure insanity, and I cannot allow it."

Rayna stops dead. She removes her helmet, giving Ayan the blackest look I've ever seen. "You had no problem with the madness of the plan when it was *you* I was saving from the Tunnel."

Ayan raises an eyebrow. "At the time, we weren't responsible for the well-being of one hundred and thirty-four women. We were only responsible for ourselves." She gestures to the women. "You're choosing the life of one over the life of many."

Rayna looks at them. "Please stand if you believe I should leave Grace in the Tunnel."

None of the women move.

Rayna looks back at Ayan. "I'll be back before dark."

Ayan's face remains neutral, but her eyes betray her. She's terrified for us and rightly so.

Mary hugs all of us before we enter the dark hallway that leads to the street. "See you soon, Mina," she says. "If you don't come back, I'll kill you."

Tabby, surprisingly, hugs me and Silas. She says nothing, but worry darkens her features.

I'm relieved when Dekker says, "Let's go." I don't want one more second to change my mind.

FORTY-THREE

Soon we're standing on 35th Street, four Twitchers surrounding one married girl in a veil.

We head west, but instead of continuing across 35th toward the Tunnel, I lead them up 7th Avenue. The old bus station where Rayna wants to go is only eight blocks away, but we have a stop to make first. I hope my idea works.

When we arrive at the Matron Sanctuary on 37th Street, I'm impressed with the old, elegant building. Made up of large red and white stones, the front is completely intact with arches over the doors, like at the Cloisters.

"Can we just knock?" I ask Rayna.

"I think you should knock and we should hide," she says. "Twitchers are not likely to make them friendly."

"Don't go far," I say.

"We'll be able to hear you if you yell," she says, leading the boys away.

An imposing knocker sits in the middle of the old door. Do they still use it? Reaching up, I grasp it, and, feeling the weight, realize I'll need both hands. Feeling foolish, I stand on tiptoe, grab it, and pound it against the door. The bang is loud enough that I don't think I need to do it twice.

The vibrations haven't finished when the door cracks open.

"Who's there?" an older woman says.

"Mina Clark. I'm here to see Sekena Husk, please."

"It's not Tuesday."

"Excuse me?"

"Visiting day is Tuesday."

"I didn't know. Please. I have something for her."

"What do you have?"

"Perhaps you would like one, too?" I lean forward, showing her a battery. This was Rayna's idea.

The door opens a bit more. "How do I know it's live?"

"I swear on the Prophet."

"You shouldn't swear," she says, snatching the battery from my hand. "You have ten minutes. Go up the stairs to your left; she's the second door on the right."

When I walk into the building, I'm a bit astonished by the space. It's like a grand room from the Cloisters, but the ceiling is much higher and the colors are much brighter. The chamber is so quiet and peaceful that I find myself wanting to stay for a while, to sit and absorb everything that's happened over the last week. To think about Father.

But there's no time.

I go up the staircase and arrive at Sekena's door, hoping she isn't angry at me for leaving without saying good-bye. I wouldn't blame her.

Knocking gently, I hear, "Yes?"

When I enter, I'm shocked to see the most barren room I've ever encountered, starker even than Jiol's apartment. A small mattress fills up almost the entire space.

Sekena sits cross legged on the mattress. She wears a simple brown sheath and her hair has been cut to her chin.

Without her floral pajamas and warm smile, she looks a decade older.

"Can I help you?" she asks, confused.

I remove my veil.

Even then, she doesn't recognize me at first, which breaks my heart. But as soon as I say, "Sekena, it's—" she cries, "Mina!"

Hopping up, she grabs a strand of my dyed hair. "Is that really you?" She laughs, so I laugh, too. "Red? Really? I was always so jealous of your blonde!"

I hug her as hard as I can. "I missed you *so much!*"

"I missed you, too."

"Are you okay? How are they treating you?"

"I'm fine. It's all . . . fine."

I hold her out in front of me. "Fine? You're a Matron. How can it be fine?"

"I was terrified the first week. I expected the women here to be monsters. But most of them are actually kind of sweet, and I like the quiet and the time to pray."

"What about the horrible Matrons at all the prayer centers?"

"The Matrons that volunteer for those jobs are very ambitious and no one likes them. They keep to themselves here."

"You're sure? I came here to rescue you." This is half of my plan: break out Sekena and send her to the Laurel Society.

She laughs. "I don't need rescuing. Truly."

"Oh."

"I'm still very happy to see you," she says. "I feared the worst."

"The worst might still happen."

"Why?"

"I came to rescue you but also to ask for your help."

"Me? How could I possibly help you?"

301

I'm embarrassed to ask her for something when I haven't seen her in so long. "I need Tasers. Lots of them. And the only place I could think of that would have them . . . was a Matron Sanctuary."

She screws up her mouth. "Your logic isn't bad, but I don't have access—"

"We're going to break into the TUNNEL," I blurt.

Her eyes grow huge. "That's crazy." She pulls me onto the mattress to sit beside her. "Who is 'we?'"

"Dekker and a few others. We *have* to save our friend Grace. If we don't get Tasers, then we have to use guns, and then we might end up killing people."

She shakes her head, looking terrified. "Murder is the worst sin."

"I know, which is why I came to you. I knew you'd understand and help us." I feel awful taking advantage of Sekena's God-fearing nature, but I don't have any other ideas. "What will happen if you get caught helping yourself to Tasers?"

She shrugs. "I don't know. I don't think anyone has ever done it before."

"Tell me where they are, and we'll break in and steal them. Then you won't be in trouble." I feel better about this idea.

"Meet me in back of the building in fifteen minutes," she says.

"What? Why?"

"I'll bring you as many Tasers as I can find."

"I don't want you in trouble. I—"

"God will protect us, because it's for a just cause: preventing death," she says, nodding with certainty. "Fifteen minutes."

She scoots me out the door.

Leaving, I walk in the direction I saw Rayna go with the boys. They must be watching out for me, because they appear almost at once on the next block. I walk around to the back of the Sanctuary and they follow. A rancid garbage bin provides a feast for dozens of rats who scatter when we appear.

I explain Sekena's instructions to the others, and we wait.

"This helmet is really hot," Dekker complains in a muffled voice.

"At least you can't smell the garbage," I say, nauseated by the stench.

I'm nervous to be standing here long, but with four Twitchers, who's going to mess with us?

Finally, the back door opens, and Sekena comes down the ramp wheeling a laundry cart. She has a proud expression on her face until she sees the Twitchers next to me. She quickly puts on her brown veil.

"It's okay," I say. "They're friends."

Pushing the cart toward us, she pulls out a few dirty sheets to reveal dozens of silver Taser tubes.

"Whoa!" Dekker says. "Nice job, Sekena!"

Sekena recognizes Dekker's voice and the back of her neck goes as red as a cherry tomato.

"How did you get so many?" Juda asks. He, Silas, and Dekker load their pockets with the tubes.

"A Sanctuary on Lafayette Street shut down, and they sent us all their supplies."

I put Tasers in my cloak pockets, and then we add more to the two black canvas bags that Rayna brought. "What will happen when the other Matrons figure out these are missing?" I ask, worried.

"I'll just say that an order came in from Uncle Ruho to send them somewhere else," she says with a smile.

"She doesn't know," Silas says.

Before I can say it with any gentleness, Dekker says, "Man, Ruho is *dead*."

"What?" Sekena says, shocked. "That's impossible."

"It's true," I say. "I'm sorry." She always had great respect for our Divine Leader.

"But we would have heard," she says.

Of course the men know before the women. "They told the Twitchers a couple of hours ago. I'm sure they're going to tell you soon."

"What will it mean? He has no son!" she says.

I take both her hands in mine. "Everything will be fine." I tell her about Mrs. Hypat and then warn her about the bombing.

"We need to pray," she says. "We ALL must pray at once."

"Praying is fine, but you have to do it somewhere safe," Rayna says. "Do you have someplace underground to go?"

"Uh, yes," Sekena says. "Our storeroom is downstairs."

"Perfect," Rayna says. "Make all the Matrons go there now."

"They'll want to know why," Sekena says.

"Tell them I told you about the bombing . . . that um, Uncle Ruho had a vision before he died about the city being destroyed." The Matrons are more likely to believe this than the reality of Ram and the Ascension.

"You should join us," Sekena says, "if it's so dangerous."

"Time for us to go," Rayna says, taking one of the bags.

I hug Sekena again. "You're amazing. I knew you would come through." When I release her, she looks more agitated than ever. "I'm sorry to come and go so quickly and to deliver such bad news."

"It's not your fault," she says. After a moment, she adds, "Is it?"

Even now, as my oldest friend, she's able to sense a bit of the truth of things. I'm not sure how to answer. How can I ever know if my actions led to Ruho's death? I pick up the remaining bag. "Take care of yourself," I say. "I love you."

"I love you, too, Mina. Please be careful."

When we're back on the street, I don't feel good about what I've done. We got the Tasers, but we left Sekena behind, terrified. We've given her the horrible task of telling her fellow Matrons that their Divine Leader is dead. My only consolation is that despite the harsh living conditions, Sekena seemed happy, and that warms my heart. At least she is surrounded by people she cares for.

I have to stop thinking about her, because getting the Tasers was the easiest part of our plan. Now we have to get into the Tunnel without being noticed, which seems as likely as drilling a hole into a hive without disturbing any wasps.

FORTY-FOUR

Rayna holds my elbow like a prisoner as we walk across 37th Street. Juda walks ahead while Dekker and Silas bring up the rear.

My mind buzzes with frightened energy, and I need distraction. "When we left Manhattan," I say to Rayna, "you whispered something in Grace's ear. What was it?"

"She'll tell you herself," she says, looking up and down 7th Avenue.

Working up the nerve to ask the bigger question, I say, "I was wondering, um, what job you did when you worked in the Tunnel?"

When she says nothing, I'm not surprised.

"Does it matter?" she says half a block later, startling me.

"No. I just wondered how you knew so much, and like Dekker said, it's illegal for women to work, so . . . "

She looks at me, then looks away. "I may not make it out today, so who cares what I tell you. I know so much . . . because I was a Twitcher."

I can't see her face and she can't see mine, but my expression is complete and total awe. "What do you mean? They never noticed you were a woman? How could they overlook your voice? Grace and I pretended, but it was only for a few hours, and we didn't have to talk to anyone and—"

"I wasn't a woman, okay?" she says, her characteristic growl taking over her voice.

My awe turns to confusion. Rayna believes she used to be a man?

"In olden times," she says, "it happened a lot. I mean, it still happens . . . Women are born in men's bodies and vice versa. I was born in the wrong body. It's not a big deal."

"Then why don't you tell people?"

"It's not a big deal to me or the people I love. It's a big deal to the government—a capital offense."

How can something I've never heard of be punishable by death? I remember Silas and our conversation on the way here —his fear of being discovered as a molley in the Cloisters.

"Do you like girls or boys?" I ask.

"What does that have to do with anything?"

"I don't know. I just—"

"Who I like doesn't define who I am."

"Right." I feel stupid for asking the question. "Is that why you don't trust men? Because you used to be one?"

"That's stupid. I don't trust men because I worked with them 24/7 and heard the way they spoke when women weren't around. I saw the way they treated female prisoners and took advantage of their helplessness. I suffered at their hands because I wasn't the kind of man they wanted me to be."

"But those were *Twitchers*, not normal men."

"Twitchers *are* normal men."

"I don't believe that's true."

"Obviously, or you wouldn't be hanging out with these

moronic boys. You're going to live a lot longer if you dump them."

I take a deep breath. I won't get into this fight again. She has her reasons for distrusting males, and I've already said that I refuse to make a blanket judgment against their entire sex.

"Once we're inside the Tunnel," she says, "only worry about yourself and Grace. If you concern yourself with everyone, you don't have a good chance of surviving."

"But your plan . . . You said we could all get in and get out again."

"I never said that. I said we could get Grace out. I never said how many of us would be with her."

Turning my head to look at the boys, I sense bile creeping up my throat. "They need to know that."

"They do. I made it very clear when you went in to find your Matron friend."

"They're very brave."

"I confess I was impressed they still came. Especially your brother."

"He, uh, seems to have some feelings for Grace."

Rayna snorts. "She can do much better."

"I know."

I think about everything Rayna has said and everything she's experienced. I have a lot of other questions, especially about how she looks so much like a woman now, but I decide I'd better keep them to myself or I might really piss her off.

Out of nowhere, she says, "Remember to be a pickle."

"Huh?"

"That's what I whispered to Grace when the two of you left. Her whole life, she was so goddamned nice, I worried about her. I thought if she ever had to go up-top, she'd be eaten alive. When she was young, I'd say, "Sweet is fine, but sometimes you have to be a pickle. You have to know how to be acidic, if you're going to survive."

Straining to remember a time Grace was disagreeable, I say, "I don't think she listened very well."

"No. She's a cupcake, through and through."

We turn up 8th Avenue, and soon the decrepit old bus terminal comes into view. My heart beats harder and louder, like raindrops becoming hail.

As Rayna said, the bus station was abandoned decades ago. The building is huge, and I don't know why it was never turned into something new. I haven't been inside it before. With its broken windows and stained walls, it always struck me as a place for vagrants and thieves.

As we enter through a busted door, I feel better with one hand on a Taser. The scent of urine and canned beans assaults me from all sides. I was right about vagrants living here.

Rayna guides us up a broken escalator and then another. When the darkness becomes overwhelming, she flips up the light on her helmet. The boys begin to do the same, but she stops them, whispering, "Let's stay as unnoticed as possible."

As she takes us up yet more escalator steps, I'm amazed at the magnitude of the building. It looked big from the outside, but from the inside, I feel like we're back at Madison Square Garden. We pass tiny restaurants in stalls that are rotting from the inside out. I'm sure if I explored, I'd find at least one family of raccoons living like kings.

A board overhead says Albany, Amherst, Baltimore, Boston, Falmouth—all the places you could go without thinking, back in Time Zero.

We enter what looks like a parking lot. The skeleton of what was once a bus lies in a corner, stripped of all its parts. The remaining two sides lean against each other, and a flickering light inside throws moving shadows against the wall.

People sit inside with a lit fire. As soon as I have the thought, I smell some sort of roasting animal. I don't want to know what it is.

"This is where the busses picked up passengers," Rayna says, ignoring the people by the fire.

We cross the parking lot and, just as Rayna promised, paved ramps lead outside the building.

"One of those will take us to the Tunnel?" Dekker says.

Nodding, she walks toward the one on the left. I swallow, telling myself everything is going according to plan. As soon as I step outside, I'm unnerved by how high up we are—probably three stories. The ramps form a little roadway in the sky. Unfortunately, they're not made for pedestrians. They're narrow with no sidewalks, and if a bus drove up, we'd all be pancakes. *Mina, no bus has driven this way in decades.* I concentrate on Rayna, who marches boldly ahead. *Her purpose is your purpose. Think of Grace.*

We walk further and the ramp curves. Before long, we can see the Tunnel.

The front part, the control room, is a gray square box not much wider than a one-way street. This is where the Twitchers bring prisoners in—it's the only entrance—and you have to pass through No Man's Land to get there. Rayna described No Man's Land as nothing but concrete and barbwire, but she hadn't explained that it's ten feet below street level, making it look like the most ominous empty swimming pool you've ever seen. By putting it lower than the control room, the Twitchers have guaranteed that they can fully see everyone approaching and easily take a shot if they need too.

The building behind it is huge and more modern. Neither structure scares me. It's what's behind them—the cells that reach under the water. What if we're inside and the tunnels are so old and weak that they collapse on top of us?

Stop it, Mina.

Think of Grace, sitting in a cell, alone. If not for me, she would still be in Macy's, reading in the library, sipping tea. I owe her this.

Rayna stops walking, and I don't know what she's doing. We haven't reached the end of the ramp. In fact, we're still very high above the ground. She walks to the ledge, looking over.

When we join her, I see that we're practically above the control room.

"Why are we stopping?" Juda asks.

"We're waiting to see if your girl Mary does her job," Rayna says, looking at her watch. "It's ten till noon."

"How will we know if it—?" Silas asks.

His question is interrupted by the prayer bell, which comes out of his Twitcher helmet. Shocked, he takes a step back. Juda and Dekker stand frozen as the bell blasts their ear drums. When this happened to me, I thought I was having a seizure. I hope Rayna warned them.

I grab Silas' arm and tell him everything is okay. Although he can't hear me, I assume he can read my lips.

He nods.

The bell finally stops, meaning people have ten minutes to reach a prayer center.

Rayna points down to the front of the building where Twitchers are starting to stream out the door.

Recovered, Dekker says, "Let's just shoot them as they come out."

Rayna's head turns slowly to him. "The whole point is to make our odds better. We can't win against a hundred men, even if you're Billy the Kid."

"Who?" Dekker says.

Tempted to duck, I ask, "Can they see us?"

312

"Get in back of me," Juda says. He's right. I'm the only one who looks out of place here.

From behind him, I ask, "How many are leaving?"

"It looks like a lot," Dekker says.

"Forty-seven so far," Silas says.

I'm impressed he's counting, but that doesn't sound like much. "They aren't finished yet, right?"

"They're still exiting." Juda sounds frustrated. "But the numbers are thinning."

Another few minutes pass. I find myself praying unreasonably that they'll *all* leave, that the prison will be empty, and that we'll be able to waltz in and nab Grace.

"It's noon," Rayna says. "No one else will be leaving. We have maybe an hour until those guards come back." She then throws her bag across the chasm that separates us from the guardhouse below. It lands with a thud on the roof.

"What are you doing" I ask.

"Time to jump," she says.

FORTY-FIVE

"Jump?"

The building is not below us. It's five feet south, leaving a *substantial* gap between it and us. The length of my arms end to end would cover the gap, but not by much, and because of the ledge, you can't even get a running start. And the distance to the ground is . . . not survivable. "Are you insane?"

"This is the only way," she says.

"It can't be," I say. "What about the rest of the ramp?"

"Look for yourself," she says, gesturing forward.

I walk ahead, telling myself that there's another way—we can take the ramp to the street level and then climb up the side of the guardhouse onto the roof. I'm much better at climbing than I am jumping.

I stop short when I see what Rayna sent me to see: the ramp ceases to exist. Someone has blown an enormous hole into it so that it's impossible to walk one step further. Dizzy, I take in the chunks of steel and concrete fractured on the streets below.

I storm back to Rayna angrily. Why didn't she warn us

about this? If making a deadly leap was part of the plan, she should have told us. I could have prepped myself.

The boys are gathered around Rayna, who's already climbed onto the ledge of the ramp. As soon as I see her standing up there, I know that I *never* could've prepared myself for this.

"Why didn't you warn us?" I ask her.

"I told you the street was closed off," she says, much too calmly. She bends her knees, swings her arms, and leaps into the air. I close my eyes, waiting for her scream as she falls to her demise.

When there's no sound but feet landing on gravel, I peek. She's safely on the roof of the guardhouse.

I can't believe it.

"I sure wish I had some StickFoot," Silas says, lifting a leg onto the ledge.

How can he be so brave? Maybe it was all those nights climbing in and out of his bedroom window.

He counts to three and jumps, landing almost as quietly as Rayna.

Dekker, Juda, and I are left.

"You should go next," Juda tells me.

I can't do this. No way.

If I don't jump what will happen? I'll sit here in the dark, waiting to see if the others have found Grace, knowing that they're one person short of our plan?

"It's Dekker's turn," I say.

To my astonishment, Dekker says, "Okay." He heaves himself onto the ledge. He's so tall, he seems to be higher up than the others. "If I don't make it, tell Grace . . . I mean, just make sure you get her out."

With a grunt, he jumps and I feel like I'm soaring with him. He lands on the guardhouse, heavy and awkward, tumbling onto his knees. I flinch, imagining the gravel cutting into his flesh. He doesn't cry out, just stands and brushes off his jumpsuit.

"It's your turn," Juda says.

"Why isn't it yours?" I say.

"Because I want to help you," he says.

"You can't." He can't lift me or carry me or do anything to help me get across this abyss. I can only leap.

"But I want to."

"Then get across safely," I say. Watching him fall would be as bad as falling myself.

"We'll do it together," he says. "Like crawling down the side of the Forgiveness Home."

The Forgiveness Home. A lifetime ago. Solomon and Kalyb were so frightening. In the face of this lair of Twitchers, they seem like kittens.

"You don't have to do it," Juda says.

Grace is waiting inside. Bombs are going to fall. "Yes, I do."

"Give me that," he says, and I hand him my bag of Tasers. He hurls it over to Rayna, where it lands next to her feet, skidding on the gravel. If only I could make it over as easily.

My whole body trembles as I put my veil into my pocket. For this, I need to fully SEE. I pull up my cloak and climb clumsily onto the ledge.

"Don't look down," Juda says. "Concentrate on the other side."

I breathe deeply.

"All the power will come from your legs. So bend deep and get lots of spring."

"Have you done this before?" I ask.

"What? You haven't?"

Picturing his wry smile underneath his helmet, I bend my knees as low as I can go.

He counts. "One . . . two . . . three!"

We fly into the air.

The roof is impossibly far. There's no way I'm going to make it. Juda's shadow darts by me. I can't reach out for him or anyone else. There's nothing to do but fall.

I shriek as my hands catch the edge of the building. I dangle from the roof, ready to lose my grip and slide to my death. A hand comes shooting down to grab me. It pulls me up like I weigh no more than a pillow.

As I lie on the gravel ground, I expect to see Juda's face hovering above me, but instead I see Rayna's. "Thank you," I say.

"If you'd fallen, the entire control room would've seen you. You would've ruined our plan."

"That would've been terrible for you," I manage to say between breaths.

She pulls me up to standing. "Let's hope they didn't hear your squeal." To everyone, she says, "No more talking."

I bend over. I don't want to talk; I want to cry at how close I just came to dying. I gulp in large mouthfuls of air, trying to ease my stinging chest.

Juda, who seems to have had no problem with the jump, rushes to me.

He whispers, "Are you all right? That was—"

I grasp him. He grips me tightly in return.

"You scared me to death," he says.

"Never make me do that again," I say, knowing full well he didn't make me.

"Never," he says. He hugs me closer. "Can you keep going?"

Does he think that after I survived that jump I'm going to give up? "Of course."

He taps his helmet. "Rayna's telling me to hurry."

She's walked off with Dekker and Silas.

The roof is flat, with air vents scattered about. After all the solar panels of Kingsboro, the space looks bare and wasteful.

We creep along, trying to make as little noise as possible, toward the eastern corner where the X was on Rayna's map. Juda's boots crunch with each step on the gravel, and I remember how difficult they were to walk in. Surely the Twitchers below can hear us.

Arriving at the right spot, Rayna kneels on the ground. Scanning the roof, Dekker and Juda pull out their guns, while Silas takes out his Taser. I pull a Taser out of my pocket, searching the area for danger.

Is someone here? I type to Juda with my Tact.

He doesn't answer, continuing to search the roof. Is his helmet interfering with his Tact? What will happen if we get separated and I can't communicate with anyone?

I try Dekker. *What's happening?*

It takes a moment, but he types back: *Rayna make hole. We guard.*

Breathing a sigh of relief, I respond, *Send MSG 2 Juda. Tact not working.*

Rayna pulls a hunting knife out of her bag. After clearing away gravel, she feels the surface of the roof with her hand. She finds a blistered area, which she explained indicates water damage. She hacks at the exterior layer with the knife, peeling it away like old cardboard. As soon as she hits wood, she signals Dekker, who joins her in pulling out the rotted plywood. I want to help, but I'm not wearing their protective gloves.

The whole process takes longer than I'd like, but to my amazement, when they finish, there's a hole leading into the building. I confess, I'm nervous to stick my head down there. What if a Twitcher is standing with his gun, just waiting for a target?

Before I know it, Rayna has disappeared into the hole. I rush to look down. She's standing in a dark room surrounded by large guns hooked into the walls. She was right about the location. *Bless her.*

Juda throws Rayna's bag down after her and she catches it.

Now u, Dekker tells me in a Nod.

Determined to be brave this time, I return my Taser to my pocket. Juda offers me his hands and lowers me into the unlit room. When he releases me, I fall several feet, but it's nothing compared to the leap I made from the ramp.

After Juda tosses me my bag, he hops down. I'm amazed by his agility. Dekker comes next and then Silas. Looking around the weapons room, I see nothing to stand on to get back up to the roof. If our plan doesn't work, we're trapped.

I want to go through the layout of the Tunnel one more time, but Rayna is busy examining the guns on the wall. She's like my mother trying to choose the freshest produce. She touches and turns each one, picking them up and feeling them in her hand. I wouldn't be surprised if she thumped one like a melon.

She finally decides on a massive, scary-looking thing that I saw some of the guards carrying at Ruho's wedding. Approaching the wall, Dekker reaches out to grab the same enormous gun, but he jerks back his hand, looks at Rayna, and walks away. I wish I knew what Rayna just said to him. I bet it was withering.

Rayna motions to my face. What does she want?

Dekker messages me: *Put on veil.*

It's already so dark. I don't want to see even less, but I take the veil out of my pocket and put it on. Rayna walks to the large metal door to our left and is about to enter a code into the keypad, when I say, "Wait!"

She freezes.

320

I'm not sure what I need to say—I just know I'm not ready for her to open the door. "No matter what happens, I love you all."

Rayna told us not to speak, so the boys place their hands on my shoulder. I take this as "We love you, too."

Rayna, not interested in our circle, secures her huge gun into a strap on her back. She raises her fingers to form a four and a five. She's telling us we have only *forty-five minutes* left.

She punches a red button, and I hear the metal door hiss open.

FORTY-SIX

When we walk out of the weapons room, we're in a shadowy hallway with a bright light beckoning us at the other end. Rayna explained that we'll pass the mess hall and kitchen before reaching the control room and intake area. The prison cells branch out from intake, where five Twitchers are normally posted. We're hoping that at least one of them has gone to pray.

We stride quietly down the hall, Juda holding my right arm, Rayna holding my left. I wish I had a Taser in my hand, but it would blow our cover. I don't even have my bag anymore; Juda is carrying it across his back. I feel helpless.

We reach the control room, where the majority of the Twitchers are—a nest of vipers that we *cannot* disturb. The door is thick and metal, so at least they can't see us passing. We turn left, and soon I'm blinded by bright light. As my eyes adjust, I see a guard tower standing in the middle of a hangar big enough to hold the row of tanks we saw in Bryant Park. The illumination is caused by floodlights, which reflect off corrugated steel walls. The ground is a resurfaced blacktop, nicer than any street in Manhattan.

"It's so empty," I whisper.

"Nothing for anyone to hide behind," Rayna says.

She's right. You can see every corner of this room; a roach couldn't pass by without being noticed.

On the wall is the largest portrait of Uncle Ruho I've ever seen. One story tall and one story wide, his face seems to rebuke me, as if it knows why I'm here.

I try to remind myself that he can't hurt me anymore.

The portrait is not nearly as daunting as the doors that lead to the cells. As we walk toward the guard tower, the doors, originally built as floodgates, appear larger and larger. They're more immense than I could've ever imagined, each as big as the side of a house. We'll never be able to open one on our own, so this part of the plan is very delicate.

The Twitchers look down from their tower as we approach. I'm relieved there are only two of them, but with their semiautomatic weapons in hand, they look as lethal as twenty men.

The taller guard walks down the tower steps.

"He's annoyed they didn't know we were coming," Juda whispers to me.

The Twitcher is communicating using his helmet. Everyone but me will receive his messages, which makes me very anxious.

When the guard reaches us, Juda, as rehearsed, says, "Prisoner for tunnel three."

The Twitcher snorts. "We're running out of room. How old?"

"Fifteen."

"We'll see." His Senscan powers on, turning red.

I feel lightheaded. Juda gives my arm a subtle squeeze of support.

As the guard scans me from head to toe, the portrait of Ruho disappears and is replaced with data about me.

Mina Clark, 15, Deserver, 5' 5", 134 lbs. FUGITIVE. PRIORITY ONE. MURDER ON TWO COUNTS.

Please, God and everything holy, don't let them scan me again. My naked body would show up on that huge screen. I couldn't bear the degradation.

"She's a bona fide murderer," the man says, grabbing my ear. "Maybe she shouldn't go in a cell. Maybe she needs to go straight to the executioner."

"I have my orders, sir." Juda's voice is full of aggression.

The pinching on my ear is unbearable, and I don't know if it's better to acknowledge the pain or stay silent. Which will satisfy this man?

I whimper, and he seems to be happy, because he says, "Put her in cell block eight."

I swear my heart beats for the first time in minutes.

He releases my ear. I assume he messages the second guard, because the other man leaves the tower, walking down the narrow steps with what looks like a length of pipe in his hand. He's a short but muscular man. He and the first guard walk to the floodgate on the right, which has a thick metal wheel in the middle. The short Twitcher attaches his pipe to a spoke of the wheel, creating a long handle. Grunting, he pulls down, which forces the wheel to slowly turn. At the same time, the other Twitcher releases several huge valves along the seam of the door.

During Time Zero, these doors were used to keep the tunnels from flooding, so they had to be air tight. Large vents have been cut into the wall above, I guess so the prisoners can breathe. As the floodgate unseals, it releases a loud wheezing sound. Taking in the size of these men, I know that the door could never be opened with less than two people. Rayna warned us each door weighs *twenty-five tons.*

Our group is moving toward the open entrance, when the

325

short Twitcher says in a mocking tone, "You need four guards for that scrawny girl?"

I look to Rayna, panicking. Dekker's the first to respond. "She's important. We were ordered to see for ourselves that she ended up in a cell."

"We've got it from here," the Twitcher says. "Go pray for his Holiness."

"We have to follow orders," Juda says.

"Your Divine Leader is dead," the guard says. "You should honor him."

"We need—" Dekker says.

"You have your new orders," the tall guard says.

A tense silence fills the air. We can't use our guns against them, or someone in the control center might hear. We can't use our Tasers, because the men could use their helmets to send out a warning before they're struck.

"Y-yes, sir," Dekker says, backing away.

"I'll make sure she makes it to the cell," Juda says.

"Fine," the short Twitcher says. "The rest of you report to the prayer center."

My hands shake. *This isn't the plan.* If Rayna, Dekker, and Silas leave, how will Juda and I make it out?

Rayna says nothing, because her voice will give her away. It must be killing her to let the boys do all the talking. She, Silas, and Dekker walk back toward the control room.

"Let's go," Juda says to me with brusqueness. Taking my arm, he leads me quickly through the opening in the floodgate. Any second I expect one of the guards to tell him to leave, too, but behind us I hear the closing of the door, its gears squealing like a dying pig.

Once it has sealed us in, I say, "What are we going to do—"

"Rayna sent a message while the men were talking. She said they'd go back to the weapons room to wait for us."

"Do you think the guards will notice they didn't leave the building?"

"We don't have time to wait and see," he says.

"Ask her if she knows how to open the door from the inside," I say.

After a few moments, he says, "She's not responding. Maybe the signal can't pass through the door?"

I try contacting Dekker with my Tact, but he doesn't respond either.

Nyek.

I try to stay calm. We have to take things one at a time, and how many of our forty-five minutes have already gone by?

"Let's keep going," I say, determined not to think about the door yet.

We walk into the tunnel, which is badly lit. The air on this side of the floodgate is heavy and damp, smelling of mildew, unwashed bodies, and disease. I hear people ahead, but nothing that sounds like conversation—only the small gasps and moans of those who can barely breathe. I'm filled with a deep terror at what I may see as we walk forward.

The first cells we come upon are crammed with young girls. Sour, fetid hay lines the floors, probably to sop up the water dripping from the fine cracks in the ceiling. Thinking of the water damage on the roof of the weapons room, I can only imagine how old and wrecked this tunnel must be. How long until the roof caves in and the river crushes everyone inside?

I force myself to stop picturing it.

I scan the faces for Grace. The girls are of every age, color, shape, and size. Some sleep, some stand, some sit and stare at nothing. You can guess how long each girl has been here by the state of her clothing—some cloaks are long and barely stained, and some are so threadbare they look like lace.

"Stay close to me," Juda says. "There could be more Twitchers in here, and you're supposed to be my prisoner."

None of the girls look at us as we pass, telling me that a guard bringing in a new girl is not an event of note. Grace must be terrified, sure she will never leave this place. I think I would be screaming, or crying, or both. We keep walking; the number of cells is staggering. Each one is filled to bursting.

"This is so awful," I whisper.

I spot a girl who can't be older than five. Her delicate face, covered in muck, makes me want to weep. What in the world can she have done to have landed here? Most likely, her mother committed a crime and this ill-fated child was born inside that cell.

How will we be able to search the whole tunnel in the time we have left? Rayna said it's a mile and a half long. The more time we take, the more likely we'll be caught, and then we too will have to live in one of these hellholes. "We have to split up," I say. "I'll run ahead and check the cells further down."

"But what if—"

"I have Tasers," I say, pulling two out of my pockets.

"Okay." His voice is displeased. "If you see a guard, speed up and ram your Taser right into him. Then signal me."

"I'll send you a Nod."

"Yell, just to be sure," he says, handing me my bag.

Not wanting to waste another second, I take off running. I quickly decide to put one Taser back in my pocket and use my left hand to hold up my cloak. Now I can run twice as fast.

Passing cell after cell, I consider what my plan is. Run to the end and work backwards? That will take forever. Making a bold decision, I rip off my veil and reveal my face to all the girls I pass.

I keep running. I have no idea how far I am from the end of

the tunnel, but I've probably passed twenty cells when I hear "Mina!"

I stop as fast as possible, nearly stumbling to the ground.

When I spin around, I have no idea which cell the voice came from. "Grace?"

"Over here!"

My heart skips as I sprint to her cell. Every girl inside is wearing a cloak in good condition, so this must be the place for new inmates. Worried faces and puffy eyes look to me as I approach the bars. "Grace?" I cry out again.

"Mina!" she says, running to meet me. She grasps my fingers through the bars. "They caught you, too. I'm so sorry." Her hair is frizzy and wild; her eyes are sad and bleak.

I lower my voice. "I'm here to break you out."

She looks at me with sympathy. "I wish that were true. But you can't possibly—"

"You have to trust me. We have a plan." Other girls are listening now. I find the keypad on the cell door and raise my voice to address them. "Who here knows the name of one of your guards? It doesn't matter which one."

"Why would we pay attention?" a girl with freckles says.

"You have to have heard them addressing each other at some point," I insist. This is vital information. "Just think . . . Captain so-and-so? Sergeant . . . who?"

The girls stare at one another with blank eyes. Their minds have been on much more important things than names.

"What's the name of the really big guy?" an athletic girl says. "Johns? Johnson?"

"Jones," her friend says.

"You have to be sure," I say.

"Miller," a small girl in the corner says. "The man who brings us water is called Miller."

A few others nod in confirmation.

"Perfect. Thank you."

Saying a small prayer, I type the code into the cell's keypad: MILRUHO.

Rayna explained that every Twitcher has a door code, and it's the first three letters of their last name plus "Ruho." But she hasn't been here in years, so we don't know if the protocol has changed.

Everyone seems to hold their breath as we wait. The keypad beeps three times.

"That's it!" Grace says.

I push on the cell door, but nothing happens. My stomach sinks.

"*Pull* it," Grace says, frustrated.

I pull on the bars and the door swings open. *I don't believe it.* It worked.

Grace stares at the open doorway. "The two of us can't possibly escape from here," she says.

"I brought Rayna and the boys."

"The six of us can't possibly break out of here."

"We're going to be a lot more than six." Taking my bag from around my shoulder, I place it on the ground. "Pass these out." I pull out Tasers and we pass around thirty-four of them, one to each girl, until we run out.

"When we leave this cell," I tell the girls, "you're going to help me unlock all the other doors. Use the same code: MILRUHO. We have to move fast."

"If we get caught, the punishment will be much worse than being locked up," one girl says, and many others nod.

"You have weapons. Over half the Twitchers have left to go to prayer. We outnumber the ones left, like, four to one."

"God sent us here," says a tall girl in the corner. "He'll be angry if we defy Him."

The girls' faces show hesitation and fear. What would

Nana tell them?

"God didn't decide to put you here. Men did," I say, "men who are power hungry. They saw you as a threat, as forceful girls who would one day become forceful women. They couldn't risk you growing stronger or more independent, so they locked you away. The crimes you've been accused of— running away from husbands, getting an education, not wearing a veil—are not in the Book. I know, because I've read it."

Girls gasp.

"I've also been outside the Wall. I've met Apostates. There are many ways to live our lives, but rotting in these cells shouldn't be one of them. Come with me! We'll only succeed if we do it together."

A handful of girls approach. "We'll come with you," a dark-haired girl says as the others hold up their Tasers.

"I'll come!" says an emaciated girl in the next cell who's obviously been here a long time. "And those of you who don't are cowards."

Grace speaks to her cellmates. "You don't know me or my friend, but I trust her with my life, and I know this is the last chance I have of ever leaving here. I'm willing to take that chance if it means I might see the sun again."

A clamor begins two cells down where girls rattle the bars. "We want to come, too!"

"I want to see the sun!" a young woman says.

"We have to leave *now*," I tell Grace.

She walks out of the cell and all the other girls stream out behind her, their faces set in determination.

"Turn the Tasers on!" I say. "The button is at the base."

I'm about to send a Nod to Juda telling him that I've found Grace, when, from the shadows, comes the biggest Twitcher I've ever seen.

FORTY-SEVEN

"Halt!" the Twitcher yells.

We can't give him time to grab his gun. I charge him, screaming, "Aaaaaiih!"

Having the element of surprise on my side, I manage to brush the Taser against his thigh. He roars in pain, knocking me aside as he drops to the ground. "Get him!" I cry.

I look up to see all the girls frozen in place, gaping at me and the convulsing man.

"Hurry!" I say. "Before he gets up!"

"What should I do?" Grace asks.

"Zap him!" I say.

She runs over to the giant man, who is already trying to stand. "Touch me, Saitch, and I'll kill you!" he bellows.

She stabs her Taser briefly into his arm. Flailing, he returns to his knees. Grace runs away, and only seconds later, he begins to stand *again*.

"Hold it there longer!" I say. "He needs a big shock!"

The guard spins to snarl at me. "I need a big shock, do I? How about you first?"

He reaches me in one enormous step, grabs my wrist, and easily wrenches the Taser from my hand. I scream as I realize that he's aiming it toward my face. "How about one in the eye?" he asks with a nasty laugh.

One of the small girls suddenly leaps like a bullfrog onto his back. "Stop it!" she shrieks.

Another girl reaches around his waist. Two girls wrap themselves around a leg each. They shock him over and over with their Tasers. He screams like a wounded bull.

When he falls this time, he's unconscious, and he lands hard on his back. The girls who attacked him cry out as he collapses on top of them. The rest of us rush to help.

It takes seven of us to roll the man off of the girls trapped underneath. They insist they're fine, but I think one has a sprained wrist.

I get my Taser from the man's hand.

"Mina?" Juda is running toward us.

He looks like another Twitcher arriving to fight. The girls raise their Tasers, ready to attack.

"He's with us!" I say.

The girls squint at me with doubt.

"I heard screaming," he says, flipping up his visor.

"Juda!" Grace says.

"Grace!" He rushes to her, lifting her into a huge embrace. "You're safe!"

"Not yet," she says.

Juda looks at the huge Twitcher on the ground. "We have to hurry before that guy wakes up."

"Are there any more Twitchers inside this tunnel?" I ask, frustrated that they didn't warn me about this one.

"No," Grace says. "He has the only day shift."

This seems like one thing that's going our way. "Okay. You know the door code: MILRUHO," I say.

"MILRUHO," the girls repeat.

"Who's a fast runner?" I ask.

The small girl who remembered the name "Miller" says, "I used to run alongside my sister's bike to the market, fifteen blocks away."

"Perfect. What's your name?"

"Katerina."

"Katerina, you run to the end of the tunnel and unlock the last cell. Then you have those girls help you unlock all the ones between here and there, okay?"

She's off and running.

"The rest of you, head for the entrance and unlock every cell on the way. GO."

The girls stumble into one another as they hurry off. They unlock the next cell, and, a few minutes later, the cell after that. The process seems excruciatingly slow, and I have to remind myself of the starlings, who, although they moved through the trees only thirty feet at a time, managed to cross the entire country without leaving behind a single bird.

"What do we do about him?" I ask Juda, pointing to the behemoth on the ground. "He won't stay unconscious for long."

Juda unbuckles his holster, revealing his gun.

"No," I say, alarmed. "Don't kill him."

With a frustrated look, he takes out his Taser instead. "I'll watch him. If he starts to wake up, I'll shock him again."

"Then I'll wait, too."

"No. You need to go lead."

"I'm not the leader . . . "

"Yes, you are. I heard you." He stands over the motionless guard. "I'll wait until all the cells are open and Katerina has passed me. Then I'll come."

I wish I could kiss him through his helmet. "Thank you."

I run toward the floodgate, trying not to worry that the

guard will wake up and overpower Juda. Instead, I focus on the fact that we found Grace, which two hours ago seemed totally impossible.

I check the empty cells, making sure no one has been left behind. I catch up quickly to the freed prisoners, who have stopped for some reason. "What's happening?" I ask.

They stand in front of an opened cell, but no one is leaving. "They don't think they can make it," Grace says.

"That's twaddle. They just need help."

Inside the cell, a perspiring girl says, "You should stay away. We have the plague."

"It's not contagious." I walk inside, where the hay smells of rot and human waste. I tell the girls standing outside, "I need ten strong girls."

No one moves.

"It was mercury in the water. You *cannot* catch this. I promise. *Please.*"

A handful of girls step forward.

"Thank you," I say, relieved beyond measure. The rest of the group moves on to free the others. I pick up a sick girl easily. She can't weigh more than a sack of flour. "What's your name?" I ask.

"Leanne."

"You'll feel better as you soon as you get fresh air, Leanne."

Our group of ten manages to get the ailing girls out of the repulsive cell. We walk up the tunnel with them as quickly as possible. The sick girls moan in pain or despair. We hurry along, whispering encouragement to them.

We arrive at the floodgate and a swarm of girls awaits me. I'm berated by questions:

"How do we open it?"

"What next?"

"Who'll help us?"

I put Leanne down gently against the wall, asking Grace to look after her.

Like the others, Grace's eyes are filled with panic. "What about the guards on the other side?"

"We defeated that Twitcher with six girls," I say. "We can beat two guards. How many of us are there? A hundred? Two?"

"And here come more," Grace says, pointing.

Katerina sprints toward us leading another herd of girls, and none of them can be older than six. I hold back tears, seeing these poor children who've spent their lives in the dark, without parents. Juda brings up the rear. He's taken off this helmet, I assume to reassure the children. I'm so happy to see his face.

Grace taps me on the shoulder. "The *door*, Mina?"

I need to concentrate on the task at hand. Rayna isn't here to open the door and we can't contact her for instructions. The guards who greeted us would've assumed that Juda and the titan Twitcher on duty could open the door together to let Juda out.

Think, Mina. The floodgate looks the same on this side as it did on the other. It has a wheel and many valves. "Somewhere around here is a pipe—a metal stick type thing—" I say, "and we need it to open the door." I *hope* there's one on this side. We need *leverage*, as Father once taught me.

Everyone looks at the person next to them, confused.

"Step away from the door and search the ground!" I yell. I don't remember that the short Twitcher took his from a special place. He seemed to have it with him when he came down the stairs.

Getting hundreds of girls to back away from the one door that could lead to their freedom is no easy task, but eventually we clear ten feet around the door. Seeing nothing, I'm despondent.

Juda makes his way through the throng to reach me. "We may have to try it without the leverage pipe."

Raising my eyebrows, I say, "You know that won't work."

"We have to try. Come on." Approaching the wheel, he says, "I need the strongest girl here!"

"Patricia," someone says, and several people agree.

Soon a major tall girl with cropped hair and a crooked nose steps forward. She has broad hips and broad shoulders. She joins Juda and places her hands on the wheel. We all take a deep breath as Juda says, "Pull!"

She pulls on two spokes as he pushes from the other side. As they put all of their strength into turning the wheel, they go red in the face, and a vein in Juda's neck looks ready to burst.

The wheel won't budge.

They let up, gasping.

"We'll try again," he says. "Ready?"

He has optimism in his voice, but anyone watching can see that there is no way that they'll be able to move those spokes. Even the brawny Twitcher needed leverage.

Grace peers at me, her look a question that's close to a reprimand: did I really execute this plan without a way to open this door?

Leanne, unable to hold herself up, is slumped against the wall next to her. What if I got these sick girls out of their cells for nothing?

We were supposed to have more people! We were supposed to have Rayna and all of her knowledge!

"One, two, three!" Juda says, throwing all his weight into the wheel.

Patricia pulls with all her might.

Suddenly, the valves of the door release. How did they do that? I swear the spokes never moved.

A second later, the door hisses and begins to squeal.

"Stand back!" I say, understanding that the floodgate is opening from the other side.

Girls huddle together in alarm, while a few run toward their cells.

The mammoth door swings toward us.

Juda gets his gun out, ready to shoot whomever is on the other side. I put a Taser in each hand and tell the girls to do the same. We have to be ready for anything.

FORTY-EIGHT

When the door finally groans open, Dekker stands there with his visor flipped up, grinning like a dope.

"Greetings, losers. Who needs weapons?"

He holds up Rayna's bag of Tasers.

The girls look to me, baffled. A Twitcher is insulting them, yet offering them help?

"He's my brother. I apologize for his behavior. Take a Taser if you don't have one."

"Don't apologize for me!" he says, frowning. "I'm—"

Before he can finish, hundreds of girls are running past him. Some grab Tasers.

"Wait by the far wall!" I tell them. "Form a straight line." We have to get them ready to leave the building in the most efficient way possible.

Dekker's smug expression disappears when he spots Grace. His mouth opens, his eyes go wide, and he reverts to the five-year-old boy I once knew.

"Grace!" he yells.

"Dekker!" she says.

He rushes to her and embraces her. "Thank the Prophet you're safe!"

She's bewildered but then produces a massive grin. "Who knew I'd ever be so happy to see you?"

"I know!" he says, and she laughs. "I mean, I'm really happy to see you, too . . . safe and everything."

"We're not safe yet," she says.

His face grows dark as he releases her. "You will be. I promise."

I join them and so does Silas.

"How did you know it was time to let us out?" I ask Silas.

"We didn't. Rayna told me and Dekker to give you fifteen minutes and then open the door."

"We were getting worried." Scanning the empty tower, I ask, "Where are the guards?"

Dekker answers. "Rayna shot them from, like, sixty yards away. It was amaz—"

"What about the noise?" I ask.

"Took over the control room first," he says. "It was glorious. We must have taken down, like, fifteen men. Took 'em totally by surprise."

Silas looks sick and I don't blame him. We'd hoped to execute our plan using Tasers, not guns, and that's not the way things are turning out. We have to get out of here before the rest of the Twitchers come back from prayer or the situation will become much worse.

"I have to get back to Rayna," Silas says, "help her keep a lookout." He sprints across the hangar.

"Tell her we're on the way!" I yell after him.

"All the girls are out," Juda tells us. "We need to shut the floodgate."

Using the pipe, he and Dekker proceed to close the door, making sure our unconscious guard can't give us any more trouble. When I look away, I see that the girls are not lining up at the far wall, like I asked. Instead, they're gathering in front of the other two floodgates.

"What are you doing?" I yell. "We have to GO!" The girls don't move. Running over to them, I ask, "What's wrong? "

"We're waiting for him to open the other floodgates," Patricia says, pointing to Dekker.

"We came for you!" I explain. *Get Grace. Get the girls. Get out.* That is Rayna's plan.

"My mother is in there!" Patricia says. "And so is hers." She points to the girl next to her and one behind her. "And hers."

Grace walks up. She says nothing, but her face tells me everything. The mother she has never met may be behind that door as well.

As Dekker and Juda approach, I tell them, "We have to let out the women."

Dekker glares at me. "We don't have time."

"They won't come with us otherwise," I say, knowing it's the truth as soon as I say it.

"My father is there!" a girl yells, pointing at the third flood-gate. "What about him?"

"And my brother!" Patricia says, putting her hands on her hips.

What were we thinking? How could we have thought that we could come here and only free one third of the prisoners?

"We only have ten minutes left!" Juda says.

If we miss our window to leave the building, we'll be faced with the returning Twitchers, a small army. We may never escape. I look from Dekker's angry face, to Juda's stressed expression, to Grace's pleading eyes.

"We're opening all the doors!" I yell.

The girls clamor with approval.

Dekker curses but takes his pipe to the middle floodgate.

Juda follows. Dekker connects the pipe to the wheel while Juda releases the valves. Maybe it only takes a minute, but the opening feels like an hour.

U ok? Silas asks in a Nod. I'm relieved our Tacts work again.

Need more time, I type.

U don't have it, he responds.

The valves release with a hiss and even with the tiniest of space, half of the girls are ready to cram through. I stop them. "There's probably at least one guard in there. Dekker and Juda should go in first with their guns."

Alarmed, Dekker looks at me. He nervously takes out his gun and cocks it. He and Juda walk into the tunnel together. Will the same door code work? If not, the women in the cells should be able to tell them the names of their guards, right?

I manage to make the girls wait outside the door, but it isn't easy. They're dying to go inside. I check on the sick girls, who are sitting on the ground near the guard tower. They're tired but happy to finally be outside of their cells.

Leanne says, "I was sure I would die in there."

My fear is that she might die right here.

Reading my face, she says, "Even sitting here is a million times better than being in that crap-filled cell."

I wish I had food and water to give her.

I get a new Nod from Silas: *They're here. NEED AMMO.*

Nyek. We've taken too long. The Twitchers are back. We no longer have a clear exit.

I snag two healthy looking girls. "You and you, come with me."

Without a word, they step in line behind me. We run across the hangar until we reach the hallway. We pass the now-open door of the control room, and I ignore the sounds of gunfire as I sprint to the weapons room. When I get to the door, I punch in

MILRUHO, but nothing happens. I'm filled with a new level of despair. Sergeant Miller only delivered water. Maybe he didn't have access to weapons.

I take a long, slow breath. The girls said there was a guard named Johnson or Johns. I enter JOHRUHO.

Nothing.

I have only one name left: Jones. I press JONROHU. The keypad beeps three times.

"Praise God," I whisper.

The girls and I rush inside. Not knowing which bullets Rayna needs, I grab every kind I see. I hand all of them to the two girls. I gather guns, holding them awkwardly in front of me like a pile of firewood.

When our hands are full, I lead the girls down the hall to the control room. It's a square space filled with computer panels and surrounded by windows. Dead Twitchers line the floor. I try to keep my wits about me and not focus on the blood.

Rayna is kneeling by a large gun which passes through the wall to reach outside. "Stay down!" she yells as she fires.

Before I dive to the ground, I see the terrifying swarm of Twitchers approaching the building. Their bullets spray against the windows, but, miraculously, the glass doesn't shatter.

"What the Hell were you doing back there?" Rayna shouts.

I hesitate to tell her. I yell above the howl of guns exploding. "We brought you bullets!!"

Taking boxes from the girls, I slide them across the floor to Rayna.

"Not enough!" she screams back. "Have you seen how many Twitcher are out there?"

Silas crouches under a computer panel, looking terrified.

"Help her, Silas!" I say, offering him a gun.

"Why me? How about you?" he yells.

"Give me a gun!" says one of the girls stooping behind me.

I offer up my whole bundle and she takes a rifle from the top. She cocks it expertly, and seeing my bewildered look, says, "Squirrel hunting." She crawls over to Rayna. *God bless the girl's squirrel-eating soul.*

"The bulletproof glass will only hold a minute longer," Rayna tells her. "Then you start shooting, got it?" She looks at me. "Send Dekker and Juda here NOW! I need more shooters."

I can't do that. They're in the second tunnel, but the words won't form.

I place my pile of guns on the floor. "I'm getting you back-up!" I say, crawling out of the room as quickly as I can.

FORTY-NINE

Sprinting back to the floodgates, I see that no one has emerged from the second tunnel yet. I can't worry about that. I have to find help for Rayna.

"Who here can shoot?" I shout.

A handful of girls raise their hands.

"We need your help!"

I direct them to the control room, instructing them to stay down and approach slowly.

I spot Grace. "Come with me!"

Grabbing the pipe that Dekker left on the ground, I lead her to the third tunnel. We can't wait. We have to free the boys and men right now.

I connect the pipe to the wheel and Grace and I both pull down on it. My arms feel like they're about to come out of their sockets, but with both of us pulling, the wheel begins to turn ever so slowly.

"Don't stop!" Grace says from behind me. We're intertwined in such a way that if we keep turning she might squash me. Before I'm crushed, I step out. She continues to lean on the pipe, and I hover over her, grabbing the pipe again to lend her some extra strength. The wheel continues to turn and we hear the hiss we want.

I'm staring at the valves, trying to figure out how to release them, when a woman walks tentatively out of the second tunnel. She's dirty and confused, and, judging by her cloak, she's been here for a very long time.

A moment later, dozens of women come pouring out. They range in age from eighteen to eighty. Seeing them, I assume that Juda and Dekker took care of the guard inside. My stomach unknots slightly.

As the women spot the group of girls, they begin to yell out names: "Madeline?" "Priscilla!" "Martha?"

The girls push one another aside, reaching their mothers and embracing them fiercely. Girl after girl finds her mother or her sister. They're laughing and crying. I'm jealous that they have mothers they're so happy to see.

The number of women coming out of the tunnel slows to a trickle. Finally, Dekker and Juda appear.

"What happened?" I ask.

"The guard is down but not out. We need to shut the door!" Juda says.

He assures me all the women are out as he and Dekker close the floodgate behind them.

I point to the third door. "Time for the men," I say.

"Let's do it," Dekker says, now in the swing of things.

He and Juda are impressed that Grace and I have turned the wheel, and it only takes a moment for Dekker to release the valves. Several girls have come over, anxious to see fathers and brothers. They know now they'll have to wait for Dekker and Juda to go first.

The boys approach the floodgate, guns raised, with Dekker

in the lead. He steps through the doorway and a second later a shot comes out of the dark.

"Dekker!" I scream, moving toward the tunnel.

"Everyone back!" Juda says. He carefully peeks around the floodgate. More shots come from inside. Juda pulls back. As soon as there's a pause, he turns into the dark and fires six fast shots. He snaps back and waits.

"Dekker?" he says.

When there's no answer, my whole body goes cold. *I sent him in there. We were supposed to leave. We stayed because I said to free the men.*

"You there?" Juda says.

"Ahhh, yeah," Dekker says, with a moan.

I breathe again. Thank God.

"That Twitcher still standing?" Juda asks.

"Noooo," Dekker says.

Juda and I race inside. Dekker lies on the ground; twenty feet away lies the body of a Twitcher. Juda hit him with almost every shot.

"That didn't go as planned," Dekker says, holding his side.

I'm relieved to hear him speak, but then I see the blood seeping through his jumpsuit.

"Don't talk," Juda says. "I'm going to help you up."

As he carries Dekker out of the tunnel, I shout at the waiting girls, "Unlock the cells!" They flood past me.

We find a clear area and Juda lays Dekker out on the blacktop. "I have to stop the bleeding," Juda says. "I need clean fabric."

My cloak is covered in dirt from the fight with the big guard. The prisoners are filthier than I am. Realizing no one else has anything, Juda unzips his jumpsuit and takes off his shirt. Girls who were watching us look away, deeply embarrassed. He balls the shirt up and holds it against Dekker's side. "You're going to be okay," he tells him.

"Is it bad?" I whisper to Juda.

"Only if we can't stop the bleeding"

I lean in close to Dekker's face. "You were really impressive in there. Grace was major dazzled."

He doesn't smile. He's in pain.

An old women approaches us. "Let me help you."

I give her a look of frustration. "Do you have clean fabric?"

"No, but I was imprisoned for practicin' medicine. May I see?" She kneels next to Dekker. "I'm Agnes," she tells him as she peers at the wound. "What's yer name?"

"Dekker," I answer for him.

"It may've hit his spleen," Agnes says.

"What can I do?" I ask. Sweat pours down his face. I wish I had water.

"Get him outta here as soon as possible," she says. She puts her hand over the T-shirt that Juda is pressing into Dekker's body. "Let me do that." She calls over two women to help her, telling them she needs the cleanest cloth they can find. They run around the room, asking everyone.

"I've got this for now," Agnes tells Juda, who lets her take over.

"Mina," Dekker says.

I lean down so I can hear him.

"I don't want to marry Delilah Delford," he whispers.

I smile. "I know."

"Will you tell her for me?"

"Sure." I'm glad he thinks one of us will get out of here alive. "Father would be very proud of you."

His eyebrows rise in disbelief. "For running into a dark tunnel and"—he winces with pain—"getting shot like some bonehead?"

"He always wanted to help the people of this city and look what you did!"

He's considering this when Grace approaches. "Is he all right?" she asks, looking rattled. "What can I do?"

Dekker tries to pull himself together. He takes a few deep breaths as Agnes continues to apply pressure. "You could, uh, tell me a story."

"Take it easy," Agnes tells him.

"Like what?" Grace says, at a loss.

"Like one of those books you're always talking about. Like *Jane Air*."

"Of course," Grace says, sounding relieved to have a job she can actually do. "You were major valiant today."

He rests his head back down. "I'll pretend I know what that means."

I hear new male voices. Panicked, I look around to discover men and boys coming out of the tunnel. They're thin, dirty, and dazed, just like the women.

Within a short time, however, several of them start giving orders.

A chubby man with a thick black beard yells, "The men will go first and then the women and children. Deservers will be at the head of the line, then Convenes!"

Furious, I leave Dekker and walk straight up to him. "You're not in charge here."

"Where's your veil, child?" he asks, averting his eyes.

"Back in the cells. Would you like to go and fetch it?" I ask.

His face hardens. "I will not be spoken to like—"

"You will be spoken to like you are an equal." I face the others. "We are ALL EQUAL here. If that is not satisfactory to you, you may return to your cell and await a rescue party that is more to your liking!"

Many of the men grumble, frowning. They seem torn between being in prison and taking orders from a girl.

"We only have a few people holding off the guards at the front," I say. "They need reinforcements."

"I'll take people to the roof," Juda says. "If you can use a gun, I need you."

"Why are we attempting this?" a man asks. "Even if we defeat these guards, more are on the way. They'll kill us for insurrection."

Many prisoners nod their heads in agreement. We're losing them.

The small runner, Katerina, says, "If the girls are willing, you should be as well. We overpowered our guard with no guns."

The belligerent man has nothing to say in response.

"I won't be separated from my daughter again," Patricia's mother says. "I'm not going back in that cell."

A roar of agreement ripples among them.

"If you can fight, follow me or him," I yell, pointing at Juda. "Otherwise, help those that are sick or injured and prepare them to walk out as soon as we give the signal!"

I ask Grace to stay with Dekker, saying, "Come get me if he gets worse."

When I return to Rayna, I'm followed by dozens of men, women, and girls. We cluster in the hallway as we wait for a safe moment to enter the control room.

The glass is gone from nearly all the windows. Rayna and the girl are shooting and then ducking under the meager protection that the computer panel provides. Silas, lying on the ground, hands them ammunition as they need it. Rayna's helmet is off. Her brow is slick with sweat and her eyes are wide with anxiety. Things must be going badly.

I crawl on my stomach to the pile of guns I brought in earlier. Carefully, I hand them back to the people behind me who claim they know how to use them.

When Rayna spies the men, she snarls. "What's going on? Where's Grace?"

"They're ready to fight" is all I say. She can yell at me later. I slide boxes of ammunition toward the door and watch as men and women load the guns. Do we have enough people to defend ourselves? It seems impossible.

Once armed, my freed prisoners creep on the ground into the room.

Dozens of Twitchers are inside the barbwire fence. Luckily, they have nowhere to hide in No Man's Land. Rayna pops up and shoots one of them in the chest. He goes down hard.

I feel sick. I'm relieved and yet horrified.

One of my men, who has apple cheeks and a huge mustache, sidles in next to Rayna. He sits up, and fires off four shots. He hits three men.

Rayna looks impressed before she hits one more of her own.

They are taking men down, but there are so many of them. For every Twitcher that goes down, another seems to take his place. I brought lots of people who can shoot, but we don't have enough guns for all of them.

Out of the blue, several Twitchers seem to fall for no reason. As two more go down, I realize that the shots are coming from above. It's Juda and the group he took to the roof.

I have a surge of hope, but minutes later our situation has become much worse. Two of our men and one woman lie on the floor, bleeding from bullet wounds. The Twitchers have gained ground. They're only thirty feet away. It's clear even to me that there's no way we can hold them off.

"Get the prisoners back to the cells!" Silas yells. "They're coming in!"

We can't possibly get people back inside the tunnels in time. We don't have time to open even one floodgate, let alone three.

We've failed the prisoners, every one of them. They'll be punished, probably executed for disobedience. I didn't stick to the plan. If we'd only opened the one floodgate, we could've gotten out.

I have to at least try to get the *children* back into their cells, right? I'm leaving the control room when I hear a strange whistling sound followed by the loudest thundering crack I've ever heard.

Smoke fills No Man's Land.

I'm still trying to figure out what's happened when I hear another whistle, and I see an explosion two blocks away.

The bombing. It's begun.

FIFTY

Another boom fills the sky and the guardhouse shakes. A fleet of drones circles overhead. Each one is half the size of the Ostrich, with whirling blades and no space for passengers—they only carry explosives.

The smoke in No Man's Land begins to clear, revealing an enormous crater in the middle of the concrete. Most of the Twitchers have disappeared into the hole. Those who were blown back by the blast stand, moving slowly, dazed.

Rayna's mouth is moving, but I can't hear the words. My ears buzz. She looks like she's yelling at me. I move closer to her, and she pulls me in until her mouth is right at my ear. "If they hit the tunnels, the whole building will flood!"

My nightmare over all these years is going to come true: I'm going to drown in the Tunnel. "We have to get out of here!" I yell. It's a stupid thing to say. It's exactly what she's been trying to do for the last hour.

I send a Nod to Juda: *Come down NOW.* On the roof, he has no protection from the drones.

I survey the remaining Twitchers. Some are helping wounded men, but others are pulling themselves together to resume their attack. Why are they so willing to die? Don't they have families? They don't live in the Tunnel—there are no beds here. They must go home to regular lives, right?

I have a strange idea. "Is there a way to communicate with them?"

"Who?" Rayna yells, obviously as deaf as I am.

"The Twitchers!"

"With my helmet!" Her helmet lays on the ground behind her, still connected to her jumpsuit.

"Put it on!" I tell her.

She must be out of ideas, because she does what I ask. Once she has it secured, I say, "Send a message. Make sure it goes out to all of them!"

She nods, fingers ready to type.

I dictate: *Apostates are bombing the island. If you want your family to survive, you must move them underground. Go home and make them safe.*

She finishes the message and a second later, the Twitchers freeze. They've received our information. A few look at one another. They don't know what to do.

A drone drops a bomb north of here, and this time I can see it falling—thin, pointy, and bright orange, it's like a huge neon pencil. It races through the sky, landing with a roar as everything it hits is decimated.

Again, our building shudders. I think of the cracks in the ceiling of those cells—the water dripping through. How much shaking can the tunnels handle?

One of the Twitchers runs out of No Man's Land and sprints toward 9th Avenue. Others look at the sky, seeking confirmation that the bombing is truly happening. They spot the orange missiles, and they, too, run toward the street.

Amazed, Rayna says, "It's working."

A guard who was helping injured Twitchers straightens up and walks toward us, firing shot after shot. The prisoner with the big mustache kills him with one bullet.

Why couldn't that Twitcher leave like the others?

Seeing their fellow guard fall, the remaining Twitchers seem to decide this fight isn't as important as the bombing. They begin to leave, taking their injured with them.

I want to celebrate the victory, but we have to evacuate the building before the tunnels collapse. Silas and I return to the hangar, ready to start barking orders, but the prisoners are organized and prepared to go. The children are at the front of a long line, ready to leave first. Their mothers, if available, walk next to them. Behind them are women and men who are helping the elderly and infirm, and after them are the healthiest of the group.

A large man passes close to me carrying Dekker. Agnes and Grace walk next to them. Smiling, Agnes says, "I don't think it hit his spleen. The bleedin' slowed."

Another explosion comes from above, causing the hangar to shake, but this time it's different. The vibration keeps reverberating. A deep rumble comes from the tunnels.

"Run!" I yell.

People start to scream in panic, but we try to keep them in their line as we rush them out of the hangar and into the control room. The sound behind us is like a series of busses being knocked over. The tunnels are collapsing. And we didn't shut the last floodgate.

People stumble and trip in their fright, slowing the line down. "Be careful!" I shout. "But don't stop moving!"

Where is Juda? Has he come down from the roof?

I watch, nerves in knots, as the line slows. I run into the control room to find the problem. People are helping the frailest prisoners out the door, causing a bottleneck. Not willing to wait for their turn, healthier people are jumping through the blown-out windows.

Dekker is carried in next to Agnes and Grace. As they head for the door, Rayna shouts, "Grace!"

Grace turns, her face lighting up when she sees Rayna.

"Hurry!" I shout.

"Get outta here, kid!" Rayna tells her, motioning at the door.

As I watch them escape into No Man's Land, I hear shrieking noises come from the hangar. The remaining prisoners shove into the control room. "Water's coming in!" a woman wails. People begin to push en masse out the door, while I help dozens out the windows.

Silas appears. "That's everyone! Let's go!"

Rayna and the mustached man sprint out the door. Grabbing my hand, Silas pulls me after them.

"I'm waiting for Juda!" I say.

"That's bonkers. We're out of time!" He tugs at me again.

Why didn't Juda come down when I told him to? Where *is* he? Going back inside would be suicide. But I can't make myself go with Silas either. How many times has Juda risked himself for me?

A gurgling crash erupts in the hangar. Silas and I look at each other. *The water is coming.* No more time for thinking. We run out the door and cross what remains of No Man's Land as the giant wave surges through the control room, breaking all the remaining glass. We sprint up the stairs while the high-speed, spitting devil continues to chase us.

We reach the top, panting and terrified, and watch as No Man's Land floods—first the bombed crater and then the rest of the concrete block. We watch in horror as the water grows deeper and deeper, knowing that if it reaches the streets, no one will have anywhere to go.

"We need boats," a girl says. "From the canals."

If only we had time to get them.

The water reaches the top of the stairs, and then it stops. Hay, detritus from the prison cells, and the bodies of dead Twitchers and prisoners float to the surface.

That's when I see them.

Juda and the prisoners he took with him are still on the roof. I wave. Juda waves back. They're trapped, completely surrounded by the enormous pool of muck that's one block wide and more than five hundred feet long. Plus they make a terrific target for the drones.

I'm gaping at them, hope draining from my body, when Juda puts down his weapon and takes off his boots and jumpsuit. Once down to only his trousers, he dives into the foul water. The other men do the same.

What are they thinking?

I try not to watch every stroke they take, but I can't tear my eyes away. Is the water still rising? I can't be sure. From here, the distance looks vast; do the prisoners have enough strength to make it?

Bombs strike on the horizon, and I watch in awe as chunks of the Wall are blown apart.

Behind me is chaos as the prisoners look for cover from the drones. Silas says, "Where do we take everyone?"

"We could have taken the *girls* to Macy's," Rayna says, "if Mina hadn't blown our plan."

"If we'd left the men and women inside, they'd all be dead right now!" I snap.

I keep my eye on Juda. Maybe we can take the prisoners to the bus station? It seemed to have several floors below ground and the building seems sturdy.

Children cry, and adults comfort them. Some men begin to fight about where the safest place to go is, while other people simply begin walking home to their families, braving the bombs for a chance to see their loved ones.

I tune them all out until Juda reaches our end of No Man's Land. Two stairs still peep out of the water, and he and his men use them to crawl out of the flood.

I run to meet him. "I was so scared," I say, embracing him.

"Me, too," he says.

"Why didn't you come down?" I ask, my fear turning to anger.

"We tried," he says, "but our exit had flooded."

Of course he tried. I'm being ridiculous. Their bravery helped us tremendously. "Thank you," I tell the wet men and women behind him.

Grace has found Rayna and is squeezing her. "I never thought I'd see you again," Grace says.

"You weren't supposed to, knucklehead. And then you had to go and get arrested."

Grace is sheepish. "Thank you for rescuing me."

"I would say 'anytime,' but I think this was a one-time deal," Rayna says.

"I have to confess something . . . " Grace says, pulling away. "I got *Nancy Drew* wet. I kind of, like, ruined it."

"No wonder they locked you up!" Rayna says, punching her in the arm.

Grace smiles.

"We're figuring out where to go," I tell Juda.

"That's absurd," Juda says. "The bombs will be back any second." Dripping wet, he marches up to Rayna. "We have to take them to Macy's. It's the safest place in the city and you know it."

I brace for her angry reply, but instead she says, "You're right."

I'm stunned. She's going to allow these men and boys to enter the Laurel Society? Seeing Grace must have melted her icy heart.

Afraid she'll change her mind, I don't say one word. I walk along the sidewalk, waving the prisoners south along 9th Avenue, telling them the address of Macy's. It's close—only four blocks down—but then we have to cross two very wide avenues.

All of a sudden, a city bus is careening down 9th Avenue, heading straight for us. The driver is probably trying to outrace the bombs.

"Look out!" I tell the prisoners.

Just before barreling through a line of elderly men, the bus screeches to a stop. As the door of the bus opens with a burst of air, I look around me for Rayna and her large gun.

Shocking me more than the landing of the bombs, Tabby and Mary step out of the bus. "We thought you might need a lift," Mary says. Looking at the number of prisoners, she loses her wide smile. "We might need a bigger bus."

I run to her, throwing my arms around her. "I'm so happy you're here!"

"It was my idea," Tabby says.

"It was a joint effort," Mary says.

I don't care whose idea it was. "One of you drove that thing?"

"I did," Mary says. "Luckily not many people are on the road at the moment."

"She was incredible," Tabby says, putting her arm around Mary's shoulder. "Like, major benny genius."

Mary laughs. They're both glowing with their accomplishment. As I notice how happy they look, I realize they aren't wearing veils, and I couldn't give a goat's ass.

"We need you to take the injured back to Macy's," I say, pointing them out a block away, "Before the bombing starts again."

Looking at the entire throng of prisoners, Tabby says, "I can't believe Rayna's plan worked. Where's Silas?"

I scan the crowd. "Up ahead, with Juda."

"And what about Grace?" Mary asks.

"She's helping with Dekker."

"Why? Is he okay?" Mary asks.

"We're not sure yet. He needs attention."

"As usual," Mary says.

"I meant—"

"I'm kidding," she says.

How can she be kidding at a time like this? "You know bombs are falling, right?"

"So hurry up!" Tabby says, getting back on the bus. Mary follows her, getting behind the wheel.

I'm actually smiling as I run to tell the ailing prisoners. I can't believe the girls are here. Mary isn't as much as a surprise as Tabby. Mary always wanted to help more, but Tabby seemed content to stay safe with the Laurel Society.

"If you have difficulty walking," I shout at the crowd, "get on the bus!"

No one hears me, so I run another block south. When I catch up to Dekker and the other injured, I'm panting. "Mary and Tabby are here with a bus. They can drive you to Macy's!"

Dekker gives me a look of disbelief, and then we hear the roaring of a drone and the whistle of a bomb. The explosives head straight for the bus.

"Get down!" Dekker yells.

Instead, I run, screaming for Mary and Tabby to get out.

The next thing I know, I'm knocked off my feet.

For a time things go very quiet, maybe I'm unconscious. When my eyes open, the buzzing in my ears is back. People are screaming; they sound miles away. I sit up, but it hurts. Looking down, I see that my body is covered in cuts.

I look around for the bus, but it's gone.

FIFTY-ONE

It's okay, I tell myself as I struggle to stand, debris sliding off my body. *Mary must have somehow driven away in time. It's fine.* Smoke fills the air, and people around me are on the ground covered in the same rubble.

I walk toward the Tunnel, where the bus was, and there's a crater a block wide. The world starts to spin as I understand that Mary didn't drive away. Whatever remains of the bus is in the bottom of this hole.

"Mary!" I yell into the trench. "Tabby!"

Rayna runs up behind me and looks down at the wreckage. She puts her hands on my shoulders. "They can't have . . . no one could survive that."

"MARY!" I shout louder.

"I'm sorry, Mina," she says.

"No!" I say. "They're here!"

She pulls me to face her. "No. They're gone."

Gone? They can't possibly be gone. I was talking to them seconds ago.

Silas runs up, face blackened with soot, and gapes at the

decimated bus. "Juda said Tabby was in there. She couldn't have been. She wouldn't have come. Not Tabby."

"Oh God, Silas. She and Mary came to help us. They were *right here.*" I grab him and hug him as hard as I can.

"I'm making sure these people get to Macy's," Rayna says in a gentle voice. "You need to get underground."

A minute later, or maybe an hour, Juda approaches. "Please let me get you somewhere safe."

I'm still holding onto Silas. I'm numb.

Juda, in a voice of military command, barks, "Let's go!"

It makes us move. We disentangle and follow him without speaking. As we walk south, bombs go off around us, but they don't matter, because I'm seeing the world through someone else's eyes. The rumbling drones, the thundering explosions, the wailing children—someone else is hearing them. The actual me is back on 38th street talking to Mary and Tabby. I'll never be that real me again. We march along with the prisoners like we're half dead.

When we finally arrive at Macy's, Rayna disappears inside, I assume to talk to Ayan. While we wait, many prisoners try to hide amid the rubble of the building, hoping to become less conspicuous targets for the drones. Silas and I sit on a curb out in the open, not caring.

Rayna returns with Ayan fast on her heels. Ayan looks truly taken aback by the army of prisoners we've brought, but she soon snaps back into her usual commanding self. "Bring in the wounded first and then the children!" she hollers.

She's going to let them in. Even Ayan can find her heart in desperate times.

The injured men and women who have to be carried are given precedence, and a line of healthy prisoners begins to convey them up and over the hill of debris that leads to the door of the basement.

All of these men and women can't possibly fit inside Macy's, can they?

A drone buzzes overhead, and soon I hear the crack of its bomb, which sounds like it landed less than a block away. People scream, and many sprint in the opposite direction. I don't run. What's the use? The next bomb could land on our heads, and there's nothing any of us can do.

Silas leaves me to go help the wounded reach the basement. His face looks soulless, as if helping these people has no meaning for him. The look makes me wonder if anything will ever have meaning for him again.

I know I should help, too, but my feet won't move.

Grace sits next to me. "I haven't had a chance to say thank you yet." When I don't respond, she says, "If I'd known what was going to happen, I would've told you to leave me there."

"Then you'd be dead, too," I say.

She chews her lip. "They were so brave."

I'm going to cry again. "They weren't even supposed to be there."

She scoots closer. "Maybe you should go see your Nana."

Nana might make me feel better, but I sense if I faced her, I'd feel ashamed. "Maybe in a bit."

"It wasn't your fault," she says.

"Yes, it was." I broke Mary out of the Forgiveness Home, and I got her tangled up in Ram's cruel scheme. I promised Jeremiah I would protect her, and I failed. And Tabby . . . she was at Macy's because I insisted on going there. She should be at Dodo's right now, safe and complaining about the food.

"Don't be arrogant. Not everything happens because of you and not everything happens for a reason. Ram made a decision to drop those bombs. *He's* responsible." She sweeps her arm toward the prisoners. "But there's something you can take

367

credit for. The tunnels flooded, and we all would've drowned without you."

I drop my head onto my knees. "I just want to go back and tell them to *stay here.*" My shoulders tremble as I sob for Mary and Tabby, and, for the first time, my father.

"They're with God now."

I look up, wiping my eyes. "Do you really believe that?"

She takes a long time to reply. "When someone dies, I think it's all we have."

"That's not an answer."

"It's been a confusing time, but, uh, yeah, I still believe. How about you?"

I want to believe *so badly.* I want to think that my father, Mary, and Tabby will soon be together, sharing stories, but the idea currently comes across as a child's fantasy.

Sometimes I think I hate God.

Wait. No. I hate the people who tell me they represent God. And that's different. I have to hang on to this distinction.

"Something's changed," Grace says, standing.

I stand, too. What's wrong?

"When was the last time you heard a bomb?" she asks.

She's right. The evening's gone quiet.

"Maybe they flew to a different neighborhood," I say.

Just as the words leave my mouth, a formation of drones flies overhead and the prisoners around us scream in terror. Juda and Silas rush the wounded man they're carrying to a doorway. But the machines don't release any explosives. Forming a perfect V, they glide east.

"They're headed back to Queens!" Grace cries.

What's happened? Did Ram decide he's inflicted enough destruction for the day?

No one, myself included, really trusts that the danger is gone, so people stay pressed against walls and huddled in doorways. After another ten or fifteen minute has gone by, we start to have faith in the silence. As we are tentatively stepping back into the street, doors start to open up and down 35th Street.

I've never really thought of people living around Macy's. I always considered the area to be abandoned, but as people stream out of the buildings, I realize how wrong I was.

The residents look shell-shocked, as if they've been hiding underground for months and not hours. An older man holds up a radio, yelling as he walks toward our group. "It's Jordan! He's saved us!"

Confused, we gather around his radio. Jordan Loudz's voice crackles loudly:

. . . therefore the crisis is over. Check on your neighbors and help in any way you can. Many will need medical care. You may take them to any hospital—be it for men or women. I repeat, the bombing is over. I have spoken to Ram, the head of the Apostates, and we have come to terms.

Grace and I look at each other, speechless. How is this possible? How did Jordan speak to Ram and why would Ram negotiate with him?

Everyone else in the street smiles with relief. Jordan continues:

We will rebuild our city. We will work together, in love. God has told the Convenes from the beginning that no man is divine. Only God is. A man should only rule if he is worthy, if his people want him to rule.

Ayan's shoulders have gone back, causing her to stand ramrod straight. She didn't like these last words—"A *man* should only rule if *he* is worthy." Having heard enough, she marches back inside Macy's.

The Ruho dynasty has come to an end, Jordan continues. *He and his heirs have been destroyed. We will no longer be subjected to their reign of terror.*

He *and his heirs* have been destroyed?

Oh God. He's killed Mrs. Hypat, just like he wanted. I can't believe it.

Stay tuned for further instructions. I am here for you. I am your servant, Jordan Loudz.

Grace appears as shocked as I am. Juda joins us, still sodden from his swim. I'm about to talk to him about the appalling news when I notice something disturbing. He doesn't look surprised.

I'm afraid to ask him the question, but I do. "Did you know he was going to kill Mrs. Hypat, even after we told him not to?"

"I . . . I wasn't sure."

"How did he contact Ram?" Grace says, baffled. "He didn't have the means to—"

He bows his head.

Oh my God. All this time that I couldn't send Juda a Nod, it wasn't because his Tact was broken; it was because *Jordan had it.*

Rage fills every cell in my body.

Seeing my expression, Juda says, "I know you're upset, but—"

"Upset? A woman was murdered, Juda, a woman who saved my life, and you helped it happen."

"Do you want more of your friends to die? I don't. And I don't want anything to happen to my uncles or to you."

"So now you get to decide who lives and who dies?" I can't look at him.

"Of course not. I didn't know what Ram and Jordan would work out. All I did was give them the means to have a discussion."

"You knew exactly what Jordan would propose. He told us what he wanted to do."

Poor Mrs. Hypat. She'd finally been released from her

father's cruel reign. She was going to find a new way to rule, and now we'll never get to see it. She once said *I want one thing in this world and that is to leave it for the next*. I hope she didn't suffer.

"You're angry. You're sad about Tabby and Mary. I think in a few days you'll understand why I did it."

"You think wrong. Let's go, Grace."

Her eyebrows are furrowed as if she's trying to understand how this could've happened. She walks away with me, but Juda grabs my arm. "Mina, please. Let's talk about this."

His eyes plead with me, but I can't look at his face for a minute longer. "Not now."

My mind muddy with sadness and anger, I rush through the crowd into Macy's, not even waiting for Grace. I have to find Nana.

The floor of the main hall is full of wounded bodies scattered like dead leaves underneath a tree. Ayan is holding court in the corner, surrounded by members of the Laurel Society and female former prisoners.

"It's time a woman led this city!" she shouts. "We've had enough of the men. Within the Laurel Society, we already have a system of government in place that works. We will expand upon it and have a female leader with a female parliament, and we will rewrite the laws that have been repressing women for a hundred years! "

Her audience cheers.

Ayan is going to challenge Jordan for the leadership of the city. I suppose I should be happy, but instead I feel sick. Her language sounds just as extreme as Ram's.

I turn around and go back outside.

When I reach the street, I yell to the remaining crowd: "I'm leaving the island. Anyone who wants to join me is welcome!"

Questions bombard me: "Where will we go?" "What's out there?" "What about the Apostates?"

Avoiding Juda's stunned look, I answer, "I don't know what's out there, but I've met Apostates and most of them are the same as you and me—no better and no worse. The drones blasted a hole in the wall behind the Tunnel and that's where I plan to go. We'll pick up boats from the canal on the way."

"We can go West!" Silas says. "It's where I've always wanted to go."

Sounds fine to me. I don't care really, as long as it's not here.

A group of around fifty people wants to join me. Not wanting to wait and see if the ceasefire is real, they're ready to leave immediately, but I still have a few things to prepare. "Spread the word inside the basement that people can join us if they want to," I tell Silas. "Ask for any blankets and clothes that can be spared." I lament the lack of food for us to grab. He rushes inside.

"And I need a horse and cart," I tell some of the women who sound like Convenes. At some point, they must have carried water into their neighborhood with horses.

An older women says, "Closest stable is probably Chelsea Park."

"We'll go," says a man next to her. He grabs his friend and they disappear down the street.

Before Juda can speak to me, I scramble back inside Macy's.

FIFTY-TWO

I search for Dekker. I'm unhappy to hear he's been put in the same room as Mother. I was hoping to leave without seeing her again.

I enter without knocking.

Mother hovers over Dekker, who's now in the bed. She presses a washcloth to his side. Glaring at me, she says, "This is your fault!"

"It's not," Dekker whispers. "I wanted to—I mean we had to save Grace."

"How is he?" I ask.

"Regina says he'll live, as long as the wound doesn't get infected."

"Praise the Prophet," I say, at a loss for other words.

Dekker moans as she dabs at his wound.

"I'm leaving and I'm not coming back," I say.

Mother scoffs. "That's what you always say."

"This time I mean it. And I'm taking Nana with me."

Mother looks at me incredulously. "Whatever your crazy scheme, she'll never survive."

"It's what she's always wanted, and I won't leave her behind again."

"You're the most foolish—"

"I came here to say goodbye to Dekker, not you." Approaching the bed, I kneel next to him. "You were major heroic."

"So were you." After a pause, he adds, "For a girl."

"I'm going to punch you in the bullet wound," I say.

He smirks. "No, you won't."

I stun myself by saying, "Do you want to join me? I can wait for you to get better."

He looks around the room and asks in a nonchalant voice, "What's Grace doing?"

"I'm pretty sure she's staying here." I can no longer picture my life without her, but the decision isn't mine. "She'll want to help Ayan start her new government."

"I don't think I'm cut out for Apostate life," he says.

"You're going to stay and initiate a female-led government?" I ask. Maybe I should hang around just to see this.

"Your brother's prospects are wonderful," Mother says. "Many girls will want to marry him after what he did, freeing all those prisoners."

"What *he* did. Right."

"That tone has always been very unattractive, Mina," she says.

"Give her a break, Mother," Dekker says. "Would it kill you to be nice to her for once?"

Mother's chin drops.

I'm flabbergasted. This is the first time he's ever stood up for me. Maybe that bullet shot some compassion into him. Or maybe it's like Silas said, and Dekker's been hiding who he really is under layers of aggression and nastiness. I hope this more sympathetic version lasts. I give him as much of a hug as he can handle.

"Good luck," he says.

"You, too," I say. "Take advantage of the library. I think you'll like it there."

He looks indignant, like I'm suggesting he needs to read more books; I'll let him discover for himself that this is where he can always find Grace.

"I'm going to get Nana now," I say, heading for the door. "And you should get word to Delilah Delford that you're not coming back." I have no intention of going back to Kingsboro myself. "She really likes you." I remember the adoring way she looked at him at Promise Prom.

Mother's face loses all color. "What's this?"

"I was engaged, Mother, but don't worry. It's off."

"To an Apostate?" she says, placing a hand on her neck. "Are you brainwashed or just *insane*?" She begins a long rant on the wickedness of heretics.

Dekker gives me a look of irritation for bringing up the subject. I produce a wicked smile. I'm almost out the door when I decide to interrupt Mother's screeching. "Why don't you tell Dekker the story about how Nana is your mother and not Father's? And about how well you can read? I'm sure it will keep him very entertained."

Mother's chin drops once again as I leave the room.

I arrive at the infirmary. Nana is sitting up in bed while Herra feeds her broth. Regina is taking care of the wounded in the main hall.

"You're up!" I say.

"Barely," she says. "But I could hardly stay asleep with all the racket!"

"Where did all those people come from?" Herra asks.

"The Tunnel," I say. "We broke them out."

Herra's mouth tightens. "Then Twitchers will be on the way."

"I think they're focusing more on Ram and his bombs right now than they are on us. Their prison is destroyed. Their leader is dead. Even Memon won't be able to organize them anytime soon."

Nana beams. "You remarkable girl!"

"I wasn't alone," I say. "I was with—"

"I don't care. You've become an extraordinary young woman, and I'm so proud of you."

No words have ever meant more.

"I'm leaving Manhattan," I say, "and you're coming with me."

"I'm too weak."

"I've got transportation waiting outside."

"I'll slow you down."

"I'm not in a hurry. This is your dream, Nana. This is your last chance to see the other side of the Wall!"

Her head drooping, she looks down at her frail body and then up at Herra. "What do you think?"

"It doesn't matter," Herra says. "You're going to do what you want no matter what I say."

Nana purses her lips.

I hold my breath as I wait.

"How would you get me outside?"

"The usual way." I yell into the hall, "Rayna!"

Rayna walks in. "I hear you need a lift," she says to Nana. "And don't try to say no, old woman."

Nana throws the sheet off her bed. "Get my clothes, Regina."

I smile for what feels like the first time in weeks. "You have no idea how happy you've made me."

"Don't get excited. I may turn to dust before we reach the door," she says.

After Nana is dressed, Rayna easily scoops her up; Nana looks like she weighs half of what she used to.

Before we're allowed to leave, Herra insists I take a first aid kit with me. "It's very basic, but I'd feel terrible if I gave you nothing." The kit attaches to a belt that I can wear under my cloak.

"Thank you," I say, thinking of the prisoners who want to join me who have cuts and sprains. "We need it."

"Thank you, Herra, you've been a doll," Nana says. As Rayna carries her out of the infirmary, Nana waves goodbye to several friends.

When we reach the main hall, the room is a mass of wounded bodies, along with the women helping Regina with the injured prisoners.

Rayna weaves in and out of the crowd until she finds Ayan, who's shouting orders at anyone who looks healthy enough to help. When she sees Rayna and Nana, she freezes.

"What's she doing out of bed?" she asks Rayna.

"She's coming with me," I answer.

"Where?"

"Who cares?" Nana says. "As long as it's *far* from here."

Ayan looks astonished and then pleased.

"You've been an excellent leader," Nana tells her. "And an even better friend."

I watch in wonder as Ayan gets tears in her eyes. "You're one of the good ones, Ura. I'll miss you desperately." She kisses

Nana once on each cheek. "If you can, send word back. Tell us what's out there."

Nana nods, saying, "A bunch of dolts I imagine. But if it's anything interesting, I'll let you know."

I remember the miles and miles of nothing I saw from the Ostrich. *Please, let there be something more.*

Ayan squeezes Nana's hand. She then kisses me on both cheeks, just like she did Nana. We haven't always seen eye to eye, but she gave me shelter when I needed it, and she's taught me a lot about leadership and responsibility. Standing in front of her, I find that her opinion of me matters a lot.

"Good luck, Mina," she says. "You've shown great promise; I'm sure you have a lot of adventures in front of you."

I don't want adventures. I want peace. But I nod with respect. "Thank you for all your help."

She smiles at us, then snaps back into efficiency mode, turning her attention to the prisoners.

When I turn around, Grace is there, apology in her big shining eyes. "Ayan is building a new government and . . . " She scans the female prisoners spread across the room. "I want to look for my mother."

"I know." I didn't expect her to leave again.

"But I can't imagine being here without you."

"Look at all the company you'll have," I say, gesturing to the swarm of people. "And now you won't have to stay underground. It'll be great."

"If it's going to be so great, you should stay."

I smile. "It'll be great for you, not for me."

"How's Dekker? Is he going with you?"

Did she just turn a little pink? "No. He's staying. I think he won't be able to leave Macy's for a *long* time."

"That's too bad," she says, but she doesn't look unhappy at all.

"You changed my life," she says. "You took me up-top, and I'll never forget it." She dives into my arms. "Thank you."

She did so much for me, I don't even know where to begin. "I'll miss you *so* much."

"Promise me you'll write?"

I smile in wonderment at the idea of a Manhattan that accepts mail from the outside world. "All the time!"

"Do you need the address?"

Is she kidding? "One five one west thirty-fourth street, New York, New York, one zero zero zero one. You're talking to someone who memorized *Time Out*, remember?"

She laughs, releasing me, and then her face grows serious. "Are you sure you want to give up on Juda? He made a big mistake, but he loves you so much."

"I'm not just leaving because of him."

"Then what's it about?"

How can I explain it? "Remember in the Cloisters, how Mrs. Hypat was all excited about that resurrected unicorn? It didn't make sense to me. It was alive, but it was still locked up. I hated that tapestry. I just . . . hated it."

"Like, what's the point of being reborn if you can't be free?"

"Yeah. Exactly." She always knows what to say.

We say good-bye and she hugs me again. I walk away before I can change my mind.

As I leave, I grab two of the large pillows that dot the floor. I follow Rayna as she carries Nana through the hallway that leads outside. I remember the first time that Rayna led Juda and me through this poorly lit passageway—how frightened I was, how I had no idea that Nana was still alive. *She survived because she was safely inside of Macy's.* I consider telling Rayna to turn around and put Nana back in her bed.

Rayna takes Nana carefully up the stairs and then slides open the metal door at the top. A shaft of light streams in, blinding us all. Once outside, Nana raises a hand to block her face, squinting as if she hasn't seen the sun in decades.

I'm worried that getting her up and over the mound of rubble will be impossible, but Rayna manages it easily. She knows this wreckage like the back of her hand, and she hops over the fallen concrete and beams like she's doing a dance.

When we reach the street, Silas waves me over. Twenty more people want to join us, which makes me feel overwhelmed. I'm hugely relieved to see that the Convene men have returned with the horse and cart. Thanking them, I place the pillows in the cart on top of the blankets Silas found, creating a soft nest for Nana. Rayna lays her inside, and, once situated, she doesn't look strong, but she looks content.

Juda watches us from the sidewalk. His expression suggests that he's waiting for a signal—a smile that tells him I've forgiven him and that I will stay—but I have no such signal to give. He decides to approach anyway.

Leaving Nana alone to say goodbye to Rayna, I meet him in the middle of the street.

"Will you ever come back?" he asks.

"Depends what's out there I suppose." My gut tells me I won't, but I can't look into his miserable face and tell him so.

"I'd come with you, but Ma . . . I have to bring her home to my uncles, help take care of her."

"I understand."

"Is it my fault?" he says.

"What?"

"That you're leaving."

Partly, I think. "I just can't live here anymore."

"I love you."

"I know. I love you, too." And the horrible thing is, I do.

"Why can't that be enough?"

"You know why."

"Promise me, if after a few days you change your mind, you'll come back, even if you're still furious with me. We can work it out. I'll take care of you."

Why can't he understand how much I don't want anyone to take care of me anymore?

Grabbing my hand, he pulls me into a tight embrace. "I don't know what I'll do without you."

My anger subsides for a moment as I feel his body against mine. Am I being an idiot? Am I giving up the best thing that's ever happened to me over something I might one day forgive?

"Let's get moving!" Nana cries from the horse cart.

Pulling away from Juda, I can't help but smile. Since coming outside, Nana's energy has already soared.

"Time for me to go," I tell him, worried I'll lose my nerve.

He nods without speaking.

Ignoring the stares around me, I kiss him long and hard, determined to memorize his face, smell, and taste forever. He responds like it's the last kiss of his life—every touch of his lips filled with love, desperation, and heartbreak. My inner longing pulls toward him, begging me to forgive him, to wipe my mind clean of anything that might keep us apart. But a flash of Mrs. Hypat's wretched face brings me back to reality, and I pull away.

I clear my head, saying, "When you get to Kingsboro, tell Jeremiah and Adam what happened to Mary and Tabby. They deserve to hear it from someone who was there."

"Of course," he says, voice hoarse.

Unable to say more, I walk away, returning to the cart.

"You okay?" Silas asks. I'm sure he watched the whole thing.

I take the reins of the horse. "You should head to the front of the group. Tell people it's time to start walking."

He frowns. "Okay. But we *will* talk about this." He jogs off.

Rayna says goodbye to Nana, and when she sees me, she straightens up and walks over. "It's real stupid to take her away." I keep her gaze. "But she seems happy about it, so . . . good job." She heads back to the basement.

I know this is as much of a goodbye as she'll give me, and I'll take it. Her approval is hard to earn.

I order the horse forward, leading it west with my small army of Convenes, Deservers, and one member of the Unbound. Even though I'm determined not to, I turn around one last time to look at Juda. He's standing in the same spot, watching me go. As I catch his eye, he yells, "Peace and light!"

I can't help but smile. "Always!" I yell.

FIFTY-THREE

Reaching the Hudson River will be simple, but crossing it is complicated. Our best bet is to head to the canals and grab as many canoes and rowboats as possible. Despite what Jordan said, we don't know if the bombing will begin again, and we have no idea if Twitchers are patrolling the streets.

The nearest canal is 11th Avenue, so we walk a straight shot across 35th. After we've walked only two blocks, I stop the horse, asking Nana, "How are you doing?"

"Never better," she says, but she looks pale.

"Do you need food? Do you want to rest?"

"Don't mollycoddle me, Mina, or I'll walk and *you* can get in this cart!"

"Yes, Nana." We continue on our way.

Due to our slow speed, we're among the last people to reach 11th Avenue. The rest of the group is untying boats, paddling, and rowing to the other side of the canal. The Wall is within sight, but the hole I saw the bombs make is further north. These people will have to get out of the canal and carry their boats four blocks.

How will we get our boat? I can't carry one alone, and if we use the cart to transport it, Nana will have to walk. I don't think she's strong enough yet. I'm about to panic when Nana says, "Find someone to lift me onto that horse."

I ask a muscular former prisoner to help us. He hoists Nana onto the back of the saddle. She isn't sitting up straight, but she is sitting.

"I'm impressed," I tell her.

"Go get us a canoe before they're all gone," she orders.

I hurry to the canal's edge. I'm searching for a decent boat when I see Silas. "I got us a rowboat. It can definitely hold three."

"Thank you," I say, immensely grateful. I've never been so happy to see his pretty face.

"What's that?" he asks, pointing east.

I follow his finger into the sky, frightened of more bombs. A drone is coming from the direction of Queens, but it doesn't appear to be one of the assault models. As it moves closer, I recognize the Ostrich.

"It must be Jeremiah!" Silas says.

"How do you know it's not Ram?" I ask.

"You think Ram has the nerve to show up here when he just bombed your city? Not a chance."

We watch the Ostrich land in midtown.

"Having second thoughts?" I ask.

"None," he says.

The two of us carry the rowboat and oars to the cart. Once everything is secured, we walk up to 37th. Most of our people have already crossed the canal in the boats and should be waiting for us at 39th.

We start seeing chunks of concrete when we reach 38th Street. The bomb hit the Wall and threw the rubble more than half a mile. Smoke fills the air, and tiny concrete particles grate my lungs like sandpaper. Nana coughs. Mother was right. I'm going to kill her.

We finally reach the Wall. I'm distressed to discover that to reach the new opening, we'll have to climb up and over decimated concrete, barbwire, and rebar sticking up in every direction. Our people are carrying their boats up the mountain of debris, a harrowing task. As they make their way up the hill, the concrete and stone shift under their feet, causing them to slide back down. If they drop their boat and damage it severely enough, they'll have to walk back to the canal to grab another. One man drops a canoe on his foot and his daughter is so convinced that he's broken it, she announces that they'll have to stay on the island.

The group seems to be making no progress, but, finally, after an hour, men, women, and children are making it down the other side and launching their boats into the water.

"What's on the other side of the river?" a girl asks.

"Weehawken," Silas says, taking our boat out of the cart.

"Do you know anything about it?" I ask, knowing my knowledge is extremely outdated.

"Not really. Ram says the people are evil, just like he says about you." He grins.

I scan the heap of wreckage, wondering how we'll get Nana to the other side. If only Rayna had wanted to join us. Just then a group of former prisoners, two good-sized middle-aged men and a tall woman, approach us. The largest of them, a scowling man with a brown beard, says, "We'll carry her over if ya want." He nods at Nana.

I'm staggered.

"I don't know why you're so amazed," Silas says. "You freed them from the Tunnel, after all."

"We all did," I say.

"I can't wait to hear the story," Nana says, as we help her off the horse.

We wait until almost everyone else has gotten to the other side. A handful of girls my age and younger loiters behind. I think they don't have any relatives and feel close to Silas and me for freeing them. They provide solid encouragement as the two burly men, Liam and Kailen, help Silas to slowly convey our rowboat up the hill. Behind them, the brawny woman called Inga carries Nana. When they start the journey down the other side, I'm sure I'll have a heart attack. If Inga loses her footing, she and Nana will careen to the bottom and crash into the river.

The young girls and I are standing at the top watching their progress, and Inga is halfway down, when I hear a familiar voice say, "I knew I would catch up with you, Mina Clark."

I don't have to look behind me to know it's Mrs. Asher.

"You don't look surprised, so you must have known it, too," she says.

She couldn't be more wrong. I'm shocked down to my marrow. How in the world did she find me? I was *so close* to escaping. This is like when her husband found me and Juda by using Rose; Rose had on that necklace he was tracking. My body sags as I realize that when the Twitcher scanned me at the Tunnel, Mrs. Asher must've been alerted. The dumbest thing I could do was return anywhere near the prison, and that's exactly what I've done—the remains of the Tunnel are only a few blocks away, and Mrs. Asher probably spotted our large group from there.

I turn to look at her. Like me, she's not wearing a veil. Her hair is wild and blowing in the wind. She holds the enormous rifle of a Tunnel guard.

None of the girls around me dare to move.

"Where did you get that gun?" I ask, stalling for time. I

want Silas and Nana to have time to get into our boat. I don't think Mrs. Asher can see them from where she's standing, and why should she care about them anyway?

"I found it by the Tunnel. All those dead Twitchers." She tilts her head. "I assume that was your doing?"

Technically it was Rayna, but I don't think Mrs. Asher cares about technicalities.

"Before I kill you," she says, drawing out her words, "you're going to tell me exactly what happened to my husband and son."

"Why? You won't believe me."

"Yes, I will. We were friends once, remember?"

"You pretended to be nice and got me drunk so you could manipulate me. That's not friendship."

"Oh my! Little Mina has grown hard since the last time I saw her." She looks at a small girl who stands wide-eyed to my left. "Actually, I think she was always hard. How else could she have murdered my family?" The girl looks up at me, terrified.

"I didn't shoot your husband," I say, knowing that the truth is useless. "Your son did. When Damon tried to shoot Juda, Mr. Asher got in the way, because Juda is his son. But you know that."

"You want me to believe that *Damon* killed Max?" She smiles, and she is stunningly gorgeous. "That would be convenient."

"I said you wouldn't believe me."

"I don't believe Max would die to protect a bastard. And you should know, I'm going to find Juda and kill him, too."

"If you love your husband so much, why do you want to kill his last remaining relative?"

"Because that boy's mother is a whore," she says.

I snort. "You wish. That would make you feel better. She was a nice girl and is a nice woman, and Mr. Asher loved her."

She steps closer to me. I shouldn't have said that.

"I didn't like my husband. He bought me for cash. But my son was the only person I loved in this world. And you killed him."

"He was chasing us, and he drowned."

"Same thing."

Keep stalling, Mina. "You once told me that we were the same, that my parents had sold me just like yours sold you. That's true, except now we don't belong to anyone. You have *money.* Uncle Ruho is dead, so no one can take it away from you. Leave this island. Or stay and help build a new government. Do WHATEVER you want. Look at these girls . . . " I gesture to the frightened faces around me. "They've been in the Tunnel for years because they disobeyed their husbands, or wanted to learn to read, or fell in love with the wrong person. Aren't you sick of it? Your husband wasn't a good man. He was poisoning thousands of people. Your son knew about it and did nothing. I'm sorry that Damon died. I really am. And I've asked for God's forgiveness many times. I wish things could've ended differently. But if you murder me, you're only creating a new prison for yourself. You'll never escape the agony of having killed someone."

She's listening to me. I can tell from the intense expression on her face. As she looks at the young girls, her face softens, and I can see the exquisite thirteen-year-old who was bought off the street and sent away from her family forever. She looks up at me, and her face goes hard. She's once again the mother who lost a son. She raises her gun.

"Leave the girls alone," I say, stepping forward.

All at once, she collapses. She's spasming on the ground. Standing behind her is Katerina, the tiny girl I rescued from the Tunnel. She holds her Taser in her hand.

"The button is at the base!" she tells me.

"Yes," I say. "Very, very good."

Rushing forward, I take the rifle away from Mrs. Asher.

"Hurry!" I tell Katerina and the other girls. "Into the boats!"

Mrs. Asher moans, and before she can come to completely, I use the elastic bandage in my first aid kit to tie her wrists behind her back. It won't last forever, but it might last long enough for us to get away.

We rush down the hill of rubble, half running, half sliding. I ignore the cuts and bruises the concrete wreckage makes down my legs as I concentrate on keeping the rifle pointed away from any people. When we reach the bottom, Silas has put the rowboat in the water. Nana is tucked inside with her pillows.

"You took long enough!" Nana says.

"Where'd you get that gun?" Silas asks.

"Tell you later."

"Are you taking it with us?" Nana says.

I look at the enormous weapon. I feel safer with it in my hands. We have no idea where we're going or who will be there. What ideas and values will they try to force upon us this time?

Looking at Silas and Nana, I realize I know what my ideas and values are—no one can change them. I throw the rifle in the river.

The boat rocks as I step inside and settle myself onto a wood slat.

"Go!" I say.

Silas begins to row. Nana watches him from her comfortable spot at the stern. The sun is dropping west, but we should make it across before sundown. Nana recites dramatically:

*Take a romantic paddle around the Lake (one-hour $15)
—or let someone else do the work during a Venetian
gondola ride at Loeb Boathouse (available April through
November).*

Silas gapes at her like she's lost her mind, and I realize he's never heard about the Primer. Realizing we've made it, we are *in the water*, I join Nana in finishing the paragraph:

*While you're there, absorb the picturesque view of the
Lake at the Central Park Boathouse Restaurant, for fine
—if pricey—fare like fish, crab cakes, salads and an
assortment of wines.*

When we finish, we giggle like little girls.

"Do you think we'll go somewhere we can try fish, Nana?" I ask.

"Maybe."

Growing serious, I watch the other boats making their gradual way to Weehawken. They'll soon land and all these prisoners I've rescued will learn what comes next.

"And do you think," I say, looking at her, "we'll find a place where men don't want to tell us what to do?"

"Oh, Chickpea. Isn't it wonderful to think so?"

EPILOGUE

I walk up the hill to my makeshift cemetery. The view, first thing in the morning, is always spectacular. When I reach the four rocks, I pull the weeds that have begun to obscure them.

Nana wants to have a special breakfast for my sixteenth birthday, so I can't stay long. Nowadays, she seems really into celebrating every little thing. Being mobile again has given her new life.

The West Coast doctors have had a slew of treatments to offer her; they even managed to fix the knee that's bothered her for twenty years. Nana said it's become embarrassing to explain the level of our medical treatments to these men and women who've been using lasers and artificial intelligence to do surgery for decades. They've also introduced us to pills for mercury poisoning, and we've been mailing them back home (with no confirmation they're arriving.)

In the nine months we've been here, we've found a lot to love and be amazed by: the abundant food, the driverless cars and planes, the total lack of crime. Maybe the thing that astonishes us the most is the atheists. Back in Kingsboro, Frannie said they'd be here, and I didn't believe her, but probably eighty percent of the population of California doesn't believe in God.

At first, I was afraid they might reject or punish us for having different beliefs, but they leave us alone, happy to let us live however we want. My neighbor, Mrs. Harris, has even asked me about the Prophet, and we've had some interesting conversations about my past.

I had a lot of questions for her, as well. I didn't quite understand how she developed any morals growing up if she didn't believe in God or Hell. She didn't seem insulted by my curiosity and told me that she trusted her "inner compass" to tell her the right thing to do. She's urging me to do the same.

She knows I've lost people, and it's hard not to get sad when her ideas suggest that they aren't in Paradise. But she argues that life has more meaning when we aren't counting on an afterlife, which is sort of interesting. Nana seems to be pursuing the notion that every day is sacred, so I'm trying to follow her example.

Once I'm satisfied that the weeds are clear, I sit in the grass in my usual spot. Shortly after we moved here, I built a shrine to the people I'd lost, nothing fancy—just four rocks, each a slightly different color and shape. From left to right, I greet Father, Tabby, Mary, and Mrs. Hypat.

"I start school in two months," I tell the rocks. "Well, technically, it's seven weeks, four days, and twenty-three hours. I've never had a first day of school before, and I wish you could give me advice." I bet Tabby was never nervous about going to school.

One day, I plan to enroll in the medical school, which is open to everyone. I've never gotten over my admiration for Dr. Rachel or forgotten how helpless I felt when Dekker got shot. I can't think of anything that I want to learn more than medicine.

Besides, you have to go to school for a *very* long time to become a doctor, which sounds wonderful.

"Silas has met someone," I tell them. "His name is Vincent." Without the fear of judgement or arrest, Silas thrives more each day.

I've been so happy that he's still with us. Many of the people in our original group have spread across California. A lot of them never made it this far, settling in communities along the way. I wonder if this new boy means Silas won't live with us forever.

"He's coming to school with me in the fall, but he's not ready to commit to something like medical school."

I imagine Tabby snorting.

"I wish I had news from home but still no word. Maybe the mail just hasn't caught up with us yet."

An empty ache surges through my stomach. I don't want to focus on it too long, since it's my birthday, but I can't help but let my mind wander to everything that might be happening back home.

Is the Laurel Society fighting with the Convenes? Has Captain Memon taken over the Cloisters? Has Grace been able to see her host-family again? What's happening between her and Dekker? If something becomes official, will they let me know?

Juda is the most difficult to think about for multiple reasons. It's hard to know we have medicine to help Rose and not be sure if it's reaching her. And, of course, I wonder if he still thinks about me.

I don't talk about him often in front of Silas or Nana. My feelings are so complicated. One day, all I can remember are the amazing things Juda did for me, the moments I wanted to spend my life with him, and I'm filled with the deepest love. The next, I'm thinking about Mrs. Hypat, and his betrayal, and

I'm consumed with a rage so deep I can taste bile on my tongue. Nana says that this is frequently the way with love—a twisted knot of conflicting emotions—and that we either find peace with our feelings or we don't. I asked what happens if we don't, and she said, "We take deep breaths, keep our hearts wide open, and read, read, read."

Ready to focus on the days ahead and not the days behind, I say goodbye to the rocks and walk back down the hill to our house. Silas is making pancakes, and Nana is topping them with bananas. Has anyone ever savored a sixteenth birthday more than me?

NOTE TO READER

If you've made it this far in the Time Zero trilogy, you know that I like to cite real world examples of the rules and social practices I use in the books. In *Time's Up*, Ram recites holy scripture to sanction the bombing of the Propheteers.

I've listed below a small sampling of murder and violence which has been justified by a difference in religious beliefs.

For sources and more examples, please visit www. timezerobook.com/religious-rules.

The Tree of Life Shooting

In October of 2018 a mass shooting occurred at a Pittsburg synagogue during Shabbat morning service. The Christian shooter yelled, "All Jews must die" as he killed eleven people and wounded seven.

Boko Haram in Nigeria

This terrorist group follows an extremely strict form of

Sunni Islam. They see members of other forms of Islam, such as the Sufi and Shiite sects, as infidels. Since 2009, Boko Haram has killed tens of thousands of people and displaced 2.3 million others from their homes. Many Americans know the name of this terrorist organization because in 2014 they kidnapped 276 teenage girls from a boarding school in Borno. Many of these girls are still missing.

The Genocide of Rohingyas in Myanmar

Nearly one million Rohingya Muslims have been fleeing persecution and the destruction of their homes since August 2017. One study estimates that during this genocide, the military and the local Rakhine Buddhists killed at least 24,000 Rohingya people and committed forms of sexual violence against 18,000 Rohingya Muslim women and girls. Additionally, 116,000 Rohingya were beaten, and 36,000 Rohingya were thrown into fire.

The Eradication of Native Americans

Yes, this happened a long time ago, but I'm including it here because most people don't know that the Bible was used to justify the murder of Native Americans when Christians first arrived in America. In 1452 Pope Nicholas V issued a papal bull called Dum Diversas that granted Portugal and Spain "full and free permission to invade, search out, capture and subjugate . . . the pagans and any other unbelievers and enemies of Christ wherever they may be." The Northern Native American population went from an estimated 12 million in 1500 to barely 237,000 in 1900.

ACKNOWLEDGMENTS

I need to give special acknowledgment to Amy Elliott. Amy acted as my beta-reader throughout the creation of *Time Next* and *Time's Up*. She was the one person who read each unedited chapter as I wrote it, who championed the plot when it was working and who was an honest critic when it was not. Good beta-readers are hard to find and if you're lucky enough to have one, I suggest you buy them dinner whenever possible. Amy, I am forever indebted to you for your enthusiasm, brutal honesty, and unending fascination with religious cults.

Thank you also to Roberto Cipriano, Lori Levy, Kailen Cohagan, Harper Javery, Lucinda Tedesco, Megan Treacy, Catherine Shattuck, Anne Bingham, Bailey Morrison, Claire Campbell, Susanne Grabowski, Rebekah Manley, Emma Finch, Kelly Steele, and my copy editor Katherine Catmull.

A special thank you to all the young writers at Kids With Pens, who patiently waited for their own anthology to be published because I was finishing this book. You all inspire me daily with your lavish imaginations and captivating voices. KEEP WRITING.

ABOUT THE AUTHOR

Carolyn Cohagan began her writing career on the stage. She has performed stand-up and one-woman shows at festivals around the world from Adelaide to Edinburgh. Her first novel, *The Lost Children* (Simon & Schuster, 2010) is a middle grade fantasy which became part of the Scholastic Bookclub and was nominated for a Massachusetts Children's Book Award. The first book in her YA trilogy, *Time Zero* (She Writes Press, 2016), won eight literary honors, including the 2017 Readers Favorite Award and the 2017 International Book Award. She is the founder of Girls With Pens, a creative writing organization in Austin dedicated to fostering the individual voices and offbeat imaginations of kids ages 8-16. www.girlswithpens.org

To receive Carolyn's monthly newsletter containing what she's watching, reading, listening to, and writing, please go to www.timezerobook.com.